"*Hot Wheels and High Heels* draws you in, then blasts off! Fasten your seatbelt for a fun, rollicking ride!"

—**Stephanie Bond,**
author of the Body Movers series

"[Jane] Graves writes with charming wit. Her characters make you smile and the situations her heroine, Darcy, faces will make you howl with laughter . . . an entertaining and delightful read." —**Armchairinterviews.com**

"Funny as can be and I had a blast reading it . . . it's on my short list of best romances for 2007 . . . a delight in any season." —**AllAboutRomance.com**

"This book is . . . a woman's self-discovery while she learns what's really important in the world. The author does a fantastic job at her characterization of Darcy . . . hilarious . . . The last page of this book was turned with a true sense of contentment." —**ARomanceReview.com**

"Fans will enjoy the antics of the high-heeled Darcy as she sasses her way into the heart of stark loner John who, though he knows she is not his style, loves her spunk; so will readers." —*Midwest Book Review*

BOOKS BY JANE GRAVES

Hot Wheels and High Heels

Tall Tales and Wedding Veils

"I was thinking about the limousine," Tony whispered.

Flashback. Mouths, hands, kissing, touching . . . "What about it?"

"There's no reason we can't pick up where we left off that night."

He hooked his finger around a strand of her hair, easing it back over her shoulder. Then he dipped his head, leaned in, and kissed her neck. Heather was so stunned, she couldn't move. *Stop him. Right now. Nothing good can come from this.*

But for some reason she sat there, frozen in place, as his lips moved along her neck, remembering how it had felt before. But it was even better now because she wasn't anesthetized with champagne. He moved his lips next to her ear, and she could feel his hot breath as he spoke.

"You have no idea how much I wanted to make love to you. Right there in the backseat of that limousine."

"I wouldn't have let you," she said, a little breathless. "I don't do that sort of thing."

"Heather, you were so hot for me I'm surprised you didn't tear the clothes right off my body."

And if this goes on, he's going to tear the clothes right off yours.

～

"Jane has a gift for making outrageously comic situations seem plausible, and her characters shine."
—*Romantic Times BOOKreviews Magazine*

more . . .

BUCKLE UP FOR SEXY FUN WITH
HOT WHEELS AND HIGH HEELS

Tall Tales and
Wedding Veils

Jane
Graves

FOREVER

NEW YORK   BOSTON

Copyright © 2008 by Jane Graves
All rights reserved. Except as permitted under the U.S. Copyright Act of 1976, no part of this publication may be reproduced, distributed, or transmitted in any form or by any means, or stored in a database or retrieval system, without the prior written permission of the publisher.

Forever is an imprint of Grand Central Publishing. The Forever name and logo is a trademark of Hachette Book Group USA, Inc.

Art direction by Mimi Bark
Cover illustration by Mike Storrings

Forever
Hachette Book Group USA
237 Park Avenue
New York, NY 10017
Visit our Web site at www.HachetteBookGroupUSA.com

Printed in the United States of America

First Printing: June 2008

10 9 8 7 6 5 4 3 2 1

To Brian, with all my love

Tall Tales and Wedding Veils

Chapter 1

They were the ugliest bridesmaid dresses Heather Montgomery had ever seen, and she'd seen her share of them. When you had a family that could fill Texas Stadium, somebody was always getting married, and it was family law that cousins asked cousins to be bridesmaids, even if it meant blood relatives had to stand in line behind five of the bride's sorority sisters.

This time around, it was Heather's cousin Regina tying the knot, and she'd chosen these dresses for one reason only: Her high-priced wedding planner had convinced her they were the height of fashion. To Heather, they simply looked ridiculous.

"Regina!" squealed Bridesmaid Number One as she fanned out the skirt of one of the six petticoated, puffy-sleeved, waist-hugging creations. "They're *fabulous*!"

Two and Three voiced similar opinions, while Four and Five stroked the satin reverently, making breathy little noises of approval. Heather had given up trying to remember the five names all ending in *i*—Cami, Taci, Tami, whatever—and which blond woman belonged to each one. In the end, she'd simply assigned them numbers according to hair length.

In the wake of all the *oohs* and *ahhs,* Heather traded furtive eye-rolls with her mother. Barbara Montgomery had come along on this dress-fitting excursion, even though she didn't particularly like her sister *or* her niece. She was there because family weddings always stirred things up, and if she stayed in the thick of things, she was sure to be around when the pandemonium began. The whole family thrived on chaos in a way that boggled Heather's mind. Given her own preference for a calm, tidy, organized life, sometimes she wondered if the stork had taken a wrong turn twenty-nine years ago and dumped her down the wrong chimney.

"Oh, yes," Barbara said. "The dresses are simply adorable. Don't you think they're adorable, Heather?"

"Yes," she said, sounding almost as Stepfordlike as her mother. "Adorable."

"Of course they're adorable," Aunt Bev said as she fluffed the skirt on Three's dress. "They're by *Jorge.*"

"Well, pink must be Jorge's signature color," Heather said. "I mean, look at how much of it he used here."

"They're not *pink,*" Regina said with a toss of her head that sent a shudder through the mountain of lace attached to it. "They're *salmon.* It's all the rage this season." She fluttered her hands. "Go ahead, girls. Try them on."

Heather went to a dressing room and stuffed herself into the dress. The sleeves drooped to her elbows, at least six inches of hem dragged on the ground, and it fit so snugly around her waist that breathing was a chore.

She pulled back the curtain. One through Five morphed into gushy, grinning quintuplets with perfectly toned abs that didn't make the slightest bulge in the waistlines of their perfectly hideous dresses. It was like watching models on a Parisian runway wearing ridiculous clothes, yet for some reason, nobody laughed.

The seamstress smiled as she fanned her gaze over the flawless members of the wedding party. Then she zeroed in on Heather.

"Hmm," she said, running her hand over the waist of Heather's dress and shaking her head. "It's a little tight."

Heather sighed. "I told Regina to get a fourteen, just in case. I knew it would have to be taken in, but—"

"A fourteen?" Regina said, blinking innocently. "I'm sorry, Heather. I swore you said size twelve."

There was nothing wrong with Regina's hearing. It was just her way of coercing her cousin into a smaller size so she wouldn't have five pencil-thin women walking down the aisle followed by one who looked like a gum eraser. So what if Heather wouldn't be able to breathe? As long as enough oxygen went to her brain that she stayed upright during the ceremony, that was all that mattered to Regina.

"I can let it out a little," the seamstress said. "But only a little. There's not much seam allowance."

"Can't you order the fourteen?" Heather asked.

"Too short of notice."

"The wedding's not for a month," Regina said. "I'm sure you can drop a size by then."

Drop a size in a month? When she hadn't been able to drop a size in the past ten years?

"Try the Hollywood watermelon diet," Four said with a vacuous smile. "I once lost six pounds in a weekend on that one."

Great. Not only did Heather have to be in a wedding she was going to hate, she had to starve herself for the privilege. As the seamstress knelt down to mark the hem of her dress, Heather wondered how many celery sticks she'd have to eat in the next month so she wouldn't look like ten pounds of potatoes in a five-pound sack.

"So, Heather," Aunt Bev said. "Are you seeing anyone right now?"

The eternal question. One whose answer never seemed to change. "No, Aunt Bev. Nobody right now."

"What a shame. But don't worry. I'm sure you'll meet Mr. Right very soon."

The subtext was so thick, Heather could barely wade through it, and all of it was directed squarely at her mother. *My Regina's getting married, and your Heather isn't even dating anyone.*

"Actually, Heather is concentrating on her career right now," Barbara said. "A lot of young women are waiting until their thirties to marry."

"Is that what all the women's magazines are saying?" Aunt Bev said, looking befuddled. "If so, I'm afraid I wouldn't know about it. It's all I can do to get through every issue of *Modern Bride*."

"What they're *saying*," Barbara said, "is that some women choose to be successful in their own right before settling down and getting married."

"And I think Heather is very smart to do that," Aunt Bev said with an indulgent little smile. "That way, if the worst happens and she doesn't find a man, at least she won't be struggling for the rest of her life to put food on the table."

Heather had long since learned to let Aunt Bev's comments roll right past her. Her mother hadn't. Heather could almost feel her mother's brain working, trying to manufacture a comeback, but when it came to sheer bitchiness, she couldn't hold a candle to Aunt Bev.

Heather took off her dress and put her clothes back on. As the seamstress marked the other bridesmaids' hems for alteration, Heather sat down on the bench next to her mother.

"Don't listen to Aunt Bev," Barbara muttered under her breath. "She's just jealous that you have a fabulous career while Regina barely made it out of college."

Truthfully, there was a limit to the fabulousness of a career as a CPA, if it even counted for anything in the first place where her family was concerned. Career women weren't put on the same pedestal as those who chose matrimony and the mommy track. What was valued the most was the ability to wed, procreate, raise progeny to adulthood, maintain a clean house, and sustain enough of a relationship with your husband that he doesn't leave you for his secretary.

"Why don't I just tell Regina that I don't want to be in the wedding?" Heather whispered. "She doesn't want me there in the first place. If I backed out, it would make both of us happy."

"No. If Regina asked, you have to do it."

"Angela told her no. Why can't I?"

"Angela is with the Peace Corps in Uganda."

"So that's all I have to do to get out of this? Live in squalor in a foreign country?"

"You're being unreasonable."

"What about Carol? She said no, too."

"You know Carol is having trouble getting her meds straightened out. God only knows how she'd behave the day of the wedding."

"So if I pop a few Prozac, I'll become ineligible, too?"

"As if anybody would actually think *you're* unbalanced."

True. Everybody in her family had a reputation for something. Heather's was being sane.

"If you come up with some story now," her mother went on, "everybody will think you're jealous of Regina because she's getting married and you're not."

Heather started to say she didn't care what her family thought, but she knew her mother did. In front of Aunt Bev, she portrayed her daughter as a high-flying career woman who couldn't be bothered with something as mundane as marriage. But Heather knew the truth. Her mother didn't want to say, *Meet my daughter, the CPA.* She wanted to say, *Meet my daughter, her handsome husband, and her four lovely children.*

Fifteen minutes later, after the fittings were over and they'd suffered through a lecture from Regina on the jewelry they were expected to wear for the wedding, Heather and her mother left the bridal shop. As soon as the door closed behind them, her mother rolled her eyes.

"Can you *believe* those dresses?" she said. "My sister may have money, but she has no taste. None whatsoever. But it doesn't matter. You still looked beautiful in that dress, despite how horrible it was."

Beautiful? No. Heather was nothing if not a realist. She wasn't beautiful. But that didn't stop her mother from continually professing it, as if repetition would make it come true. While Heather was growing up, she could only imagine how her mother must have watched and waited for her ugly duckling to blossom into a swan. Instead, Heather had ended up somewhere between a chicken and a cockatiel. She had a headful of curls the color of a paper sack that she spent ten minutes every morning taming with a flat iron, a bump on the bridge of her nose she kept swearing she was going to have fixed, and a body polite people called "curvy." In the past ten years, she'd lost approximately fifty pounds. If only it hadn't been the same five pounds ten times, she might actually have gained a foothold on being thin.

On the positive side, she had clear skin, blue eyes everyone commented on, and nice white teeth that had never needed braces or fillings. But she'd always felt as if the bad outweighed the good, and if attention from men was any indication, she wasn't the only one who thought so.

They stopped beside Heather's car. "You *are* going on the bridesmaid trip tomorrow, aren't you?" her mother asked.

Heather groaned inwardly. A weekend jaunt to Las Vegas with Regina and her five picture-perfect friends? She couldn't wait.

"Yeah, Mom. I'm going."

"Good. Aunt Bev and Uncle Gene are footing the bill. Take advantage of it." She gave Heather a quick hug. "Where are you off to now?"

"I'm meeting Alison for a quick drink at McMillan's."

"You'll have a good time in Vegas," her mother said, then shrugged nonchalantly. "And who knows? Maybe you'll meet a nice man."

There it was again. Heather could say she was going to a gay-pride parade, and her mother would still say, *Maybe you'll meet a nice man.*

Heather hated to burst her mother's bubble, but for her, this trip was going to consist of going to a few nice restaurants, sitting by the pool, catching up on her reading, and

watching a lot of men watching five blond bridesmaids
instead of watching her.

⁓

There was nothing like having a drink at McMillan's to
put Tony McCaffrey in a good mood. He loved everything
about the place—the antique bar with the inset mirrors,
the big-screen TVs, the polished oak tables, the clacking
of pool balls, the beat of the music, the hum of the crowd.
When he went to heaven, he imagined God would welcome him inside the Pearly Gates and escort him to a bar
and grill just like this one. Somebody would hand him a
beer and a pool cue and surround him with a host of tall,
leggy women with halos of blond hair and whose only
desire was to keep him company in paradise.

As soon as he bought this place, he wouldn't have to
die to go to heaven.

Two weeks ago, he'd told his boss, John Stark, that
he was leaving. John ran Lone Star Repossessions, where
Tony had worked as an auto repossession agent for the
past few years. It was a good fit for his skills and personality. He kept his own hours, the money was good,
and on the rare occasion when dangerous deadbeats tried
to cause trouble, he generally managed to talk his way
out of the situation with a smile and a little bit of Texas
good-ol'-boy charm. But when this bar had come up for
sale, he realized he was destined for bigger things. For
once he'd be running his own show rather than being part
of someone else's.

John told him he was sorry he was leaving, but he ad-
mired that Tony wanted to go into business for himself.

Then he'd pulled a bottle of Scotch out of his desk drawer, poured each of them a drink, and toasted Tony's future success.

God, that had felt good.

Tracy came to the table and slid his usual Sam Adams in front of him. She'd started working there about a month ago, and she was just his kind of woman—quick with a beer, out for a good time, and *very* nice to look at, with long blond hair and legs to die for. Someday soon, he intended to do more than just look.

"You're sure in a good mood," she said. "Could it be because you're getting ready to buy a certain bar and grill?"

He smiled and took a sip of his beer, which tasted even better than usual. "You bet it is. Monday's gonna be a red-letter day."

"Everybody around here is thrilled that you're going to be the new owner." She leaned in and spoke confidentially. "Frank is such a tight-ass."

She was right. Frank was a tight-ass, and that was the last kind of person Tony intended to be. There was no need to be a slave driver. A happy employee was a productive employee. That was going to be his motto from now on.

He couldn't believe how everything had fallen perfectly into place. He'd put in an offer, and after a week of negotiation, Frank had finally agreed to finance the majority of the sales price, only to have their negotiations hit a stalemate when Tony was twenty thousand short of what Frank insisted on for a down payment. That was when he asked his friend Dave to loan him the twenty thousand, and in return, he would become a silent partner.

Tony performed the necessary due diligence. He checked out the current demographic trends and the projected business growth in the area. Hired somebody to do a projected profit/loss statement. Ordered inspections of the building and the facilities. Everything had looked good, and they were set to close escrow on Monday morning.

He couldn't wait.

As Tracy walked away, Tony turned and looked out over the room. Even though the crowd was light at five o'clock, he knew it would pick up considerably in the next hour. Right now, two guys were drinking beer and playing pool. A young couple was deep in conversation at a table near the door. And Tracy had just set a couple of martinis in front of two women sitting in a booth against the wall.

The women weren't exactly his type—a little too ordinary-looking—but anyone who came through the door with money in his pocket and looking for a good time was going to be his new favorite customer. He intended to become Mr. Hospitality, courting every one of them with great food, drink specials, and a big, welcoming smile. A neighborhood bar was all about making people feel right at home, and that was exactly what he intended to do.

He turned to see Dave come through the door. Tony had arranged to meet him here to get a check for the twenty thousand, which he was going to deposit this afternoon, which meant he'd be right on track for the Monday morning closing. Tony waved at him, and Dave made his way over to the table and sat down.

"Beer?" Tony said. "I'm buying."

"No, thanks."

"Aw, come on. Have one with me. I feel like celebrating."

Dave shifted uncomfortably. "Yeah? Well, you're not going to feel like it in a minute."

Tony froze, dread creeping through him. "Dave? What are you talking about?"

Dave blew out a breath. "Bad news, man."

"What?"

"I can't give you the twenty thousand."

Chapter 2

Bridesmaid dresses are supposed to be ugly," Alison said as she twirled the spear of olives in her martini glass. "It's the law."

Heather took a healthy sip of her own martini, hoping by the time she reached the bottom of the glass, the memory of those dresses would be obliterated.

Oh, hell. Who was she kidding? She could chug an entire bottle of gin and still wouldn't be able to forget.

Alison tucked a strand of her straight brown hair behind her ear, then put her elbow on the table and rested her chin in her hand, listening to Heather get the bridal-shop experience out of her system. Alison had perpetually widened brown eyes that made her look as if she was interested in anything a person was saying, even when she wasn't. This was probably one of those times when she wasn't, but she was too good a friend to say so.

"It wasn't just that the style was weird," Heather said. "It was the color, too. They were *pink*."

Alison's forehead crinkled. "Pink's not really your color."

"That pink wasn't anybody's color. Take a blender.

Throw in a chunk of watermelon. Toss in a dozen flamingo feathers. Top it off with a bottle of Pepto-Bismol. Hit the button, and there you go."

"How about we make a pact?" Alison said. "When we get married, we have veto power over each other's bridesmaid dresses. That'll lessen the chances of either of us making a tragic mistake."

"Sounds like a plan to me," Heather said.

They locked pinky fingers, entering into the umpteenth pact they'd made since junior high. The first one had been a pinky swear that unless they both got dates to the Christmas dance, neither one of them would go, which turned out to be a nonissue since nobody asked either of them.

"Do you remember when we were in high school," Alison said, "and we made lists of the qualities we wanted in the men we married?"

Heather remembered. Her list had included *intelligent, well dressed,* and *good sense of humor.* Alison's list had consisted of *nice body, good kisser,* and *well hung.* Even though they'd both been virgins at the time, Alison's intuition told her that size really did matter.

"Yeah," Heather said. "I wanted a professional man. You wanted a porn star."

"Hey! Stamina is a very worthwhile quality in a man. I mean, if it's over in five minutes, then what's the point of doing it at all?" Alison looked across the room. "And speaking of men we'd like to marry..."

Heather turned to see one of McMillan's regulars sitting at a table with another man she didn't recognize. Her heart always skipped a little whenever she saw Tony McCaffrey, but only because there were certain basic reactions a woman couldn't fight.

"Marriage?" Heather said. "A man like him?"

"You're right. Forget marriage. I'd settle for a nice, steamy affair."

Which was about all a man like Tony would be able to deliver, since guys like him were all about playing the field. With those captivating green eyes and dazzling smile, he could have a woman stark naked before she knew what hit her.

"Yeah, he's gorgeous, all right," Heather said. "But would you really want a man like him?"

"Please. Would *you* kick him out of bed?"

"I'd never go to bed with him in the first place."

Alison rolled her eyes. "You are such a liar."

"No, I'm not. I like men with brains. Guys like him are so good-looking they've never had to rely on anything else."

"I don't know about you," Alison said, "but I'd be having sex with the man, not asking him to derive a new law of physics."

"Fine. Why don't you hop over there and see if he's free tonight?"

"Right," Alison said. "And the entire time we were talking, he'd be looking over my shoulder at one of the waitress's butts."

"Exactly. What's the future with a guy like him?"

"Forget the future. I'd be perfectly willing to take him one night at a time." Alison sighed wistfully. "Why is it women like us never get men like him?"

"Because we're B-cups with three-digit IQs."

"Seriously. Look what we have to offer. We're college graduates. We have good jobs with 401(k)s. We're not in therapy. Maybe we're not Miss America material, but we don't scare small children, do we?"

Heather frowned. "Next you're going to say we have good personalities and childbearing hips."

"Trouble is, we have boring professions. You're an accountant, and I'm a loan officer. What man wants to date either one of those?"

"So what should we do? Become flight attendants? Exotic dancers? Dallas Cowboy cheerleaders?"

"I was thinking Hooters girls. Just once I'd like a man to love me for my body instead of my mind."

And that was exactly what it took to get the attention of a man like Tony: a hot body in low-slung jeans and a tight T-shirt that showed off perky breasts, a belly-button ring, and a lower-back tattoo. A woman whose intelligence was inversely proportional to her bra size.

Tracy swung by and asked if they wanted another martini. Heather just asked for the check.

"Leaving so soon?" Alison asked.

"Soon as I finish this one. I have to get up early in the morning. Regina's picking me up at seven to go to the airport."

"So you're actually going on the bridesmaid trip? You said you'd rather sit through a time-share presentation in Death Valley."

"Well, it is a free trip, and I've never been to Vegas." Then she sighed. "And my mother really wants me to go. It reminds me of when she wanted me to try out for the high school drill team."

"So you could be around all the popular girls?"

"I think she's hoping that if I hang out with Regina and the other bridesmaids, there'll be men all over the place.

That way, at least I'll have a shot at getting one of their castoffs."

"Actually," Alison said, "that's not a bad plan."

"Wrong. It's the sign of a desperate woman. And my mother is more desperate than most. It drives me crazy."

But if Heather was honest with herself, the reason it drove her crazy was because she *was* beginning to feel a little desperate. The closer she got to thirty, the more she felt a million years of evolution bearing down on her. No, she didn't want Og smacking her over the head with his club and dragging her back to his cave to make little Oggies, but she wasn't immune to the forces of nature. A forward-moving relationship with a man that eventually led to marriage would be nice, but so far it hadn't happened.

She glanced back at Tony. Yeah, he was hot, all right, but men like him had never been part of her dreams, just as she'd never been part of theirs. She'd always figured that the man she married probably wouldn't be all that handsome, but he would be reasonably attractive. He might not be wickedly charming, but he'd certainly be a good conversationalist. They'd settle down, have a couple of kids, take summer vacations, and plan for retirement.

Heather had always prided herself on being a realist, and *that* was reality.

⌒

Tony couldn't believe this. Three days before closing, and suddenly Dave was pulling the rug right out from under him?

"Come on, Dave," Tony said. "You can't do this to me. You said you'd loan me the money."

"It's my wife. We had a big fight last night, and she told me I couldn't give you the twenty thousand."

Tony took a calming breath, trying to keep his panic under control. "Dave. You told me you talked to her. You said she was okay with it."

"She was. Then she got to talking to her girlfriends. They told her that if I was part owner of a bar, I'd be spending all my time there."

"That's crazy! You're going to be a silent partner. I'll be running the place."

"I tried to tell her that, but she wouldn't listen. She's convinced I'll want to be here all the time. She already thinks I play too much golf."

"So tell her you'll play less golf. Tell her you'll throw your damned golf clubs into the lake. For God's sake, tell her something. I'm set to close on this place Monday morning!"

"Sorry, man. I can't help you."

Tony sat back, reeling with disbelief. "Dave? How long have we been friends?"

Dave looked away. "A couple of years."

"Six years. *Six.* Ever since we worked at Charlie's together. And this is what you do to me?"

"You're a friend, Tony. She's my wife. I have to *live* with her. And trust me, sometimes that ain't easy." He checked his watch and sighed. "I have to get home. If I'm late for dinner, I'll catch hell."

As Dave started to get out of the booth, Tony grabbed his arm. "Come on, Dave. I'm begging you. Do something. You *know* how much I want to buy this place."

When Dave looked at him sadly, Tony knew he was sunk. "Sorry, buddy. I really am. But I just can't help you."

Dave walked away, leaving Tony alone with his beer, his frustration, and a dream that was falling apart at the seams. If he didn't show up with the entire down payment at the closing on Monday morning, the deal was dead.

Think. Think! How can you come up with twenty thousand dollars by Monday?

He sat there a long time, trying to formulate a plan, but nothing came to him. He was completely tapped out himself, and he had no other friends he could borrow that kind of money from, particularly on such short notice. No friends, and certainly no family members.

He didn't own a house, so a home equity loan was out.

He glanced over at the pool tables. He knew he could bet on a few games and come out a winner, but betting on pool in a neighborhood bar wouldn't net him twenty grand until the beginning of the next millennium, much less by Monday.

He dropped his head to his hands, letting out a sigh of disappointment. By the time this place came up for sale again, he'd probably be collecting Social Security.

Then slowly he raised his head again as a thought occurred to him. There *was* a way he could conceivably put twenty thousand dollars in his pocket before Monday. Betting on pool might be out, but there were other kinds of gambling....

No. He was crazy even to consider it.

But as the minutes passed and his desperation grew, even a crazy plan seemed better than no plan. It was a long shot—such a ridiculous long shot that no reasonable man would even consider doing it—but it was his *only* shot at keeping this opportunity from passing him by.

He took out his cell phone, dialed American Airlines, and booked a flight to Las Vegas, praying that Lady Luck would follow him all the way there.

~

The bridesmaid entourage arrived in Las Vegas around noon on Friday. They took a cab to the hotel, and by the time everyone paired up for rooms, Heather of course was the odd woman out. But that was okay. She didn't mind a room by herself if the alternative was to be stuck with a woman who chattered incessantly, complained about her nonexistent cellulite, and hogged the bathroom.

After checking in, Heather spent the afternoon at the pool with the other women, who looked sleek and svelte in their designer swimsuits. Heather finished the novel she'd bought at the airport before the flight, all the while listening to One through Five flirt with every man in the vicinity. Regina did the same, only her flirting was accompanied by a giggle and a flash of her three-carat diamond. *Sorry, guys. I know you want me, but I'm taken.*

That evening they went to dinner, and then the other women sashayed across the casino floor, gambling just enough to allow them to sidle up next to any handsome high rollers who might be looking for a good time.

Thanks to a statistics class she'd had in college, taught by a Vegas-addicted professor, Heather knew quite a bit about gambling. How to play the games. What the odds were. Which games were more favorable to the bettor even though they were all stacked in favor of the house.

She'd even tried gambling once on a day trip with Alison to a Shreveport casino, and she'd actually won a hundred dollars playing craps. But since it was all about luck, she knew when to quit. At the end of the day, she'd reached the conclusion that gambling was at best expensive entertainment and at worst a horrible addiction, which meant she had no desire to do it again.

The bridesmaids' other recreation of the evening—picking up strange men—held no appeal for Heather, either. So instead of trailing after them, she strolled up and down the Strip to do a little people-watching, ducked into a few shops, and then took in a comedy show.

Later, as she was going back up to her room, she found a ten-dollar chip on the floor outside her room, which she stuck in her purse to take home as a souvenir. *There.* She'd gotten lucky in Vegas. Only it wasn't the kind of "getting lucky" her mother had hoped for.

On Saturday morning, they all slept in, then had lunch at a café in the hotel. Heather learned that Five hadn't returned to her room until after three o'clock, and One hadn't made it back until dawn. Both of them described their sexual escapades in graphic detail, and the longer they talked, the more Heather realized how white-bread her sex life had been up to now.

Heather passed on the spa excursion with the other women, then met them for dinner that night. One and Five were still talking about their exploits from the night before, and as Heather sipped an after-dinner martini, she found herself wondering if there might be a decent pay-per-view movie she could watch in her room that night.

"Heather," Regina said. "You don't seem to be having a good time."

Heather looked up, a little startled. "I'm having a wonderful time."

"You haven't said ten words all weekend."

"I'm fine. Really."

"I know what your problem is."

"My problem?"

Regina fanned the bridesmaids with call-to-arms expression. "Girls, we need to find Heather a man."

Heather almost choked on her martini. "What did you say?"

"Yes!" Four said. "I *love* matchmaking."

"Me, too," Five said. "This hotel is full of single men. We'll have you hooked up in no time."

Heather was flabbergasted. Were these women out of their minds? "No. Really. I think I'm just going up to my room to watch a movie or something."

"Oh, come on, Heather!" Regina said. "Do you have to be such a stick-in-the-mud? Let us help you find a man."

"No, thanks," Heather said. "One-night stands aren't my thing."

"You know what they say," Two said, wiggling her eyebrows. "What happens in Vegas stays in Vegas."

Heather doubted that. The STD she was likely to acquire would probably follow her all the way back to Texas.

"Come on," Three said. "Don't you want to hook up?"

"Thanks for the offer," Heather said, "but I think I'll just go back to my room." She downed the rest of her martini, then rose from her chair, wobbling a little as the alcohol rushed to her head.

"You know, Heather," Regina said, "it's pretty clear

why you can't find a man." Heather froze. "It's because you don't even try."

Well, *hell*. What was Heather supposed to say to that? If she said she *did* try, she looked like a pitiful woman who couldn't get a man's attention. But if she agreed that she didn't try, she looked like a pitiful woman who'd *given up* on getting a man's attention.

"I told you I'd rather just go back to my room," Heather said.

"Well, if that's the way you want it," Regina said. "Don't say we didn't try to help."

Rationally, Heather knew Regina acted the way she did because she dealt with her own insecurities by putting other people down. *Ir*rationally, Heather wished she could wrap her hands around her cousin's neck and squeeze until her eyeballs popped out.

"And I appreciate that," Heather said, with sweetness edging into sarcasm, "but like I told you, I'm calling it a night."

As she turned and left the restaurant, she could feel Regina's smirk following her all the way out the door.

Actually, Regina was wrong. Heather *did* try to meet men. She did everything the women's magazines said single women were supposed to do. Get out in the community. Do volunteer work. Take up a hobby. Join a church group. Meet men at work. Hang out in the produce section of the grocery store. She'd done it all, with no results. Now, not only was she stuck being in Regina's wedding, but she probably wouldn't even have a date to bring to it.

Heather turned the corner into the elevator lobby, where a man stood with his back to her. The UP button had already been pushed, but he reached over impatiently and jabbed it again. She came up beside him.

"The elevators are really slow here, aren't they?" she said.

"Yeah," he muttered. "I could walk the stairs faster than this."

"I'm on the twenty-second floor," she said with a smile. "I think I'll wait."

As she spoke, she turned to look up at him, and for a moment she thought she must be seeing things.

Tony McCaffrey?

She turned away quickly. No. It couldn't be. He couldn't possibly be standing next to her in this elevator lobby a thousand miles from home. Identical twin, maybe?

She peered at him out of the corner of her eye. Nope. It was Tony. Even an identical twin couldn't be *that* identical. He was dressed the way she'd always seen him—casual and comfortable, this time in a faded blue polo shirt, well-worn jeans, and Nikes.

Her heart rate picked up a little, as it always did whenever she saw him. But what woman's wouldn't? Some men were so handsome that any woman between puberty and the grave would stop to stare, and Tony McCaffrey was one of them.

Then all at once, Heather realized something wasn't right. Instead of the electric smile he wore most of the time, his mouth was turned down in a frown, and his face was tight and drawn. He stabbed the UP button again, then turned and leaned against the wall, closing his eyes with a heavy sigh, a beer bottle dangling from his fingertips.

"Bad night?" she asked.

He opened his eyes. They were heavy with gloom. "They don't get much worse."

"What's wrong?"

"I needed to win tonight. I really, *really* needed to win."

Uh-oh. She'd seen him hustle plenty of games of pool, but she'd never taken him for a gambling addict.

"Loan shark?" she asked.

"No. Nothing like that."

"Then what?"

He took a sip of his beer, still looking morose, and for a moment Heather thought he wasn't going to answer.

"Have you ever had something you wanted really badly?" he finally said. "So badly you'd do anything to get it?"

Heather shrugged. "Well, yeah. I guess."

"No. I mean, something that was *really* important to you."

"Like what?"

He let out a breath of resignation. "I was going to buy a bar."

"A bar? What kind of bar?"

"A little place called McMillan's. It's a neighborhood bar in Plano, Texas."

Heather blinked in surprise. He was going to *buy* McMillan's?

Then she remembered hearing that the bar was going up for sale. Tony spent a lot of time at McMillan's—drinking, playing pool, and hitting on women—but she'd never imagined him actually owning the place.

"You don't recognize me, do you?" Heather asked.

"Uh...should I?"

"I'm from Plano. My friend and I go to McMillan's sometimes. I've seen you there."

When he stared at her blankly, it confirmed exactly what Heather had always thought. The moment she walked through the door of a bar, she slipped right into a cloak of invisibility.

"Yeah," he said finally, "I think I remember seeing you there," even though she knew he didn't.

"So what happened?" she asked. "Did the deal fall through?"

"A friend was going to loan me the last twenty thousand I needed. He backed out. If I don't have the money to close the deal by Monday morning, it's dead in the water. I came to Vegas thinking maybe..." He exhaled. "Oh, hell. It was a stupid idea."

"You thought you could win the money?"

"Even long shots pay off every once in a while." He drained his beer and tossed the bottle into a nearby trash can. "This wasn't one of those times."

Heather couldn't remember the last time she'd seen anyone looking quite as miserable as Tony did right then, and suddenly she knew that buying McMillan's wasn't just a whim of his. He was desperate to have it.

Desperate enough to risk everything on a trip to Vegas.

"Why don't you try again?" she asked.

"Nope. I'm completely tapped out. I shouldn't be spending one more dime tonight."

Heather heard the *ping* of the elevator, and the doors finally opened. Tony started to get on.

"Wait," Heather said.

"What?"

"Just wait."

He held the elevator as she dug through her purse and came up with the ten-dollar chip she'd found in the hallway outside her room. She held it up. "Here. Play this."

"No. I can't take your money."

"Play the chip. If you lose, you owe me ten bucks. If you win, I'll take back my ten and you can keep on betting with the winnings."

He laughed, but there was no humor in it. "Thanks, sweetheart. But I need a bigger stake than ten bucks if I expect to turn it into twenty thousand."

He got onto the elevator. Heather followed, still holding the chip. The doors closed. She punched 22. He punched 24.

The elevator ascended. Silence, except for the mechanical noise of the elevator and the *ping, ping, ping* as it passed one floor after another.

"You're making a mistake," Heather said.

"I doubt that."

"I think this is a lucky chip."

"Yeah? What makes you say that?"

"I found it in the hall near my room. Maybe there's a reason I found it, you know? Fate, or something."

He turned away again. "Sorry. I don't believe in fate."

Stubborn, *stubborn* man.

This was making Heather crazy. She could think of very few situations where gambling was a logical thing to do, but this was one of them. When a person had only one shot left at something that was important to him, no matter how small, wouldn't he be smart to take it?

When the elevator doors opened on her floor and he still hadn't given in, she casually let the chip fall out of her hand. It clicked against the marble tile floor, then came to rest near Tony's foot.

"Oops," she said. "Look at that. I dropped it." Then she smiled sweetly. "Good night."

She left the elevator and walked in the direction of her room, listening intently for the doors to close behind her. They didn't.

"Wait," Tony said.

She turned around to see him holding up the chip. "Do you have any idea what the odds are of turning this into twenty thousand bucks?"

"Zero if you don't play."

"It's one chance in a million."

"Beats no chance at all."

"The way my luck has been, it's not worth the trip downstairs."

She walked back to the elevator and got on. "Then I'll play it for you. I once won a hundred dollars at the El Dorado in Shreveport."

"That's a far cry from twenty grand."

"I wasn't shooting for twenty grand."

"What's your game?"

"Craps. I don't like blackjack, and it's got the next lowest house advantage."

Tony nodded. "That's my game, too. Hope you have more luck with it than I've had tonight."

Heather was a realist. No doubt about that. But as she stood in that elevator giving this tiny bit of hope to a man who five minutes ago had had none at all, she felt an amazing surge of optimism. Or maybe it was a surge of gin to her brain.

Either way, it felt *wonderful*.

As the elevator descended, Tony took a deep breath and let it out slowly, all the while tapping his fingertips nervously against his thigh. He'd told her this was a chance in a million, but by the look on his face, she knew just how much he was counting on it.

Chapter 3

Tony knew there was no way under the sun they could turn ten dollars into twenty thousand. So why was he standing at a craps table next to a woman he didn't even know, waiting for her to play a ten-dollar chip so he could go home an even bigger loser?

"How are you playing it?" he asked her.

"You leave that to me."

As the shooter prepared to roll, she placed the chip on the pass line. When the come-out roll was a seven, Tony's heart skipped. An automatic winner. But it didn't mean a thing. Anybody could win one roll of the dice.

She tucked one of the chips back inside her purse and held up the other one. "Now you have money to play with."

"It's a far cry from twenty grand."

"Gotta start somewhere."

"Fine," he said. "Play it again."

"It's your turn now."

"Nope. I told you how my luck's been running."

"As long as you avoid the sucker bets, you have as good a chance of winning big as I do."

But right now, Tony wasn't so sure about that. He'd

told her he didn't believe in fate, but he had to admit it was more than a little strange that he'd met this woman in the elevator who was from his home town, who hung out in the bar he wanted to buy, who had found a chip outside her room that she insisted on giving him when he was all tapped out himself.

Very strange.

When Tony first saw her, he'd immediately dismissed her. Average features. Plainly dressed. Nice-girl type, which meant she wasn't his type. But he wasn't looking for a date for the evening. He was looking for a miracle, and right now, she was the only one who might be able to give him one.

"Listen to me…uh…What was your name again?"

"Heather."

"Heather. Like I told you, my luck has left the building. I want you to play for me."

"And if I lose?"

"I'd already lost. I'd be no worse off than I was ten minutes ago."

With a shrug, she placed the chip on the pass line again. When the shooter rolled a six as a come-out and his next roll was another six, which doubled Tony's ten to twenty, he felt a little tremor of excitement.

"What now?" Tony asked her.

"Hmm," she said, surveying the table. "A come bet."

"Why?"

"Just a hunch."

She placed a bet, this time against the shooter. When the man crapped out, Tony turned to Heather with disbelief.

"You won," he said.

"It's nothing but luck."

"But some people's luck is better than others'. Do it again."

The dealer passed the dice to Heather. She placed a bet, and on the come-out roll, she threw an eleven. Another winner. And because she'd played the odds, she'd more than doubled his money.

Unbelievable.

Then, on the next roll, she lost, and Tony felt a tremor of apprehension. But still she smiled up at him.

"No big deal," she said. "As long as we win more than we lose, we'll be fine."

Over the next forty-five minutes, she didn't win every roll, but her piles of chips grew bigger. The strangest little tremor slid across the back of Tony's neck. He did a quick count, and to his astonishment, he was up nearly fifteen hundred dollars.

This was starting to get serious. He had a decent stake now, one that could actually get him where he needed to go.

As long as their lucky streak held.

～

Heather was trying to play it cool, but she'd underestimated how nervous it would make her to see this much money on the line. She was into conservative investments that grew over time, not large chunks of money that could appear or disappear with the random roll of a pair of dice.

She became aware of other women hovering around the table, watching the action, but mostly they were watching Tony. There was nothing like a handsome man on a winning streak to catch the attention of a horde of women. Heather might have been the one playing, but he was the one they were watching. To her surprise, she felt the funniest little twinge of possessiveness.

Back off, she wanted to say. *He's with me.*

No matter what she'd told Alison about not being attracted to Tony, she just couldn't help herself. She liked the feeling of having the attention of the most handsome man in the room. Still, she knew the truth. She had his attention only because he was winning.

So make sure he keeps winning.

The cocktail waitress came by, and because Heather's usual good judgment was seriously slipping, she asked for another martini. Anything to settle her jangled nerves. Tony, on the other hand, didn't seemed jangled at all. With every addition to their pile of chips, he seemed more relaxed, more animated, more hopeful.

When the waitress brought their drinks, Tony took a few sips of his beer. Heather downed half of her martini in one gulp. Okay. Now she felt better. Not quite so shaky. A little more optimistic. Only slightly more woozy. She told herself that people showed up in Vegas all the time with pocket change and left millionaires. She and Tony didn't need a million dollars. They needed only twenty thousand.

When she thought about it that way, it didn't seem so insurmountable. In fact, it seemed downright probable. That made her feel even luckier than before, so she played a bit of a long shot. Tony's smile slipped a little as he realized what she was doing, which made her nervous, but she held her breath and rolled the dice.

And won.

Tony let out a little whoop. Then he wrapped his arm around her shoulders and gave her a big, smacking kiss on the cheek. "My good luck charm," he said, and flashed that broad, beautiful smile. "Thank God I ran into you."

Heather's heart went wild, her cheek on fire from that single touch of his lips. Tony was handsome and exciting and fun, and being with him made her feel as if she were glowing from the inside out. Suddenly it was as if another woman had taken over her body, a dice-throwing, risk-taking alter ego who was going to get that twenty grand for him no matter what.

Over the next few hours, she lost some, but she won more, and their winnings grew. The loud voices in the casino and the steady *pinging* and *shuffling* of the slot machines and the effect of the three martinis she'd had lulled her mind, and soon the nervousness she'd felt earlier had transformed into an edge of excitement that blasted away any thoughts of losing. Rationally, she knew that that was how all Vegas losers felt before the bottom fell out, but then Tony smiled at her again, and that thought floated right out of her mind.

When they were approaching the eight-thousand mark, Tony leaned over and whispered, "We'd better watch our step. This kind of luck can't hold forever."

"Nope. We're on a roll. It's time to ramp things up."

"Ramp things up?"

"Bigger bets."

Tony looked at her in surprise. Then his eyes brightened, and his lips edged into a smile. "I like your style."

Heather felt as if she were hovering a few inches above the ground, buoyed by the exhilaration he made her feel. She could do this. She could get to that twenty grand.

After all, they'd won eight thousand dollars in a matter of a few hours. What was a few thousand more?

Pretty soon, eight thousand became ten.

"Sweetheart, you are *hot,*" Tony said, resting his hand on her shoulder. Then he leaned closer and murmured in her ear, "Can you bring it home for me?"

Heather felt a delightful little shiver run from her neck all the way to her toes. He was right. She was hot. She couldn't lose. Sometimes everything in the universe lined up behind a person and pushed them in the right direction, and that was exactly what was happening tonight.

"Yeah," she said. "I can do it." She took a deep breath. "As a matter of fact, it's time to go for broke."

Tony froze. "What?"

"All of it on the next roll," Heather said. "The whole pot."

"Are you sure?"

She knew it was a crazy thing to do, but conviction filled her mind like a lion's roar, silencing that whiny little pip-squeak that usually ran her day-to-day activities, the one who wanted her to toe the line, play by the rules, and in general lead a boring, repetitive, mundane life.

Tonight she was listening to the lion.

"All ten thousand," Heather said. "Trust me. I feel it. We can't lose."

She gave Tony a challenging stare, showing him she meant what she said. Then her gaze moved to his lips. Lordy, he had such nice, *nice* lips, particularly when he used them for something besides talking. She wanted to feel them again, anywhere he wanted to put them. If he'd kissed her on the cheek earlier for winning a few hundred bucks, what would he do if she won the whole twenty thousand?

It made her dizzy just to think about the possibilities.

Her gaze drifted back to his eyes, and for a moment she thought he was going to say no. Then a tiny smile played around his mouth, becoming a full-fledged, full-speed-ahead grin.

"Okay, sweetheart. I can't argue with success. Go for it."

Yes!

She turned back to the table and shoved the whole pot onto the pass line, which made everyone at the table fall silent and stare at her as if she was the most courageous woman alive. And right at that moment, that was exactly how she felt. She gave Tony a confident smile. She shook the dice. Threw them. Heard them hit the table. A gasp went up from the crowd, signaling that something astonishing had happened.

"Four," the dealer said.

Heather froze. No. It couldn't be.

Time seemed to grind to a sluggish crawl, with everything moving in slow motion. She couldn't have heard him right. It was supposed to be a seven. Or an eleven. Anything but a four. People were supposed to be *cheering.*

But there it was. Four black dots staring up at her like tiny demonic eyeballs.

Her head felt as if she were submerged in swamp water, where everything was murky and she couldn't hear a thing and she couldn't breathe. Tony just stood there, his jaw slack with surprise, his hands hovering in the air as if he'd expected to sweep an armload of chips toward him, only to watch the dealer sweep them away instead.

No, no, no! This can't be happening!

People around the table started murmuring among themselves. She couldn't hear most of their conversation.

The words *moron* and *nutcase* came through loud and clear, though, and the truth struck Heather so hard, she was sure she heard the *thwack*. People hadn't been staring at her before because she was courageous. They'd been staring at her with the same sense of lurid compulsion they generally saved for train wrecks and five-car pileups. They knew something disastrous was only seconds away from happening, and they hadn't been able to look away.

Heather took a few clunky steps backward, blinking with disbelief. How stupid could she possibly have been? It wasn't like her to get carried away. It wasn't like her to even *be* in Vegas, much less betting thousands of dollars. What was the *matter* with her?

She glanced at Tony. His slack jaw had constricted, and he was clutching his beer bottle so tightly she was afraid it was going to shatter. Then he turned around and walked away.

"Tony! Wait!"

She caught up to him, striding along beside him as he headed for the elevator lobby. "I'm sorry. I'm so, *so* sorry. I never should have bet it all. Never."

"That's right. You shouldn't have."

"I don't know what got into me."

"I think gin got into you."

"I thought I could do it," she said. "I really thought—"

"Hey, it wasn't my money to start with. You could do anything with it you wanted to."

"I *wanted* to win the money for you!"

"I don't want to talk about it."

"But—"

He stopped short and faced her. "Look, if it makes you

feel any better, I'm mad at both of us. I let you do it, so it was just as much my fault as it was yours."

But she could tell by the look on his face that he didn't believe that for a moment. He blamed her now, and he would blame her through the rest of eternity. And she had eternity left to feel horrible about it.

"Wait." She dug through her purse and found the original ten-dollar chip. She held it up, giving him a shaky smile. "We still have this."

"You're kidding, right?"

"No. If we did it once, we can do it again. Only this time—"

"Forget it, sweetheart. I'm done."

And this time, she knew he meant it.

The sick, sinking sensation in Heather's stomach was more than she could bear. She hated that she'd been the one to steal that smile right off Tony's face, to dangle his dream in front of him only to yank it away again.

He turned and headed for the elevator lobby, leaving her standing there feeling worse than she ever had in her life. Somewhere in this town tonight, somebody was going home a big winner.

She'd give anything right now if that somebody could be Tony.

She turned and looked out at the gaming floor. Bright lights. People laughing. People *winning*. Okay, maybe not twenty thousand dollars all at once, but . . .

Then something caught her eye. A slot machine sitting less than an arm's length away. Her gaze panned up, and when she saw the maximum payout, she couldn't believe it.

Twenty thousand dollars?

As she stared at the machine, her heart skipped crazily, then settled into a heavy, thudding rhythm.

Maybe fate wasn't through with them yet.

～

Tony punched the button for the elevator, then turned around and leaned against the wall. Hadn't he been here only a few hours ago feeling just like this?

No. He hadn't felt like this at all. He hadn't felt as if an elephant were sitting on his chest, squeezing the breath out of him. Everything he'd ever wanted had been within his grasp. He'd been so close to it, so *close*...

And then he'd trusted his future to a crazy woman.

All he wanted to do was go upstairs, climb into bed, and pretend this day had never been. And then Monday, he'd go back to stealing cars for a living and wondering if he'd be old and gray before the next opportunity like this one came along.

He punched the button again. Where was the damned elevator?

Suddenly he heard a commotion coming from the gaming floor, with a noise level even greater than usual. Wild *pinging* and people cheering. He knew those sounds. Somebody had won, and won big. *Damn it.* Why couldn't it have been him?

Finally the elevator came. He drained his beer, tossed the bottle in a nearby trash can, and got on.

"Tony! Wait!"

He looked between the closing elevator doors to see Heather hurrying toward him. He jammed his hand between the doors until they opened again. She stepped into the elevator, grabbed his hands, and pulled him out.

"Heather? What are you doing?"

"You'll never guess what happened!"

"What?"

"I did it, Tony. I did it!"

"Did what?"

"I won twenty thousand dollars!"

He blinked dumbly. If this was a joke, it was a really bad one.

"You couldn't have," he said. "It would have taken you hours to win that much money."

"Not when I plug a ten-dollar slot machine that has a payoff of twenty thousand!"

She was right. Those could have big payoffs. They happened only once in a blue moon, but the possibility was there. But the likelihood...

"Tony?" she said, jiggling his hands. "Did you hear me? I *won!*"

"Come on, Heather. Nobody walks right up to a slot machine and wins twenty thousand dollars."

Her face fell. "But I did! Look at this!"

She showed him the receipt. She was right. Twenty thousand dollars.

When he finally realized she wasn't delusional, that maybe she really did win all that money, envy shot through him so sharply he nearly doubled over from the pain. She'd been reckless at the craps table when she was playing for him, leaving him with nothing. Then as soon as he left the gaming floor, she'd won big. Yeah, she was lucky, all right. At all the wrong times.

With a heavy sigh, he turned around and hit the

button to call another elevator. "Good for you, sweetheart. Congratulations."

"What do you mean, good for me? It's good for *you!*"

"What are you talking about? We were finished. That was your ten bucks. Which means it's your twenty thousand."

"No! I'd have won it for you at the craps table if I hadn't gotten so wound up in the moment. That was stupid." She smiled brightly. "But this makes up for it, right?"

Tony couldn't believe it. She was giving the money to him?

He felt an edge of excitement, but he wasn't ready to accept the fact that this was really happening. She'd been drinking, which, as she'd already demonstrated, made her do dumb things. Still, when he studied her face for any reservation she might have, he just didn't see any.

"Twenty thousand is a lot of money," he said. "I never would have known you won it if you hadn't said something. Why did you?"

"Because if I hadn't, twenty thousand dollars' worth of guilt would have followed me around for the rest of my life. I don't like feeling guilty. Take this money off my hands. *Please.*"

Even though she said it dramatically, he didn't miss the smile that played across her lips, and his own excitement escalated. "You really want to give me this money? No strings attached?"

"It may have been my ten dollars, but I was still playing for you. And think about it. What were the odds that the first machine I saw had a jackpot of exactly the amount you needed? It was fate, Tony. Fate!"

He'd never believed in fate before, but she was right.

What were the odds? The funniest little shiver crept across his shoulders, telling him that maybe it was time to quit questioning the why of it and just enjoy the fact that this evening had turned out way, *way* better than he'd ever expected.

He matched her smile. Then he started to laugh. With a whoop of excitement, he put his arms around Heather, picked her up, and spun her around. When he set her down again, she was laughing, too, and her cheeks were flushed pink.

"You're going to buy the bar," she said breathlessly.

"Thanks to you."

"I got lucky."

"It's not luck, remember? It's fate."

"But you told me you don't believe in fate."

"In the past few minutes," he said, "I've been reevaluating a lot of things."

Not the least of which was the woman he held right now.

How many women would have chased him down to give him twenty thousand dollars when she could have kept it for herself without him ever knowing?

None of the women he usually went out with.

As he stared down at Heather, something seemed to shift inside him. He noticed for the first time how clear and blue her eyes were as they sparked with excitement; how her broad, brilliant smile caused tiny crinkles around her mouth; and how her skin felt so soft beneath his hands.

He stroked her arms, assuring himself that this whole thing wasn't a figment of his imagination. That *she* wasn't a figment of his imagination. He remembered thinking earlier that she wasn't his kind of woman, but for the life of him, he couldn't see why now.

Maybe it was the alcohol he'd had, or the roller-coaster ride this evening had become, or the fact that she'd walked into his life and made all his dreams come true. Whatever it was, he didn't want to let her go. Instead, he grabbed her by the shoulders, dragged her up next to him, and kissed her.

Chapter 4

When Tony's lips landed on Heather's, she couldn't have been more shocked. But her gasp of surprise was immediately stifled as he curled his hand around her neck and pulled her to him, engulfing her mouth with his. She put her hand blindly against his chest and caught his shirt in her fist, her other hand winding automatically around his neck. She clung to him helplessly, losing herself in the pleasure of it.

This was it. This was what it was like to be kissed by a man who really knew how. The taste of him was intoxicating—like beer and sex and victory all rolled into one—and she couldn't get enough of it.

She sensed that other people were watching, people who'd wandered into the elevator lobby, never expecting to see a full-fledged public display of affection. Or in this case, appreciation. She figured Tony probably kissed women all the time for just about any reason, and the money she'd won for him was a better reason than most. She couldn't have imagined what a twenty-thousand-dollar kiss felt like, but now she knew.

It was *amazing*.

"Heather, what in the world are you doing?"

Heather spun around, surprised to find Regina standing behind her. *Great.* Leave it to Regina to interrupt the best kiss she'd ever had in her life.

But then she noticed Regina had stopped dead in her tracks, staring at her with an expression of dumb disbelief. She was flanked by One through Five, all of whom looked equally incredulous. In that moment, Heather discovered there was only one thing on earth that even approached the pleasure of a kiss from Tony McCaffrey, and that was Regina watching her get a kiss from Tony Mc-Caffrey. Heather felt positively giddy. *Ahhh.* This night just got better and better.

"Hi, Regina," Heather said, then gave the bridesmaids a little wave of her fingertips. "Hi, girls."

"Friends of yours?" Tony asked Heather.

"Uh...yeah. Well, Regina's my cousin. She's getting married in a month. The rest of us are her bridesmaids. We're here to party a little before the wedding."

"Congratulations," Tony said to Regina, then turned to the others. "Nice to meet you, ladies."

When he gave them one of his thousand-watt smiles, the women's knees seemed to get a little wobbly. For a moment, Heather felt a twinge of foreboding, thinking maybe Tony was on the verge of scooping up all the bridesmaids, picking out the one he liked the best, then tossing the rest away and spending the remainder of the evening with that one. It certainly wasn't unprecedented behavior. Instead, he turned to Heather.

"Why don't you go fill out whatever paperwork you have to and get the check? In the meantime, I'll get the limousine."

Heather blinked. "Limousine?"

"It's time for us to celebrate," Tony said. "A little champagne, a tour of Vegas, and"—he gave her a wink—"whatever else we can think of to do. How does that sound?"

Six heads whipped around, waiting for her response. Was this really happening? Tony had a smorgasbord of beautiful women right there in front of him, and he wanted to spend the evening with her?

"Sounds great," Heather said. "We do have a lot to celebrate."

"You bet we do." Tony leaned in and gave her a quick peck on the cheek. "Meet me in front of the hotel."

With one last smile, Tony headed for the concierge desk. The women watched him walk away, expressions of total astonishment on their faces.

"My God," Three said, once Tony was out of earshot. "Regina. Did you see that guy? He's *gorgeous*."

"I suppose he is," Regina said. "If you like pretty boys."

"No boy there," Five said. "I'm pretty sure that one's all man."

"Wow, Regina," Two said. "Guess she didn't need our help finding a man after all."

Never in Heather's wildest dreams could she have imagined a scenario like this, and she wanted to wallow in it. To bask in the glow of Regina's disbelief. To let the wild torrent of her own elation spill over her cousin like a bucket of cold water.

Okay, so she was being spiteful in a way she usually wasn't, but since the opportunity might never present itself again, she wasn't above enjoying it to the fullest.

Four turned to Heather. "Where did you hook up with *him?*"

"In the elevator lobby after I left the restaurant."

"What are you celebrating?" One asked.

"Tony just won twenty thousand dollars." Sort of. Close enough. Regina certainly didn't need to know the details.

Regina's mouth fell open. "Twenty *thousand* dollars?"

"That's right."

"And now you're leaving here with him?" Regina asked. "In a limousine?"

"That's right."

"I don't think that's a good idea."

"Why not?"

"Isn't it obvious? You don't even *know* that man."

Which struck Heather as really dumb, since Regina hadn't given One and Five any warnings like that when they went off with men they didn't know. And it wasn't as if Tony was a total stranger.

"Actually, I do know him. Sort of. We go to the same bar back in Plano. McMillan's. It's down the street from Chantal's." *You know. That pretentious, overpriced place you always go.*

"He's from Plano?" Four said. "You meet a hot guy in Vegas and he's from your home town? How lucky is *that?*"

"That's all you know about him?" Regina said. "That he shows up at the same bar you do?"

"I know something else," Heather said. "He's one *hell* of a kisser."

"Heather," Regina said sharply. "He's clearly preying on you for some reason. I'd watch my purse if I were you."

Heather laughed. "He just won twenty thousand dollars. Why would he bother to steal from me?"

Regina couldn't take this. She couldn't take seeing her wallflower cousin with such a handsome man. It went against the order of things in her world. Hell, it knocked her world right off its axis.

"Come on, Heather," Regina said, a note of desperation in her voice. "For all you know, he could be a serial killer."

Heather laughed. "Serial killer?"

Regina raised her chin. "It's just not a smart thing to do. That's all."

"Fine. Then I think I'll go be dumb for a while." Heather fluttered her fingers at the bridesmaids. "'Night, girls."

Feeling delightfully inebriated, she went to the cashier and got a check for twenty thousand dollars. She had to wait for a while, so she started getting a little worried that maybe she'd go outside and Tony would be gone. But when she went through the revolving door of the hotel and stepped onto the sidewalk, there he was, leaning against a long, shiny, black limousine wearing a smile as bright as the Sunset Strip itself.

He stepped away from the car, and the driver opened the door. Tony got in first, then took Heather's hand and helped her inside. She nearly gasped when she saw the interior. Soft leather seats, a television, a stereo system, and a wet bar. A bottle of champagne was chilling in an ice bucket, with a couple more in a rack beside it.

He sat down on the seat along the back of the car and pulled her down next to him, his thigh resting against hers.

"Where to, sir?" the driver said.

"Just drive," Tony told him. "The Strip, downtown, anywhere you can find lights and action."

As the driver pulled away from the curb, Tony fished through a few CDs, picked one out, and stuck it into the

CD player. Classic rock poured through the speakers, just loud enough that the bass thudded nicely along Heather's nerves.

Tony uncorked the champagne, and it fizzed down the side of the bottle. He quickly grabbed a glass, filled it, and handed it to her. She had a passing thought that maybe she'd had enough for tonight, only to tell herself that a glass or two of champagne couldn't hurt. After all, they were celebrating, weren't they?

She took the glass. He filled another one and held up his glass. "A toast to you, sweetheart. For being my good luck charm."

They clinked glasses, and she took a sip. Hmm. Not bad.

She took a bigger sip, and a bigger one after that. Then an even bigger one. She didn't remember liking champagne before, but this was *wonderful*.

Tony chugged his champagne and poured more. Heather tipped up her glass and drank the rest in a few big gulps. Little bubbles popped all the way down her throat, alcohol oozing into her stomach, making her feel warm from the inside out.

"Mmm," Heather said. "That's *really* good."

She held out her glass, and he filled it up again, and this time he proposed a toast to Las Vegas, that wonderful desert oasis where dreams come true. Heather sighed at the sentiment and tossed down more of the bubbly. Next she proposed a toast to McMillan's, which she said was going to be an even better place under its wonderful new owner. Before she knew it, her glass was empty again. As Tony filled it up, she nodded her head to the beat of the music. By the time Tony toasted Carlos Santana for his damned fine guitar playing and the driver for taking the corners really smoothly, Heather was feeling more deliciously fuzzy than she ever had in her life.

Somewhere in the back of her mind, a little voice was saying, *He's the kind your mother always warned you about. The kind who takes advantage of nice girls like you.*

Nice girl. Heather didn't realize until this moment just how much she hated being one of those. It was bad enough being an accountant because of all the stereotypes that went along with it. But for the most part, men made her nervous. What amazed her, though, was that Tony didn't intimidate her at all. He was free and fun and not the least bit hard to talk to, and she felt more comfortable with him after a few hours than she had with some men she'd known for months.

And he was so incredibly handsome, he took her breath away.

"Oh! I almost forgot." Heather handed him her glass, reached into her purse, pulled out a check, and handed it to him.

Tony stared down at it for a long time, and when he looked back up, she almost melted under the sheer force of his luminous smile.

"I still can't believe it," he said. "Sweetheart, you are something else."

"I'll deposit my check first thing Monday morning. As soon as I do, that one will be good." She pulled the original ten-dollar chip from her purse with a smile. "I played a ten-dollar bill at the slot machine, so I get to keep this as a souvenir."

"I guess I owe you ten bucks, then, huh?"

She laughed. "Just give me a free drink or two at Mc-Millan's, and we'll call it even."

"A free drink or two? Nope. I want you to come to McMillan's, and I want you to come a lot. And when you do, your money's no good there. Ever. Understand?"

"Now, how are you ever going to make a profit if you give away your food and drink?"

"How was I going to buy the bar in the first place if you hadn't come along?"

"Tony," she said, swaying a little as she leaned toward him, "if you don't watch out, I'll bankrupt you on champagne alone."

When he laughed at that, Heather felt a flush of warmth all the way to her toes, and God, it felt good. She'd never been one of those beautiful, witty women who had the instantaneous and undivided attention of handsome men. It was a heady feeling she never wanted to come down from.

"This reminds me of high school," Tony said. "Limousines on prom night are all kinds of fun."

"I didn't go to my prom," she said.

"Yeah? I didn't think they let you out of high school unless you went to the prom."

"I was valedictorian. They decided it was okay to give me a diploma anyway."

"Ah. One of the smart girls. I didn't date many of those."

"Yeah? Why not?"

"Because they didn't like to get crazy."

Heather laughed a little. "There's some truth to that. I was never really a crazy kind of girl."

"Don't worry. I can fix that."

Tony grabbed her champagne, set it down with his, then reached up to open the limo's sunroof. He got on the seat, grabbed her hand, and pulled her up to stand next to him. He stuck his head out of the sunroof and coaxed her to do the same. The wind caught her hair and whipped it behind her like a flag in a hurricane-force wind.

"My God, you *are* crazy!" she said.

Tony put his arm around her shoulder and gave her a smacking kiss on the cheek. "Heather, sweetheart, you have *got* to learn how to have a good time!"

And just like that, she was sold on crazy.

They waved and shouted to people on the sidewalks. Some waved back; some looked at them as if they were nuts. Some pretended not to see them at all, although how they could have missed two weirdos sticking their heads out of a stretch limo, Heather didn't know. In some still-sober, still-sane part of her mind, she knew she was behaving like a lunatic, but the insane part of her mind told those other parts to shut up.

Finally they collapsed back down onto the seat together, laughing, and Heather couldn't seem to wipe the grin of delight off her face. Tony was right. Crazy was good. Crazy was fun. She couldn't believe she'd gone through her whole life driving straight down the freeway when there was so much fun to be had on the side roads. Then Tony leaned forward to talk to the limo driver.

"The woman of my dreams," he said. "And to think she was right under my nose the whole time. Can you believe it?"

"No, sir," the driver deadpanned. "That is indeed unbelievable. I'll drive straight to the courthouse so you can get a marriage license."

Heather giggled. "Well, that's Las Vegas for you. Instant riches, instant weddings."

"But you're not a spontaneous person?" Tony said.

"Me? Nope. No spontaneity here. I used up all my spontaneity sticking my head out the top of the car."

His hand crept over to her thigh. "You sure about that?"

At that moment, a lightning bolt could have zapped Heather, and she wouldn't have felt the pain. Locking his eyes with hers, Tony inched his hand upward, slowly and tantalizingly, teasing his fingertips along her inner thigh. She tensed, and a tiny shudder shook her whole body. Just when she was about to jump out of her skin, he smoothed his hand back down again until it rested just above her knee.

Angling his body toward hers, he shifted his hand from her leg and draped it along the seat behind her head. Leaning in, he brought his other hand up to cradle her face.

"You have beautiful eyes," he said, his thumb stroking her temple. "And such soft, soft skin." Then he teased his fingertip along her bottom lip. "And look at this *beautiful* mouth."

And then he leaned in and kissed her. It wasn't anything like the spontaneous I'm-twenty-thousand-dollars-richer kiss he'd given her in the casino. It was a long, slow, hot kiss that made her muscles liquefy and her mind turn to mush.

Still cradling her in his arms, he leaned away a little and touched her collarbone, then dragged a single fingertip all the way to her cleavage, his gaze following it. She felt a glorious, swoopy sensation in her stomach, her breath coming faster.

"Do you really live in Plano?" he asked.

"Yeah. I really do."

"And you go to McMillan's?"

"Yeah. Don't you believe me?"

"So why do I not remember seeing you there? Shouldn't I have noticed if an angel had dropped straight down from heaven?"

He's drunk. He's delirious. He's deluded. He's anything but serious.

"I'm no angel," she said.

"I'm not so sure about that," he said, stroking his hand up and down her arm and then kissing her neck. "Have you seen that Jimmy Stewart movie? The one they always play at Christmas?"

"*It's a Wonderful Life*? I wouldn't have taken you as somebody who likes sentimental movies."

"Ah, sweetheart, there's a lot you don't know about me." He kissed his way along her neck, then swirled his tongue over her earlobe. "There was that guy who was Jimmy's angel. He came down from heaven, fixed what was wrong in his life, and then when Jimmy turned around, he wasn't there anymore."

"So I'm an angel who's out to get my wings?"

"Hope not," he said, his breath tickling her ear. "I don't want to turn around and find you gone."

Tonight did seem like the kind of miracle that only the presence of an angel could explain. And what else but a miracle could explain her being in a limousine right now with Tony's arms around her?

As he drew her into another kiss, all coherent thought left her mind, and Las Vegas became just one big swirl of light and sound and fairy-tale possibilities.

Tony had never felt more exhilarated in his life.

From the moment he'd met this woman in the elevator lobby, he felt as if he'd been on a roller coaster, swooping and turning, up and down. And now—finally—he was on a straight shot all the way to the top. For years now, he'd been waiting for an opportunity that would get his life going in the right direction. Careerwise, that was going to happen. He was going to buy the perfect business. Had he lucked out and found the perfect woman at the same time?

She felt so good beneath his hands that he couldn't stop touching her. She was hardly a wisp of a woman, but the longer he held and kissed her, the more enticing she became. He wanted more of her. *All* of her. Right here, right now, in the back of this limousine.

But from their first kiss in that elevator lobby, he knew he wasn't dealing with the kind of woman he usually dated—party girls who provided breathtaking sex with no strings attached. Any one of those women would have been ripping her clothes off the second the limo door shut behind them. This one, though, had sat down and looked around, her eyes wide with wonder, and when he so much as put his hand on her leg, she'd practically jumped out of her skin.

Take it easy, he'd told himself. *This one is different.*

She wore a loose-fitting blouse, a skirt that was a respectable length, and shoes that were way too sensible. And even though she had breasts that would turn any man's head, she didn't flaunt them. She wasn't *trying* to be sexy.

Maybe that was what was so damned sexy about her.

Not only that, but she was smart too. He'd dated enough dim bulbs to know the difference. He didn't remember the last time he'd been with a woman who had more going on upstairs than he did. That should have done some serious damage to his male ego, but for some reason, it just drew him to her even more.

The excitement of winning that money combined with the alcohol that had gone to his head in conjunction with kissing this wonderful, wonderful woman in the back of a darkened limousine made him feel on top of the world. This was good. This was *very* good.

This was extraordinary.

As he kissed her, he slid his hand to her breast, and when he found her nipple with his thumb, it was already hard and swollen. When he stroked it, she moaned against his mouth and pressed her breast harder against his palm, asking for more. It was all he could do not to rip open her blouse, hike up her skirt, and take her right here on the seat of this limo.

No. You can't do that. Not with this one.

He pulled away, took her face in his hands, and stared at her. She looked back at him, her breath coming in soft little gushes, her pale blue eyes blinking dreamily.

"What?" she murmured.

"You're different than other women I know."

"Good different or bad different?"

"For where I am right now in my life, sweetheart, you couldn't be better."

She smiled at him with those full lips and perfect white teeth, and he thought, *This woman. She's the one.*

The women he'd dated over the years had been just for fun. They'd been out for a good time, and so had he. But this was different. Suddenly he was experiencing the kind of mental clarity he was sure most men never did, that indescribable feeling that he'd finally found his direction in life. Come Monday, he was entering into a whole new phase. He was going to be a responsible businessman, maybe eventually even a pillar of his community, and it was all because of the woman he held in his arms right now, the one with the clear blue eyes and the generous heart and the quick mind and the soft, full mouth that begged him to kiss it. Under normal circumstances, he'd have passed right by her as if she were just an extra in the story of his life, but tonight she'd taken center stage, the spotlight swinging around to pick her out of a crowd of thousands.

Suddenly he needed this woman in a way he'd never needed one before. There were women you had casual sex with, and there were women you married.

Married?

As he drew her into another kiss, his mind went into a pleasant fog. He thought about the future, about this woman in it, and the luck that had followed him all the way to Vegas....

When Tony opened his eyes the next morning, shafts of sunlight stabbed through the window, penetrating his eyeballs and lodging directly in his brain. He snapped his eyes shut again and rolled away, which evidently was the cue for a jackhammer to start pounding away at his head.

He'd died and gone to hell.

But a few minutes later, when flames didn't seem to be lapping around the bed, he tossed the hell theory and decided he just had a hangover.

Just a hangover. That was like saying he had *just* a brain tumor.

Slowly he eased his eyes open again. For several seconds, he wasn't even sure where he was. Not home, that was for sure.

A hotel room. But where?

Vegas. Okay. Yeah. Vegas. Now it was coming back.

He turned over, only mildly surprised to find a woman lying next to him. Wasn't the first time that had happened. His head was so foggy, though, that he wasn't sure which woman it was.

Then he remembered. A woman with clear blue eyes who had turned a ten-dollar chip into twenty thousand. Even with his head pounding and a case of dry mouth for the record books, he smiled at the thought of all that money and how it was going to change his life. He'd have to do something very nice for her. Something to show just how much he appreciated everything she'd done for him.

Just as soon as he could remember her name.

He rolled over and sat on the edge of the bed with a soft groan, his head feeling like a clogged-up drain somebody was beating on with a wrench. He looked down at himself. He'd taken off his shirt, but he was still wearing his jeans. He'd slept with a woman and hadn't gotten laid?

Red flag. You're getting too old for this.

After a night of drinking, he used to be able to bounce

back from near-comatose to a somewhat functional state in a matter of a few minutes, but he could tell functionality was still a long way off.

Bathroom. Water. Shower. Coffee. Repeat as necessary.

He rose from the bed and staggered toward the bathroom, only to stop short when he saw something unfamiliar on the dresser. A piece of paper he didn't recognize. He picked it up, blinking his eyes into focus.

No. He had to be hallucinating.

His gaze slid down the page. Two names. Tony McCaffrey and Heather Montgomery. Together.

On a marriage license.

For at least ten seconds, Tony stood there motionless, clutching the page, panic buzzing inside him like a swarm of angry bumblebees. It couldn't be the real thing.

Could it?

Then all at once, he had a fuzzy, dreamlike memory of being someplace last night that looked remarkably like a courthouse. And somewhere in his head were stars and cherubs against a nighttime sky—what was that all about? And he vaguely remembered two people saying "I do," and one of them just might have been him.

No. No way. Impossible. He could *not* have done this.

But there it was in black and white. He, Tony McCaffrey, who, to avoid inadvertently landing in that lifelong trap, rarely had more than a few dates with any one woman, had gotten *married?* What the hell had he been thinking?

Well. At least now he knew her name.

He took a deep breath to ward off the feeling of suffocation, telling himself that this was fixable, that people got divorces every day. He fully intended to be one of them.

Surely the woman he'd married would feel the same way. Anyone who did something as crazy as this would want to take it back.

Wouldn't she?

He turned around and looked down at her.

Maybe not.

She lay on her side with one arm tucked under her pillow and her other hand beneath her cheek, her hair spread out across the pillow. She looked sweet and kind and trusting, like Mother Teresa without the advanced age and the religious overtones. He remembered thinking last night that she was a member of that species of woman on the endangered list: a nice girl. Last night, that had seemed like such a good thing. This morning it meant he was in trouble.

Big trouble.

Right now she was probably dreaming of a white picket fence, a pair of SUVs with car seats for the kids, and family vacations to her grandparents' farm in Iowa. She was going to wake up like a bride on her honeymoon, all sweet and smiley and assuming all was going to be well until their golden wedding anniversary. When he told her he wanted to spend their first day of their marriage getting a divorce, she'd be in tears. She'd helped him win twenty thousand dollars last night—hell, she'd essentially *given* it to him—and now all he had to say about their wedding was...*oops?*

She might even want the twenty thousand back. He didn't even want to think about that.

He laid the license down and went to the bathroom to slap water on his face to wake up his brain so he could find a way to deal with this situation, because the last thing he wanted in this life, and maybe in the next couple as well, was to be a married man.

Just please, God, don't let her cry.

When he came out of the bathroom, he was surprised to find her awake. Her brown hair was sleep-mangled, and she had mascara rings under her eyes. She was sitting up with her back against the headboard, one hand holding the covers to her chest, the other holding the marriage license.

She knows. And now you have to tell her you want out.

But before he could say anything, he realized the gooey smile he'd expected to see on her face was strangely absent. Her sweet slumbering serenity was nowhere to be seen. He'd been afraid of tears. Now he was praying for them, because anything would be better than the homicidal look on her face right now.

She held up the marriage license. "What the *hell* is this?"

Chapter 5

Heather's mind was so hangover-fuzzy that she could think of only one explanation for the piece of paper she was holding. Somewhere in Vegas they sold fake marriage licenses you could take home and show your friends. *Ha, ha, ha! Look! We got married!*

"This is a joke, right?" she said sharply. "Tell me this is a joke."

She waited for Tony's face to break into that million-dollar smile so they could both have a good laugh over it.

It didn't.

Panic shot through her. "Are you telling me this is the real thing? We actually got *married?*"

Tony squeezed his eyes closed. "No shouting, sweetheart. If you shout, my head is going to explode."

No kidding. If she shouted again, *her* head was going to explode.

"Why are you in my room?" she asked.

"Uh...we're married?"

She swallowed convulsively. "Did we...?"

"Have sex? Don't think so. I woke up still dressed."

Wincing a little, she lifted the covers and peeked

beneath them. *Clothes, thank God.* Relief gushed through her.

"Tell me what you remember," Tony said.

She bowed her head. Closed her eyes. Bits and pieces gradually came back to her, a jumble of images fading in and out. It was hard to make sense of them, though, when little guys with battering rams were trying to get out of her head.

"I remember winning the twenty thousand dollars," she said.

"Good," he said on a breath. "I was afraid I'd made that part up."

Heather remembered driving up and down the Strip in the limousine. Lights flashing. Neon blaring. And champagne.

Lots and *lots* of champagne.

"I remember the stuff in the limo," she said, hoping her face wasn't as red as it felt.

"How about after that?"

Then they were standing on the seats, poking their heads out of the sunroof, waving to other cars, to people on the street, to stray dogs, to inanimate objects. And then they were back down in the seat together, and . . .

Just thinking about what came next made her face heat up. She'd found out last night what it felt like to be with a man who was charming and sexy and really knew how to kiss, whose hands were gifts from God, whose smile shone brighter than the neon on the Sunset Strip.

She closed her eyes. Like a film going from fuzzy to sharp focus, she saw an office of some kind. Bright lights. People at desks. She and Tony filling out forms. Then they were in the limousine again. There were stars and moons and little flying cherubs. What had been up with *that?*

"There was a courthouse," she said, panic rising in her voice. "Then a wedding chapel. It's all kinda vague, but..."

Slowly the images coalesced. Came into focus. Organized themselves into a discernible timeline. And when they did, they led her to one horrible, undeniable conclusion. She put her hand to her throat, gasping out the words. "My God. We're really married, aren't we?"

"Looks that way."

"But why did they let us do it? We were in no condition to know what we were doing!"

"If they refused to let drunk people get married in this town, half the wedding chapels would be out of business."

Panic was setting in. Heather wasn't used to panic. She hated the muscle tension. The crawly feeling in her stomach. Panic was for people whose lives were disorganized messes. Who didn't know how to plan ahead. It was for people who were *spontaneous.*

Then she thought about those stars and moons and flying cherubs against a canopy of a night sky, and suddenly she realized where she'd seen that. She closed her eyes in humiliation. "Please tell me we didn't actually do it at a drive-through wedding chapel."

"If I remember right," he said, rubbing the back of his neck, "they called it 'The Tunnel of Love.'"

Good Lord. Not only had she gotten married in Vegas, but she'd done it in the most tasteless way imaginable.

"This can't be happening. This isn't me. I'm the *sane*

one in my family. I've never done anything like this before!"

Tony shrugged. "I once woke up naked on a beach in Cancun. I still don't remember the flight from Dallas to Mexico."

"Did you end up married?"

"No."

"Then it's not as crazy as this. Congratulations. You now have a new personal best."

She threw back the covers and started to get out of bed. He grabbed her arm. "Will you take it easy? This isn't that big a deal."

"Not that big a deal?" she said, shaking loose. "We got *married!*"

"But we can get unmarried. All we have to do is get an annulment."

She stopped short. An annulment?

Yes. Of course. That was all they had to do. Nobody else even knew they'd gotten married. They could keep this to themselves, get a quiet annulment, and then get on with their lives as if last night had never happened. No one but the two of them would ever have to know.

For the first time since she saw her name on that marriage license, Heather's heart stopped hammering in her chest. It was just as Tony said. No big deal. Just a little paperwork to cancel out the wedding, a bottle of aspirin to cancel out her monumental hangover, and pretty soon this whole experience would be nothing but a bad memory.

"You're right," she said, feeling so much better. "An annulment. That solves the problem. There can't be much to one of those, right?"

"Right."

"People do it all the time. How hard can it be?"

"Then it's settled?" Tony said. "We're getting an annulment?"

"Of course."

"Thank God," he murmured.

She turned back. "What?"

"Uh...nothing."

"No. What?"

He laughed a little. "I thought maybe you were going to be upset."

"About what?"

"You know. About the fact that I don't want to be married."

Heather blinked. "You thought I would be *upset* by that?"

"Uh...maybe," Tony said. "But you're not. That's the important thing."

"No. The important thing is that you dodged that bullet, right?"

"No, I didn't mean—"

"You actually thought I'd *want* to be married?"

He frowned. "I thought it was a possibility."

"In Vegas? To *you?*"

He looked offended. "For your information, there are a lot of women who would *love* to be married to me."

"Will you get *over* yourself? How dumb would a woman have to be to think a guy like you is suddenly ready for that little house with the white picket fence?"

"What do you mean, a guy like me?"

"You've dated half the women at McMillan's. And the other half are waiting their turn."

"How do you know that?"

"Newsflash, Tony. Women talk. Men may not carry on conversations in the bathroom, but women do. I hear all kinds of things. But just for the record," she said, rising from the bed and heading for the bathroom, "I'm not one of the women waiting her turn."

"Yeah? You didn't mind taking your turn last night."

She looked back to find him staring at her hotly, a knowing look in those gorgeous green eyes. He knew. He knew just how easily she'd fallen for him last night and how she'd reveled in every hot, sexy moment of it.

"I was drunk," she said. "People do stupid things when they're drunk."

"So that's the only reason you were making out with me in the back of that limo?"

"Why else?"

"Because it's fun?"

"Forget fun," she snapped. "We need to concentrate on fixing this stupid thing we did."

"Sure, sweetheart. Whatever you say."

He gave her a cocky smile that really irritated her. Of course it had been fun. But it was the kind of fun crazy, irresponsible people had, and she'd had enough crazy and irresponsible in the past twenty-four hours to last her a lifetime.

Last night Tony told her she was the woman he'd been waiting for all his life, punctuating every word with warm hands and warm lips in all kinds of inadvisable places. In her champagne-induced delusional state, he was a fun, charming, blindingly handsome man, and just being with him had turned her into a brainless, airheaded idiot. It was as if she'd been saving up her entire life to do one outrageously dumb thing, and this was it.

All at once the room phone rang, rattling Heather's already painful skull. She grabbed the receiver.

"Hello?"

"Heather, what are you doing?" Regina said. "Your cell phone's turned off. Where are you?"

"Uh..."

"You were supposed to meet us in the lobby at ten so we could catch cabs to the airport."

Heather looked at her watch. Ten after ten? *Damn it*. "I must have overslept."

"But we have a plane to catch. We're leaving right now!"

She put her hand to her forehead. "I'll catch a later one."

"But you rode with me to the airport."

"I'll pick up a cab back to Plano."

"Heather? What's going on? Are you with that man?" She gasped. "My God. You didn't *sleep* with him, did you?"

Well, wasn't this ironic? Yeah, she'd slept with Tony. As in, they'd occupied the same bed. Given that they were still clothed, apparently they'd been too drunk to do much else *except* sleep. But Regina didn't know that. She was clearly picturing something considerably more carnal, and in spite of everything, the thought of that almost put a smile on Heather's face.

"I might have," she said coyly.

"Heather!" Regina said. "It isn't like you to sleep with strange men! What would your mother think?"

Heather couldn't believe this. Her *mother?* Did Regina tell the other bridesmaids that their *mothers* were going to be horrified if they slept with strange men?

"For God's sake, Regina," she said. "Will you give me a break? I'm almost thirty years—"

Heather stopped short. Wait a minute. *Mother?*

The tiny hairs on her arms stood straight up, little vibes of dread sprinting along every nerve. No. She couldn't have done what she thought she'd done. She *couldn't* have.

She told Regina she'd see her back in Plano and hung up. She grabbed her cell phone, powered it on, and hit the CALL HISTORY button. And there it was. Last night, at eleven thirty, she'd called her mother. And not just to say hello.

"Oh, no," she moaned.

"What?" Tony said.

"No, no, no!"

"What?" Tony said again.

"I called my mother last night!"

"You did?" His eyes shifted back and forth. "Oh, yeah. I remember that. After we left the wedding chapel. I even talked to her, didn't I?"

She'd called her mother. How could she have forgotten that?

Because by that time last night, she'd guzzled about a gallon of champagne. By all rights, she should be in a coma right now.

"I take it this is going to cause a problem?" Tony said.

He had no idea.

In her drunken state of pure ecstasy, she'd told her mother all about their wedding. How wonderful her new husband was. How handsome. How entrepreneurial. On and on and on.

It was all coming back, and it horrified her.

At first her mother had sounded stunned. She'd asked the questions any sane mother would have under the circumstances, questions designed to determine whether her daughter had lost her mind. But when Heather had assured her that her new husband was from Plano, that he wasn't a total stranger, and that she did indeed know what she was doing, her mother had let wishful thinking take over, probably writing off her daughter's drunken delirium as the exhilaration any new bride would feel. After all, Barbara was getting something she'd wanted since Heather turned eighteen years old: a married daughter. Then she'd told Heather, *You be sure to bring that new husband of yours by the house the minute you get back in town!*

And Heather had promised to do just that. Only now she was going to have to tell her mother that she really didn't have a son-in-law after all, and those grandbabies she wanted so much weren't going to be popping out anytime soon. Could this situation get any worse? Was there any *way* it could get worse?

"So you regret everything you did last night?" Tony said.

"I think I've made that pretty clear by now, haven't I?"

Tony reached into his wallet and pulled out the check she'd given him. "Even this?"

That really irritated Heather. "I wasn't incapacitated the entire evening. I knew perfectly well what I was doing when I gave you that money. It's yours, Tony. You can keep it."

He looked at her warily. "Are you sure about that? I don't want you coming back later and telling me I cheated you out of twenty thousand dollars."

"I *said* you could keep it, didn't I?"

"It's just a lot of money, that's all. You said last night you'd feel guilty if you didn't give it to me. To tell you the truth, I'm feeling a little guilty for taking it."

"No," she said. "I know how much you want to buy McMillan's. I'd never take that money back from you. I really do want you to have it."

Finally he nodded and returned the check to his wallet.

Heather took a deep, calming breath, trying to put this whole thing in perspective, telling herself this situation was manageable if she handled things logically. She ticked off her to-do list in her mind: *Order coffee from room service. Drink three cups. Change plane reservations. Find out how to get an annulment. Mentally review your CPR training so when you get home and tell your mother the truth, you can bring her back from heart failure.*

And do not, under any circumstances, fall into the hands of a man like Tony McCaffrey ever again.

⸺

Four hours later, Tony shoved his carry-on into the overhead compartment on the airplane, then sat down in his aisle seat and stuffed a pillow behind his head. He'd taken enough aspirin before getting on the plane to gnaw a hole through his stomach lining, but his head was still pounding.

He turned to see Heather coming up the aisle. The instant their eyes met, she looked away, taking her seat two rows up on the aisle across from him.

He hated that. He'd expected her to at least speak to him. Then again, he'd also expected her to collapse in a useless heap of emotions this morning, and that hadn't happened, either.

Instead, she'd ordered coffee from room service, then got on the phone and changed her plane reservation. After that, she called a twenty-four-hour legal advice line and learned they could complete an online form to get the annulment ball rolling. She told him she'd go to the business center at the hotel to do that. It had amazed him that in spite of her tremendous hangover, she'd still taken control of the situation and handled things quickly and efficiently. He couldn't fathom how competent she might be if she'd actually been clearheaded.

Later she went to the airport by herself, and if she hadn't happened to book a seat near him, he wouldn't have seen her at all. Besides some distress about passing on the news to her mother, there had been no regrets. No tears.

Not so much as a wistful backward glance.

Tony didn't know whether to be relieved or insulted. Yeah, he wanted out of this mess. And he wanted Heather to want out, but not quite so insistently. Was the idea of being married to him really all that awful?

Stop it. You're lucky she's not a basket case right now, crying her eyeballs out.

After all, she wasn't his kind of woman. Right now, she wore a pair of jeans and a blue shirt, but everything about her was beige. Every strand of her long, straight hair was like a soldier lined up for inspection. She wore makeup, but it blended into her face rather than making a statement all its own. She moved in a quiet, reserved manner, as if she'd scripted every step she'd taken since birth.

Uptight women bugged him. He never knew what to do to make them happy, because nothing ever did.

Okay. A gallon of champagne had made this one pretty happy, but how often did a woman like her pop the cork and go after it?

She buckled herself in, and as they took off, she became the only passenger in the history of air travel to actually watch the flight attendants' safety speech. Then she pulled a copy of *Forbes* magazine from her tote bag and began to read.

Forbes? Weren't women her age supposed to read *Cosmo* and *Glamour* and that Marie-whatever magazine?

Definitely not his kind of woman.

He leaned his head against the pillow and closed his eyes, but even though he felt tired enough to sleep for a week, he couldn't doze off. Over the next few hours, he listened to music, ate stale peanuts, sipped a soft drink, and chatted with one of the flight attendants who was friendly beyond the scope of her job responsibilities. When she gave him her phone number, he smiled automatically and stuck it in his shirt pocket. Later he was going to tear it into tiny pieces, shove it into his garbage disposal, and flip the switch. Casual flings had lost their appeal about the time he woke up this morning a married man. Worse, he was a married man who hadn't even gotten a wedding night to go along with it.

Oh, hell. What difference did that make? He wouldn't have remembered it, anyway.

When they finally landed, Heather got up right away, retrieved her bag from the overhead compartment, and got off the plane ahead of him. When he walked through the jetway and emerged in the terminal, he didn't see her. He rode up the escalator to the parking garage level.

He went through the automatic doors and stepped outside, and when he did, he caught sight of Heather standing at the front of a line of people waiting for a cab. He started to cross the street to head to the parking garage, but his conscience nagged at him. Cab fare for the thirty-mile trip back to Plano was going to cost her a bundle.

Not your problem. Keep walking.

But he couldn't get his feet to move. He just stood on the curb, looking at Heather and feeling really crappy about the whole thing. After everything she'd done for him, was it right to let her pay to get home when he could take her home himself?

A cab pulled to the curb, and the driver got out to grab Heather's bag. Tony walked over and took it from the man's hand.

Heather spun around. "Tony? What are you doing?"

"A cab will cost you a fortune."

"I don't care."

"We're both going back to Plano. I'll give you a ride."

"That's not necessary."

"It's also no big deal."

She opened her mouth to protest, then closed it again. "Fine," she said, "I'll ride with you," even though she didn't seem the least bit happy about it.

Ten minutes later, Heather and Tony were in his Explorer heading east on 635. And being with him felt every bit as awkward as Heather had expected it to.

After the plane landed, she'd grabbed her stuff and gotten off as quickly as she could so she wouldn't have to talk to him. She'd spent the past three hours thinking about him sitting two rows behind her, telling herself the whole time not to turn around, not to look at him, not to give him even the tiniest indication that she couldn't get last night out of her mind.

Because she couldn't. Not for five consecutive minutes.

And she hated that. When she should be smacking herself for her spur-of-the-moment wedding, all she seemed to think about was every sizzling moment that had led up to it.

But apparently she was the only one who felt awkward. Tony didn't seem uncomfortable at all. He'd jacked up a country-and-western CD and was tapping his fingers on the steering wheel along with the music. She glanced at the speedometer. The speed limit was sixty. He was going almost seventy. It didn't surprise her that he was one of those men who took traffic signs as suggestions, not rules.

"You were reading *Forbes* on the plane," he said.

She looked at him warily. "Yeah."

"I don't think I've ever met a woman who read that before."

"Then you probably don't know many women who are CPAs."

"You're a CPA?" He laughed a little. "Somehow that doesn't surprise me."

Heather sighed. Just once she'd love to hear a man say, *CPA? No way! I would have sworn you were a supermodel!*

Maybe in her next lifetime.

"What I mean is that you seem pretty detail oriented," Tony added.

She shrugged.

"Not me. Guess I'll have to learn to be, though, right? Running a business and all?"

"Uh-huh."

Silence, except for the country music twanging through the speakers.

"So where did you go to college?" Tony asked.

Did he *always* chatter like this? "Rice University."

"Good school. I went to the University of Texas. Only one year, though." He smiled. "I majored in tequila drinking and minored in class skipping. As soon as they offer a degree in those things, I'm going for my Ph.D."

She didn't respond, so he kept talking. He was clearly one of those people who didn't like dead air and felt obligated to fill it. She would have asked him if he'd consider becoming the strong, silent type, but she couldn't get a word in edgewise.

"Tell me why you're not talking to me," he said.

She whipped around. "What?"

"You didn't speak to me on the plane. You've barely said anything to me since we left the airport."

"I'm just tired after last night."

"A little conversation might be nice."

"I'm really not in the mood."

"Come on, Heather. It really doesn't take much to—"

"Look, Tony. I know we spent last night together, doing God knows what, because I still don't remember everything, but I barely *know* you. What more could we possibly have to talk about?"

His smile evaporated. "Okay. I just hoped there weren't going to be hard feelings."

She turned away to look out the window again, only to feel her conscience nag at her. She was just as responsible for this mess as he was, yet she was treating him as if it was all his fault.

"I'm sorry," she said. "I don't mean to be snippy. But it's easy for you, you know? All you have to do is walk away. I'm the one who has to deal with the fallout."

"Your mother."

"Yes."

"So what are you going to say to her?"

Heather sighed. "I don't know exactly."

"Does she know you drink?"

"Yes. She knows."

"Does she know you drink a lot?"

"I *don't* drink a lot!"

"You did last night. And that's your excuse. 'Mom. I got blasted and lost my mind. You understand.'"

"Just because she knows I drink doesn't mean she's happy about it. About the only alcohol she ever has is half a glass of champagne every New Year's Eve. Telling her I did something stupid because I was dead drunk wouldn't exactly win me points."

"I don't get it," Tony said. "What mother wants her daughter to elope in Vegas? Don't they like that whole wedding thing?"

"She just wants me to be married. Preferably before I'm too old to give her four or five grandchildren. She'll take it any way she can get it. I'm just dreading having to tell her it's not going to happen this time around."

Evidently Tony didn't know what to say to that, because he finally stopped talking, which made Heather feel exactly like the snippy person she'd just apologized for being.

Never mind. Just get this mess over with.

She directed him to her parents' house in east Plano, and as he pulled up to the curb, she had to resist the urge to tell him to just keep on driving. Preferably right off a cliff, so she wouldn't have to deal with this.

They got out of the car. Tony opened the back hatch and retrieved her suitcase.

"I'll contact you when I hear more about the annulment," Heather said.

Tony handed the bag to her. "Good luck."

She nodded, then looked at the house. *It's now or never. And never's not an option.*

Then all at once, the front door opened, and her mother stepped onto the porch. Then her father. Then she saw Uncle Burt. Aunt Sylvia. Her cousin Kelsey. Grandma Roberta. Grandpa Henry. And other assorted aunts, uncles, and cousins.

Heather froze. What was going on?

They were coming down the steps. Hurrying along the sidewalk. Spilling across the lawn. Given the size of her parents' house, it was like watching circus clowns climbing out of one of those tiny little cars, and more kept coming.

Oh, God. No. *This couldn't be happening!*

"What the hell is going on?" Tony said.

"I don't know," Heather said warily. "But it doesn't look good."

"Why are all these people at your house?"

"It's not my house. It's my parents' house."

Her mother reached the car first, grinning like a lunatic. She stepped off the curb, walked right up to Tony, and stopped in front of him, her hand fluttering against her chest.

"Oh, my God, Heather! He's every bit as handsome as you said he was!" She threw her arms around him and gave him a big, smacking kiss on the cheek. "Welcome to the family!"

Chapter 6

Tony couldn't move. He couldn't speak. He just stood there, his mouth hanging open. Cameras sprouted in everyone's hands and began snapping, as if they were the paparazzi and he and Heather were superstars du jour.

"I'm Barbara," the huggy-kissy woman said, grinning like a lunatic. "Heather's mother."

She was dressed like a mom, wearing a flowered cotton shirt, baggy jeans, and sandals, with her bobbed hair tucked behind her ears. She grabbed a man's sleeve and pulled him over.

"And this is Heather's father, Fred."

Heather's mother was smiling. Her father wasn't. He was a tall, solid, chunk of a man, the kind who ripped phone books in half for fun.

"What are all of you doing here?" Heather said.

"Your mother called to tell us you'd gotten married," one of the women said. "Of course, we all want to meet your new husband."

Translation: They all wanted to see if Heather really had lost her mind. From the way a few of them were looking at her right now, the jury was still out on that, but that didn't stop them from drawing her into hugs and Tony into handshakes, introducing themselves as Aunt this and Uncle that and Cousin somebody-or-other. Tony wanted to say something, but then he and Heather were sucked into a vortex of bodies moving toward the house. He shot her a helpless get-me-out-of-here! look, but she appeared to be just as flabbergasted as he was.

They went up the steps, through the door, and into the living room, surfing along on the tide of humanity. He had a vague sense of the room around him. Neat and clean but very dated, with a flowered sofa that had to be twenty years old and walnut veneer furniture. Over the fireplace was a horrendous portrait of some old woman, the kind of thing some oddball families displayed rather than cramming in a dark corner of the attic. And somewhere in this house there had to be doilies. And in the bathroom, one of those crocheted toilet-paper covers. He'd stake his life on it.

Two people were sitting on the sofa who hadn't greeted them at the curb. One was an older lady Tony didn't recognize. The other was Heather's cousin Regina, whom he'd met last night.

Regina rose from the sofa, looking as impeccable as before. Sleek hair, perfect figure, flawless skin, breasts she'd probably paid a fortune for—the kind of woman he usually went for. But her snooty expression backed up what Heather had told him about her last night, which meant if he ever cracked that gorgeous shell, she'd be bitchy all the way to the bone.

The family parted, and Regina came to stand in front of Heather and Tony, smiling sweetly even as insincerity oozed from every pore. "Well, it looks as if congratulations are in order. Heather, you could have told me when I talked to you this morning that you'd gotten *married*."

She shot a nervous glance at Tony. "I ... I guess I was still half-asleep."

Regina turned to Tony. "I had no idea when I met you last night I'd be welcoming you to the family today. Imagine that."

Yeah. Imagine that.

The older woman rose from the sofa. She wore beige pants and a silky blouse with lots of gold jewelry, her hair an unnatural shade of red-blond.

"I'm Heather's Aunt Beverly," she said. "Regina's mother."

Sweet smile. Calculating brain. Tony could smell that kind of woman at twenty paces. Like mother, like daughter.

"So tell us about your wedding," Bev said. "I can't think of *anything* more lovely than a spur-of-the-moment midnight wedding in a Las Vegas wedding chapel."

"Yes!" Barbara said with a heavenly little sigh. "Isn't it romantic?"

Tony didn't know if Barbara was always a little dim or whether she was so caught up in the blessed event that her sarcasm detector had stopped functioning.

"So tell us all about it!" one of the women said. "We want to hear every detail."

"There's not much to tell," Heather said.

"You might start with how you ended up married after only four hours," one of the men said, and the woman next to him jabbed him in the ribs. He whipped around and whispered, "Cut it out, Sylvia! It's a fair question!"

"Hush, Burt!" she whispered back. "It's none of your business!"

Then Sylvia turned and gave Tony and Heather a smile that said she was trying really hard to believe this was all for the best. Looking around, Tony realized everybody else's smiles had that same tinge of hopefulness. He figured only one thing was keeping the rest of the crowd from expressing the suspicion they obviously felt: Heather's reputation for being sane, smart, and logical, no matter how much it looked as if she'd lost every one of those qualities the moment she'd stepped foot in Vegas.

"Regina told me you two knew each other before you went to Las Vegas," Bev said.

"Uh, yeah." Heather glanced at Tony, speaking carefully. "Tony's a regular at a bar where I go sometimes."

"How nice," Bev said, then turned to Barbara, crinkling her nose as if she'd caught a whiff of sulfur. "They met in a bar."

"And now he's buying the place," Barbara said. "Heather told me last night. Did I tell you that, Fred? He's going to be an entrepreneur!"

"Yup, you told me," Fred said. "About ten times." And then he turned to look at Tony, his eyes narrowed and his heavy brows scrunched up. *You had better be on the up and up,* that look said. *Or I'm squashing you like a bug.*

Tony had gotten stuck in some pretty odd situations in his life, but this was getting a little weird even for him. Somebody—preferably Heather—needed to stop the madness, but she looked just as stunned as he felt. And he wasn't sure if saying the wrong thing would turn this large crowd into a large, angry mob.

He leaned over and spoke softly. "Heather? Can I talk to you for a minute?"

"Uh...sure. Will you all excuse us for just a bit?"

Heather took Tony into another room, which turned out to be a den that contained a lot of man furniture—a walnut desk, a leather sofa, and a hefty coffee table piled with magazines. *Guns and Ammo. Hunting Illustrated. Shooting Sportsman.*

But the manliest things of all were the hunting trophies that filled nearly every square inch of wall space. Deer. Elk. Buffalo. A few other creatures Tony didn't even recognize. Judging from the sheer number of them, Fred Montgomery had put his taxidermist's kids through braces, college, and funded a wedding or two for good measure. The only wall space not occupied by hunting trophies held gun racks.

"Holy shit," Tony said, looking around.

"My father likes hunting." She paused. "And he's a retired cop, so he has a thing about guns."

Oh, this was just great. A cop. The moment Fred found out Tony had married his daughter and wanted a divorce all in the same weekend, he would not only want to blow Tony's head off, he'd also have the means to do it. Times twenty. And then successfully hide the body.

"Does your family actually believe our wedding was the real thing?" Tony asked.

Heather shrugged weakly. "I don't really know who believes what. I only know how much my mother wants to believe. And after I told her about ten times last night how happy I was and how perfect you were for me, I think I actually have her convinced."

"Then you need to *unconvince* her."

"I know."

"I don't believe it," Tony said, shaking his head. "All I did was take you home, and now I'm in the middle of *this?*"

"I'm sorry."

"I don't get uptight about much, but facing angry men with guns isn't my idea of a good time."

"My father isn't angry."

"Oh, yeah? He's looking at me as if I'm at the top of the FBI's most-wanted list."

"He isn't a violent man."

"Not a violent man? Look around you. The man's shot more stuff than a freakin' survivalist!"

"That's not violence. That's hunting."

"And he was a cop."

"That was his *job,*" she said with an eye roll. "And in his whole career, he only fired his weapon once."

"Uh-huh. Shot the guy dead as a doornail, didn't he?"

"Uh...yeah."

"You have to tell your family the truth."

"I know, all right? It's just that..."

"What?"

She sighed. "It's just that I've never seen my mother like this."

"Like what?"

"She's just so *happy.* If I go out there now and tell everyone our marriage isn't the real thing, she's going to be humiliated. And you can bet Aunt Bev will be catty to her about this for the rest of her life."

Tony blew out a breath. *I don't want to hear this.*

"See, Bev is my mother's sister," Heather went on. "She has a rich husband. A big house in West Plano. A gorgeous daughter who's getting married. My mother is married to a retired cop. They live in a twenty-year-old tract home in east Plano; I'm their only daughter. Marriage isn't even on the horizon. Aunt Bev never lets my mother forget any of that. So imagine how my mother's going to feel when I go out there now and tell her, in front of everybody, that our wedding wasn't the real thing."

This was it. This was the reason Tony was careful about getting too involved with women. The minute he was *involved*, he had to deal with their families, their problems, their emotions, and he just wasn't very good at it.

He looked back at Heather. She was frowning. And—oh, God—her eyes were glistening.

"What's the matter?" he asked.

"Nothing." She fished through her father's desk drawer, grabbed a tissue, and dabbed her eyes.

Run. Leave now. It's her family, so it's her problem. But then he realized something else. Her mother wasn't the only one who was going to be humiliated.

"You told me what it's going to be like for your mother when you tell them the truth," he said. "What's it going to be like for you?"

She met his eyes, then looked away again. "It doesn't matter. It has to be done."

"Tell me."

She sighed. "Well, let's see. I expect Aunt Bev and Regina will pretend to sympathize with me, but really they'll be secretly glad that Regina's wedding isn't getting upstaged after all and that I'm still the plain-Jane cousin they can keep putting down."

"What about everyone else?"

"They won't be mean. It won't be like that. They'll just

'bless my heart' until the cows come home and wonder how such a smart girl could get involved in a situation like this. I must have been desperate, you know? And then there's Regina's wedding. I'll be úp there in a month as a bridesmaid. Again. Everyone will remember my wedding that wasn't. They'll 'bless my heart' all over again and pledge to each other that they have to find poor Heather a man before she's too old for anyone to be interested anymore. And then come the blind dates with forty-year-old men who still live with their mothers and play video games."

"You're kidding."

"I wish I was."

"Is that really what it's going to be like?"

"That's the sanitized version. But it's no concern of yours."

"Wrong. It is my concern. I owe you, Heather. After what you did for me last night, the last thing I want is for you to get hurt by all this."

"It can't be helped." She tossed the tissue into the wastebasket. "Why don't you just go? I can handle this. There's no need for you to hang around."

As Heather turned and left the room, Tony blew out a breath of frustration. He was getting everything out of this situation he ever wanted, and all she was getting was an overdose of humiliation.

No, he thought with sudden conviction. *You have to do something so Heather can save face in front of her family.*

He just wished he knew what that something was.

Heather walked back to the living room to find her mother still grinning.

"Heather! Where's Tony? I have coffee and cheese-cake!"

Heather cringed. Her mother had always been an exclamation-point kind of person, but this was ridiculous.

"I have something to tell you," Heather said, then turned to the rest of the family. "Actually, I want to tell all of you."

"Whatever it is," Aunt Sylvia said brightly, "it can't top what you told your mother last night."

Everybody laughed. Then the laughter died away, and Heather stood there in the yawning abyss of expectation, waiting for the words to come to her.

"So where's your husband?" Regina said, looking around, practically sniffing like a bloodhound.

"Uh...that's what I need to talk to you about," Heather said.

A calculating look came across Regina's face. "He didn't... *leave,* did he?"

Heather started to say yes, only to hear Tony's voice behind her. "Of course not. I'm right here."

When he walked over to stand next to her, she figured he must have a masochistic streak a mile wide. But that didn't change anything. She had to tell the truth, and she had to do it now.

"It's about our wedding. This is not exactly what it appears to be."

Her mother's smile dimmed considerably. The relatives stopped smiling altogether.

A gleam entered Regina's eyes.

"See, what happened was—"

Tony put his arm around her shoulders. "Let me."

She started to speak again, but he gave her arm a squeeze to quiet her. "Heather's right," Tony said. "This is not exactly what it appears to be. It appears that we were two impulsive people doing something really stupid. I mean, we barely knew each other, and yet we ended up married."

Regina's eyes shifted wildly back and forth between the two of them, clearly hoping for a catastrophe. Heather looked at her mother, whose hand was on her throat, her eyes wide with dread.

"And you would have thought that I'd have woken up this morning thinking what a crazy thing it was to do," Tony went on. "I mean, married in Vegas? How insane is that? But then I took one look at Heather, and I thought..." He turned to stare at her. "And I thought, how in the world could something that should have been so wrong have led to something so right?"

With that, he took Heather in his arms, bent her backward, and kissed her.

Several gasps went up from her family, and Heather might have gasped herself if Tony's lips hadn't been smothering hers. For a few seconds, she forgot she was in her mother's house, forgot she was surrounded by her family, forgot everything except Tony and his wonderfully talented mouth.

As he slowly brought her back to her feet, everybody clapped. Catcalls all around. Finally Heather came to her senses. She wasn't dumb enough to believe that somewhere between the den and the living room Tony had fallen madly in love, so what in the world was he up to?

Tell them the truth. You can't let this deception go on. Fix this ridiculous, out-of-control situation right now.

Then she looked around the room. Her mother was beaming. Uncle Burt was giving her a thumbs-up. Aunt Bev looked positively ill. Regina's mouth hung open in shock. Grandpa Henry was eating a handful of Cheez Doodles, but nothing ever got his attention.

The words just wouldn't come out of Heather's mouth. All she could do was stand there in a daze, staring at her family staring back at her. Like sounds muffled underwater that she could barely make out, she heard Tony telling her mother thanks for the offer of cheesecake and coffee, but they were going to decline.

"But you must be hungry," her mother said. "They couldn't have fed you anything decent on the plane."

"Barbara," Aunt Sylvia said with a raised eyebrow. "They want to be *alone.*"

Tony gave Aunt Sylvia a confirming smile and wink, and she tittered like a Japanese schoolgirl. Regina's jaw fell the rest of the way to the floor. Heather's mother smiled like a woman with visions of baby booties dancing in her head.

Say it, Heather told herself. *Tell them the truth. Tell them he's not really your husband, that he just played one in Vegas.*

But then Tony was hustling her out the door, and her tongue was still in a knot, and it wasn't until they got inside his car and the doors were closed that she found her voice again.

"What the *hell* was that?" she said. "I thought you wanted me to tell them the truth!"

"I thought about it, and I realized there's no need. At least not right now."

"What are you talking about?"

"Here's the plan," Tony said. "We can wait until after Regina's wedding. By then the heat will be off. We can tell everyone it just didn't work out. By then our annulment will be official, but as far as everyone else will know, we just got a quiet divorce. You can even tell them you're the one calling it quits."

"What in the world is that going to accomplish?"

"You said it yourself. You don't want to stand up at the front of that church with everybody pitying you. This way, you don't have to. If we wait a month, it means this was a real marriage. We meant to do it. Telling them after a month that we really aren't compatible is way better than telling them we barely remember getting married in the first place."

Heather drew back. "Are you *completely* out of your mind?"

"Come on, Heather. Do you really want to go back in there now and say, 'He got drunk and married me, and now he wants out'?"

"No, but—"

"Do you really want to tell your mother how blasted you had to get to do something this nuts?"

"No, but—"

"If we wait a month, you can give that nasty cousin of yours a big smile and a wink and say, 'Our marriage might not have worked out, but it sure was fun while it lasted.'" He grinned. "See? Big difference."

"Yes, but—"

"Then it's settled. Staying married for a month really isn't that big a—"

"Tony!"

He stopped short. "What?"

"Did you ever stop to think that your brilliant plan just *might* have a tiny flaw?"

"Flaw?"

Heather's cell phone rang. She grabbed it from her purse and answered it. "Mom? We just left. What's up?" She listened for a moment. "Uh...yeah. Okay. I'll get back to you on that." A pause. "Yes. I'll call you later. I promise."

She hung up the phone, her hand falling limply to her lap.

"What was that?"

Heather turned slowly to face him. "My mother wants your address."

"My address? Why would she want my—" He stopped short, his eyes widening. "Does she think we're going to be *living* together?"

"Of course she does! We're married! Are you telling me that didn't even *dawn* on you?"

"Oh," he said, a little sheepishly. "I'm guessing that's the flaw?"

"I was all set to tell them the truth, and now everything's a big, fat mess all over again. How could you *do* this?"

"But your mother will never know we're not living together."

"Oh, yes, she will."

"No. If your parents come by your place and wonder

where I am, you can just tell them I ran an errand or something. They'll never know the truth."

"Nope. I'm pretty sure they'll know you're not living with me."

"How?"

"How?" Heather said, her voice escalating. "Because *I'm* living with *them!*"

He drew back. "You still live with your parents?"

"I don't *still* live with them! My apartment lease was up. I want to buy a condo, but I haven't found one yet. In the meantime, I'm staying with them." She reached for the door handle.

"Wait a minute," Tony said, grabbing her arm. "Where are you going?"

"To tell them the truth like I should have done in the first place. Of course, after your Oscar-winning performance in the role of my loving husband, I'm really going to look like a fool."

"No. You don't have to tell them."

"Yes, I do!"

"Will you take it easy?"

"Will you stop saying that? The last time I took it *easy,* I ended up married!"

"Here's plan B. I have a spare bedroom. Just stay with me until after Regina's wedding."

She stared at him dumbly. "*What* did you say?"

"As soon as I close the deal tomorrow, I'll be at the bar most of the time. We'll barely even see each other. If anyone comes by, we can pretend to be happy newlyweds." He shrugged. "Problem solved."

"Problem solved? Me living with a man I don't know for a month *solves* the *problem?*"

"Well...yeah."

She shook her head in disbelief. "Is there *anything* that's a big deal for you?"

"Buying the bar. That was a big deal. You helped me with that, and now I'm helping you with this."

"You *caused* this!"

He grinned. "Which is all the more reason I should help you with it."

She held up her palm. "Look, I know in your own convoluted way, you're just trying to be nice, but I can't live with you for a month. That would be *weird*."

He smiled. "I'm sure you mean 'weird' in the nicest way possible."

She bowed her head with a groan of frustration. For all her protesting, if she went back in there now, she really was going to look pitiful. She pictured Regina's snarky face. Imagined tears rolling down her mother's cheeks. Saw the horribly geeky blind dates lining up at her door from now through eternity.

She had to deal with this sooner or later. But with her head still pounding and her mind muddled from lack of sleep, later sounded much better than sooner.

"I don't even know you," Heather said.

"We got to know each other pretty well last night."

"Hey, there'll be no more of that, so don't even think—"

"Roommates. That's all we'll be." He started the car.

"Wait a minute. I haven't said yes."

"But you haven't said no."

"Tony—"

"What's the matter?" he said, eyeing her suspiciously. "Are you *afraid* to live with me?"

She blinked. "Afraid?"

"You don't trust yourself. That's the problem. For all this talk about no more 'getting to know each other,' you're afraid you can't keep your hands off me."

She started to bite back, only to see a sly smile inching its way across his mouth. She sagged with resignation. "You never quit, do you?"

"Look, Heather. I went to Vegas and ended up with twenty thousand dollars. All you got was a hell of a hangover and a husband you didn't ask for. Letting you live with me until the heat dies down is the least I can do."

This man scrambled her brain until she couldn't think straight to save her life. She felt as if she were sinking in quicksand, and every effort she made to grab on to something to pull herself out only made her sink that much deeper.

But when she glanced back at the house, she had the feeling Tony was right. A real wedding that didn't work out sounded a whole lot better than a drunken mistake. And the truth was that she'd loved the look of amazement on Regina's face when Tony kissed her. That was petty and small and ill-advised in every way, but still it made Heather feel good right down to her toenails.

"Okay," she said. "Sure. Why not? If I was crazy enough to marry you, why shouldn't I be crazy enough to move in with you?"

"Exactly," Tony said, as if he'd missed the sarcasm, which of course he hadn't. "What about your stuff?"

"I don't want to go back in there now. I'll do it tomorrow. I have all the stuff I need for now in the suitcase I took to Vegas. Most of my stuff is in storage until I find a new place to live, so I have just a few things to get, anyway."

As Tony pulled away from the curb, Heather told herself everything was going to be all right. In a month, Regina's wedding would be over, they'd have their annulment, and they could tell everyone they were parting amicably.

Our marriage might not have worked out, but it sure was fun while it lasted.

With the right voice inflection, she could sell that. She could make herself out to be everything she wasn't: a hot single girl who'd had a whirlwind romance, lived it up, and was now moving on to her next adventure. For once in her life, that was who she wanted to be, not poor, plain, pitiful Heather who couldn't get a man to save her life.

Chapter 7

As they pulled into Tony's apartment complex, Heather let out the breath she'd been holding. She'd felt uptight all the way there, wondering what she'd gotten herself into. What if he lived in a slum? What if criminals lived next door? What if she was going to be living someplace she wouldn't even think of going after dark, or maybe even in the daytime?

But this seemed okay. Red brick. Black shutters. Recent paint. Grounds well-kept. Late-model cars in the parking lot. It was nice. She could stay here. She could do this. Then she followed Tony into his apartment.

How had a tornado trashed only his place without destroying the rest of the apartment complex?

Newspapers were strewn on the sofa. A pair of tattered jeans and a shirt were thrown over the back of a dining room chair. Bills and ad circulars were scattered across the dining room table. A big plastic bowl sat on the coffee table, empty except for a few popcorn kernels in the bottom. An overflowing laundry basket sat on the floor beside the sofa, and she had no idea if its contents were clean or dirty. Possibly both.

The fireplace was nice, with a raised hearth and a mantel inset with emerald green tile, but it looked as if it had never been used except as a place to stack old issues of *Hot Rod* and *Sports Illustrated*. The walls were empty. Nothing decorative. Nothing homey. No pictures, no photographs, no nothing.

And the kitchen. She couldn't see all of it from the living room, but she saw the trash can. The *overflowing* trash can. A little shiver of *ick* slithered down her spine.

The only pristine thing she saw was a plasma TV the size of a Times Square billboard, which completed the picture to make Tony's apartment every cliché of bachelorhood all rolled into one. Heather knew there had to be a decent apartment beneath all the mess, but it would take somebody with a hell of an imagination to see it, and she'd never been all that imaginative.

"Nice place you've got here," she told him.

"Watch it. I know sarcasm when I hear it." Tony wheeled his suitcase against a wall and smacked down the handle. "I like the 'lived in' look."

"Is that what this is?"

"I should have known. You're a neat freak, aren't you?"

"There's nothing freaky about being neat."

"Other women who come here don't seem to mind."

"Well, there's a fetish I've never heard of. You sleep with blind women."

"They're not looking at the décor," he said with a smile. "They're too busy looking at me."

Egomaniac.

He grabbed her suitcase. "Come on. I'll show you to the Presidential Suite."

He led her to his spare bedroom. Boxes were scattered

everywhere. A beat-up dresser sat along one wall, and an orange plaid sofa the size of the *Titanic* sat along another. A neon Budweiser sign leaned against the sofa, its cord lying in a tangled heap. It looked as if a dorm room had exploded.

"Well," Heather said, "this is nice."

He shoved a few boxes aside. "I use this room for storage."

She looked into one of the boxes. It was full of *Sports Illustrated* annual swimsuit editions. "Yeah, you sure wouldn't want to throw those away."

"I tried once," Tony said with a sad shake of his head, "but then I pictured all those beautiful women facedown in a Dumpster, and I just couldn't do it."

Heather started to suggest that maybe paper women wouldn't care, only to realize there was a more pressing issue. "You didn't tell me there was no bed."

"This is a sofa bed."

He nudged a few more boxes aside and opened it up to reveal a mattress that was a twisted-up orthopedic nightmare.

"Wow," Tony said. "I don't remember it being quite this ... squashed. Maybe you'd better take my bed."

"No. It's okay. You didn't promise me luxury."

"Are you sure?"

She was. Sleeping in Tony's bed while he slept in here would make this already strange experience even stranger. "Yes. I'm sure. I'll be fine."

He grabbed some sheets, pillows, and a blanket out of the closet and tossed them onto the bed. Heather winced at the thought of the dust they'd undoubtedly collected at the top of that closet, but as tired as she was right now, she could probably fall asleep in a filthy chair at the bus station.

Just then, Tony's phone rang. He looked at the caller ID. "Excuse me," he said to Heather. "Gotta take this."

He slipped out the door, leaving her alone to survey the hideous sofa bed and the boxes full of mostly naked women and the depressingly bare walls. She could certainly straighten things up a little, but no matter what she did, she was still going to feel as if she were living in a cross between a frat house and a homeless shelter.

Then she peeked into the adjoining bathroom to discover that the bedroom was the least of her problems. Without constant cleaning and proper ventilation, Texas humidity could make a bathroom a moldy mess in a hurry. And in the case of this bathroom, it had.

Just as she was searching under the sink for cleaning products, her cell phone rang. She grabbed it from her purse.

Alison.

Heather debated only a moment before letting the call ring through to her voice mail. Alison might be her best friend, but she dreaded telling her about what had happened in Vegas and about her living arrangements now. She could only imagine the barrage of questions, everything from *What does he look like naked?* and *Is he as good in bed as everyone says he is?* and worst of all: *You actually want to divorce him? Are you nuts?*

Tomorrow. She'd deal with it tomorrow. Tonight she had more pressing things to worry about.

She headed for the living room, intending to ask Tony if he had a can of Ajax and an industrial-strength sponge. If that offended him, so be it. She simply could *not* spend the next month using a bathroom that looked like a science experiment.

As she circled around the doorway and came into the living room, she saw him flopped on the sofa, still talking on the phone. Even in the midst of his chaotic apartment, with his shoes kicked off and his shirt rumpled and his feet on the coffee table, he still looked incredibly handsome.

Stop staring at him. He's not really your husband. And would you really want him to be?

She started to duck back into her bedroom, where she'd wait until he was off the phone, only to have him hold up a finger, asking her to wait.

Then he turned away, lowering his voice, but still she could hear what he was saying. "Take it easy, sweetheart," he said. "Of *course* you have a right to be upset." A pause. "Why, sure! I can be over there in twenty minutes... yeah, I know. You really could have used that thirty million."

Finally Tony hung up and shoved the phone into his pocket. "I have to step out for a little while," he said, reaching for his shoes.

"Is there a problem?" Heather asked.

"You might say I have a friend in need."

"A friend?"

"Rona. Every once in a while she needs a shoulder to cry on. She isn't very good in a crisis."

"A crisis? What's going on?"

"Well, usually it's something like getting dumped by her boyfriend. Or getting fired. Or having a fight with her roommate. Or getting a bad haircut." He slipped on his shoes and tied the laces. "This time she missed the big jackpot in the lottery by four numbers."

"That's a crisis?" Heather said. "Half the city missed it by four numbers."

"Yeah, but see, she had this flash of what the winning numbers were, but then her sister called, and by the time she went to buy her tickets, she couldn't remember what those numbers were."

"If she couldn't remember them, how did she know that they were the winning ones?"

"Now, Heather. You're being logical. That'll get you nowhere with Rona. In situations like this, logic only makes her cry."

"Let me get this straight. You're going to console a woman who's crying because she thinks she got cheated out of a multimillion-dollar jackpot?"

"Yep."

Heather stared at him dumbly. She knew Tony's motives weren't exactly like other people's, but that seemed weird even for him.

Then she understood.

"Let me guess," she said. "This woman who was almost the multimillionaire. She's really hot."

"Uh . . . yeah."

"And eventually her crying stops and the sex begins?"

When he finished tying his shoes and rose from the sofa without responding, she knew she'd hit the nail on the head.

"Wait a minute," Heather said. "Have you forgotten you're a married man?"

"No. I haven't forgotten that."

"If you're with another woman, someone from my family is liable to see you."

"Come on, Heather. That's not going to happen. We don't exactly run in the same circles."

"It's still a possibility."

"A remote one."

"Look, Tony. I know you. It won't be just Rona over the next month. You hit on every woman in sight."

"You're exaggerating. I don't hit on *every* woman in sight. If that were true, I'd be pulling cars over on the freeway."

"It's only for a month," Heather said.

"Do you have any idea how long a month is when you're talking about no sex?" He headed for the door.

"Hey!" Heather said. "I thought we had a deal!"

Tony turned back, looking exasperated. "We do. And the deal is that we're married in front of your family. That's it. No one else needs to know."

"This situation is already crazy enough, and now you want to make it worse?"

"If we're with your family, we're married. If we're not, we're not. What's so crazy about that?"

"A marriage that goes on and off like a lightbulb? You're right. That's not crazy at all."

"Okay, so it's a little crazy, but—"

"Did it not even occur to you that seeing other women might be a problem?" Heather said. "Could that be another flaw in your brilliant plan?"

He frowned. "Sarcasm doesn't really suit you."

"If you're going to see other women, tell me now, and we'll call this whole thing off."

He cocked his head, staring at her as if he was actually considering that. Then his body heaved with a sigh. He sank to the sofa and kicked off his shoes again.

"You're staying home?" Heather asked.

"Yes," he said resignedly. "After all, all this was my idea. If I'm going to be your fake husband, I guess I should be your *faithful* fake husband."

"It's only for a month."

"Yeah," he said wistfully, as if she'd said, *It's only for the next twenty years.* He pulled out his phone. "I'll call Rona back right now and talk her off the ledge. That and a little phone sex should perk her right up."

"What?"

He grinned. "Why, Heather. I do believe you're blushing."

She looked away. "I don't blush."

"Uh-huh. Don't you like phone sex?"

She paused. "Phone sex is juvenile."

"Juvenile?" Tony laughed. "Sweetheart, there's nothing juvenile about the things I've been known to say over the telephone. I take it you've never tried it?"

"Could you *be* any more rude? That's not a question you should ask a lady."

"If you really do talk dirty on the phone, you're no lady, so I'd say the question is fair game."

"Okay, Tony. You win. I've never had phone sex. I've also never had sex on a beach at midnight or in an airplane bathroom or in a car. Anything else you'd care to know?"

"No, but I do have a little advice for you."

"What's that?"

"Don't bother with any of those things. They're highly overrated. Sand...tight quarters...a gearshift poking you in all the wrong places..." He smiled. "But phone sex. Now *that* can be a lot of fun."

Heather dropped her arms limply to her sides. "You never quit, do you?"

"No, I'm done. I need to call Rona." He started to dial again, then paused. "Hey! I know. How about I set up a conference call, and we can make it a threesome?"

Heather shook her head in disbelief. All she wanted was a clean bathroom. Was that really too much to ask? "Forget phone sex. I need cleaning products."

"What are you going to do? Wash my mouth out with soap?"

"The bathroom, Tony. It's a mess."

"It is?"

"You know perfectly well it is."

"Sorry. I've just never felt the need to put bathroom germs at the top of my list of things to worry about."

"Maybe you should."

"You know what would make you forget all about the bathroom?"

"What?"

"Phone sex."

With a roll of her eyes, Heather marched back to the bedroom and into the bathroom, where she found a bar of soap and a washcloth. If that was all she had, it would have to do.

She went to work scrubbing the sink as best she could. Just because Tony didn't think it was important didn't mean it wasn't. Sooner or later, he was going to catch some horrible disease because he didn't have the sense to keep things clean, and who would have the last laugh then?

But after a few minutes, she started to imagine him out there laughing and shaking his head at the nerdy, too-serious, overly sanitary person she was. She slowed down her scrubbing, and pretty soon she tossed the cloth aside, rinsed her hands, and sat down on the toilet lid, feeling dumb.

Ajax. *God.* She was talking about cleaning products, and he was talking about phone sex. That, right there, was a microcosm of their relationship.

Heather buried her head in her hands. *Microcosm.* Just the fact that she'd *thought* that word meant she was one of the most boring women alive.

If she listened hard, she could just make out the sound of Tony's voice. Undoubtedly he was having a hot conversation with Rona, one that had nothing to do with germs and everything to do with sex. And just for a moment, she wished she was the kind of woman who said to hell with the necessities of life and dove right into the fun, even though she couldn't imagine a scenario in which that would ever happen.

When Tony told Rona he wasn't coming over after all, it elevated her whining to an unprecedented level. He tried joking with her to shake her out of her bad mood, but still she kept yammering that somebody else was rolling in millions of dollars that were rightfully hers.

Finally he couldn't take it anymore and told her exactly what Heather had said—if she couldn't remember the numbers, how did she know they were the winning ones? He should have taken his own advice and skipped the logic, because Rona said she just *knew* and that he was a horrible, horrible person for being so unsympathetic, and if she did win a million dollars someday, she wasn't giving him a dime of it. In light of that, he figured phone sex was out.

More evidence that he didn't know when to keep his mouth shut.

Then, out of nowhere, another woman popped into his mind. Babette. Oh, God. *Babette.* How could he have forgotten her?

Babette was an Air France flight attendant, a woman who made the average nymphomaniac look like a cloistered virgin, the kind of woman who brought the sexual experience to a whole new level with no strings attached. And she'd be here in a couple of weeks for their monthly rendezvous. Tony looked forward to being with her the way a kid looks forward to Christmas. Unfortunately, after promising Heather there would be no other women, seeing Babette would be out of the question.

He lay back down, trying to resign himself to being celibate for the next month, no matter how painful that was going to be. It was a very small price to pay in return for all Heather had done for him. In fact, it just might be a blessing in disguise.

Yeah. That was it. A blessing in disguise.

A month of celibacy meant his blood would stay in his head rather than moving south to take care of other needs, which meant he could stay focused, moving forward with his new business in a clearheaded, decisive manner. Nobody at the bar would even know he was married. If anybody pointed out that he wasn't being his usual self, he would just say he had to concentrate on his new business for a few weeks, and once everything was running smoothly, the old Tony would be back. Everybody would buy that, wouldn't they? It wouldn't be a problem. The month would be over before he knew it.

And if he said that about a hundred more times, maybe he would believe it.

~

At ten till eight the next morning, Heather jumped off the light-rail and dashed to the door of the building where she worked, her head consumed by a bad-sleep headache she'd known was coming the moment Tony opened that sofa bed last night. She juggled her briefcase and her Starbucks cup and the umbrella that was keeping the faint drizzle from frizzing her hair. After spending fifteen minutes every morning fighting to make it straight, she sure didn't need rain to cancel out all her effort and turn her back into Bozo the Clown.

A few minutes later, she was making her way through the cubicle city at Greenfield & Associates, turning left and right like a rat in a maze. No cheese when she reached her desk, though. Nothing but a pile of files, a blinking voice mail light, and a note from her boss that she wanted to see her as soon as she got in. Because Heather already felt like crap, it was probably something about the Morehouse account. It never failed. If she was having a bad day, the account from hell reared its ugly head and stuck out its tongue.

Heather had just set her briefcase and her coffee down on her desk when her phone rang. She looked at the caller ID. Alison. Again.

No. Not right now. She couldn't tell Alison what had

happened while she was sitting in cubicle city where anyone could hear.

A minute later, she heard her text-message ring tone. She pulled her phone from her briefcase. Not surprisingly, it was Alison. *Been trying to call you. What happened in Vegas?*

If she texted her back and told the whole story, she'd wear her fingers down to the knuckle. She texted back: *Downtown Deli. Noon. I'll tell you all about it.*

A minute later, Alison responded: *Did you do something really crazy?*

Heather's heart jumped. Then she told herself to calm down. There was no way Alison could possibly know anything. She texted back, *Why do you ask?*

Almost immediately, Alison responded: *I talked to your mother.*

Oh, my God.

Heather strode to the conference room, hitting speed-dial two on the way there. Alison answered and launched right in.

"Heather, tell me right now, and don't lie. Did you or did you not get m-m-marr…" She let out a breath. "God, I can't even say it."

Heather closed the conference room door, figuring there was no way to dance around this. "Yes. I got married."

"In *Vegas?*"

"Yes."

"Oh, my God." Big pause. Then, very carefully, "Who did you marry?"

If Alison had talked to her mother, she already knew the answer to that question. She was just looking for confirmation. Heather took a deep, calming breath. "Tony McCaffrey."

"No way!" Alison shouted. "There is no way in hell that you married—"

"No! Don't say it. *Please.* And for God's sake, don't *tell* anyone!"

The door to the conference room swung open. The senior accounting manager came in with several people trailing behind him. "Uh...I believe we have the conference room at eight?"

"I'm sorry," Heather said. "I'm leaving now."

Brushing past them, she went into the hall and whispered, "Alison. I can't talk now. Meet me for lunch, and I'll tell you everything. Don't say a word to anyone. Do you hear me?"

"I hear you. But, Heather—"

"The Downtown Deli at noon," Heather said, and hung up.

Chapter 8

As Heather walked into Downtown Deli, the heavenly smells of all the decadent food made her mouth water. She thought about the prospect of stuffing herself into that too-small bridesmaid's dress, cursed Regina, and passed by the dessert case without stopping to look. She slid into a booth across from Alison.

"I swore your mother was delusional," Alison said. "But you're saying what she told me is *true?*"

"Why did you talk to my mother?"

"I got worried when you wouldn't answer my calls. Swear to me you're not making this up. Swear to me—"

Heather held up her pinky.

Alison clasped her throat. "You tell me how this happened. You tell me how last week you could be bitching that you hadn't had a date in six months, and now you got a man like Tony to marry you in *one night.*" She closed her eyes. "God, this is too weird for words."

"It's not what you think."

"What I think is that you're the luckiest woman on the freakin' planet!"

"No. It's not a real marriage."

"Not real? Do you have a piece of paper?"

"Yes."

"Then it's a real marriage." Alison groaned. "My God, Heather! Do you know how painful this is for me? It's like you got that date to the Christmas dance with the hottest guy in school, and even though I was stuck at home dateless, you *went*. We had a *pact!*"

"For God's sake, Alison. That was junior high. You're going off the deep end."

The waiter came by, and Alison ordered a hot brisket sandwich with potato salad. Heather gritted her teeth and ordered a salad with dressing on the side. While they were waiting for the food to arrive, she told Alison the whole story, from winning the twenty thousand to the limo ride to the chapel to her and Tony passing out in the same bed. And then she told her the part that was going to send her to hell for lying to her mother.

Alison sat back, stunned. "You gotta be kidding me. So it really isn't a real marriage? As in love, honor, and cherish?"

"No. It's more like drink, deceive, and divorce." She shook her head. "I should have said something the moment he kissed me. I was telling myself to. The words were right there in my head. But then I looked at my mother, and Regina, and I just…" She shook her head helplessly. "I just couldn't do it."

"Hey, if Tony had kissed me, I'd have lost my mind, too." Alison smiled. "I wish I'd seen the look on Regina's face when he did it. I bet her eyeballs popped right out of her head." She giggled. "This is *so* cool."

Heather couldn't help the tiny smile that crossed her lips. "It was kinda fun to watch." Then her smile evaporated. "But it's all a lie."

"Yeah, but it's an *inspired* lie. So Tony was the one who came up with this plan?"

"Yeah. But this isn't the first time he's done something crazy. Do you know he once woke up naked on a beach in Cancun and doesn't remember flying to Mexico?"

"Hold on. I have to get a visual on that." Alison closed her eyes, sighed, then opened them again. "And you have him to yourself for an entire month."

"To myself? No, not really."

"You're living with him, right? Just because you didn't have sex on your wedding night—an opportunity I can't believe you passed up, by the way—"

"I was unconscious!"

"—it doesn't mean you can't take that opportunity now."

"No way. It's not like that. It's not as if he's going to start treating me like his wife just because his name accidentally ended up on a marriage license with mine."

"Wife? Forget wife. How about friends with benefits? *Seduce him.*"

"I don't *want* him. The man is a mess. I don't think he's cleaned his apartment since the turn of the century."

Alison looked positively crazed. "Are you telling me you'd find him *more* attractive if he was holding a sponge and a can of Ajax?"

Actually, Heather had always fantasized about marrying a man who actually helped out around the house. Did that make her weird?

Okay. Maybe it did. Hadn't she already come to that conclusion last night?

"You can't tell anyone about this," Heather said. "Only my family knows."

"You're keeping this to *yourself?*"

"It was a dumb thing to do. I want as few people as possible to know about it."

"Are you kidding me? You should be shouting it from the rooftops!"

Heather grabbed Alison's sleeve and yanked her forward. "Not a word, Alison. *Not one word.*"

Alison clenched her teeth, scrunching up her eyes, glaring at Heather. "Okay," she said finally. "I won't say anything." Then she got a thoughtful look on her face. "Did Tony ever strike you as the kind of guy who'd do something like this?"

"You mean, something like marry a woman he doesn't even know? Actually, yes."

"No, like concoct this whole plan just so you won't be humiliated in front of your family. I never would have thought it of a guy like him."

For the first time, Heather really stopped to think about that. Yeah, he'd made a real mess of things, but his heart had actually been in the right place. Was it possible that there was more to Tony McCaffrey than met the eye?

But even if there was, she'd told Alison the truth. He wasn't the kind of man she wanted. Sure, if she could get a guy who looked like Tony, who smiled like Tony, who laughed like Tony, who *kissed* like Tony, but was actually down-to-earth and steady and responsible, she wouldn't turn him down. But those things rarely went hand in hand, and they certainly hadn't wound up together inside Tony McCaffrey.

At two o'clock that afternoon, Tony signed the papers, transferred the funds, and became the new owner of Mc-Millan's Bar and Grill. After leaving the title company, he went directly to the bar, where he pulled into a parking space, killed the car engine, and just sat and stared at the building. It looked friendly and welcoming, the kind of place where you could come in, sit down, and relax. Maybe someday he'd build a deck on the north side where people could sit to enjoy a meal or a drink outdoors. Frank occasionally hired local bands to play, and Tony intended to do even more of that. Maybe he could shake things up with a little karaoke. Have an open-mic comedy night. Anything to bring people in to eat and drink and enjoy themselves.

It felt good. No, it felt *great*. He was doing something with his life. Something big. A lot of people dreamed of being their own boss, but he'd actually done something to make that dream come true.

When he went inside, Tracy, Jamie, and Kayla were at the end of the bar, chatting with Lisa. Kayla was cute, smart, and efficient, the kind of waitress who could do three things at once and look for more. Lisa was a good bartender who hustled drinks like a real pro. Jamie, waitress and assistant manager, was normally just as competent, but at eight months pregnant, she had understandably slowed down a little. And Tracy . . .

Actually, Tony had never really stopped to assess her competence. He was too busy admiring her long, gorgeous legs and spectacular breasts.

Hands off. One month. You can do it.

Everyone looked at him expectantly as he approached. He pulled out a barstool and sat down.

"It's a done deal," he said. "You're looking at the new owner of McMillan's Bar and Grill."

The women cheered. Hugs all around. And Tony felt as if he were flying.

Chuck poked his head out of the kitchen. "Do we have a new boss?"

"Tony just closed the deal," Kayla said. "He's officially the new owner."

"Hey! Great news!" Chuck said, hurrying out of the kitchen to shake Tony's hand. Chuck was a middle-aged guy who'd spent his entire adult life in one restaurant kitchen or another, and he could turn just about anything into a meal to die for. Emilio followed behind him, a younger guy who was learning from Chuck, and from what Frank said, he was doing a good job. Tony intended to make sure both of them stayed with him from now on.

"We gotta get back to the kitchen," Chuck said. "Lunch hour's coming up."

"Dedicated employees," Tony said with a grin. "I like that."

"I hope you're thinking about raises," Kayla said. "Frank was a tightwad. You'll be much more generous, won't you?"

"Sure, sweetheart," he said, his head still floating in the clouds. "It'll be the first thing on my list."

As well it should be. What was more important to a business than its personnel?

As the waitresses scattered to get ready for the lunch shift, Tony sat at the bar a few minutes longer, basking in the pleasure of owning his own business and being his own boss. And in a month, after he got that annulment, he'd no longer have a roommate, which meant he could invite Tracy straight to his king-sized bed and resume his life of happy bachelorhood.

~

Heather was dead tired by the time she caught the train for home at the St. Paul station. It had been a hellish Monday at work, with dissatisfied clients right and left. The Morehead account had been only the beginning. She still hadn't recovered from her Saturday-night debauchery in Vegas. Maybe she never would. Maybe she'd stay permanently hungover as a punishment from God for doing something so incredibly stupid.

Heather collapsed on a seat on the train, intending to pull out her mystery novel and escape into somebody else's problems. But when the train stopped at the Pearl Street station, Heather looked up to see an enormous woman wearing black stretch pants and a leopard-print tank top. She trundled down the aisle and plopped down next to Heather, filling her own seat and half of Heather's, then proceeded to sing along with the gospel music oozing from her iPod. Heather sighed. Sometimes the train truly sucked. But her only alternative was to brave Central Expressway traffic from Plano to downtown and pay a hundred and fifty bucks a month to park her car.

On days like today, that didn't seem like such a bad option.

Heather stuffed her book inside her tote bag and closed her eyes, hoping to zone out the rest of the way home, but as they were about to enter the Cityplace tunnel, her phone rang. She grabbed it from her purse and looked at the caller ID. Her mother.

With a heavy sigh, she hit the TALK button to answer the call, only to lose it as soon as they entered the tunnel. When they emerged a few minutes later at the Mockingbird station, Heather saw that her mother had left a voice mail.

"Hi, sweetie," her mother said. "I tried to get a hold of you at work, but you must already be heading home. I thought maybe you'd like to join Aunt Bev and me for a friendly drink."

Heather's mind went on red alert. Aunt Bev? Since when did her mother and Aunt Bev stop off somewhere for a friendly drink? And where her mother was concerned, a drink of what? Hot tea? And since when did *friendly* describe anything the two of them did together?

Then came the punch line: "If you get this message, meet us at McMillan's. Can't wait to see the place!"

Apprehension slammed into Heather like a hurricane-force wind. Her mother? Aunt Bev? *McMillan's?*

In the next second, Heather understood. It wasn't her mother's kind of place. But now that she finally had a handsome, entrepreneurial son-in-law to show off, she couldn't wait to do it—in front of one person in particular. Her snooty sister.

And the minute she walked into McMillan's, Tony was going to flip out.

Heather speed-dialed her mother's house. No answer. Aunt Bev's. No answer, either. Good Lord, they'd already left.

Tony. You have to warn him.

She didn't have a clue what his cell phone number was, so she called directory assistance to get the number for McMillan's. It seemed as if an eternity passed before the recorded voice told her the number. She hit the button to have it dialed for her automatically.

The phone rang. And rang. And *rang*. Finally someone answered.

"McMillan's. May I help you?"

Thank God. "I need to talk to Tony."

"Who's calling?"

"Tell him it's Heather. I have to talk to him right now."

"I'm sorry. He's not here."

"No. I know he's there. You have to put him on the phone."

"I said he's not here."

"Where did he go?"

"I don't have a clue."

No. After closing on the place that morning, Heather couldn't imagine that he wasn't there now. "Do you have his cell phone number?"

"Sorry. No. Why don't you check back tomorrow? Maybe you'll get lucky and catch him then."

"But—"

Click.

This was a disaster. Even if Tony wasn't there, what was her mother going to tell the people who worked for him?

Heather smacked her cell phone closed and stuffed it into her purse, cussing under her breath.

"Sweetie? Can I give you a little advice?"

Heather turned to the enormous leopard-spotted woman sitting next to her. "What?"

"Don't you be chasing men like that," she said with

a shake of her finger. "Not a single one of them is worth it."

With that, she went back to singing about the glory of God, and Heather started praying to God she could get off this train, hurry to McMillan's, and stop the train wreck that was getting ready to happen.

Back at McMillan's, Tony was in his office, getting things organized now that Frank had moved out. Frank hadn't been the best record-keeper, and the office was a mess even by Tony's standards. As much as he hated housekeeping of any kind in his personal life, this was business, and he was determined to keep things in good order.

Then he looked underneath the desk and saw about two dozen power cords wrapped around each other like spaghetti. He pushed the chair away and ducked under the desk to straighten things out. Fifteen minutes later, he was starting to make sense of it, but he still had a mess on his hands. It seemed as if all he was getting for his trouble was a cramp in his neck.

"Hey, Tony."

He peered out from under the desk to see Jamie at his door.

"I'm kind of in the middle of something here," he said. "Can it wait?"

"Uh...no. Maybe you'd better put that on hold."

"What's the matter?"

"There's a customer out front who wants to talk to you."

"Who is it?"

"She says she's your…uh…"

"What?"

"Mother-in-law."

Tony came out from under the desk so fast, he banged his head. Mother-in-law?

Crap. Barbara Montgomery. Who else? And what the hell was she doing here?

He scrambled to his feet and hurried out of his office, and when he saw Barbara and her sister, Bev, sitting at a table, his heart slammed against his chest. Kayla and Tracy were looking over Barbara's shoulder at something she held in her hands. Their eyes grew progressively wider. In unison, they turned those eyes up to meet Tony's, and for one of the only times in his life, he didn't have a clue what to say.

"And look at this one," he heard Barbara say as he drew closer. "One of Heather's uncles snapped it. Do they look cute together, or what?"

Tony felt a shot of dread. Photographic evidence.

He was a dead man.

Chapter 9

Heather leaped off the train, threw her briefcase and tote bag into her car, and then ran through the parking lot and around the corner to McMillan's. With luck, her mother hadn't made it there yet, and she'd be able to stop her before she went in. Then she saw a white Toyota out front with a dent in the driver's door.

Too late.

Taking a deep breath, Heather opened the door and went into the bar, and what she saw made her nerves tighten with dread.

Her mother sat at a table near the window, talking excitedly. Aunt Bev sat next to her with a sour look on her face. They were surrounded by a rapt audience of three waitresses, and everybody was passing photographs from one person to another. And Tony was standing nearby, looking as if he was on the verge of mixing himself an arsenic cocktail.

"Heather!" her mother said, just a little too loudly. "You got my message. Come here and sit down with us, sweetie!"

Heather made her way to the table, feeling as if she was having one of those absurd nightmares where nothing made sense. Tony slipped up beside her, put his hand on her shoulder, and whispered in her ear, "We have a problem here."

Oh, boy, did they.

"See?" her mother said, pointing to Tony and Heather. "Aren't they just the *cutest* couple?"

Tony pulled his hand away from Heather. Quickly. Too quickly, which gave her the most sickening feeling that they were about to be found out. There was no way this could possibly end well.

Then she noticed the plate in front of her mother. "Mom? What are you eating?"

"Poppers," she said, tossing another one into her mouth. "And they're *wonderful*."

"Fried jalapeños? What about your esophageal reflux?"

"That's what I asked her," Bev said.

"And you're *drinking?*" Heather said.

"Why, yes, I am!" her mother said. "Jamie told me Cosmos were delicious, and darned if she wasn't right."

"I don't know what you think you're doing," Aunt Bev snapped. "You don't even drink."

"You don't follow me around every minute of every day, Bev," her mother said, slurring a word or two. "You have no idea what I do."

"I'm not talking about sniffing the cooking sherry. What's gotten into you?"

"For heaven's sake," Barbara muttered. "Will you lighten up and have a good time?" She turned to Jamie. "Bring us another drink."

"Mom—"

"And one for Heather. Ever had a Cosmo, sweetie?"

"This will be her third drink," Bev told Heather.

Heather whipped around. "Mom? *Three* drinks?"

"It's okay. They're itty-bitty. Martooni"—she stopped and cleared her throat—"mar*tini* glasses don't hold much."

"Barbara, you're drunk," Bev said.

Barbara raised her chin. "No, Bev. Drunk is what you were the night of Regina's engagement party. Six gin and tonics? *Really.*"

"I was *celebrating*," Aunt Bev said.

"Well, so am I," her mother said, then turned to Jamie with a big smile. "Another Cosmo," she said, then whispered, "There's a big tip in it for you and the baby."

Jamie smiled and headed for the bar. Heather couldn't believe this. She just *couldn't*.

Bev turned her gaze across the room to Tracy, who was bending over wiping a table, her skirt hiked up to the very tops of her thighs.

"Your waitresses dress very skimpy," Bev said to Tony. "But I suppose that's what it takes to get the attention of the kinds of customers who come to places like this."

"Bev," Barbara said, "will you stop being such a prude?" She smiled at Tony. "I think they look adorable."

Adorable? Crop tops and miniskirts? Was this her mother talking? The woman who thought any girl in a two-piece swimsuit should wear a T-shirt over it? The woman who didn't see her first R-rated movie until she was forty years old?

"So," Aunt Bev said to Tony and Heather, "I'm not sure I've ever known anyone who got married in Vegas before. Especially after knowing each other only a few hours. That's a little impulsive, isn't it?"

Barbara smiled indulgently. "Now, Bev. Don't take it too hard that it took Jason two years to propose to Regina. I'm sure it doesn't mean he loves her any less."

Aunt Bev opened her mouth to respond, but nothing came out. Heather felt a surge of delight. *Direct hit, Mom! Way to go!*

"People are going to be flocking to this place," Barbara gushed to everyone within hearing distance of her voice, which was growing louder by the moment. "Tony is such a nice boy, and he has that beautiful smile. He's going to be *such* a success."

Heather glanced at Tony. He looked like a man standing in the path of a bulldozer with nowhere to run.

"And this place is such a worthwhile pursuit," Aunt Bev said. "Bartending is such a respected profession."

Barbara laughed. "Please, Bev. To say Tony is a bartender is like saying Donald Trump is a carpenter."

Good one, Mom! You got her again!

"Oh!" Barbara said. "I almost forgot. Your father and I have a wedding gift for you two."

"You do?" Tony said.

"We'd like to bring it by your apartment tomorrow night. Will you be home about six?"

"Uh...I'm afraid not," Tony said. "New business, you know. I'll probably be here night and day for a while."

"Oh, that's okay," Barbara said with a wave of her hand. "Fred and I can bring it here."

"No!" Tony whipped his gaze to Heather and back again. "No, that's all right. I can come home for a little while. No problem."

"Good," Barbara said with a big, loopy smile. "We'll drop by about six."

Tony slipped his arm around Heather's shoulder, gripping it just a little too tightly. "Heather? I need you to take a look at something in my office. Could you come with me?"

"Uh...sure." She turned to her mother. "We'll be back in a minute."

All the way down the hall to his office, Tony felt as if he were going to explode with irritation. He dragged Heather inside, closed the door behind them, and let her have it.

"What the hell is going on? Did you know they were coming here?"

"I picked up a voice mail from my mother when I was on the train. I tried to call her back, but she had already left the house."

"Did you try her cell phone?"

"My mother? Cell phone? She's lucky to be able to dial a touch-tone phone."

Tony gripped the back of his desk chair, closing his eyes with frustration.

"Hey, I tried to call to warn you," Heather said.

"Wrong. I've been here all afternoon. You didn't call."

"Oh, yes, I did. Whoever answered said you weren't here."

"Yes, I was. I've been here since I closed on the place this morning."

"Not according to the woman who answered."

"I've been in my office for the last hour. Why didn't she—" Tony stopped short, his eyes falling closed. "Oh, boy."

"What?"

"Never mind."

"What?"

He opened his eyes. "I guess old habits die hard."

"What are you talking about?"

"See, the bartenders and waitresses here...well, they know to..."

"To what?"

"If a woman calls here looking for me..."

Heather looked at him blankly for a moment. Then her mouth fell open. "Oh, you have *got* to be kidding me. They cover for you? Tell women you don't want to talk to that you're not here?"

"Uh...yeah. Something like that."

"So this is your fault," Heather said.

"My fault? *My* fault? It was your mother who came in here with a fistful of photographs! What is *with* her, anyway?"

"She's just glad I'm married."

"Yeah? Well, I'm glad somebody's glad about that."

Heather glared at him. "Hey, buster. This was your plan. Not mine."

"But I didn't expect everyone I know to find out!"

"You think *I'm* happy about that?"

"You don't get it, Heather. Did you see the looks on their faces? Me being married changes everything!"

"Okay, so we didn't expect anyone but my family to find out. But what if they did? You'll be divorced in a month, and you can go back to playing the field, so I don't see why it's so..." Her voice trailed off, and a knowing look came over her face. "Ah. Now I understand."

"What?"

"What you really mean to say is that being married to *me* changes everything."

Tony froze. "What do you mean?"

"Tell the truth. It really screws up your reputation for people to know you married a woman who isn't a perfect ten."

"That's not true."

"I saw the looks on your waitresses's faces. And I'm very self-aware, Tony. Men like you don't go for women like me."

"There's nothing wrong with a woman like you."

"I never said there was. You're the one with the problem."

He drew back. "Me? What are you talking about?"

"As far as you're concerned, unless a woman has a pair of 38Ds, she might as well not even be in the room."

"You think that's all I look for in a woman?"

"Oh, God, no. That's just the baseline. After that comes the blond hair and the perfect tan and the cute little ass and the *space* between her *ears*."

"Are you saying the women I date are dumb?"

She looked at him pointedly. "Rona and the lottery?"

"Okay," he muttered. "So some of them aren't exactly rocket scientists. So what? I like beautiful women."

"Here's a thought. You might want to look above the neck for a switch. Find a woman who can add two and two together and come up with something that's at least close to four."

"You mean, like your average CPA?"

Heather raised her chin. "You could do a hell of a lot worse. And from what I've seen, you frequently do."

"The women I date are no concern of yours."

"Look, Tony. You and I both know that if I were some gorgeous but airheaded bimbo you'd married, you wouldn't be so pissed off that everyone found out. All the girls would be jealous, and all the guys would be back-slapping you. But because it's me—"

"That's not true."

"Admit it. Being married to me embarrasses you."

Tony opened his mouth to refute that, but he opened it a second too late.

"So I'm right," Heather said, making a scoffing noise. "Do you have any clue how shallow that makes you?"

Tony wished he could deny the whole thing. But when he'd been standing there next to her, with her mother going on and on about what a cute couple they were...

Heather was right. It had embarrassed him. He'd hated the way everyone had looked at him in that confused, confounded way that said, *You could have had any woman in the world, and you picked* her?

He heard a knock on the office door, and Jamie poked her head inside. "Heather? Your mom's in the bathroom."

"Yeah?"

"She's looking a little queasy."

Tony turned to Heather. "I thought you said your mother doesn't drink."

"She doesn't very often." She turned back to Jamie. "I'll be there in a minute."

Jamie nodded and left the office.

"If she doesn't drink, why did she have three Cosmos?" Tony asked.

"Do you honestly not know?"

He frowned. "I honestly don't know."

"It's her stamp of approval for what you do, particularly in front of Aunt Bev."

"Stamp of approval?"

"Don't you get it? If you'd bought a sex-toy shop, she'd be praising the virtues of vibrators and glow-in-the-dark condoms."

"Huh?"

Heather waved her hand. "Oh, never mind. I don't expect you to understand."

"Just get her to stop gushing to everyone about how wonderful I am and what a big success I'm going to be, will you?"

"There's something wrong with that, too?"

"She was actually talking about me and Donald Trump in the same breath."

"Let me get this straight. Her saying nice things about you embarrasses you?"

"She doesn't even *know* me!"

"She doesn't have to know you. You're family."

"Family? I'm *not* family!"

"She thinks you are. And do you know why? Because you kissed me in front of them all and told them I was the love of your life!"

And Tony was regretting that more with every passing moment.

"I'm sorry my mother embarrassed you," Heather said, even though it was clear she wasn't sorry at all. "But no matter what you think of her, she likes you. That's why she goes on and on. And I'm sorry *I* embarrassed you in front of all the people here and screwed up your reputation."

"I never said that. You're putting words in my mouth."

"That's right. The ones you're thinking and not saying. But you know what? Just between you and me, your reputation could use a little screwing up."

"What?"

"I can't say I'm looking forward to spending the next
month with an overgrown frat boy, but spending a month
with me might actually do you some good."

"Good?"

"Yeah. You might actually start to see a woman as
something more than collections of body parts. It's not
likely that you will, of course. But miracles do happen."

Heather yanked open the door and left his office, and
he felt the heat of her anger trailing in her wake. She
thought he was shallow? Fine. But it was his life to live
the way he wanted to. He liked things easy and mindless and feel-good, with nobody telling him what to do.
But for the next month, somebody else was scripting
his life, and that made him uncomfortable like nothing
else.

So she thought she was good for him, did she? Wrong.
She was an anally retentive number-cruncher who had
a family that gave the word *intrusive* an entirely new
meaning. It would take months of excavation just to uncover her sense of humor, if it existed at all, and she
had a superiority complex as vast as the plains of West
Texas.

Tony sat fuming in his office for several minutes,
and by the time he came out, Heather had collected her
mother and they'd left, taking Bev with them. He slid
onto a barstool and asked Lisa for a Coke, dreading the
rest of the evening when he should have been looking
forward to it. Not only did his employees now know
he was a married man, but they would spread the news
to the regular customers, too, until the whole damned

world knew. And there wasn't a thing he could do to stop it.

~~

Heather drove toward her parents' house with her mother in the passenger seat. She looked a little woozy after her bathroom episode, leaning her elbow on the console and resting her chin in her hand.

"I guess those Cosmos are a little more powerful than they taste, huh?"

"Yeah, Mom. A little bit."

"Was I just awful? I bet Tony thinks I'm just awful."

"Of course not," Heather said. "He likes people to have a good time. That's why he bought a bar."

"Bev wasn't having a good time at all." In spite of everything, Barbara managed a shaky smile. "Too bad about that, huh? But when I asked her if she wanted to go, she couldn't very well say no without looking like a bad sport." After a moment, though, her smile faded into a look of concern. "Heather?"

"Yeah, Mom?"

"This is a good thing for you, isn't it?"

"What do you mean?"

"You know how suspicious your father is. He says it's not like you to do something this impulsive. He's worried."

"Dad was a cop. He's suspicious about everything."

"I know. He can't even walk into a convenience store without thinking there are hostages tied up in the back." She looked at Heather with an anxious frown. "Tony is the right man for you, isn't he?"

Oh, boy. What was she supposed to say to that? *Yeah, he's perfect. How do I know? After nine glasses of champagne, my judgment always becomes crystal clear.*

"There are never any guarantees, Mom. Even when people date for a long time." She smiled. "I guess time will tell, won't it?"

"Yeah. I guess so."

About a month's worth of time, and it'll tell more than you can possibly imagine.

"You've always been a smart girl, Heather. If you say this marriage is a good thing, it's a good thing." She took a deep breath and let it out slowly. "I'm just going to rest my eyes a little now, okay?"

"Okay."

As her mother's eyes drifted closed, Heather wondered if there was any way this situation could get any more complicated. She had hoped to become a single woman again with only a few people knowing she'd ever been married, but after what had happened tonight, that number would be increasing with every passing hour.

But she knew that as much as it bothered her, it bothered Tony more.

At the time, it had been very satisfying to tell him exactly how she felt about his taste in women, but now she wished she hadn't pushed him quite so hard. Because now the plain, glaring truth had been spelled out for her. Tony, along with everyone at that bar, thought she wasn't good enough for a guy like him.

She wished she could say she didn't care. Intellectually, she didn't. But still there was that little emotional tug, the one that told her she was somehow lacking because she wasn't pretty enough to be seen with a man as handsome as Tony. But the truth was that while Tony was nice to look at, that was where Heather's interest in him ended. He was the kind of man with nothing on his mind but seven hundred cable channels, cold beer, and naked women. When it came to having the qualities she wanted in a man, he didn't even come close.

~

As happy hour progressed, Tony's prediction came to pass. Word spread fast, and soon he was getting as many congratulations for his marriage as he was for buying the bar.

Just before seven o'clock, he saw a couple guys come through the door who usually showed up on the same nights Tony did for the purpose of doing three things: drinking hard, watching sports, and chasing women. Tracy was heading to their table, which meant that any moment now, they'd know everything.

Sure enough, barely thirty seconds passed before Andy turned and yelled at him. "Hey, Tony! Come here!"

Tony sighed with resignation and walked over, pasting a big smile on his face. "Hey, guys! How's it going?"

They both stood up and shook his hand, congratulating him on being the new owner, then tossed out all kinds of smart-ass suggestions, like telling Tony he should have a free beer night, or a Jell-O wrestling event, or maybe even a *no* T-shirt contest.

After the questionable hilarity wound down, Kyle turned to Tony. "Tracy just told us something, and we want to know if it's true."

Tony sighed inwardly. "What's that?"

"She said…" Kyle stopped, laughing a little. "Okay, I know you're not going to believe this, but she said that over the weekend, you got *married*."

Tony hated this. *Hated* it. It was as if he'd hopped on a freight train in Vegas that picked up more steam with every moment that passed, and there was no way off.

"Yeah. I got married."

Andy blinked in disbelief. "You did not."

"Yes," Tony said. "I did."

"So who did you marry? I don't remember any woman you dated more than a few times."

"You don't know her."

Andy shook his head. "What happened, dude? You buy a bar, which means you get your alcohol cheap, and you're surrounded by women every night. And you go and get *married*? That's crazy!"

"The same woman every night?" Kyle said. "I thought you liked variety."

Tony could barely get the words out of his mouth. "Variety is overrated."

Kyle turned to Andy with a look of disbelief. "Did he actually say that?"

"I think he did. Hell must have frozen over." Then Andy gave Tony a sly smile. "So…when do we get to meet the little woman?"

"Someday soon, I'm sure. You guys drink up. I have something I need to take care of in the kitchen."

As Tony walked away, Andy and Kyle were still muttering with disbelief. Tony didn't blame them. He was experiencing a little disbelief of his own. Somehow he'd ended up having to deal with a surly wife, a drunk mother-in-law, an intrusive family, and the confused stares of people who wondered how he could be playing the field one day and married the next.

He repeated his mantra, one he was sure to wear out before he became a single man again: *One month. Just one month, and it'll all be over with.*

Chapter 10

It was almost six o'clock the next evening when Tony got out of his car and hurried into his apartment. He'd been praying all the way home that Barbara and Fred would show up on time, give them the ugly silver candlesticks or whatever, and then leave.

He saw Heather's car out front, which meant she was already there. He'd left the bar so late last night that by the time he got home, she had gone to bed, and by the time he got up this morning, she'd already left for work. That gave him hope that after this visit from her parents, they would go their separate ways until Regina's wedding and their annulment, and his life could get back to normal. He unlocked his door, went into his apartment, and stopped short.

What the *hell* had happened in here?

It was as if a gigantic wind had blown through and swept away every bit of clutter. The hearth was clear. He could see the top of the dining room table. A few magazines were precisely fanned out on the coffee table, making his living room look like the waiting room of a doctor's office.

He looked down at the floor. So *that* was the color of the carpet?

The walls even looked whiter, but maybe that was just because there was nothing piled in front of them. And hanging in the air like swamp gas was the smell of bleach and ammonia and all those other products that belonged only in hospitals and public bathrooms. Tony hated the smell of disinfectant the way other people hated the smell of rotting corpses.

"Heather!"

He heard some shuffling in the kitchen, and Heather poked her head around the doorway. Her hair was pulled up to the crown of her head in one of those scrunchy things, but a few strands had pulled free and fell along her cheeks. She wore a pair of pink rubber gloves and a stubborn expression.

"I'm just about finished," she said. "I still have to scrub the sink."

She ducked back around the doorway. Tony strode into the kitchen, blinded by the light reflecting brightly off every surface.

"What have you *done?*"

"So it's true. You really don't know clean when you see it."

The pantry door was open, and Tony peered inside. Boxes and cans were lined up according to height, like little soldiers all in a row—unhappy little soldiers who were never allowed any R and R.

"My God, what happened in here?" he said.

"Well, mostly I threw stuff out."

He whipped around. "You threw out my stuff?"

"Only if it was moldy. But don't panic. Your Twinkies are still there."

He yanked open the refrigerator. "My God. There's nothing left!"

"Sure there is. Fruit. Produce. Good food. *Fresh* food." She gave the sink a final rinse, then pulled off the gloves. "Isn't that nice for a switch?"

"Where did all this come from?"

"I stopped at the grocery store this afternoon on my way home. I took off a few hours early." She gazed around with a weary sigh. "I probably should have taken off a few more. After dropping by my parents' house to get more of my things, I didn't have much time left."

"I don't suppose you got the gift when you were there," Tony said.

"No. My mother wanted to give it to both of us in person."

"So we're still on for tonight."

"They'll be here in a few minutes."

Great.

Then he had a horrifying thought. "You didn't mess with the stuff in the other room, did you?"

"Only the ugly stuff. And if it was clearly trash, I threw it out."

"What about the boxes that were in there? The magazines?"

Heather rolled her eyes. "Will you calm down? The girls are alive and well."

"Do *not* mess with my swimsuit editions," he said, pointing at her. "They're *collector's items.*"

"They're in a box in the closet. Along with *Hot Rod* magazines that are five years old and a pair of softball trophies." She shook her head. "You actually played on a softball team sponsored by Luigi's Little Bit O' Italy?"

"Hey, we beat the team from Mr. Wong's Dry Cleaners to win the championship that year. Those guys are tough."

"Grown men playing softball. *God.*"

"You need to stop moving my stuff."

"Sure. Next time I'll dust *around* the socks on top of the TV."

"Why are you doing this?" Tony asked.

"Because clean is nice," she said. "And because if my mother had seen me living in your apartment the way it was, she'd have had a heart attack."

Her mother. Of course. He should have guessed that. "Can't you just clean the part that shows?"

"No. My mother's a real snoop. If she tells you she's just going to the bathroom, she's lying." Heather brushed her hands together and swept her gaze around the apartment. "There," she said with a smile of satisfaction. "Shipshape."

Shipshape. God, how Tony hated the sound of that word.

All at once there was a knock at the door.

"They're here," Heather said, yanking the scrunchy thing out of her hair. "Can you at least try to smile? You're really very good at it. Just do what comes naturally."

"There's nothing natural about my in-laws showing up."

With a roll of her eyes, Heather opened the door. Barbara flitted into the apartment, and Fred trudged in behind her. Heather proceeded to do the huggy-kissy thing with her mother. And now that Tony was caught in that sphere, Barbara did the huggy-kissy thing with him, too.

Fortunately, Fred was neither huggy nor kissy. He just stood there holding a large, flat package wrapped in exactly the kind of paper Tony had dreaded. Shiny silver with wedding bells and flowers.

I'm never getting married. Not for real. Never, never, never.

Heather escorted her parents to the sofa, then sat down on the love seat next to Tony.

"Oh, my!" Barbara said, her gaze traveling around the apartment. "Fred! Will you look at this? Tony keeps things so nice and neat! This is just amazing. I mean, it's so rare these days to find a young man who knows how to keep house."

"Why, thank you, Barbara," Tony said. "Just because I'm a man doesn't mean I can't keep things shipshape, right?"

Heather gave him a subtle knock-it-off-smart-ass look, which he ignored.

"Can I get you something to drink?" Heather asked her parents.

"Your mother had more than enough to drink last night," Fred muttered. "If she shows up again," he said to Tony, "give her ginger ale."

Barbara stuck her nose in the air. "I'll drink what I want to, when I want to, Fred Montgomery. And you don't have a thing to say about it."

"Fine. Find somebody else to take you to get your car the next morning."

Barbara turned to Tony. "Don't mind Fred. His arthritis is acting up. It always makes him crabby. I had a lovely time last night. The appetizers were just a little too spicy for me, that's all." She waved her hands at the package. "Go ahead, you two. Open it!"

Tony dutifully scooted over and helped Heather rip the paper away. And when he saw what was behind it, he was stunned. He'd been afraid of toasters and blenders and bath towels, but this?

Courtesy of Barbara and Fred, they now had a very large, very old portrait of the ugliest woman on earth, which Tony recognized as the portrait that had been hanging over their fireplace. And now he and Heather were stuck with it?

"Oh, my God," Heather said, staring at it dumbly. "It's Grandma Frances!"

Barbara smiled. "I don't know why you're surprised. You knew one day it would be yours."

"Well, yeah, but..." Heather glanced nervously at Tony. "But she's been hanging over your mantel since you and Dad got married. You can't give her up."

"Nonsense. I'm supposed to give her up. That's the way family heirlooms are. Fred's mother passed her down to us, and now we're passing her down to you." She turned to Tony. "You know, she was considered quite a handsome woman in her day."

"Yes," Tony said. "I can see why." Actually, he couldn't see it at all. If this was handsome, what did the ugly women look like?

"But she stayed a spinster until the day she died," Barbara added. "She ran the newspaper in Sorrento, Texas, for fifty-two years. She was a feminist before there were feminists. Men weren't exactly ready for that at the time."

"Well, I'm all for feminism," Tony said. "I like strong women."

Heather gave him another one of *those* looks, which he also ignored.

"And you have just the place for her." Barbara poked Fred. "Try it out above the fireplace. Let's see how it looks."

No. No way. The last thing Tony wanted was sour-faced Grandma Frances staring down at him for the next month. But Barbara was smiling again, and Fred was frowning, and both of those things told him that a confrontation over the issue just might end in tears and bloodshed.

Fred picked up the portrait and rested it on the mantel. Barbara put her hand against her cheek, staring up at it with a bittersweet smile.

"She looks beautiful up there, doesn't she?"

"Yeah," Heather said, looking a little sick. "Beautiful."

"Grandma Frances would be thrilled to be here."

"Thanks, Mom," Heather said. "It makes me feel right at home. For her to be looking down at me. You know. Like that."

Tony thought about a horror movie he'd seen once where the eyes on a portrait followed anybody who walked by. He swore Grandma Frances's eyes were doing a little tracking of their own.

"You've met a lot of our family," Barbara said to Tony. "Will we be meeting yours anytime soon?"

Tony froze. "Uh...no. None of my relatives live here."

"Oh, that's too bad," Barbara said.

"What does your old man do?" Fred asked.

"He's a retired Navy officer. Lives in Fort Lauderdale."

Fred gave him a curt nod. "Good career."

Tony wasn't surprised by Fred's opinion. Cops and military officers were cut from the same cloth. As a matter of fact, Tony could see a lot of his father in Fred. Unsmiling. A man of few words, and what few words he did speak made Tony feel as if he was judging every move he made.

"And what about your mother?" Barbara asked brightly.

"She died when I was a kid."

"Oh, I'm so sorry!"

Tony shrugged. "It was a long time ago."

"How old were you?"

"Ten."

"So young," she said, then smiled. "Any other family?"

"A few aunts and uncles on the East Coast. I don't see them very often."

"I'm sorry you have so little family in town. But just think. Now you have all the family you'll ever want."

"Yeah, Tony," Heather said. "Isn't that great? And maybe the rest of that great big family would just love to come see your new business."

He slid his hand to her thigh and squeezed. "I'm sure most of them wouldn't be interested in coming to a sports bar."

"Fred would," Barbara said, then turned to Fred. "There are big-screen TVs."

"There had damn well better be if it's a sports bar," Fred said.

"Come on, Fred," Barbara said. "It's time for us to go. Tony needs to get back to the bar. Just let me go to the little girls' room first."

Tony shot a look at Heather, who shot one back at him: *I told you so.*

While Barbara was gone, Heather talked to her father about something going on with one of their relatives. Or, rather, she talked *at* her father. As usual, Fred didn't say much. And all the while, Tony imagined Barbara stealing glances into his bedroom, peeking inside his medicine cabinet, and lifting the toilet lid to make sure when he said "shipshape," he meant it. She came back to the living room a few minutes later, all smiles, which meant his apartment had passed inspection.

She and Fred rose to leave. As they were walking out the door, Fred glanced back at the portrait, then leaned toward Tony and whispered, "She's been glaring at me for the past thirty-two years." His mouth twitched into something that looked almost like a smile. "Now she's all yours."

The only satisfaction Tony felt right then was the thought of it ending up back over Fred's mantel. *Give it a month, Fred, and she'll be glaring down at you all over again.*

As soon as Tony clicked the door shut, he turned on Heather, who looked frustratingly unconcerned about any of this.

"Tell me it's not just me," he said. "Tell me that portrait is the creepiest thing on earth."

"That portrait is the creepiest thing on earth. When I was a kid, I swore the eyes followed me. I'm still not so sure they don't."

The old woman's face made Tony's skin crawl. "We'll put it in your room. Facing the wall."

"No. If my mother drops by and doesn't see it, she'll

be hurt. And at least it fills the space. There's nothing there now." She put her hand to her mouth. "Oh, my. It looks as if we've found one more flaw in your brilliant plan, doesn't it?"

He glared at her, then turned his expression of disgust back to the portrait, imagining what it was going to be like to come home to it every day. Yep. Excruciating. But since this whole experience was excruciating, did it really matter?

"Okay, Franny," he said with resignation. "You've got a home for a month."

"Frances," Heather said. "She hated being called Franny. Have respect for the dead."

"Granny Franny."

"She'd have castrated you for that."

"A battle-ax swinging a battle-ax. Doesn't get much badder than that."

"Texas is a community-property state," Heather said. "You're entitled to fight me for her when we split up."

"Nope. She's all yours."

"Maybe we could divide her down the middle. Then she'd only be half as ugly. Oh! I know. If you agree to take her, I'll throw in my grandfather's collection of magnets from all fifty states."

"As tempting as that is," Tony said, "I think I'll pass."

"Tell me what awful things you have from your family. Maybe we can trade."

"Nothing, actually. Like I told your parents, my family's pretty small." He checked his watch, then grabbed his keys. "I have to get back to the bar." Halfway to the door, he turned back around and pointed at Heather. "And *don't* clean anything while I'm gone."

Heather just folded her arms and gave him that sweet smile again, which meant he'd probably walk back through his door later to find she'd scrubbed the bathroom grout with a Q-tip and sterilized his TV remote.

Good God. Three days ago, he'd been a nice, normal bachelor with his underwear on the floor and nothing in his fridge but beer and day-old pizza. Now he had terrifying wall décor and a wife with a cleaning fetish, along with a terrible feeling that the weirdness was just getting started.

Chapter 11

The next Saturday evening, Heather was drinking martinis with Alison at Chantal's, which was down the block from McMillan's. It was a loud, hard-edged club with lots of chrome and glass and yuppies on the prowl. Pretension hung in the air, as thick and choking as tear gas. Regina went there a lot, which was a really good reason for Heather to stay away, but since she'd told Alison that McMillan's was off-limits for now and maybe forever, they had to drink somewhere.

"This place sucks," Alison grumbled. "The men are creepy, and the waitresses are conceited bitches. And paying ten bucks for a martini is stupid."

Heather didn't much like that herself, but she wasn't going to McMillan's, and that was that. Still fresh in her mind was the way the waitresses had looked at her, then at Tony, their expressions practically shouting, *Her? You gotta be kidding me.* The truth was that they were all hopelessly shallow people who cared more about looks than what was inside a person, so why should she subject herself to that?

Then she realized that sounded like one of the nauseatingly uplifting e-mails her friend Kathy forwarded to her all the time, the ones with smiley faces and baby animals and animated images that told her what a special and unique person she was. Heather was getting a little tired of being the kind of person who other people thought needed pick-me-ups like that.

Alison peered out the window. "There sure is a big crowd at McMillan's tonight. Looks like fun."

Heather knew Alison could see McMillan's from their booth, which was why Heather had declined to sit on that side of the table. Now, though, she was beginning to wish she hadn't. It was too hard to steal glances when Alison wasn't looking.

"Business must be good," Alison said.

Heather shrugged and took another two-dollar sip of gin.

"I mean, look at all the cars in the parking lot."

"There are more people here."

"Yeah. Horny men and slutty women."

"There are plenty of those at McMillan's, too."

"The difference is that these horny men and slutty women think they're high class." Alison tapped her fingertips on the table. "Speaking of horny men, how's your husband?"

"If you don't stop referring to him as my husband—"

"Okay. Then how's that horny man you're cohabitating with?"

Heather looked down at her drink. "I wouldn't know."

Alison eyed her carefully. "This is nuts. First you insist we come to this neon meat market, and now you're pretending not to care about Tony even though you've looked over your shoulder at McMillan's so many times your neck is going to cramp."

"I'm just wondering if things are running smoothly since he bought the place. That's all."

"If we go over there, we can find out. Why don't we?"

"Things are going to be a whole lot easier if Tony and I stay as far away from each other as possible."

"But you're living with him. How far away from him could you possibly stay?"

"We don't see much of each other. He doesn't get home until late every night, and I'm up early to go to work."

"So stay up late one night and seduce him."

"Alison, will you *stop?*"

"I bet it wouldn't take much, considering he's stuck without sex for a month."

"I don't sleep with men because they're horny and I'm handy. I don't like being used."

Alison turned her gaze heavenward. "Please, God, just once in my life, let a guy like Tony want to use me."

"That's demeaning."

Alison folded her arms on the table and looked at Heather. "You know what your problem is?"

Heather had plenty of problems. She just wasn't sure which one Alison was going to point out.

"You don't recognize opportunity when you see it. It's like you're standing in front of a great big wall-to-wall buffet, and you decide you're not going to eat."

"No buffet references," Heather said, glaring at the scant pile of field greens, tomatoes, shredded carrots, and low-fat dressing in front of her that wasn't worth one-tenth of the fourteen dollars she'd paid for it. "I still have to drop a size by the end of the month."

"Heather. *Focus.*"

"I am focused. I'm focused on what an idiot I was to go along with Tony's plan in the first place."

"You weren't an idiot. You get to go to your snotty cousin's wedding with a really hot guy."

Heather started to tell herself it wasn't worth it, only to think about Regina's snarky face and realize that maybe it was.

Their waitress came to their table, balancing a tray full of drinks on her fingertips. She wore the house uniform— a black catsuit cut halfway to her navel that fit condom-tight, a heavy silver chain around her hips, and a pair of black spike heels. She looked like Catwoman with a sado-masochism fetish. She gave them a look of sheer boredom she'd stolen from Paris Hilton and asked if they wanted another martini.

"No, thanks," Alison said, glaring at her glass. "One more drink at these prices and I won't be able to pay my rent."

The waitress lifted her chin and looked straight down her nose. "You could go down the street to McMillan's. I hear it's two-dollar beer night."

Alison turned to Heather. "See, I told you we should have gone there."

"Just the check," Heather told the waitress, who dismissed them with a not-so-subtle roll of her eyes as she slinked to the next table, where she gave three guys in power suits the drinks on her tray while they stared at her breasts and conjured up their favorite dominatrix fantasy.

"Yet one more reason I hate this place," Alison muttered. "I wish we could go back to...whoa. What's going on there?"

Alison had shifted her gaze to the window. Heather

swiveled around and looked down the street to McMillan's. She saw an ambulance pulling up to the front door, its red lights swirling in the darkness, and a feeling of dread swooped through her.

"I don't know," Heather said.

"Let's go find out."

Heather paused only a few seconds before tossing money on the table to cover the check and grabbing her purse.

As they left Chantal's and approached McMillan's parking lot, Heather saw people standing around like people do when there's an emergency, talking among themselves, speculating about things they know nothing about, and generally getting in the way. Then the door opened, and the EMTs brought out a woman on a stretcher. Heather peered over somebody's shoulder.

It was Jamie, Tony's very pregnant assistant manager. She was wide awake, and since there was no blood and no screaming, Heather figured it couldn't be too bad. But there was the baby to think about. About a thousand things could go wrong there.

Tony followed the EMT guys out the door. He gave Jamie's hand a quick pat and said something to her as they loaded her into the ambulance. Then they closed the doors and took off. The sirens weren't blaring, so Heather took that as a good sign, too. But when Tony put his hand to his forehead, squeezing his eyes closed as if he had a monumental headache, she took that as a bad one.

She squirmed through the crowd and caught him before he went back inside. "Tony? What's wrong? What's happening?"

"Heather? What are you doing here?"

"We were having drinks down the street at Chantal's and saw the commotion."

"Chantal's?" he said with a look of disgust. "What were you doing there?"

"That's what I asked her," Alison said. "The men are slimy, the waitresses are bitchy, and ten bucks for a martini? Are they kidding?"

"Tony, this is my friend Alison, who's going to shut up now. What's wrong with Jamie?"

"She's okay. She just went into labor and couldn't get hold of her husband. She's six weeks early, and I didn't want to take any chances. So I called nine-one-one."

"That was a smart thing to do."

"Oh, yeah. It was great. There hasn't been enough chaos around here this evening, so I thought, Hey, why don't I call an ambulance and bring on a little more?"

Heather drew back. "What are you talking about?"

"Sorry. Can't stay and chat. See, I have a business falling apart inside, and I'd like to say good-bye to it. Or maybe I'll just burn the place to the ground and collect the insurance money. If you ladies will excuse me?"

The crowd parted and Tony went back inside. Alison turned to Heather. "What's up with him?"

Heather didn't know, but sarcastic defeatism wasn't his style. "I don't know, but I'm going to find out."

They went inside, and Heather was stunned. Every table was full, and the bar was standing room only. The place was buzzing with conversation and swirling with energy. People were eating, meeting, laughing, and drinking. Right now this bar and grill screamed *profit,* and Tony should have been over the moon about that.

Why wasn't he?

Tony pulled baskets of burgers out from under the warming lights, cringing at how dry they looked from sitting there too long. He packed them on trays for the waitresses to deliver. Assuming, of course, that the waitresses he had left hadn't thrown in their aprons and run screaming from the premises.

As an adult, he really hadn't known what stress felt like. He'd engineered his life for just the opposite, honing his surroundings, handpicking the people he associated with and the jobs he took, then smoothing out the edges into the kind of existence where he could sit back, relax, and live it up. No real pressure, no big demands. He thought that was what he was getting when he bought this place, with the added benefit of being his own boss and making a really nice profit. How deluded must he have been?

"Tony. What's going on?"

He spun around to see Heather standing behind him, and it wasn't a welcome sight. First she'd been at Chantal's, patronizing his competition, and now she was here to bug him, which would help ensure he was no competition at all. And if his waitresses or any of the regulars saw her, the speculation about his marriage would begin all over again.

"I can't talk right now," he told her. "I'm busy."

"Yeah. That's obvious. What's the problem?"

"The *problem*," he said, "is that I have too many customers and not enough employees."

"Why? Jamie's gone, but what else?"

He stopped and took a deep breath, but he still felt manic. "If you must know, Tracy called in sick at the last minute. I hired a new waitress who started today, and she's falling apart. Kayla and Danielle are here, but that's it. I was barely making it tonight before Jamie went into labor. The band who's supposed to play here tonight is pretty popular, which means a lot of people turned out; only now I can't handle the crowd."

"Get the band to start early. Take people's mind off the food and drink."

"Good plan, except when the drummer got here twenty minutes ago, he was too stoned to sit up, so they're not going on. The other guys are making calls to see if they can get a quick replacement, but it probably won't happen. This crowd came to see them, and they're going to get a little testy if they don't."

"Can you call in another waitress or two?"

"I can't get a hold of anybody else."

"You need more help."

"Yeah? You think? I haven't got the time for this, Heather. Go home."

He turned back to his task, every nerve in his body strung so tight it nearly paralyzed him. Suddenly everything seemed blurry and otherworldly. The glaring kitchen lights. Chuck and Emilio, flipping burgers in slow motion. Steam rising from the grill. Heather standing beside him, watching a guy who'd never done a damned thing worthwhile in his life reaching for something big and failing. In a daze of helplessness, Tony reached back under the warming lights and grabbed for a basket of fries. He fumbled it, tried to catch it, but succeeded only in turning it upside down and scattering fries everywhere.

"Damn it! Where's the broom?" He looked left and right, finally spying it leaning against the wall. Heather grabbed his arm.

"Tony—stop."

"Go away, Heather."

"I said *stop*." She gave his arm a hard squeeze, accompanied by a no-nonsense stare. "You're going nuts. That's not going to help. What you need is a plan."

"I had a plan when I had a staff. Now I have a floor full of French fries and a bar full of pissed-off customers."

"Then it's time to go to plan B."

"I don't have a plan B!"

"Then listen up, because I do."

"Heather—"

"*Listen* to me." She slowly released the grip on his arm. "First of all, you get behind the bar and help Lisa until you're sure the drink orders are caught up. If you keep alcohol in front of people, they tend to lose track of time and won't realize it's been too long on their food."

"Don't you understand? It's already been too long for most of them. Hungry people are angry people."

"Give every table free chips and salsa. Something to munch on until their order comes out. I'll get Alison to do that so your waitresses don't have to."

"Give food away? How am I supposed to make money?"

"Wrong question. The question is, how are you supposed to keep customers happy tonight when it takes an hour to get their food so they'll come back *next* time?" She grabbed an apron off a nearby hook and put it on. "Which section was Jamie's?"

"The booths along the west wall. What are you doing?"

"Taking her tables."

"You? Wait tables?"

"Don't act so shocked. When I was in college, I was the weekend manager at a pancake house."

"That's not the same as working in a bar."

"Beer and burgers. Coffee and pancakes. It's all the same."

Kayla hurried into the kitchen, shaking her head. "It's getting ugly out there. Are my orders up?"

"Yeah," Tony said, then looked back at the grill. "All four of them."

As Kayla hurried over to grab one of the trays, Danielle burst into the kitchen. "Somebody spilled a drink. I gotta get the mop." As she yanked open the door to the utility closet, the new waitress came into the kitchen, shoving her bangs out of her face and looking disoriented. She stopped and just stood there, looking small and scared.

"Erika," Tony said, trying to keep the panic out of his voice. "Come on. You've got a couple of orders up."

Tony saw tears filling her eyes, and he felt a wave of apprehension. *No tears. For God's sake, a crying woman is the last thing I need tonight.*

"Erika," he said. "Get it together. You have to get this food out. We don't have time for—"

Heather put her hand on his arm, silencing him. She took the girl by the shoulders and stared down at her. "Hey, take it easy, okay? Tell me what's the matter."

"They're all so demanding! I get one thing to them, and they want something else. The only place I've ever worked before is a cafeteria. On the line. Waiting on old people. *Slow* people!"

"I know, sweetie. But this place isn't usually this wild. And Tony understands that you're new. If things go wrong tonight, nobody's blaming you, okay? I just want you to do the best you can."

The girl nodded, then looked confused. "Who are you?"

Heather looked at Tony, as if she wasn't completely sure how to answer that.

"Heather's my wife," Tony said. "She's here to help out tonight."

Heather's my wife. That was the first time he'd uttered that phrase out loud. It should have given him a bad case of hives, but he was too preoccupied to wonder why it didn't.

Lisa shoved the door open. "Tony. We're out of Shiner Bock. Any more in the back?"

"Damn," he muttered. "No. I don't have a delivery scheduled for two more days."

"Talk up a different beer," Heather said. "Something they've never tried before."

Lisa looked at Tony. He turned his palms up. *Try anything.* She nodded and started to leave the kitchen.

"Lisa, wait," Heather said, then fanned her gaze over the rest of the staff. "Listen up, everybody. I know it's tough out there tonight, but we appreciate all your hard work. If you guys keep things running smoothly, there'll be fifty-dollar bonuses on your next paycheck."

Tony whipped around. *What* did she say? Hundreds of dollars in bonuses to go with the free food? What was she *doing* to him?

Heather gave the troops a curt nod. "Okay, everybody. Let's move!"

The women scrambled away, grabbing trays and mops and hustling out of the kitchen. Chuck and Emilio went back to grilling with a vengeance. Tony pulled Heather to one side, whispering angrily, "Bonuses? Are you out of your *mind?*"

"If you don't think it's worth it by the end of the evening, I'll pay the bonuses out of my own pocket. Now, get out there and make sure everybody has a drink who wants one."

"God, this is a disaster."

"If you manage things right, it doesn't have to be."

"Tell me again why I bought a bar and grill?"

"Because it's your dream come true, remember?"

"Doesn't seem too dreamy right now." Tony blew out a breath. "Maybe I'm just not cut out for this."

"Maybe you're right."

Tony frowned. "You weren't supposed to agree with me."

She moved in close and lowered her voice. "You're running scared because your new business is hard to manage. I've got news for you, buster. Hard is good. It means whatever you're going after is worth it."

As she turned and walked away, Tony just stood there in disbelief. The last thing he'd expected was for her to tell him to get over it and get moving. Actually, the last thing he'd expected was for her to be here at all.

Heather reached the kitchen door and turned back. "And, Tony?"

"Yeah?"

"Don't forget to smile."

Then she had the nerve to give him a smile and a wink of her own, as if this whole mess wasn't a mess at all. Just a little speed bump, then full speed ahead.

Smile? Was she out of her mind?

A few minutes later, he was slinging drinks as if his life depended on it and smiling as if he didn't have a care in the world. He saw Heather bring Alison an apron and send her into the kitchen to deliver chips and salsa to all the tables. She looked at Heather as if she had one foot in the loony bin, but in the past few minutes, he'd learned just how persuasive Heather could be. Before long, every table had something to munch on even if it wasn't the food they'd ordered. Once that was under control, Alison pitched in to bus tables and help out in the kitchen.

The band never found a replacement drummer, but they did find a guy in the crowd who played a little and wasn't stoned, and he got up to jam with them. It was a Band-Aid on a gaping wound, but at least the crowd didn't get ugly. A problem came up with a credit card, but Heather handled that in no time. Tony wasn't surprised. She was an accountant, after all. A money person. Of course she could handle that.

What shocked him was how good she was at handling everything else.

She took care of Jamie's tables, filling customers' orders with amazing efficiency, at the same time issuing orders to his staff that didn't sound like orders at all. More like suggestions with authority. The staff took her lead and buckled down to work. He was left to take up the slack, delivering food to tables, restocking the bar, retrieving more toilet paper for the restrooms, laughing at a few jokes, slapping a few backs, and shaking a few hands.

A couple of customers did get a little irate, but since they were women, Heather immediately came to get him, telling him it was time to turn on the charm. That he could handle.

But, it appeared, not much else.

He'd gone from being irritated when Heather showed up to being doubtful about her plan to being grateful when things smoothed out to feeling like a flunky in his own establishment. Of course, he couldn't say that her competence surprised him. That morning in Vegas, hadn't she taken charge of things and started them on the road to annulment even as his own hangover had rendered him virtually useless?

When things finally slowed down and the place started to clear out, he went to the bar and asked Lisa to give him a beer. A crawly sensation settled in his stomach, and he took a swig, trying to drown out the feeling of total inadequacy that had settled over him. And it might have worked, if he hadn't glanced over at Heather, who was still buzzing around like the Energizer Bunny, doling out help and hospitality, so capable of everything he wasn't that he was forced to face the truth.

He didn't know crap about running a bar and grill.

A few minutes later, Heather made things even worse by sliding onto the barstool beside him and giving him a playful nudge.

"So what do you think?" she said. "Everything worked out pretty well after all, didn't it?"

"Yeah. It did."

"You won't believe what I made in my section alone."

"Quite a bit, I'm sure."

"Actually, things ran pretty smoothly once we got on

a roll. Try running the breakfast shift at a pancake house. Now, *that's* a nightmare."

Yeah, but I bet you didn't have a bit of trouble handling it.

"I'm sure you're tired," he told her. "Why don't you head home? I'll close out your final checks."

"No. I'll stay and help clean up."

"That's not necessary. I can manage just fine."

"I don't mind. In fact, once you close out, why don't I get the bank deposit ready for you?"

"You don't have to do that."

"Not a problem. I'm an accountant, remember? We live for numbers. And tonight, we're going to have some big ones."

"Assuming there's any profit left after the free food and employee bonuses."

Heather's smile faltered. "Come on, Tony. You've got happy customers and happy employees. What more do you want?"

"Money in the bank would be nice."

Her smile vanished. "If you have a problem with the decisions I made, I'll cover the cost."

"No. It's my fault. I let you do it."

"Yeah, and it was the right thing to do."

"The jury's still out on that."

"No. You're going to clear plenty of profit tonight, even with those payouts. But even if you don't, it was still worth it. You bought a lot of goodwill."

"Yeah, and how much more goodwill can I buy before it sends me into bankruptcy?"

"Come on, Tony. Aren't you being a little dramatic?"

She ventured a shaky smile. "Wait until we add up the night's receipts, and you'll see I'm right."

"I'll take care of that."

"But I really don't mind. I'll just—"

"Heather, whether you know it or not, I'm still the boss around here. And that means when I tell you to go home, *go home.*"

She stared at him a long time, her expression moving from surprise to thinly veiled anger. She pursed her lips, as if she wanted to snap back at him but was holding it in. She spoke calmly, even as icicles formed on her words. "Sure, Tony. Whatever you say."

She went into the kitchen. A few moments later, she emerged minus her apron, her purse slung over her shoulder, and made a beeline for the door, refusing even to look at him.

"Heather!" Erika said. "Wait!"

Heather turned back, and the girl rushed up to her, holding two checks. "I got these messed up. I should have charged this beer to this one, but instead I charged it to this one. And it wasn't even the right beer. What should I—"

"Talk to Tony."

"Huh?"

"He'll help you with that."

"But—"

"He's the boss around here. Don't ever forget that." She looked back at Tony. "I know I won't."

With that, she went to the door, yanked it open, and left the bar, anger trailing in her wake. Tony gritted his teeth, telling himself he didn't care. He hadn't asked her to help in the first place, and he certainly hadn't asked her to take over the way she had.

Erika turned back to look at him helplessly. "I'm sorry," she said, holding up the checks. "I didn't mean to mess it up. Can you fix it for me?"

Hell, yes, he could.

Unfortunately, it took him ten minutes to straighten out a problem Heather could have solved in two. He sent Erika on her way to screw up something else, then went back to the bar and asked Lisa to give him another beer.

"Hell of a night," Lisa said.

"Yeah. It was."

"Oh, I didn't get a chance to tell you. Jamie's husband called. They had a little girl tonight. Five pounds, eleven ounces. So she'll be out for a little while."

Tony nodded.

"Thank God Heather showed up," Lisa said. "Don't know what we'd have done without her."

Thanks, Lisa. That's just what I need to hear.

"We'd have muddled through," he said.

"But with her, we didn't have to muddle." She laughed a little. "Heather doesn't strike me as someone who's *muddled* a day in her life."

Thank you, Lisa, for once again stating the obvious.

"So what does she do for a living?" Lisa asked.

"She's a CPA."

Lisa blinked. "Really?"

Her disbelief didn't surprise him. It did, however, crawl under his skin and irritate the hell out of him. "Is there something wrong with that?"

Lisa turned away, dunking a pair of wineglasses in the wash basin. "Uh . . . no. I just thought . . ."

Tony knew what she wasn't saying. She'd never expected that a guy like him would marry a smart, professional woman. Evidently the whole damned world thought that, and he wasn't sure he liked it.

Lisa set the dripping glasses on the grid. "I just thought maybe she'd run a restaurant before. She seems to know an awful lot about it."

"When she was in college, she was the weekend manager at a pancake house."

"That explains it. I worked at one of those once. If you think it was bad here tonight, try the Sunday morning shift at a place like that."

Tony let out a silent sigh. One more thing he didn't need to hear.

Lisa looked over her shoulder, then spoke softly. "I gotta tell you, Tony. Some of the girls, and I guess me included, kinda wondered about Heather, you know?"

"What do you mean?"

"I mean, you two getting married so fast and all. And no offense, but she doesn't really seem like your type. But after tonight..." She shrugged, her mouth easing into a smile. "Heather's smart. And she's nice. I don't know how the other girls feel about it, but I think you did good."

She dried her hands, then walked away to deal with a customer, leaving Tony sitting there in turmoil. He tried his damnedest to stay mad, to hold on to his conviction that Heather had taken over tonight when she had no right to. But it didn't take long for all of that to fall by the wayside, leaving him feeling like the biggest fool alive.

First Heather had handed him the twenty thousand to buy the place he was incapable of running. Then when she'd pitched in to *help* him run it, he'd gotten angry, pulled rank on her, and told her to go home. A crawly feeling settled in his stomach, and he took another swig of beer, trying to drown it out. But there was no way around it.

Heather had gone out of her way for him—not once, but twice—and what had he given her in return? A whole lot of ingratitude she didn't deserve.

He'd screwed up. Big time. And somehow he had to fix it.

Chapter 12

Thirty minutes later, when Tony arrived home, part of him hoped Heather was already in bed so he wouldn't have to face her tonight. Instead, he saw the living room lights on.

Crap. She was still up.

When he came through the door, she was sitting on the sofa wearing a horrible terry-cloth robe and equally horrible pink slippers with most of the fuzz worn off them. Her hair was wet, as if she'd just gotten out of the shower. The TV was tuned to some late-night show only insomniacs watched. She grabbed the remote, clicked it off, then turned and gave him a look that could have melted stone.

And what was that he smelled? Cleaning products? *God.* He should have known she'd take out her anger on dirt.

He shut the door behind him and locked it, then slowly turned back to face her angry scowl, heaving a silent sigh. "You cleaned something just to piss me off, didn't you?"

"I scrubbed the top of the refrigerator. Dusted the windowsills. Vacuumed under the sofa."

"Anything else?"

"Yeah. I sterilized your toothbrush."

"You *what?*"

"That thing is horrible. You should have bought a new one months ago."

"You *sterilized* it?"

Her frigid stare deepened. "It was very cathartic."

"It's going to taste like disinfectant, isn't it?"

"If I'm lucky."

Okay. He deserved that. This was one woman he intended never to piss off again, or she'd starch his underwear and scrub the numbers off his computer keyboard.

Tony could feel her wheels turning as she geared up to let him have it. He held up his palm to silence her, then sat down. He put his elbows on his knees and clasped his hands together in front of him. He stared down at them for a moment, then slowly turned his gaze to meet hers.

"I acted like an ungrateful bastard tonight, didn't I?"

She blinked those big blue eyes, her gears grinding down a little. "Yes. You did. I worked my ass off all evening for you."

"I know you did."

"And that was how you thanked me?"

"You're right. I was a real jerk."

"Yes, you were."

"The worst."

"You're right."

"On a scale of one to ten—"

"Damn it, will you stop telling yourself off? That's *my* job."

He sat up and thunked his head against the back of the sofa. "One more thing I can't do right. Apologize."

She looked at him skeptically. "So this is an apology?"

"It's late. I'm tired. It's the best I can do. But I'll go at it again tomorrow if you want me to."

"No. It'll do." She twisted her mouth with irritation. "But you could have at least let me vent a little first."

"Go ahead," he said, closing his eyes. "Vent. I deserve it."

"Well, I can't do it *now*. Not after you've already beat yourself up. How much satisfaction would I get out of that?" She settled back against the sofa. "Now, are you going to tell me *why* you were an ungrateful bastard?"

He hated having to say it, but she deserved an explanation. "You had no problem handling things tonight, did you?"

She paused. "Well, I wouldn't say *no* problem—"

"Everything ran perfectly after you showed up."

"There were glitches—"

"Which you smoothed over."

"There was that credit card mess."

"Which you took care of."

"Well, yeah, but—"

"Did you have to be so damned *competent?*"

She looked at him as if he'd lost his mind. "Competence is a problem?"

"When you have it and I don't, then yeah. It's a problem."

She looked astonished. "So that's why you acted that

way? Because I was running the place better than you could?"

He grimaced, hating the sound of that.

"You felt *threatened?*"

"Stop with the psychobabble. You sound like Dr. Phil."

She sat back with a disbelieving stare. "Why didn't you just tell me how you felt instead of biting my head off?"

"Oh, right. How many men do you know who will walk up to a woman and say, 'Do you think we could have a dialogue? I'd like to talk about my *feelings*'?" Tony rubbed his eyes with the heels of his hands, then let out a heavy sigh. "Maybe my father was right."

"Your father?"

"Yeah. The man was a walking cliché. You know, the one who tells his son he'll never amount to anything."

Heather drew back. "That's terrible!"

"Nah. Not really. I figure if I fail, I'll have lived up to his expectations."

"No. You're *not* going to fail at this."

"Don't tell my father that. It'll break his heart."

"Well, it'll just have to get broken. You were born to run a place like McMillan's."

"After tonight, I'm not so sure about that."

"Listen to me, Tony. The problems you had tonight aren't really problems. Anybody can learn how to deal with that stuff. But you've got something going for you that most people don't."

"What's that?"

"A neighborhood bar is all about the atmosphere. The hospitality. The comfortable feeling people get when they go there. You know how to relate to people. Just keep giving them that gorgeous smile, and you've got it made."

He gave her a sidelong glance. "So you think I have a gorgeous smile?"

"Of course you do. It goes hand in hand with your enormous ego."

"So all I have to do is give everybody a big smile, and I'll be a huge success?"

"No. You'll be a huge success by working your ass off. The smile is just insurance."

Hard is good. It means whatever you're going after is worth it. But he was starting to realize that going after it all by himself might be a tough thing to do.

"How would you like to be my temporary assistant manager on the night shift?" he asked her. "Just until Jamie gets back. I'll pay you, of course."

He blurted out the offer before he really thought about it, and judging from the look on Heather's face, it was the wrong thing to say. She probably made a lot of money as a CPA, and he was offering her nothing but the opportunity to work herself silly on a second job that paid peanuts.

"Never mind," he said. "That's dumb. It's just that..." He exhaled. "I need somebody around who knows what they're doing. Just until I can figure out what *I'm* doing."

"Nope. What you need to do is make Kayla your assistant manager. She's sharp and dependable and gets along with everyone. What you need from me is to be a consultant who also waits tables if necessary."

"Okay."

"But I don't want you to pay me."

"I can't let you work for nothing."

"Don't argue. If you paid me what I'm worth, you couldn't afford me."

After what he'd seen tonight, he knew just how true that was.

"Here's another recommendation. You need to have a grand opening."

"But the place is already open."

"*Re*opening, then. To let people know it's under new management and that it has a new name."

"New name?"

"I think it's time McMillan's became McCaffrey's."

Tony had to admit he liked the sound of that. He hadn't actually decided to put his name on the place, but he had thought about it, and Heather's optimism was contagious.

"Maybe so," he said.

"Definitely so. Order a sign, and we'll unveil it at the grand opening. We'll advertise. The bigger the crowd, the better, and this time we'll be ready for them. I'll write your press release. And send the invitations. We can brainstorm some food and drink specials. If we do it right, we'll have half the people in town there. What do you think about that?"

Tony's head was spinning. "I think Hurricane Heather just swept through."

"I'm choosing to take that as a compliment."

"You make it all sound so simple."

"It is."

Wrong. If it was that simple, he'd have had all that stuff in motion already. Running a bar and grill was harder than he'd ever thought it would be, but somehow, with Heather helping him, it didn't seem nearly as insurmountable.

Heather suppressed a yawn, then scooted to the edge of the sofa. "It's late. I'm going to bed."

"Yeah. I'm not far behind."

Then he noticed her hair. It was still damp from the shower, but for the first time, he saw that where it had always been straight and regimented before, it was fluffing into a zigzagging cascade of curls that spilled over her shoulders and down her back.

Before she could stand, he picked up a strand. "Hmm. What's going on here?"

She shuddered away from him and tried to smooth it back into place.

"Is this what it's really like?" he asked. "Curly?"

Heather looked disgusted. "*Curly* is the kind word for it."

"So you usually straighten it?"

"Every morning of my life."

"Why?"

"Are you kidding me? Without my flatiron, I look like a poodle."

Tony shook his head. "Will you stop being so uptight?"

She frowned. "It's not uptight to want straight hair."

"But you want everything in your life straight. And neat. And perfect."

"Contrary to what you believe, that's not a personality defect."

"No, it's not. But it does keep you from having fun. Mess yourself up a little, Heather. Walk in the rain. Roll in the mud. Sing in the shower." He grinned. "Eat a Twinkie."

"And maybe stick my head out the sunroof of a limo?"

"Say the word, and I'll rent another one."

She shook her head. "You really are crazy."

"So you've told me. But I'm not sure you really hate that."

"What would it take to convince you?"

"Now that I've seen this," he said, nodding toward her hair, "nothing will convince me."

"Because my hair's crazy, you think deep down the rest of me is, too?"

"Just makes me wonder what else you're hiding."

And he meant that. After tonight, he realized there was a lot more to Heather than met the eye. And as she stared back at him, those blue eyes shimmering like the surface of an ice-cold martini, Tony felt something trip inside him, an awareness he hadn't felt before.

It wasn't as if she'd suddenly turned beautiful. But as he looked at her cheeks still flushed pink from the shower, then shifted his gaze to the pale, creamy skin along the side of her neck that looked so warm and tantalizing, he found himself reevaluating his concept of beautiful.

"Tony," Heather said. "You're staring."

He brought his gaze back up to meet hers. "I'm just admiring my wife."

"Your wife doesn't have anything worth admiring."

"Why doesn't she let her husband be the judge of that?"

Heather's heart started to beat faster. "It's late. I need to go to bed."

She tried to rise from the sofa, but Tony took hold of her wrist. "Tell you what, sweetheart. You're helping me out, so I'm going to help you out."

"What?"

"You show me how to make my business a success," he said, leaning in and emphasizing every word, "and I'll show you how to have more fun than you've ever had in your life."

The low, seductive sound of his voice was like a soft melody to Heather's ears, sending vibes of pure pleasure pulsing along every nerve.

He's seducing you.

Impossible to believe, but she'd never been one to draw erroneous conclusions when the data was right out there in front of her. The moment that thought popped into her head, her senses came alive with anticipation, even as she knew she had no intention of getting anywhere near a bed with him.

When he spoke again, his voice was a near-whisper. "I was thinking about the limousine."

Flashback. Mouths, hands, kissing, touching... "What about it?"

"There's no reason we can't pick up where we left off that night."

He hooked his finger around a strand of her hair, easing it back over her shoulder. Then he dipped his head, leaned in, and kissed her neck. She was so stunned, she couldn't move. *Stop him. Right now. Nothing good can come of this.*

But for some reason, she sat there, frozen in place,

as his lips moved along her neck, remembering how it had felt before. But it was even better now because she wasn't anesthetized with champagne. He moved his lips next to her ear, and she could feel his hot breath as he spoke.

"You have no idea how much I wanted to make love to you. Right there in the backseat of that limousine."

"I wouldn't have let you," she said, a little breathless. "I don't do that sort of thing."

"Heather, you were so hot for me I'm surprised you didn't tear the clothes right off my body."

And if this goes on, he's going to tear the clothes right off yours.

Up to now, the memory of that limousine ride had been hazy and out of focus, but now she remembered exactly what it had felt like. But this was all wrong. Getting up close and personal with Tony was a recipe for disaster. Hadn't that been proven already?

But maybe that wasn't true. Maybe things had changed. Maybe she'd made an impression on him. Maybe after tonight, he finally saw the value in a woman who had something going for her besides scanty clothes on a model-thin body. Maybe...

But then the words faded from her mind, and she couldn't think at all.

He breathed deeply and rested his hand on her thigh, easing it beneath the tail of her T-shirt. The higher it went, the more her heart pounded in anticipation. He kissed his way along her jaw, his lips blazing a slow but scorching trail to her mouth.

"For the next month," he murmured, "I can't see other

women, and you can't see other men. It's just you and me. What do you say we make the most of it?"

Without waiting for her answer, he kissed her. *Ahhh,* now she remembered. She remembered exactly what it had felt like when he'd kissed her in the back of that limousine. *God,* this man was good.

But just as her mind was going blank with satisfaction, a few brain cells popped up again. What was that he'd said? That neither of them could have sex with anyone else, so they might as well do it with each other?

As she realized the truth of the situation, she felt a surge of humiliation. She pulled away from him and pressed her palm to his chest.

"Stop."

He froze. "What's the matter?"

She looked him right in the eye. "You're stuck being celibate for the next several weeks. I know that's painful for you. But I'm not letting you come after me just because every other woman is off-limits."

She rose and started for her bedroom, but he grabbed her arm and pulled her back to sit again. "Wait a minute. Do you really think that's all this is about?"

"Oh, please. Line up three of your waitresses and me. Which one would you pick?"

"Why do you put yourself down so much?"

"I'm not putting myself down. I have qualities those women will never have. I'm just not the kind of woman that appeals to you, so for you to come on to me like this means you just want to get laid. But I'm sorry. I don't do casual sex."

"Have you considered the possibility that I might actually be attracted to you?"

"Oh, give me a break. I must have been in McMillan's dozens of times when you were there. If you were going to be attracted to me, it would have happened by now."

"I'm there to have a good time. I notice women who like to laugh and watch sports and play pool. I don't tend to notice the ones who never get up out of a booth, sit down at the bar, and say hello."

"Aren't you being a little disingenuous? If a perfect ten walked through the door and sat in a booth by the wall, your radar would pick her up so fast it would make her head spin."

"That's a fair assessment." He eased closer to her. "But just because I didn't notice you before doesn't mean I'm not attracted to you now."

"Fine. Let's assume that's true. It still doesn't matter, because I'm not attracted to you."

"Yeah? What about that night in the limousine?"

"I was drunk."

"You can't hide the way you feel." He put his palm against her face. "Your cheeks are on fire."

She shuddered away from him. "Don't do that."

"Don't lie. You want me as much as I want you."

"No. I told you in the beginning this wasn't going to happen."

"But that was then," he said. "This is now. I like you, Heather. More all the time. I just don't see what's wrong with the two of us being together."

His gaze never wavered. She searched his face for

insincerity and didn't see even a trace of it. But that didn't mean his motives were any purer than before.

"You made it pretty clear where you're coming from, Tony. We can't sleep with anybody else, so we might as well sleep with each other. Doesn't sound to me as if anything's changed." She stood up. "I'll help you out at the bar. But all this other stuff has to stop."

"Heather—"

"Good night, Tony."

Heather went into her bedroom and shut the door, then walked straight into the bathroom. She looked at herself in the mirror.

Tony was right. Her cheeks were strawberry red.

She splashed cold water on her face and patted it dry with a towel, wishing her heart would *slow down*.

He was good. He was so good he could gear a seduction plan to any situation. She had practically been able to feel his brain working. *Let's see...I'm stuck married to an unattractive woman for a month. What does she want to hear so I can get her into bed?*

This was something she simply hadn't anticipated.

Have you considered the possibility that I might actually be attracted to you?

The sad thing was that for a split second, she'd believed him. She'd looked into those gorgeous green eyes and believed every single word he was saying.

Then she'd come to her senses.

She knew now how he could seduce so many women with just a tiny crook of his finger, because he'd come really close to seducing her. But no matter what he said, she knew the truth. They could go at it like a couple of hormone-crazed bunnies, and still the only qualities of hers he'd be attracted to would be that she was there, she was female, and she was breathing.

She hadn't been lying. She didn't do casual sex. And since that was all he *ever* did, it was good that she'd stopped this thing before it had even gotten started.

~

A few minutes later, Tony fell into bed with a sigh of frustration. He might not have noticed Heather before, but he was sure noticing her now.

He couldn't believe he'd said the wrong thing and blown it so badly. All he'd meant was that over the next month, they'd have a really good chance to get to know each other better. What could possibly be wrong with that?

He thought about following her into her bedroom and trying a little seduction all over again. But if he did that, she'd have slapped him senseless, and how much more rejection could one man take? He'd never imagined being in this situation, where his usual plan of attack was useless, where the empty phrases he usually used worked against him because she was too damned smart to fall for them.

But why did he want her so much?

Maybe nothing had changed. Maybe, like before, he just wanted to get laid.

And maybe it was more than that.

No. That was impossible. Intellect and competence and a take-charge attitude had never even been on the list of qualities he looked for in a woman. In fact, he'd always assumed those things would just get in the way of having a good time. But now...

He'd never realized just how enticing those things could be. How enticing *she* could be.

Line up three of your waitresses and me. Which one would you pick?

A week ago, he would have been able to answer that question without even thinking. Now he wasn't so sure. Maybe he'd pick the one he couldn't have with nothing more than a sexy smile and a crook of his finger, one he found way more attractive than he'd ever imagined he would.

Chapter 13

At ten the next day, Heather woke to bright morning sun, aching muscles, and the smell of coffee. She put on her robe and shuffled into the kitchen to find Tony slouched at the table, sipping coffee and reading the newspaper. He wore a threadbare Rangers T-shirt and green plaid boxer shorts. His hair was sleep-mussed. His eyes heavy-lidded. His face unshaven. Any other man would have looked shabby and unkempt. So how did Tony manage to look so incredibly appealing?

He turned and slowly looked her up and down, and then smiled. "Good morning."

For Heather, mornings meant pillow-creased cheeks, droopy eyelids, and her already-wild hair even more out of control. The fact that Tony was staring at her anyway told her he had to be even more desperate for sex than she thought. Unfortunately, every time he looked at her this way, it knocked one more brick out of the mental wall she'd built that was supposed to keep her from giving in to him. And as those bricks disappeared, the only thing that kept her from taking him up on his offer was the knowledge that the moment their annulment was final, his interest in her would fizzle faster than a rain-soaked firecracker.

I'm just admiring my new wife.

What a load of crap that had been. But even though she hadn't bought it, she had to hand it to him. He was damned good at selling it.

"Good morning," she said, pouring a cup of coffee.

"Your hair," he said.

Heather frowned. "What about it?"

"Leave it curly today."

"Nope. I haven't worn my hair like this in years, and I'm not going to start now."

"But I like it."

"You like anything that's a mess."

"Well, yeah, but—"

She faced him. "If you shut up about my hair, I'll cook you breakfast."

He mulled that over for a moment. "Okay. That's a deal."

Heather pulled out a skillet and a bowl, turned on a stove burner, and grabbed eggs out of the fridge. She whacked one of the eggs, opened it, and dumped its contents into a bowl.

"I thought eggs had a lot of cholesterol," Tony said.

"They also have a lot of protein. You balance the bad with the good. Of course, I'm saying that to a man who believes Twinkies are one of the four major food groups."

"They're not?"

"Your diet is horrific."

"Keeps body and soul together."

"I can't even imagine what the insides of your arteries look like."

"Sure you can. They're cream filled."

Heather made a face of disgust and grabbed a can of nonstick spray from a cabinet. She popped the lid and started to squirt it into the pan.

"Oh, for God's sake," Tony muttered. He got up, grabbed the can away from her, and dumped it into the trash.

"Hey!" she said. "What are you doing?"

Opening the fridge, he grabbed a stick of butter and handed it to her. "There."

She looked at the butter with exasperation. "I can't eat butter. I have to get into a bridesmaid's dress in a few weeks, and it's a size too small."

He looked confused. "Why didn't you get the right size in the first place?"

"It was Regina's doing."

"Okay. So why didn't Regina get you the right size?"

Heather sighed. "I'd have to go back to our childhood to explain that one. Suffice it to say, my diet from now until then is going to consist of celery sticks and rice cakes."

"Screw the bridesmaid's dress. Go naked."

"Oh, that'd go over big."

"I'd enjoy it."

"That's because you're a pervert." She cut off a tiny pat of butter and stuck it into the skillet.

"Don't get carried away," Tony said.

"Hush. You're lucky I'm using any at all."

Tony sat back down and eyed her carefully. "You know, I wouldn't have thought it, but there's something really satisfying about having a little woman in the kitchen, rattling those pots and pans."

She turned around with a look of exasperation. "I cook because I like decent food, not because I was born with ovaries."

"Fine. If you refuse to accept your natural-born role as a woman, then don't expect me to kill spiders."

"Fortunately, that doesn't take balls." She poured the eggs into the pan and started whipping them with a fork. "I've been thinking about the grand opening. When do you want to do it?"

"Hold on." He went to a kitchen drawer and pulled out a small calendar. "How about Saturday the twelfth?"

"That's the night before Regina's wedding."

"Is that a problem?"

"Shouldn't be, since the rehearsal dinner is on Thursday night. They were going to do it Saturday night before the wedding on Sunday, but Jason's mother couldn't get their country club that night."

"So Saturday's good?"

"Yeah. Assuming that leaves us enough time to do all the planning necessary."

"I don't want to wait too long. Once you're my ex-wife, people will think it's kind of weird if you're still hanging around to help me."

"Good point. So let's aim for the twelfth. I'll start planning today."

"That's good for me, but are you sure you don't have something else you need to be doing?"

Well, she had plenty of things she *could* be doing. On most Saturday afternoons, if she wasn't cleaning, she was clipping coupons, taking her car for inspection, shopping for groceries, paying bills, or doing any number of other things that were absolutely necessary but deadly dull.

But helping a new business get off the ground? *That* was exciting.

"If I stay home today," she told Tony, "I'll only end up washing windows and cleaning behind the refrigerator. Would you rather I do that?"

"God, no."

"Okay, then. The first thing I'll check into is ordering a new sign. I'll also have some cards printed up that we can leave on the tables at the bar. Get customers to give us their information so we can send them an e-newsletter letting them know what bands are going to be playing, what specials we're running, that kind of thing. If we keep in touch, they'll keep coming in."

Tony gave her a look of amazement. "That's a good idea. Why didn't I think of that?"

"Because you're a big-picture kind of guy, and I'm a detail-oriented kind of girl. I'll start setting up a database today. Do you have addresses for your friends and relatives?"

"Yeah. My address book is in my bedroom."

"Get it. We can talk about it while we're eating."

While he was gone, Heather popped a couple pieces of bread into the toaster.

Tony came back a few minutes later. "Sorry it's a little tattered," he said as he put the address book on the table. "And my handwriting isn't the best. I'll decipher anything you need me to."

Heather filled their plates and brought them to the table. Tony flipped through his address book.

"I have mostly women in here," Tony said.

"There's a surprise."

"I'll mark the ones you should send invitations to."

As they ate, Tony flipped pages, checking almost every name. If there were people he knew had moved, Heather told him to make a note and she'd find their new addresses. By the time he was halfway through the book, she estimated he'd checked over forty names.

"You know a lot of people," she said.

"That's because I'm a friendly guy. I lived all over the world when I was a kid. I learned how to make friends fast. It was the only way I ever had any."

"That's right. Your father was in the military."

"Yep. Sometimes I didn't even finish out a school year before we had to move again."

"That's too bad. I bet it was hard to make friends."

"Nah, not really. People warm up to the class clown pretty quickly."

"You? The class clown? Now, there's a surprise."

"That was only in grade school and junior high. When I got to high school," he said with a sly smile, "I achieved rapid popularity in a different way."

"With the girls."

"Uh-huh. I did the whole bad-boy thing. Worked like a charm."

"Bad-boy thing?"

"Just kid stuff. Graffiti. Street racing. You know." When she looked surprised, he said, "Sorry. I guess valedictorians don't know much about that stuff."

"I bet your father loved that."

"It drove him straight up the wall. But the girls loved it."

"They liked being with a juvenile delinquent?"

"Oh, yeah. As long as I layered a little bit of tortured soul on top of it. High school girls love drama."

Heather stared at him dumbly. "You're lucky you're not rotting in a foreign prison."

"Nah. My father always got me out of trouble. Otherwise, I would have been an embarrassment to him, and *nobody* embarrasses Commander McCaffrey."

"Speaking of your father," Heather said, "it's too bad he lives in Fort Lauderdale. Do you think he'll be able to fly in for the grand opening?"

"My father? No."

"Why not?"

"Because I'm not inviting him."

Heather sat back, surprised. "Why not?"

"I haven't spoken to him in three years. This is not the time to start again."

"Three *years?*"

"Yes, Heather. My family isn't like yours."

"Well, I guess if he lives out of state—"

"He lives in Plano."

Heather blinked. "Wait a minute. You told my parents he lived in Fort Lauderdale."

"That's because I didn't want your mother getting any big ideas about wanting to meet him."

"He lives here, but you never see him?"

"My father and I still don't see eye-to-eye. It's best for both of us."

"But you're opening a business. That's a big event. Surely that means something."

"Sweetheart, coming from where you do, I know this is hard to understand, but sometimes seeing your family members only once every three years is a *good* thing."

"But he's your father."

"Not so much, really. He's Commander McCaffrey, and that's about it."

"So he was hard on you growing up?"

"It was a classic case of a demanding father and a slacker son. He wanted me to 'make something of myself,' and I wanted him to go to hell."

"I bet he thought 'making something of yourself' meant going into the military."

"Oh, yeah. He hammered me about it from the time I was twelve. But he wanted me to get a college degree first. I lasted one year. That was when the real fight started. I skipped out of school and got a job as a bartender. That went over big. Looking back, I think I did it just to piss him off."

"What would he think of you buying McMillan's? There's a big difference between being a bartender and owning the place."

"I don't know. And I don't care."

But Heather knew he did care. He had to. All sons cared what their fathers thought, particularly those who had never felt as if they quite measured up.

"I still think you should invite him."

Tony looked at her in disbelief. "Did you not hear a word I just said?"

"I think he'd be proud of you."

Tony's shoulders heaved with a silent sigh. "Look, Heather. It isn't as if I didn't wish I had some kind of relationship with my old man. If I thought anything had changed, it might be different. But the older he gets, the more set in his ways he becomes."

"Sometimes the older people get, the more they realize what's important. And family is the *most* important thing."

"Three years ago, we saw each other over the holidays. For a while, things weren't too bad. Then he started in on me, asking me why I was a repossession agent. Why I had a job where I mostly dealt with deadbeats. Why I didn't do something bigger with my life."

"Maybe McMillan's is the kind of thing he was talking about?"

"Trust me, Heather. No matter what I do, it still won't be enough. So when you're making up that guest list?"

"Yes?"

"My father's name is the last one I want to see on it."

He popped the last bite of toast in his mouth and took his plate to the sink. He helped her clean up the kitchen and then went to take a shower.

Heather sat down at the kitchen table and opened the address book again. She flipped to the *M*s and saw the listing for Don McCaffrey at an address in Plano. Tony had put a great big *X* through it.

Heather didn't get it. So they'd had a little discord when he was a teenager. Okay, maybe a lot of discord. But sometimes, too, people got caught in a circle of old behavior they couldn't get out of, and because of that, they kept each other at arm's length for the rest of their lives. Tony said he had no other close relatives, so if he and his father were estranged, who did he turn to when he had nobody else?

An hour later, Tony was at McMillan's, stocking the bar, when Heather strode purposefully through the door. Her wild cascade of hair was pulled to the back of her neck in a barrette, but several strands escaped to curl down her cheeks.

She stopped in front of the bar, her fists on her hips, her voice low and angry. "Okay. Where is it?"

"Where's what?" he said.

"My flatiron."

Tony shoved a bottle of Johnny Walker Red onto the shelf. "I don't know what you're talking about."

"It was in the drawer in my bathroom. And now it's gone."

"You must have misplaced it."

"No, Tony. You may misplace things, but I don't. It's gone."

"And you think I took it?"

"I *know* you took it."

"Come on, Heather. When would I have had the chance to take it?"

"When I was cooking breakfast and you went to get your address book."

Tony paused. "Oh, yeah. I guess there was time then, wasn't there?"

Just then, Kayla came out of the kitchen and stopped short, her eyes going wide with surprise. "Heather. My God. What did you do to your hair?"

Heather spoke through gritted teeth. "This is what it looks like when I *don't* do anything to it. Tony hid my flatiron. The man is weird. He likes my hair this way."

"Well, yeah. He's not blind."

"What?"

"It's gorgeous."

"Oh, *please*."

"No, really! Do you know how much it costs to get hair that looks like yours? Hundreds of dollars. Believe me, I've checked it out. It takes all these weird perm techniques, and you have to sit there for hours."

"I'll trade hair with you any day."

"You don't know what you're saying." Kayla flicked her own hair. "Look at this. It's thin. Lifeless. I'd kill to have hair with as much body as yours."

Heather turned to Tony. "You know I'll just buy another one."

"And I'll hide that one, too."

"I *will* get you for this," Heather said, and headed for the ladies' room.

Tony couldn't get over how different that hair made her look. Instead of uptight and repressed, she looked like the kind of woman who was wild and free and knew how to get crazy. Of course, before she could do that, she'd have to get over being pissed at him.

"She doesn't see it, does she?" Kayla said.

"Nope."

"Did you really hide her flatiron?"

"Yep."

Kayla shook her head. "Bless her heart. She didn't have a clue what she was getting into when she hooked up with you."

Tony smiled. And he didn't have a clue what he was getting into when he hooked up with her.

~

Standing in front of the bathroom mirror, Heather pulled the elastic out of her hair so she could reposition it to incarcerate as much of it as possible. The instant she released it, curls cascaded around her face and tumbled over her shoulders.

Aaargh. She *hated* it.

She'd never met anyone as presumptuous as Tony. It took a lot of nerve for him to go into her bathroom and steal something. Particularly something she needed as much as she needed that flatiron.

But as she started to gather it up to put the elastic back in, she remembered what he'd told her. *Mess yourself up, Heather. Do something crazy. Walk in the rain. Roll in the mud. Sing in the shower. Eat a Twinkie.*

Well, the Twinkie was out of the question no matter what Tony said, but...

She stopped for a moment and stared at herself in the mirror, trying to see herself through Tony's eyes. Could he be right? Was it really not as bad as she thought? Should she look at it from a different perspective now that she was a grown woman and not a gawky teenager?

She fluffed her hair with her fingertips, then shook her head, watching the curls bounce back and forth.

Nope. It still looked like a wad of tangled yarn.

She dropped her hands to her sides with a heavy sigh. Something was wrong here. Maybe it was all in the attitude.

She slid her fingers deep into her hair, tilted her head back and shook it, giving herself a heavy-lidded, come-hither look in the mirror. *You're a wild woman. A wild, wicked, uninhibited woman who's dying to take great big bite out of life.*

She dropped her hands to her sides. Nope. Not working.

"Heather?"

Startled, she turned to see Kayla come through the door.

"Tony wanted me to let you know that a big party just came in."

"How big?"

"I lost count."

"Who's on for the lunch shift?"

"Lisa's at the bar, and Danielle and I are supposed to be waiting tables. And Danielle just called in sick."

Heather quickly pulled her hair back and fastened the barrette around it, telling herself she'd get a new flatiron on the way home. And to ensure Tony never found it, she'd hide it behind a can of Ajax.

The crowd turned out to be an alumni group from Ohio State that descended on the place to watch the finals of the college World Series. In no time, four parties having quiet lunches turned into a room full of balding fiftysomething men who ate like cavemen and drank like sailors on leave.

Heather grabbed an apron and took care of the sports fiends, leaving Kayla to handle the other customers and Tony to meet and greet and help Lisa keep the alcohol flowing.

Three hours later, the men finally left. Half an hour after that, when everything was cleaned up and only a few customers remained, Heather collapsed on a barstool with a huge sigh of relief.

"Those guys were maniacs," Tony said.

"Those guys were money in the bank. Pour me a Diet Coke, will you?"

"Coming up."

Tony set the Coke down in front of Heather, and she took a long sip. "You know, if you contact groups like that one and offer them specials when certain teams are playing, you might be able to bump up traffic during your slow times. Why don't I check out the sports schedules and the alumni groups who have chapters in the area?"

Tony had already thought about that once he saw the alumni party in full swing. But putting a strategy in place to get it done was another thing entirely.

"Sounds good to me," he told Heather.

She picked up her glass and slid off the barstool. "Mind if I use your computer to start setting up a customer database?"

"You've worked yourself to death already today. Take a breather."

"Nah. I just need to get off my feet for a little while. My fingers can still stay busy."

Tony glanced over her shoulder. "Your busy fingers will have to wait. Look who just showed up."

Heather turned around, and when she saw who was standing there, she considered making a run for Tony's office and ducking inside until closing time.

Regina was here. And she had her fiancé, Jason, with her.

Chapter 14

Heather!" Regina said. "How *are* you?"

As she gave Heather a phony smile and a pseudo hug, Heather thought, *There's not a damned thing that's real about this woman. Not one.*

"Regina? What are you doing here?"

"We came by to see Tony's place, of course. I was hoping you'd be here and that maybe we could—"

All at once, Regina's hand flew to her mouth, and her eyes grew big and horrified as she stared at Heather. "Oh, my God!"

"What?"

"You poor thing! Didn't you have time to do your hair this morning?"

Heather's hand flew automatically to her head. She'd forgotten. And now it was official: she really was going to kill Tony.

Regina grabbed Heather by the shoulder and turned her so she could see the puffy lump of curls that resulted from her hair being pulled back in a barrette.

"Oh, my," Regina said. "I haven't seen it like this since high school!"

High school. You know. Where you were a big, ugly dork with hair like a Brillo pad.

Heather always worked hard not to react to anything her cousin said, but still a tight little ball of nerves gathered in her stomach, the same one she used to feel whenever something happened that made her feel as if she didn't quite measure up.

"Yeah, it's kind of a mess today," Heather said, laughing a little and shoving a strand of hair away from her face. "I misplaced my flatiron."

Regina turned to Tony, teasing her fingers through her own dark, silky hair. "Genetics is such an odd thing, isn't it? Would you ever guess that Heather and I come from the same family?"

"Nope," Tony said. "You two don't look the least bit alike." Staring at Heather adoringly, he reached up and opened her barrette. Her heart seized up. What the hell was he doing?

As her hair tumbled down her back, he picked up a strand and let it fall sensually through his fingers. "Heather has all these *beautiful* curls. As soon as I saw what she'd been hiding from me, I made her promise to wear it like this for me from now on."

Heather held her breath. She knew what he was doing, but anybody with two functioning eyes could see what a mess her hair really was, so it was totally unbelievable that Tony would be smiling at her as if he worshipped her. They were going to be found out right then and there for the great big liars they were.

Heather glanced at Regina, cringing at the triumphant expression that was sure to take over her face very soon. But seconds passed, and all she did was look back and forth between Heather and Tony with a whole lot of confusion.

Then she shook herself out of her bewilderment and pasted her smile back on. "Tony, this is Jason Reynolds. My fiancé."

The men shook hands. Tony smiled at Jason, but it wasn't the people-loving grin he usually wore. Heather was pretty sure Tony smelled a rat, which meant he had very good instincts. Jason reminded Heather of those too-rich, too-handsome frat boys she'd known in college, who strutted around as if they owned the world. He wore a starched dress shirt and a pair of sharply creased slacks with his ever-present BlackBerry on his hip.

"Jason is an attorney at Reed, Randall and McCall," Regina said. "Product liability. I'm sure you've heard about that suit against Dutton Foods for mercury poisoning? That's the case he's working on right now." She leaned in and spoke confidentially. "It's not going to be long before it's Reed, Randall, McCall and *Reynolds.*"

"Regina exaggerates," Jason said with a cocky smile. "But only a little."

He and Regina laughed as if that were funny, never noticing that no one else in the vicinity joined in.

Heather heard a ring tone. Jason grabbed the Black-Berry from his belt and looked at the caller ID.

"Sorry, babe," he said to Regina. "Gotta take this."

He walked away a few feet, and Regina gave Tony and Heather a sad smile. "That's the story of my life. I'm afraid I'll just have to get used to having a husband who's in constant demand."

Why don't you just go home? Heather thought. *And take super-lawyer with you.*

"So can you two take a break and have a drink with us?" Regina said, glancing around. "It looks as if you have a bit of a lull right now."

"Uh . . . sure," Heather said, hoping Tony was okay with it. "I guess we can spare a few minutes."

"What can I get you to drink?" Tony asked.

"Hmm," Regina said. "I think I'd like a glass of Pinot Noir."

"Wouldn't you know it?" Tony said. "We're fresh out of Pinot Noir."

"Oh. Well, a German Riesling maybe?"

"Sorry. No."

Regina smiled brightly. "Maybe I should just look at your wine list."

"No need," Heather said. "I have it memorized. We have red, white, and pink. Which one would you like?"

Regina gave Heather a thinly veiled look of disgust, which pissed Heather off, since Regina was about as knowledgeable about wine as a bum in the gutter. She threw a few buzz words around to sound sophisticated, but she wouldn't know a glass of Pinot Noir from cup of cherry Kool-Aid.

"Make it a martini instead," Regina said. "You do have gin, don't you?"

Yes, and I'd like to pour it directly into your lap.

"Scotch straight up for me," Jason called out, and then continued his conversation.

"You two find a booth," Tony said, "and Heather and I will get the drinks."

As Jason and Regina walked off, Tony and Heather went behind the bar. Tony reached for the gin bottle. "You don't mind if I add a little arsenic to her drink, do you?"

"No point," Heather said. "Arsenic would only make her meaner."

"Maybe I'll just throw a bucket of water on her. She'll melt. Problem solved." He grabbed the shaker and filled it with ice. "I don't like the way she talks to you."

"I'm used to it."

"So she does this all the time?"

"Ever since we were kids. But it's her hang-up, not mine. She just has an inferiority complex."

"Looks like a superiority complex to me."

"Nah. People who know they're good don't have to put other people down the way she does."

Tony stopped and stared at her. "That's all very logical. But it still bothers you, doesn't it?"

Heather turned away. "She's always been the pretty one," she said, pouring the Scotch. "She had a hundred friends. She was a cheerleader, for God's sake."

"And you were valedictorian."

"Yeah, but there were times when we were growing up that I'd have traded every brain cell I had to look like her. Guess that's *my* inferiority complex showing."

"You have no reason to feel inferior to anyone."

"Yeah, but Regina has a way of making it happen, anyway."

Tony looked across the room. Jason had ended his conversation, but now he was poking away at that BlackBerry like a woodpecker on speed. Tony narrowed his eyes, and a calculating expression came over his face.

"Is Jason always doing something with that Black-Berry?"

"Constantly."

"Does it piss Regina off?"

"Constantly. Not that she'd admit it, of course. To hear her tell it, Jason is a very important man. Of course he has to stay in constant communication with...you know, all the other important people."

"So she makes excuses for the fact that he ignores her?"

"Yes."

Tony put the drinks on the tray. "Let's go have a chat with them, shall we?"

As they approached the table, Heather saw Regina give Jason a little poke in the ribs, and he set the BlackBerry down on the table. Heather had no doubt he took that thing with him to the bathroom, to bed, and when he died, they'd bury him with it.

Tony delivered the drinks, then stepped aside for Heather to slide into the booth before sitting down beside her.

"My mother was right," Regina said, her gaze traveling around the room. "This place is so...quaint."

Quaint. Regina-speak for "ratty little hole-in-the-wall."

"The beer posters are nice," she said, crinkling her nose. "And what's that above the bar? A boar's head? Wearing a Ranger's cap?"

"It came with the place," Tony said.

"A dead animal," Regina said, curling her lip to match her crinkly nose. "I suppose your customers like that kind of thing?"

"Yep. It's a real conversation piece."

"So tell me. How's business? I've driven by a few times and seen quite a few cars in the parking lot."

"So far, so good," Tony said.

"The restaurant business is difficult. I'm glad to see you're making a go of it."

"To tell you the truth, Regina, I'd have fallen flat on my face if not for one thing."

"What's that?"

"Heather."

"Oh, really?"

"See, I'm just the guy who smiles and shakes a lot of hands." He turned to Heather with that same adoring look he'd given her earlier. "She's the real brains behind the business."

Regina blinked with surprise. "Well, then. I suppose it was fortunate you met her."

"Yes. It was definitely my lucky day."

All at once, Regina looked relieved. "Oh! So you needed somebody smart to help you run your business. That's what drew you to Heather."

"Oh, yeah. I do love smart women. But I'm a man, Regina. I hate to admit this because it makes me sound shallow, but it takes more than brains to make me look twice at a woman." He gave Heather a smoldering look. "I have to feel the chemistry."

Even though Heather knew it wasn't real, Tony sold it so well that she felt a twinge of that chemistry herself. The question was, was he selling it *too* well? To the point where nobody would believe it?

"I'm sorry," Regina said, laughing a little. "But that seems a little odd."

Heather felt a quiver of apprehension. It was coming any minute. The accusation. *You two are in love? I don't think so.*

"Why does it seem odd?" Tony said.

"It's just that I always imagined Heather marrying somebody a little more...well..."

Ugly? Average? Ordinary? Boring?

"Traditional. After all, she's an *accountant*."

"Yeah," Tony said, staring at Heather again. "She is, isn't she? And the first thing I thought when I saw her in Vegas was, 'Sweetheart, you can check out my financial statements anytime you want to.'"

Oh, God. Now he's taking this right over the top. Pretty soon this whole thing is going to come crashing back to earth.

But every word he spoke only seemed to cement their status as soul mates in Regina's mind. She glanced at Jason, possibly hoping he'd practice a little adoration of his own. But judging by the way he was looking longingly at his BlackBerry, it was clear that to Jason, PDA stood for "personal digital assistant," not "public display of affection."

Tony draped his arm around Heather's shoulders and pulled her up next to him, until they were tucked together like two little lovebirds, her thigh pressed against his, the back of her head against his shoulder. And Regina's confounded expression said she was buying every bit of it.

"So you two met in that hotel in Vegas," Regina said, "and you were married just hours later. Imagine that. Heather, where in the world have you been hiding all this spontaneity?"

"She didn't have to be spontaneous," Tony said. "I just had to be persuasive. I'm a man who knows what he wants. And when I see it"—he turned again and looked at Heather like *that*—"I don't let *anything* stand in my way of getting it."

"That's exactly the way Jason felt about me," Regina said quickly. "The moment he saw me, he wanted me." She turned to Jason. "Isn't that right, sweetie?"

"Uh...yeah," Jason said. "Sure."

Actually, there was some truth to that. Heather had heard from one of Regina's other bridesmaids that she met Jason when he stumbled up to her at Chantal's, told her she had a nice ass, and asked her if she'd go to bed with him. Regina told him to go to hell. Then somebody told her he was an associate at Reed, Randall & McCall making almost six figures, and suddenly he wasn't nearly as crude as she'd originally thought.

"Oh! Heather, did I tell you we finalized our honeymoon plans?" Regina said. "We're cruising from Miami to the Bahamas. Seven glorious days in the sun. We're getting a suite with a balcony and a whirlpool tub, and..." She looked back and forth between Tony and Heather. "Oh, you poor things. I guess you two didn't have much of a chance to take a honeymoon, did you?"

"We'll take one eventually," Tony said. "But it certainly won't be on a cruise ship."

"Oh, really? Why not?"

"Waste of money. We'd never leave the cabin." He turned to Heather. "Isn't that right, sweetheart?"

"But we could order chocolate-dipped strawberries from room service."

"True. Think they'd send up a can of whipped cream to go with it?"

Heather gave him a suggestive smile. "I've heard on cruise ships you can have just about anything you want."

"Never mind," Tony said, dropping his lips against hers in a gentle kiss. "I already have what I want right here."

Impossible as it was to believe, the more nauseating they became, the more Regina seemed to buy it. She was lapping up every prolonged glance, every adoring look, every sickeningly sweet smile like a thirsty puppy at a water bowl.

Soon, though, she brought the conversation back around to herself, giving Heather and Tony a room-by-room description of the new house they were buying, complete with how she planned to decorate it.

As she rambled on, Tony began a mesmerizing back-and-forth motion with his thumb against Heather's upper arm, and she rested her hand casually on his thigh. It felt good sitting with him like this, no matter how big a lie it was, and she found herself wishing it was the real thing. Of course, that would require Tony to become the stable, one-woman man he was pretending to be now, and the odds of that ever happening were worse than their odds had been of winning that twenty grand.

Kayla swung by their booth. "Sorry to interrupt, Tony, but there's a beer salesman on the phone. Says he needs to talk to you right away."

"Take a message," he said, turning back to Heather. "I'm busy."

"Go ahead and talk to him," Heather said. "I have to go to the ladies' room, anyway. By the time you finish with the call, I'll be back."

"Okay," Tony said. "But I won't be gone long, so you don't be, either." He gave her another dreamy little kiss before sliding out of the booth. Heather looked after him longingly, then slid out herself.

"Wait," Regina said. "I'll go with you." She turned to

Jason with a smile. "You know girls. They always go in pairs."

Jason grunted and reached for his BlackBerry. Regina gave him a look that could have withered a redwood tree. He put his hand back into his lap as they walked away, waiting, Heather knew, until Regina was out of sight before grabbing for it again.

⁓

Tony had taken the call on the phone behind the bar, and as he was hanging up, Jason slid onto a barstool.

"Dude," he said. "You gotta help me out with something."

Tony walked over. "Sure. What do you need?"

"That call I got earlier. It was from a guy who was going to be one of my groomsmen. He's getting transferred to Seattle and can't be in the wedding."

"Oh. That's too bad."

"Understatement. The wedding's only a few weeks away. If I tell Regina, she's going to freak out."

"She has to find out sometime, doesn't she?"

"Yeah, but it's better if I tell her after the problem's already been solved. So... will you fill in?"

"You want me to be one of your groomsmen?"

"Yeah."

"Why not ask another one of your friends?"

"Regina has six freakin' bridesmaids. I used up all my friends. Will you do it?"

Tony's first inclination was to say no, but then he thought what the hell? He was going to have to be there, anyway. The only difference was that he'd be wearing a

tux instead of a suit, and he'd have a better vantage point
for the ceremony.

"Sure, man. I'll help you out."

"Whew. Thank God." Jason drained his glass, then set
it down on the bar. "Better hit me again, dude. I'm gonna
need it."

"Thought the problem was solved."

"That was only one of my problems. After we leave
here, we're going to Regina's parents' house for dinner."

"Oh, yeah?" Tony said, filling another glass with
Scotch. "That's a bad thing?"

"You have no idea." Jason looked toward the restrooms, then lowered his voice. "The women in this family will drive you nuts. Bev's the mother-in-law from hell.
She nags like you wouldn't believe. And this wedding is
making her even more insane. If you weren't solving my
groomsman problem, she'd be all over my ass right along
with Regina."

Tony slid the drink in front of Jason. "You must love
Regina an awful lot to put up with a mother-in-law like
that."

Jason shrugged. "It's just time to get married, you
know? The big bosses at the firm expect it."

So marrying Regina was simply something on Jason's
to-do list he undoubtedly kept inside that BlackBerry.
How heartwarming.

"Besides," Jason went on, "I figure any woman I marry
is going to have a mother-in-law who's a pain in the ass."

Which Tony thought was an incredibly dumb statement
to make. "Really? I like my mother-in-law just fine."

Jason chuckled. "Yeah, I know you think that now, but
trust me, Barbara's as loony as the rest of them. You just

haven't been around long enough to see it." He took a heavy swig of his drink. "So how are things going with Fred?"

"Fred? Fine. Why?"

"To tell you the truth, he scares the crap out of me. Glad he's your father-in-law and not mine. Gene's easy. All you have to do is talk golf with him, and he's happy. Fred, though... He kinda freaks me out." Jason looked toward the restrooms again, then leaned toward Tony and whispered, "Okay, man. Just between you and me. Why Heather?"

"What?"

"Marrying her in Vegas," he said with a snicker. "That was a crazy thing to do. Were you dead drunk, or what?"

A week ago, Tony might have laughed off a comment like that, because that was exactly what he'd been. Dead drunk. But something had changed between then and now, and suddenly there was nothing funny about it.

Tony put his palms on the bar. "Jason?"

"Yeah?"

"It sounds to me as if you're insulting my wife."

Jason's grin evaporated. "Hey, lighten up. It was just a joke, you know?"

"Uh-huh. You know what, Jason? In the future, when you talk about the women in this family, will you do me a favor?"

"What?"

"Leave Heather and Barbara out of it."

"Uh, yeah," Jason said. "Sure, man."

"And if you value your life, you might watch what you say about Fred, too."

Jason's throat convulsed with a hard swallow. "Yeah. I will. Hey, no hard feelings, okay?"

Tony gave him a tight smile. "Of course not. We're family, right?"

"Yeah," Jason said with a shaky smile. "Family."

Tony walked down the bar to ring up the drink, leaving Jason sitting there looking exactly like the dumbass he was. He and Regina deserved each other.

Chapter 15

Heather came out of the bathroom stall to find Regina leaning into the mirror and dabbing on lipstick. As Heather washed her hands, Regina smacked her lips, then backed off to admire herself.

"I noticed neither of you is wearing a wedding ring," Regina said.

"We just haven't had the time to shop for them."

"Well, let me know when you're ready, and I'll put you in touch with my custom jeweler."

Yeah. Uh-huh. I'll be sure to do that.

"Tony is an interesting man," Regina said, capping her lipstick tube.

"What do you mean?"

"Does he always act like that?"

Heather turned off the faucet and reached for a paper towel. "Like what?"

"You know," Regina said with a roll of her eyes. "Like he's going to *die* if you're separated for, like, five minutes."

Only when he's trying to get your goat. "Tony's just a demonstrative person."

Regina did the eye-roll thing again and tossed her lipstick into her purse.

"What's wrong?" Heather asked.

"Nothing, really."

"Okay." Heather dried her hands.

"Well, if you must know…" Regina faced Heather, folding her arms. "I think his public displays of affection are a little…excessive."

Okay. Now Heather was really pissed. Only Regina could find a way to turn Tony's affection into a bad thing, and Heather had had just about enough of it.

"To tell you the truth, Regina, I think it's a little excessive, too."

Regina drew back. "You do?"

Heather drew her face into a worried frown. "Yes. And I'm starting to get concerned about it."

"Concerned?"

"Yeah. What you're seeing today…believe me, that's *nothing* compared to how he usually is."

Regina's eyes grew wider. "You've got to be kidding."

"Nope. Like, whenever we're in the car, he won't keep his hands off me. He's always touching me and kissing me and heaven knows what else. Now, don't get me wrong. It's not that I don't like it. Tony is a good kisser. I mean, a *really* good one, and what he can do with his hands…" Heather closed her eyes with a heavenly little sigh. "But yesterday he came *this close* to sideswiping another car."

Regina's face was frozen, her mind clearly still focused on Tony's hands and lips. Then she shook her head a little and said, "Well, I can certainly see why that would worry you. He could get you both killed."

"And he always insists I take a shower with him. Yesterday I was trying to squirt some shampoo, but then his hands were all over me, and then he was kissing me, and things got really hot, if you know what I mean. Some shampoo ended up on the floor. I slipped on it and almost fell."

"See, now, that's dangerous, too. If I were you, I'd tell him to take showers by himself from now on."

"And those aren't even the worst things," Heather said.

Regina's eyes widened. "What else?"

Heather leaned in and whispered, "He has discovery fantasies."

"Discovery fantasies?"

"You know. Of making love in a public place."

"A public place? Like where?"

"Well, we went to a movie a few days ago, and he wouldn't be quiet. He kept whispering in my ear all the things he wanted to do to me in the back of that theater. You wouldn't believe his imagination. It was all I could do to talk him out of it."

"Are you telling me he wanted to have sex right there in the theater? You could get arrested for that!"

"Exactly! Now do you see why I'm worried?"

"Heather, you tell that man that sex in a movie theater is completely out of the question."

"I can't say that he'd actually do it. But he sure likes to talk about it. All the time. In lots of detail." She blew out a breath. "Sometimes for hours."

"Hours?"

"Oh, and speaking of talking, he's really into phone sex, too."

"He talks dirty to you on the phone?"

"Yeah. That's one of his favorite things."

"Well, you need to tell him to stop it. You never know what that might lead to!"

"What do you mean?"

"Think about it. You really know nothing about the man you married. Contrary to popular belief, normal men don't think about sex every single waking moment. Didn't I tell you in Vegas that you needed to watch out for him? He could be some kind of...of...*pervert* for all you know!"

"God, Regina, do you really think so?"

"It's a distinct possibility. And someday he could snap."

"Snap?"

"Snap."

Heather put her hand against her chest. "Oh, my. I really hadn't considered that. Maybe you're right. Maybe I did marry a sexual deviant."

"Maybe you did," Regina said with a look of smug satisfaction.

Heather zipped her purse, then looked up and gave Regina a sweet smile. "Or maybe he's just a man who's crazy in love with his new wife and takes every opportunity he can to show it."

Regina opened her mouth, only to clamp it shut again. A speechless Regina was a sight to behold.

"Shall we go?" Heather said.

Without waiting for an answer, she turned and walked out of the bathroom. Regina trailed along behind her.

"Jason is very affectionate, too," she said.

Heather gave her an indulgent smile. "I'm sure he is."

"Just not...you know. Excessively so."

"Right. Men as important as he is have a lot of other things on their minds."

"Of course."

"Tony only runs a bar. Jason is an attorney."

"Exactly."

"Of course he'd have a lot to think about besides sex."

"Yeah," Regina said, looking positively ill. "Of course."

Heather turned the corner, surprised to see Tony behind the bar and Jason sitting on a barstool. She put her elbows on the bar, and Tony leaned over and gave her a kiss. She stared dreamily into his eyes. "Did you miss me?"

"Every moment. Don't ever stay gone that long again."

Jason turned to Regina. "Come on, babe. We're leaving."

"We are?"

"Your parents are expecting us."

"Not for another hour."

"Traffic might be heavy."

"Their house is only three miles away."

"I said we're leaving."

Tony gave them a dazzling smile. "Sorry you can't stay. But I hope you'll be back soon. And, Jason?"

"Yeah?"

"Get back to me about that tux rental. I want to make sure I look my best for the big day."

"Uh . . . yeah. Sure, man. Regina will talk to Heather." Jason grabbed Regina's arm and ushered her toward the door.

"What's he talking about?" Regina said.

"Shut up. I'll tell you in the car."

Tony continued to smile and wave until the door was closed behind them, and then his face fell into a frown. "Asshole."

"Oh, you got that already?" Heather said. "It took the rest of the family at least a couple of hours to figure it out. What was that about a tux?"

"One of Jason's groomsmen backed out, so he asked me to fill in. Regina doesn't know it yet. He wanted to solve the problem first."

"So she doesn't freak out?"

"Exactly."

"And you're going to do it?"

"Why not? I have to be there, anyway."

"They sure did leave in a hurry," Heather said.

"I think Jason was feeling a little sick. What took you and Regina so long in the ladies' room?"

"Just a little girl talk. I led her to believe you're a sex maniac. Hope you don't mind."

"Not at all."

"I got all kinds of satisfaction out of that," Heather said. "Does that make me a bad person?"

"If it does, then we're both bad people."

"They bought it." Heather laughed a little. "Can you believe it? Regina thinks we're going at it like rabbits. She has no idea it's all a lie."

"Heather?"

"Yes?"

Tony leaned his forearms on the bar and fixed his gaze on hers. "It doesn't have to be a lie."

Heather slumped with frustration. "Tony, please—"

"Look," he said, lowering his voice, "I know we're splitting up soon. That this marriage isn't forever. But in the meantime..." He shook his head. "God, Heather. The fun we could have together."

Given the never-ending repertoire of sexual talent Tony was alleged to have, she could only imagine what kinds of things he was talking about. Suddenly her cheeks felt hot. She only hoped she wasn't blushing.

"No matter how much you deny it, you want me as much as I want you. There's a wild woman inside you who's just dying to come out and play."

"It's the hair. It gives you the wrong impression."

"It's more than the hair, and you know it."

"Happy hour is about to gear up. We need to get back to work."

"You're staying? Sunday evenings tend to be slow."

"Danielle called earlier and asked for the night off. I told her I'd fill in."

"Well, then," Tony said with a smile, "I suppose I should give you fair warning."

"Fair warning?"

"My mind isn't going to be on this place tonight. It's going to be on you."

Great. He'd done it now. By telling her he was going to be thinking about her, he'd accomplished his goal. She was going to be spending the rest of the evening thinking about *him*.

Over the next several hours, anytime Heather got near Tony, she could feel his eyes on her. It got to the point that she couldn't bus a table or deliver a tray of drinks or just punch the cash register without him watching every move she made, and it grew harder and harder to ignore him.

Later in the evening, she stopped to talk to him about a problem with a customer's food. He leaned in close, as if he couldn't hear her over the music, even though the music wasn't all that loud.

"I think we should just comp his meal," she said. "Yeah, he ate the whole burger before he complained about it being too rare, but in the interest of public relations—"

"You know what?" Tony said.

Heather stopped short. "What?"

"I never noticed that before."

"What?"

"You have a mole on your earlobe."

"Tony? Will you pay attention?"

"I am paying attention. It's shaped like a half-moon."

Heather grabbed him by the arm and hauled him into the kitchen, then opened up the storeroom door and dragged him inside. She spun around, her fists on her hips. "You have to stop this."

"Stop what?"

"You know what! You should be concentrating on business."

"Have there been any problems tonight?"

"Yes!" she said, waving the check. "This guy's burger needs to be comped!"

He slid the check out of Heather's hand. "Consider it done. Is everything else running smoothly?"

"Well, yeah, but—"

"No other problems?"

"No, but—"

"You know what they say about all work and no play. It makes Tony a dull boy. And to tell you the truth, it doesn't do much for Heather, either."

"You can't do a decent job and stare at me at the same time."

"You know, I would have thought that, too. But you know what I discovered tonight?"

"What?"

"I'm very good at multitasking."

For the umpteenth time that evening, his gaze dropped to her breasts. She folded her arms across her chest and glared at him. "Tony. Take care of the check. *Now*."

"You bet. I'm on it." He started out of the room, then turned back. "Oh, yeah. While you were dragging me in here, I saw Alison come in."

"Was she smiling?"

"Not that I noticed."

"Great. Another bad date."

"Things have slowed down," Tony said. "Why don't you go have a drink with her?"

"Not a bad idea. Maybe we should go to Chantal's to do it."

"Now, Heather. Mustn't patronize the competition. What would people say?"

"Are you going to quit staring at me?"

"What do you think?"

With one last provocative smile, he walked out of the storeroom, leaving Heather standing there feeling frustrated as hell. She'd spent her entire adult life wishing men would look at her, and now when she had one who couldn't take his eyes off her, it had to be one she refused to sleep with.

Heather went out to the bar to find Alison with an already half-empty martini glass in front of her.

Heather slid onto the stool next to her and asked the question she already knew the answer to. "So . . . how was your date tonight?"

Alison's whole body heaved with a sigh, and she turned to look at Heather, only to shrink away with a startled expression.

"*Aaack!* Your hair! What did you do to it?"

Heather cringed. "Looks like hell, doesn't it?"

Alison's shock slowly faded. She tilted her head first one way, then the other. "Actually, no. It just surprised me a little. Is this how it was in high school?"

"Yes."

"Are you sure?"

"Oh, yeah. It's pretty unforgettable."

"Why did we think that was a bad thing?"

"Because I looked liked I stuck my finger in an electrical outlet?"

"I don't know, Heather. These days, people pay good money to get their hair to look like yours."

"So I've been told."

"I just don't remember it looking exactly like that. But, then, a lot of the stuff we loved back then looks horrible today. Maybe it works the other way around, too. What made you let it go?"

"I didn't do it on purpose. Tony hid my flatiron. He says he likes it this way."

"I think he has a point."

"Never mind my hair. Tell me about your date."

Alison let out another big sigh. "What's wrong with me, Heather? Seriously. What is it about me that's a magnet for every weird, dysfunctional, or disgusting man in the Dallas metroplex? That isn't a rhetorical question. I want an answer."

"Bad karma?"

"Yeah? Well, I must have done something pretty damned wicked in a past life to get stuck with *this* life."

"What happened?"

"Well, let's see. While we were standing in line for the movie, he scratched his balls."

Heather tried not to make a face. "So he scratched his balls in public. What man hasn't at one time or another?"

"On a first date?"

"Is that really a deal-breaker?"

"No. I'm getting too old to worry about standard disgusting male behavior."

"Then what *was* the deal-breaker?"

"We went to a late dinner after the movie. He blew his nose on a cloth napkin."

Okay. *That* was disgusting.

"If he does that kind of stuff right out in public, imagine what he does in private."

"You're right. That's a deal-breaker." Heather smiled. "But don't worry. I'm sure the next one will be better."

"Will you stop? You know how much I hate cheerful optimism when I'm dating-depressed."

"Sorry."

"So how are things between you and Tony?"

"Same as always."

"So why is he staring at you?"

"What?"

"Tony. At the other end of the bar."

Heather glanced over to see Tony sitting with Andy and Kyle. The moment her attention turned to him, his gaze slithered from her face to her breasts, hovered there for a moment, then continued down to her legs crossed beneath the bar. Then it moved slowly back up again, lingering here and there, practically scorching her right through her clothes. He met her eyes for several seconds, then slowly turned back around, took a lazy sip of his beer, and continued with his conversation.

"My God," Alison said. "I think I just had an orgasm, and you were the one he was looking at. What's going on between you two?"

"Nothing. We barely even see each other."

"Nope. You're lying. Something's up. Now spill it."

Heather poked at her spear of olives, then let out a sigh of frustration. "He came on to me last night."

Alison jerked to attention. "Came on to you? What exactly do you mean by that?"

"He told me that since we couldn't sleep with anybody else for the next month, we might as well have a good time together. And then he kissed me. If I hadn't stopped him—"

"You *stopped* him?"

"Of course I did."

Alison thunked her forehead on the bar. "You're killing me, Heather. *Killing* me." She jerked her head up again. "The best I can do is a nose-blowing, ball-scratching loser, and you're living with a gorgeous guy who wants to ravish you. And you won't *let* him?"

"He only wants me because he can't have anybody else. Do you know how that makes me feel?"

Alison grabbed Heather's wrist and dragged her closer. "Heather, listen to me. And I mean this from the bottom of my heart. If you don't go over there right now, drag him into his office, and have your way with him, I'm going to."

"Do it. Then maybe he'll leave me alone."

"You know what your problem is? You're thinking about this all wrong. You're thinking if you sleep with him, he's using you."

"Exactly."

"But won't you be using him, too?"

"What?"

"Tony's a player. You know that. So stop thinking about him the same way you'd think about a man you really wanted to marry. There are men who commit, and there are men you just have fun with. Stop lumping them together in your mind."

"What are you talking about?"

"You're splitting up in less than a month, right? If it helps, think of Tony as a boy toy you married, and in a few weeks, when you get bored with him, you're going to toss him away. But in the meantime, you're going to get all the hot sex you can get your hands on."

Heather mulled that over. She really hadn't thought about it from that point of view. And since she knew exactly what kind of man he was, when their time together ended, she certainly wasn't going to expect anything more from him, so she wouldn't be falling for him and causing herself that kind of grief. They'd simply part company, and that would be that.

"Come on, Heather. What are you scared of where Tony's concerned? The worst thing that could happen is that you have wild, hot, cataclysmic sex for the next couple of weeks, then smile, shake hands, and say good-bye."

Was it possible? Could Alison be right?

There's a wild woman inside you who's just dying to come out and play.

She had to admit that there was something going on

inside her that had started that night in Vegas, and it was only getting stronger. Spending time with Tony made her feel like somebody else, somebody she used to lie awake at night wishing she could become. She'd never experienced wild, hot, cataclysmic sex before. Wouldn't it be nice to do it at least once before she died?

"Okay," she said. "I'll do it."

Alison whipped around. "You will?"

"Yes. You're right. There's Mr. Right, and there's Mr. Right Now. I just have to start thinking of myself as *Mrs. Right Now.*"

"Exactly! So when are you going to do it?"

"I don't know."

"Do it tonight. Otherwise you'll chicken out."

"But it'll be really late when we get home."

"Would you stop being so damned practical? Who cares if you lose a little sleep?"

Heather took a deep, shaky breath. "Okay. Tonight."

"I can't believe you actually came to your senses," Alison said with a smile, only to frown all over again. "God, I envy you."

"Don't. It's not like we're staying together forever. But for now—"

"It's the 'for now' I'm jealous about. Do you have something hot to wear?"

Heather froze. She hadn't thought about that. She had ratty T-shirts and white cotton panties. For all Tony's insistence that they sleep together, he'd probably run screaming from that.

No, wait. He'd tried to seduce her last night, and she'd been wearing those things in addition to her ugly robe and slippers. Clearly he hadn't been deterred. Still, showing up looking like a bag lady wasn't going to give her a whole lot of confidence.

"I'll find something," Heather said, vaguely remembering one black nightgown that might be in one of the boxes she brought from her parents' house.

"So...are you nervous?" Alison asked.

"Nervous?"

"Well, yeah. The women Tony dates are borderline anorexics who buy all their lingerie at Victoria's Secret. They probably know every sex trick in the book. I'd feel a little out of my league."

"Thanks, Alison. I wasn't feeling inadequate enough, but you solved that problem."

"I didn't say you should feel that way. I'm just telling you how *I'd* feel."

Which was exactly the way Heather felt now.

"Just be cool," Alison said. "Act nonchalant, like you sleep with hot guys every day. Tony won't know the difference."

Heather thought about her too-thick thighs, her lack of sexual adventure, and her absence of a really nice lingerie wardrobe. Tony was a lot of things, but dumb wasn't one of them. He'd know the difference, all right. From five miles away, he'd know.

She glanced down the bar. Tony had evidently gone into the kitchen, because he was nowhere to be seen. If she was going to do this, she needed some time to make sure she was in control of things. The crowd had thinned out considerably. If she left now, it wouldn't be a problem.

She circled the bar to grab her purse.

"Do me a favor," she said to Alison. "Tell Tony I left."

"Why? Where are you going?"

"Just tell him, will you?"

"Okay. But call me tomorrow. I want to hear..."

But Heather was already halfway to the door, and Alison's voice was drowned out by the music. It was going to be good. Better than good. She had a feeling it was going to be even hotter and more cataclysmic than she could even imagine.

As long as she didn't talk herself out of it.

~

As Tony drove toward his apartment, he tapped his fingers on the steering wheel, thinking he should feel tired, but he didn't. And he knew it was because of all this damned pent-up sexual energy he couldn't let out.

He'd hoped to keep Heather on perpetual simmer this evening with the goal of sparking a nice, hot blaze with her tonight, only to turn around and find her gone. She hadn't even told Alison where she was going, or if she had, Alison wasn't saying. If she'd simply wanted to go home, why hadn't she just said so?

He could get inside the head of virtually any woman on the planet. It was a skill he'd honed all these years, leaving other misguided men in the dust when it came to success with the opposite sex. But Heather...hell, they could stay married for fifty years and he still wouldn't be able to figure her out.

A few minutes later, he pulled into a parking space in front of his apartment. Heather's car was there, which meant she was at least home, and he took that as a good sign. But when he came through the front door and she was nowhere to be seen, he took that as a bad one.

He looked in the kitchen. Nothing.

He went to her bedroom door to find it closed. No light shone from beneath it. He put his ear to the door and heard nothing.

Damn. She'd simply come home, closed her door, turned out the light, and gone to bed?

Tony stood there in the hall, frustrated as hell. So much for his new, improved seduction plan. It was just as abysmal a failure as everything else he'd tried. Women lined up around the block to sleep with him, yet he was having to chase after Heather like a horny high school kid. What was *wrong* with her? Or, more to the point, what was wrong with him that she wasn't the least bit interested?

Pretty soon, though, his frustration faded, and he reached a conclusion he didn't want to face.

It was time for him to stop being so selfish.

He was getting way more out of their make-believe marriage than she ever would. What kind of jerk was he to demand more? Instead, he should be counting his lucky stars. He should be grateful Heather was helping him launch his business, because she was damned good at the things he wasn't. He needed to get over the fact that she had no intention of being his wife in every sense of the word. He was going to accept the fact that she wasn't going to have sex with him, take the shot to his ego, and get over it.

Deep breath. There. He'd done it.

Feeling rational and reasonable, he flipped off the living room light and strode to his bedroom, telling himself he was dead tired, anyway. It was a good thing they wouldn't be having sex tonight. He took pride in pleasing women, and he needed to be rested to be at the top of his game. In fact, he felt so tired he wasn't sure he could even get out of his clothes before he collapsed on the bed.

Then he opened his bedroom door, and his second wind came roaring back.

Heather was in his bed. The sheet was pulled up to her chest, but because her shoulders were bare, he could only conclude...

She was stark naked.

Chapter 16

When Tony opened the door, Heather's heart leaped, then settled into a hard, heavy rhythm. She'd heard him at her bedroom door and knew it was only a matter of time before he found her here. Now that he had, she was officially terrified.

Earlier, when she couldn't find the black nightgown, she did away with the lingerie problem by wearing nothing at all. Even if she had a nightgown on, he'd eventually take it off her, anyway. She was hoping to mask her oversized thighs by turning out the lamp and lighting the Glade French Vanilla candles she'd picked up at a convenience store on the way home. It was said that every woman looked beautiful by candlelight, and she just prayed that was true. As for her lack of sexual adventure, she hadn't found a spur-of-the-moment remedy for that.

Just be cool, she reminded herself. *Act like you sleep with hot guys all the time.*

At first Tony looked stunned, clearly unable to believe she'd done something so completely out of character. But true to *his* character, it wasn't long before a lazy smile made its way across his face.

"Hey, there, Goldilocks. Is that bed just right?"

Panic seized her. Oh, Lord. She should have known he was going to talk. Sexy banter. She was lousy at that kind of thing. She scooted the sheet higher on her chest and opened her mouth to speak, but her vocal cords were tied in a knot.

No. You can do this. What would a wild woman say?

"The bed's nice enough," she said provocatively, "but it would be better if you were in it, too."

God, that's dumb, she thought, but she forced herself to act nonchalant, as if she slept with men every day of her life and twice on Sunday.

"And here I thought you were a good girl," Tony said.

Another lob she had to return. *Think! Think!*

"I am a good girl," she said, dropping her voice suggestively. "Come on over here and I'll show you just how *good* I can be."

Damn. She sounded like somebody doing a bad Lauren Bacall impression.

But just when she was sure he was on the verge of laughing, he started toward her. His footsteps were nearly silent, but every one of them seemed to thunder in her head. *He's coming this way. All six feet of gorgeous, soon-to-be-naked man.*

Maybe she sounded sexy after all.

He stopped at the side of the bed, tilting his head questioningly, a smile still playing across his lips. "Who are you, and what have you done with that uptight CPA I married?"

"She took the night off," Heather purred. "Now it's just you and me."

Lauren Bacall, eat your heart out.

"Naked in my bed," Tony said, his gaze moving up and

down her body beneath the sheet. "Now, that's something I never expected."

She toyed with a strand of her hair, twirling it around her finger. "Well, now. It looks as if I'm more of a mystery than you realized, doesn't it?"

"Hmm." He got a thoughtful look on his face. "Speaking of mysteries, I have been wondering something for the past couple of days."

"What's that?"

"What you look like naked."

Naked? Heather nearly choked. In spite of the fact that she was naked under this sheet, she thought they'd be working their way up to the unveiling.

Trying to stay calm, she settled back against the pillow, but her heart was beating wildly. To her horror, Tony reached down and grabbed the sheet that covered her. Slowly he began to pull it toward him.

Oh, God. Did he actually intend to uncover her in one big swoop? Suddenly the candles felt as bright as spotlights in a theater, and she was center stage. Why had she lit *three* of them?

As the sheet started to slip past her breasts, she grabbed it back and sat up suddenly. "Don't."

Tony drew back. "What's wrong?"

Heather felt more mortified than she ever had in her life. Why couldn't she do something as simple as have sex without getting all uptight about it?

"I'm...uh...cold."

"Yeah? It doesn't seem all that cold in here to me."

She forced herself to smile provocatively. "So are you telling me you don't want to get *under* these covers with me?"

"Nope. I want you over them."

Her hands started to tremble, and she tightened them against the sheet. "Now, Tony. Where's the mystery in that?"

"Mystery doesn't turn me on. Naked. *That* turns me on."

He reached for the sheet again, but she grabbed it away before he could take hold of it.

"Heather? What's wrong?"

"I'm sorry," she said suddenly. "I can't do this." She scrambled to the edge of the bed, dragging the sheet along with her. "I don't know what I was thinking. I must have been out of my mind." She stood up, clumsily wrapping the sheet around herself. "This isn't me. I'm not a wild woman. I'm not even a little bit disorderly."

"Where are you going?"

"To that crappy sofa bed where I should have been in the first place. Sorry about the sheet. You'll just have to do without it. I'll wash it and return it to you tomorrow."

She headed for the door, tripping a little on the edge of the sheet and righting herself again, trying to preserve what little dignity she might possibly have left.

"Looks as if my uptight CPA is back," Tony said.

"Yes, she is," Heather said. "Whether you like it or not."

"Oh, I like it," he said. "I like it a lot."

She spun around, blinked dumbly. "What did you say?"

"For a while there, I thought the pod people came and took the real Heather. Fortunately, that's not the case."

She looked at him incredulously. "What is *with* you?

Huh? You tell me I'm too uptight, but when I try not to be uptight, you tell me that's not right, either!"

"Right now I just want you to be you, Heather. Slutty women are a dime a dozen. That's not why I'm attracted to you."

Attracted to her?

She had no idea exactly what a guy like Tony meant when he said that, but the words seemed to fuse her feet to the floor. As she stood there clutching that sheet to her chest, Tony walked over and stood in front of her, looking big and imposing and way, *way* more comfortable than she felt, which made her realize how far out of her element she really was. After the kinds of women he'd been with in his life, she'd be nothing but a big, fat disappointment. If she thought she was embarrassed now, wait until *that* happened.

She ducked her head. "I'm sorry, Tony. I thought I could do this, but I can't."

"Why not?"

She expelled a breath of frustration. "Because I'm not really into recreational sex."

He frowned. "You make it sound like a round of golf."

"You know what I mean. But you are."

"I'm what?"

"Into recreational sex."

"Is that a problem?"

"You do it a lot."

"Yeah."

"But I don't do it a lot, so this is never going to work."

"Look, sweetheart, I know you're trying to tell me something here, but I'm afraid I'm just not getting—" He stopped short, looking a little panicked. "Are you telling me you're a *virgin?*"

"Oh, for God's sake, Tony! I'll be thirty in July. What woman gets to thirty without having done it at least once?"

"So how many times have you done it?"

She swallowed hard, her voice suddenly deserting her. "Once?"

"No!"

"Two times?"

She closed her eyes. This was turning into a major disaster.

"Three?" he asked.

She exhaled. "More like two and a half."

"How do you do it two and a *half* times?"

"His roommate came home early."

When Tony smiled, then laughed a little, Heather felt like a total loser.

"See, I knew that was going to be a problem," she said. "I don't know why I did this. Temporary insanity. Bad phase of the moon. Split personality. Hell, I don't know. I just know I'm out of here."

She started for the door again, but he caught her arm. "Now, hold on there. We're going to talk about this."

"Tony? Why can't you be like other men? They don't like to talk. Women have to drag the words out of them. But not you. You never shut up. You talk and talk and—"

"Tell me why you've had sex only two and a half times."

"You're teasing me."

"No. I just want to know."

She shrugged weakly. "The first two and a half times

didn't go so well, so I thought I'd wait until I knew that it *would* go well."

"There's never any guarantee of that." He paused, his teasing smile returning. "With most men, anyway."

Heather shook her head. "Is that ego of yours *ever* going to take a vacation?"

"Tell the truth, Heather. You like my ego. You like having a man around who's sure of himself and knows what he wants." He inched closer. "And do you know what I want right now?"

"What?"

He took a step forward, closing the gap between them, then took her face in his hands. "You."

He lowered his mouth to hers in a gentle kiss, and in spite of the mortification she felt, her heart went crazy. He trailed the backs of his fingertips sensuously along her cheek and then kissed her again, this time touching his tongue to her lips, and when she opened to him, he slid his arm around her back and deepened the kiss. She clung to the sheet with both hands, her world going blurry. He kissed her again and again, taking his time, making her want him more with every moment that passed.

Finally he eased away and looked down at her hands clutching the sheet. "Tell you what. Why don't I blow out the candles?"

He backed away slowly, then went to each candle and extinguished it. She looked toward the window, where the full moon shone in like a searchlight. Even though the blinds were closed, the room was still too bright.

"I don't suppose you'd consider turning off the moon, too?" she asked.

"Sorry. My superpowers are limited to sex." He held out his hand. "Come here."

She took a deep, shaky breath and went to him. She shifted uncomfortably, tugging the sheet higher on her chest.

"I know it feels awkward," Tony said. "But I promise you it won't for long. Just let go of the sheet."

"You're not going to like what you see."

"Heather," he whispered. "Let go."

Her stomach churning with apprehension, she released the sheet, closing her eyes at the same time so she wouldn't see his face when he saw her. Seconds sluggishly ticked by. She could only imagine how disappointed he must be.

Then she felt his hand against her hip. *Oh, God. He's not just looking. He's touching.*

She held her breath as he stroked his hand upward, leaving a trail of seared nerve endings in its wake. She squeezed her eyes tightly closed, every muscle in her body tensing with anticipation. He closed both hands around her waist. She felt him shift, and a second later, his lips touched the side of her neck in a gentle kiss.

"Heather?" he said.

"What?"

"Where did you ever get the idea that I wouldn't like what I saw?"

Taken aback, she slowly opened her eyes as his gaze came around to meet hers. Every word he spoke could be a lie. Every word probably *was* a lie. But she saw nothing but sincerity in his eyes.

Tony slid his hand beneath the mass of hair at her neck, the warmth of his fingers sending tiny shock waves across her shoulders. He leaned in and whispered in her ear, his breath hot against her neck. "I've been dying to get my hands on you. And now you're all mine."

All mine. Heather felt a slow, heavy pull of desire right down to her toes.

"I thought about holding you like this," he said, moving behind her, splaying his hand across her abdomen and pulling her against him. She felt his erection at the small of her back, and even through his jeans it felt hard and demanding.

"And kissing you like this," he murmured, pulling her hair away from the side of her neck and placing a hot, wet kiss there. Shivers zoomed all the way to her toes.

"You're still tense," he said.

"A little."

"The good thing about sex is that you just do what comes naturally."

"I don't remember it feeling all that natural."

"That's because you were thinking too hard. You have to go with the flow."

He ran his hands slowly and sensuously along her waist to her hips, then slid them down to stroke the tender flesh of her inner thighs. Then he brought his hands slowly back up across her hips, moving them upward to caress her breasts, then strum his thumbs across her nipples. She swallowed a gasp. They were already so swollen and hot that the slightest touch made her squirm.

"You feel so good, Heather. I want to touch you everywhere at once."

Lost in the feeling, she dropped her head back against his shoulder, wishing that were anatomically possible. He spent what seemed like forever just touching her, his big, strong hands moving over her body, his lips moving over her neck, as if she was his to do with as he pleased. But she needed more. She needed him to be as naked as she was. She needed to touch him. She needed to move on with this very, very soon or she was going to melt away into a red-hot puddle of goo.

"Tony—"

"Shhh."

She squirmed against him, but he held her tightly.

"I'm naked," she said, breathing hard. "You're not."

"That's because I'm not finished with this yet."

"When will you be finished?"

"I'll let you know."

"But I want..."

"What do you want, sweetheart?" He pinched her nipples lightly, then rolled them between his fingers, nipping at her earlobe at the same time.

Oh, God. He was killing her. More. She wanted more. More, more, more! *Now!*

With a sudden gasping breath, she turned around. "Take your clothes off."

Tony drew back with feigned surprise. "Are you sure? Right now?"

"Yes, *now!*"

"Yes, ma'am."

Tony grabbed his T-shirt by the back of the neck, yanked it off, and slung it aside. In seconds, the rest of his clothes had hit the floor, too.

For a moment, all she could do was stare at him in awe, cursing the fact that he'd blown out the candles and she couldn't see him as clearly as she would have liked.

She could almost feel her pupils expand, trying to take in more of him.

He pulled her to the bed, where he stretched out beside her and gave her a leisurely kiss, smoothing his hand over her abdomen. Then he moved his hand lower. Then lower still, until the heel of his hand was resting on her pubic bone. She tensed, holding her breath, and a moment later, he stroked his fingertips between her legs.

No!

She grabbed his hand, stilling it. He looked up, frowning. "What's the matter?"

"It..."

"What?"

"Tickles."

"Oh. Sorry."

He moved his hand to her thigh, caressing her there for a moment until she relaxed again, then moved his fingers back. He pressed them to her and rubbed in little circles, but it wasn't long before she gasped and clutched his hand again.

"Oh, God," she said. "I'm sorry. That still..."

"Tickles."

"Yeah."

"Maybe we'd better go about this differently."

"No. It'll be okay this time. Really. I'll concentrate. Do it again. Maybe harder or something."

He touched her again more firmly, this time kissing her deeply. Heather squeezed her eyes closed and bunched the sheet in her fist, but she couldn't help it. She squirmed away from him again, laughing this time. "Stop. *Stop!*"

He sat up, throwing his hands in the air. "These are my

moves, Heather! They're supposed to leave you gasping for air! Begging for more! You're giving me a *complex!*"

She giggled.

"And now you're laughing. *God.*" He turned and flopped down on his back. "Well, now you've done it. I am *not* in the mood anymore."

"Not in the mood?" She glanced down at the contradictory evidence between his legs. "Tony, somebody could shoot you dead and bury you six feet under, and you'd *still* be in the mood."

"That's residual. From the moment right before you attacked my performance."

She laughed. "*Attacked* your *performance?*"

"You know how big my ego is. And you just shot it to pieces. To *pieces,* Heather." He sighed dramatically. "I'll never be able to have sex again."

"Oh, you poor thing. Sure you will."

"No," he said sadly. "I won't. You've wounded me for *life.*"

She gave him a sly smile. "What would it take for me to convince you that your sexuality isn't gone forever?"

He shrugged and turned away with a hurt expression.

She leaned in and whispered against his ear, "I have an idea."

He flicked his gaze back to her.

She sat up beside him. "What I want you to do first," she said, running her hand from his shoulder to his wrist, "is put both of your hands behind your head. Beneath the pillow."

With exaggerated reluctance, he did as she said. "I don't know what good this is going to do."

"Oh, you'll see in a minute." She leaned in again,

kissed him on the neck, and whispered, "Now, close your eyes."

His eyes drifted closed. She let her gaze drift down that beautiful body and back up again, watching it go rigid with anticipation. She rose to her knees, letting her hands hover over his chest...

And tickled his armpits.

His eyes sprang open. He yanked his arms from beneath the pillow and grabbed for her. Laughing, she squirmed away, but he caught her arm, pulled her back, and pinned her to the mattress.

"Why, you rotten, conniving little—"

"Tony! You're not attacking my performance, are you?"

"You're as crazy as I am. Don't you *ever* try to say you're not!"

"I am *not* crazy!" she said. "If I were crazy, I'd have tied you up and *then* tickled you."

"Now that's a hell of a good idea. Only you're going to be on the receiving end of it."

"Uh-oh. I'm out of here."

She tried to squirm away again, but he grabbed her and pulled her back. She squealed and started to laugh again, and then he was laughing, too, and then he was kissing her and they laughed some more, and then he extinguished the laughter completely with a long, slow, blistering kiss that melted the fight right out of her. The endorphin rush was almost more than she could bear. Tony was something she'd never imagined a man like him could be—sweet and kind and funny—and she wished she hadn't waited so long to be with him like this.

She pushed him to his back again, tracing her fingertip along his jaw. "How about if I do it for real this time?"

"I'm all yours, sweetheart."

As Tony lay back, Heather felt like a starving woman at a smorgasbord—she didn't know where to start first. But she had the feeling that whatever she did, wherever she kissed him, however she touched him, she couldn't mess things up.

She explored his body in a way she'd never done with a man before, finding all kinds of places that elicited a groan here, a sigh there. With every kiss, every touch, his arousal seemed to grow. Soon she got up the nerve to close her hand around his penis, feeling the length and width of him.

"That's right, sweetheart," he said, his voice hot and breathy. "Touch me."

He seemed to be waiting for her to do something specific, but the sex she'd known so far had been fast and fumbling without much of a chance for experimentation.

"I don't exactly know how," she whispered.

She felt really dumb saying that, but since she'd already confessed her lack of experience, she figured this was a good time to get rid of some of the ignorance no woman her age should have. Tony closed his palm over her hand and showed her what he wanted, and then she was stroking him up and down, over and over, loving the feel of him beneath her hand, watching the rise and fall of his chest as his breath came faster. Eventually she felt bold enough lean in and kiss the head of his penis. He sucked in a breath, his body going rigid.

"Is that okay?" she said suddenly.

"Oh, yeah," he said as he exhaled. "Trust me. It's all good."

She closed her mouth over the tip, then pulled back. When she saw his fingertips curl into the mattress, she took him deeper into her mouth, then pulled back, circling her tongue around the head as she stroked the shaft. She did it over and over, going a little deeper each time.

She heard his sharp, ragged breathing, and when she flicked her gaze up, she saw a sheen of sweat on his chest and his eyes squeezed closed and his hands clasping the sheet, and suddenly she didn't feel like the same awkward, clueless woman she'd been just a short time ago. She was a woman who could give as much pleasure as she received, and it made her feel powerful in a way she never had before.

Okay, she thought with a little bit of elation, *this is good. I can do this.*

Then all at once he let out a soft groan and sat up, taking her by the shoulders and pressing her back on the bed again.

She looked up at him with distress. "Was I doing something wrong?"

"Sweetheart, it doesn't get much more right than what you were doing. Which means if you keep it up, this is going to be over way sooner than I want it to be."

And then he was touching her again, and to her surprise, her ticklishness was long gone. He slid his fingers deep inside her, then moved them back up again to circle over her clitoris. If she was writhing this time, it was only to ask for more, to *beg* for more. The tension he created seemed to pull her tighter and tighter, her whole body trembling with need.

Oh, God. There it was. A tiny spark deep inside her. A soft, involuntary moan rose in the back of her throat, and soon her breathing turned into short, sharp gasps. He drove her higher and higher, then higher still, until the whole world finally exploded in a burst of sensation.

Before she knew it, Tony had the condom on and was moving between her legs. He plunged inside her with sharp, heavy thrusts, his breath scorching hot against her neck. It seemed as if only seconds passed before his body went rigid, and then he fell forward and clung to her with a fierce groan.

Heather had never felt anything like it.

As they rode out the last waves of pleasure together, she relished the feeling of Tony's body on hers, the brush of his hair along her cheek, the wild beating of his heart against her chest. She clung to him as tightly as he clung to her, until the last tremors died away and she could finally breathe again.

After a moment, he fell away from her, hitting the mattress with a soft thud of satisfaction. His chest expanded with a deep breath, settling down again as he slowly let it out.

Then he turned to look at her.

Their eyes locked, and Heather had the sense of something meaningful passing between them. In those few moments, she imagined what it would be like if he really were her husband. If they weren't just having sex, but making love. She felt as if she were under some kind of spell that had transported her into the future, a future where she woke up with Tony every morning of her life.

Then a smile slowly spread across his face. "That," he said, still breathing hard, "was a hell of a lot of fun."

And the spell was gone.

Recreational sex, she reminded herself. Like playing golf. Only naked. In bed. With no clubs or golf course. Pure entertainment. Nothing else was included, nor would it ever be.

"Fair warning," he said. "I intend to get you back. Next time it's fur-lined handcuffs and a feather for you. And there *will* be a next time."

This was dangerous in so many ways. She'd never been wowed by a guy in bed before. That was doing some serious damage to her logical, orderly mind. But as long as she remembered who she was dealing with, she'd be okay. Tony wasn't good for her. In the long run, he wasn't good for any woman. But in the short run...

There wasn't anybody better.

"I think you were right," she said offhandedly. "It's dumb for either of us to be...deprived."

"Exactly. We don't want that. Deprivation is a bad thing. While we're together, we'll be together."

"And when it's over, it's over."

"But think of the fun we'll have in the meantime." He grinned. "Come here, Goldilocks."

He dragged her to him and kissed her again, reminding her just how sweet and tender and seductive he could be, like a sexual Pied Piper driving her right over the cliff. And she was closing her eyes and making the leap.

Chapter 17

When Tony awoke the next morning, the bed beside him was empty. He felt disoriented for a moment, wondering where Heather was. He rolled over and looked at the clock. Ten after nine. Then he remembered that this was Monday morning, which meant she'd probably left a couple of hours ago for work, and he'd slept right through it.

He thought about last night and couldn't help smiling. Heather was nearly thirty years old, but she'd had sex only two *and a half* times? Good Lord. What had he gotten himself into? Any woman who was that inexperienced generally had him running the other way. But Heather...

The last thing he'd expected was for her to show up naked in his bed. Then the tickling thing. He'd teased that she had a wild woman inside just waiting to get out, but he hadn't known just how right he was. Against all odds, he knew now that in order to stay one step ahead of her, he was going to have to stay on his toes.

Which led him to another thought.

He got up from the bed and dug through his dresser drawers. When he found what he was looking for in the third drawer down beneath a pile of boxer shorts, he smiled. So Heather liked surprises, did she?

She hadn't seen anything yet.

~

Heather spent the morning in her cubicle, drinking coffee, trudging through balance sheets, and answering questions about her hair. No, she hadn't had it permed. Yes, it was this way naturally. And no, she didn't have a clue how a person could get hair like hers if they hadn't been born with it.

By midmorning, she was on her fourth cup of coffee, trying to keep her eyes open and her body functioning. It had been all she could do to drag herself out of bed this morning. Mostly that was because she was dead tired after being up half the night. But it was also because she'd had such a hard time taking her eyes off Tony.

She lay her pencil down for a moment and closed her eyes, thinking about how he'd been sprawled on his stomach this morning, the sheet pulled up to his hips. The faint morning sun filtering through the blinds had cast his skin in a golden glow, highlighting his lean, muscled back. She hadn't seen that many naked male bodies close up, but the few she had seen didn't even come close to being as beautiful as Tony's.

She'd finally forced herself out of bed, taken a shower, and thrown on a robe, only to curse that beautiful man when she realized she still didn't have a flatiron and was going to be forced to wear her naturally curly hair to work. She'd have to get him back for that. She just didn't know how. Shave him bald as he slept, maybe? It would be drastic but effective. He'd think twice about rummaging through her drawers and stealing things next time, now, wouldn't he?

Unfortunately, he was just insane enough to retaliate with something worse.

Heather heard her text message tone. She grabbed her phone and saw a message from Alison. *Lunch? Downtown Deli? Noon?*

Heather punched in *OK,* and Alison responded with *You're telling all.*

An hour later, Heather walked into the Downtown Deli and slid into a booth across from Alison.

"Okay," Alison said, her eyes lit up with anticipation. "Tell me all about it. And don't leave anything out."

"Alison? Do you think we could order lunch first?"

"Hey!" Alison said to the waiter, who jumped with surprise. "We're ready now!"

The waiter came over. Alison ordered the hot pastrami sandwich that Heather wished she could have, and Heather ordered a salad. Again. Dressing on the side. Yuk.

"Okay," Alison said. "Spill it. Tell me everything."

Heather thought for a minute. "Hmm. It's hard to put into words."

"Heather," Alison said sharply. "Find the words. Sexy. Erotic. Seductive. Steamy. Captivating. Hot. Romantic. Pick a few, add some verbs, and string it all together for me in some kind of meaningful way."

"One word works."

"Which is?"

"He was... sweet."

Alison screwed up her face. "Sweet?"

"I guess you had to be there."

"That's all you can say about it? That he was *sweet?*"

"No, that's not all I could say. It's all I'm *going* to say."

"Heather, you can't do this to me. You can't—" She stopped short, looking skeptical. "You didn't do it with him, did you?"

"Yes, I did."

"Then why won't you tell me about it? We've told each other everything since junior high. You can't stop now."

The truth was that it really *was* hard to put into words. "Those adjectives you mentioned…they're all kind of givens, you know? What I didn't expect was…"

"What?"

A smile made its way across Heather's face. "How much fun it was going to be."

"Fun? No. In my experience, sex is serious business."

"Not the way Tony goes about it," Heather said, and her smile just got bigger.

Alison sat back and eyed her carefully. "Heather? Are you falling for him?"

"No. But now I know why women do."

"Yeah, they fall for them, and then he breaks their hearts. You can't fall for him, or he'll break yours, too."

"My heart's going to stay perfectly intact."

"You say that now, but you have a few more weeks to go. Are you going to be sleeping together again?"

"It looks that way."

"Maybe that's not such a good idea."

Heather slumped with frustration. "Will you make up your mind? First you wanted me to sleep with him, and now you don't?"

"I just don't want you to get hurt."

"Stop worrying about me, will you? I know what I'm doing."

"I know you do. I just want to make sure." Alison sighed. "So that's all you're going to tell me about the experience?"

"Yeah," Heather said, still feeling the glow. "I think it is."

"Okay. See if I tell you about my dates from now on." She rolled her eyes. "You know. My ball-scratching nose-blowers. *God.*"

The waiter brought their food. Alison dug into her sandwich, and Heather picked at her salad.

"How's the diet going?" Alison said.

"Lousy. Tony made me eat butter."

"What?"

"Never mind. Are you going to eat all those chips?"

"Take as many as you want."

She wanted all of them. Plus a sandwich to go with them. And maybe some potato salad on the side. And strawberry cheesecake for dessert.

The only thing that stopped her from placing that order was the prospect of standing at the altar at Regina's wedding and exploding right out of that horrible pink dress. Tony would look gorgeous in his tuxedo, and she'd look like a fat freak of nature. Because of the dress, she couldn't do much about the freak-of-nature part, but at least she could try her best not to be a fat one.

⤸

Heather spent the evening with her computer in her lap, working on the database for the grand-opening invitations. She incorporated the rest of Tony's address book, then farmed contact information from Plano and Dallas food and entertainment web sites. If she could get a couple of reporters to write nice articles about the place, it would go a long way toward growing Tony's customer base and insuring that every night would be as busy as the first night she'd worked there. She couldn't print the invitations, though, since her printer was still in a box at her parents' house, but she could take them on a disk to Tony's office and print them there.

She also checked out the directories on the Web that listed local bars and restaurants and discovered the former owner had never listed McMillan's. She made a note do that as soon as she could get some good digital photos.

And a web site. They needed a web site. There wasn't any business on earth that couldn't benefit from one of those.

About ten o'clock, her stomach started to growl, but she forced herself to ignore it. Twenty minutes later, it started in again. She thought about Tony's Twinkies and chips in the pantry.

No. The dress. Remember the dress.

At ten thirty, she finally closed her computer and lay down on the sofa, thinking it might be wise to take a nap. She had no idea how late she'd be up after Tony came home, and if she wanted to be worth a damn at work tomorrow, she needed to grab some sleep from somewhere.

Shortly before midnight, her phone rang, waking her from a sound sleep. She rose on one elbow, grabbed it, and looked at the caller ID. She smiled and hit the TALK button.

"Hey," she said. "How are things going there?"

"Had a good night. But that's not what I'm thinking about right now. I was thinking about what I'm going to find in my bed when I get home."

"Maybe the same thing as last night?"

"Sweetheart, that's exactly what I had in mind. See you soon."

She disconnected the call, then sat back on the sofa, closed her eyes, and tried to imagine what he might have in store for her tonight. A few weeks ago, she couldn't have predicted anything like this. Living with Tony. *Sleeping* with Tony. She'd told him that when it was over, it was over, and she meant it, but that didn't mean she wasn't going to enjoy it while it lasted.

A few minutes later, she'd tucked herself into Tony's bed, surrounded by candlelight. And this time the candles were going to stay lit, because she was through being uptight about this. As long as it lasted, she was determined to throw out every bit of self-consciousness and live it up.

It wasn't long before she heard the front door open and close, and when Tony came into the room and saw her in his bed, the smile he gave her made her feel like the most desirable woman in the world.

"Good," he said. "You're right where I want you. Don't move."

Heather settled back with a sigh of contentment. She had no intention of going anywhere.

He pulled his wallet out of his hip pocket and tossed it on the dresser, along with his watch. He walked slowly toward the bed, crawled up on it, straddled her hips, and laced his fingers through hers. He pushed her hands to the bed on either side of her head, then leaned down and gave her a long, delicious kiss. Heather practically melted into the mattress.

"Last night," he said, a smile playing across his lips, "you got just a *little* bit out of line."

"Yes," she said smugly. "I did, didn't I?"

"And I believe I told you what I was going to do about that."

Her smug expression faded. "What?"

Before she knew what was happening, he'd scooted one of her hands down and placed his knee gently but firmly against her forearm. Still holding her other hand, he quickly reached between the mattress and the headboard, pulled something out, and clicked it onto her wrist.

Handcuffs?

Chapter 18

Tony! What are you *doing?*"

Heather squirmed beneath him, but he held her snugly and reached around to cuff her other wrist. Clearly flabbergasted, she yanked hard on the cuffs. They may have been soft and furry against her wrists, but they were bona fide handcuffs that did their intended job.

Still sitting astride her hips, he leaned back and stared down at her. Not surprisingly, her smug expression had vanished.

She laughed nervously. "Come on, Tony. Handcuffs?"

"Yep."

"I . . . I thought you were joking about that."

"Now, see, Heather, that's your problem," he said as he swung his leg over her and rose from the bed. "You should know by now just how serious I am about crazy things. And things don't come much crazier than fur-lined handcuffs. Unless . . ." He opened his closet door, pulled something out, and held it up. "It's one of these."

She blinked with surprise. "A *feather duster?*"

"Don't worry," he told her. "It's a new one. No germs. I knew that would be an issue with you."

"The *issue,* Tony, is that I'm handcuffed to your bed!"

"I decided your behavior last night warranted more than a single feather." He sauntered over to the bed, tapping the handle of the feather duster against his hand. "And since I know how turned on you get by cleaning, I thought this was just about the ideal sex toy."

She tugged on the cuffs. "Tony, this makes me a little nervous."

"That's because you're a control freak. We're going to work on that."

"Fine. Let me out of these handcuffs and we'll work on it all you want to."

"Nope. You were a very bad girl, Heather. And now you're going to pay the price."

"I don't think this is a good idea. Really. You need to let me go now."

"In good time."

"No, Tony. Seriously. *Now.*"

Tony walked over and sat on the bed beside her, still looking at her like a schoolmaster with a disobedient pupil. But then he leaned in and planted a warm, gentle kiss on the side of her neck.

"Trust me, sweetheart," he whispered in her ear. "You know I'd never do anything to hurt you."

When he pulled away, he turned his mouth up in a playful smile and gave her a subtle wink. She opened her mouth as if she was going to protest, and if she had, he'd have called a halt to the whole thing. Instead, she swallowed hard, and after a moment her fearful expression turned calculating.

"I *will* get you back for this," she said.

"No, Heather. After tonight, you'll be begging me to do it again."

Then he stood up and did what she wouldn't let him do last night. Very slowly, he pulled the sheet off her and tossed it aside. With candles lighting the room tonight and the handcuffs keeping her from covering herself up again, he could stare at her all he wanted to.

His gaze traveled from her shapely calves to the dark curls at the apex of her thighs to her full, heavy breasts capped with rosy pink nipples that were already tightening in the bedroom's cool air. Her skin was flawless, looking so soft and touchable that he couldn't wait to feel it beneath his hands. Her wild, walnut-brown hair was fanned out on the pillow, glinting like gold in the candlelight. It was as if he'd found a naked forest nymph in a darkened glen caught in a tangle of vines, totally at his mercy. And when she looked up at him with those clear blue eyes, it burned that impression right into his brain. All that was needed to complete the image was a bed of leaves and a few tiny flowers woven into her hair.

"Tony," she said. "You're staring."

"Shhh," he whispered, his finger against his lips.

She blinked. "What?"

"You're messing up my fantasy."

"Fantasy?"

"Change of plan," he said, tossing the feather duster aside.

Her eyes widened. "Uh...Tony? You're making me nervous again."

"Don't worry, sweetheart. I'm just going to tell you a story."

"You handcuffed me to a bed so you could tell me a *story?*"

"It's a very special story. Once upon a time—"

"A fairy tale?"

He sighed. "It's a standard story beginning. Recognized the world over. Will you just go with it?"

She looked at him impatiently. "Fine. Keep talking."

"Once upon a time, there was a strong, handsome, virile knight riding through a dense forest on his trusty steed."

Heather laughed. "You're kidding, right?"

"Fairy tales demand certain archetypes."

"Okay, fine. So why is the knight riding through the forest?"

"He's on a quest."

"What kind of quest?"

"I don't know. It's irrelevant to the plot." Tony began to unbutton his shirt. "Anyway, it gets late, so he stops to make camp for the night. He starts walking through the woods near his campsite, looking for wood to start a fire, when he hears a noise."

He unfastened the last button and took off his shirt, tossing it aside. Then he reached for his belt buckle.

"He listens closely. It sounds as if tiny branches are breaking, as if somebody is shuffling through the brush. The knight is sure it's an enemy on his trail. He draws his sword. He goes deeper into the woods, and the sound grows stronger. He lifts his weapon, and..."

Tony paused, and Heather's eyes widened. "And?"

"And he lays eyes on the most beautiful creature he's ever seen."

"Creature?"

"A forest nymph."

Heather laughed. "A *forest nymph?*"

"Yes. She's lying on the forest floor. Somehow she's gotten caught in a tangle of vines, and she can't get loose. No matter how hard she struggles, she isn't strong enough to free herself. And she isn't wearing so much as a fig leaf."

"Okay. I get it. I'm a naked forest nymph in bondage. You got that from a porn flick, didn't you?"

"No. My stories always have original content." He kicked off his shoes, then pulled his jeans off, taking his underwear with them, and tossed them aside. "Then the strong, handsome, virile knight—"

"You, of course."

"Yeah. What gave it away?"

"The grandiose adjectives. That ego thing again."

"Nah. It's just typecasting. *So*...the strong, handsome, *virile* knight puts his weapon away and approaches her."

As he spoke, he sat on the bed beside Heather. She looked down. "Got news for you, Tony. Your weapon is still drawn."

"This is a simple story, Heather. Metaphors aren't allowed. Shall I go on?"

"Please do."

"The knight has never seen anything quite as beautiful as the forest nymph," Tony said, dropping his gaze to Heather's breasts, "and for a long time, all he can do is stare at her." He paused. "And stare." A longer pause. "And stare..."

"Tony," she snapped.

"But soon she grows uncomfortable under his blistering gaze. The knight knows he should free her from the tangle of vines. But he also knows that the moment he does, she'll disappear into the woods and he'll never see her again."

"What if she promises not to run away?"

"Forest nymphs may be beautiful, but they're notorious liars. And he can't let her go, anyway."

"Why not?"

Tony leaned in and whispered against her neck, "Because he hasn't yet satisfied his raging...male...*lust.*"

Heather swallowed hard. "Oh, my. I bet the forest nymph is starting to get a little uptight with all that testosterone flying around."

"At first, she's terrified. She struggles to free herself, but it's pointless. The knight can do with her whatever he chooses. But then she realizes it's not pain he has in mind." He dropped his voice to a deep whisper. "Only pleasure."

With that, he cradled Heather's face in his hands and kissed her, amazed once again at how soft and sweet her lips were. He teased his tongue along her bottom lip, and she opened her mouth beneath his. He threaded his fingers through her hair, angled his mouth, and delved inside with his tongue. When he felt her stroke her tongue tentatively against his, as if she were an innocent girl still learning the wonders of kissing, he felt every contradiction that Heather was. On the outside, she was a tough, no-nonsense woman. Inside, though, she had a sweet naivety that blew him away. Just kissing her made him feel as if this were all brand-new to him, too, as if he'd found a whole new facet of lovemaking to explore.

Without taking his mouth from hers, he slid his hand

to the side of her neck, where he felt her pulse pounding like mad. He'd shocked the hell out of her with the handcuffs. It had been a devious move on his part, but it was all going to be good. He wanted to make her feel things she'd never felt before. He knew he had a lot to pick from, considering her two and a half times—three and a half after last night—and the handcuffs ensured that whatever he chose to do, her modesty or apprehension wouldn't stand in his way.

He moved his hand down to splay against her chest, his fingertips playing across her collarbone; then he passed his hand over the swell of her breast. He grazed his thumb over her nipple—once, twice—and with just that tiny touch, he felt a shudder pass through her and her soft moan hum against his lips. She was so sensitive. So responsive. The way her body reacted to everything he did—her face growing flushed, her breath coming faster, the tiny whimpers in the back of her throat—was genuine. After being with women for whom sex had been reduced to performance art, it aroused him like nothing else.

He kissed his way along her jaw, then moved lower to close his mouth over her neck in a warm, wet kiss, tugging at the flesh with his lips. She shuddered again, twisting her shoulders, but when he pulled his lips away, she tightened her grip on the straps of the handcuffs and tilted her head in a subtle invitation for him to do it again. He smiled and obliged, strumming her nipple at the same time, loving the way her body writhed gently beneath him.

Finally he stretched out beside her. He dropped a kiss against the swell of her breast, then drew her nipple into his mouth with moist suction. She let out a soft gasp and tried to shudder away, but he was relentless, teasing it with his tongue until it grew hard and stiff. Then he moved to the other one and gave it the same treatment, at the same time skimming his hand down her inner thigh to caress the tender skin there.

When he stroked his fingers between her legs, she jumped a little and shifted her hips, but he persisted, astonished to feel how hot and wet and swollen she already was. Before long, she was tightening her fists on the cuff straps and pressing against him, asking for more, but a reprise of last night wasn't what he had in mind.

He backed away and rose from the bed.

"No!" she said. "Tony! Don't leave me!"

"Take it easy, sweetheart. I'm not going anywhere." He moved to the foot of the bed and stared down at her, watching the sharp rise and fall of her chest and the way her whole body seemed to throb with impatience as she waited for him to touch her again.

He leaned over, placed his hands on her thighs, and smoothed his palms all the way down to her ankles. Then he gently pulled her legs apart and sat between them. He dropped his palms to her hips and passed his thumbs along the junction between her hips and pelvis.

Yes, yes, yes. Touch me now.

For as clearly as her body was saying that, she might as well have shouted it. But Tony was in no hurry. He stroked her thighs and hips for what seemed like forever, making her body go rigid with anticipation. Then he dipped his head and kissed her abdomen. Sliding down, he braced himself on one elbow at her right hip and sprawled between her legs. Resting his other hand on her thigh, he kissed her abdomen again, then dragged his lips lower. Kissed her again. Lower. Another kiss.

And lower still.

Heather had never been slow on the uptake, but until he parted her with his thumbs, it didn't seem to dawn on her what he intended to do. When he flicked his tongue against her, she gasped and twisted hard to one side.

"No. Oh, God, no. It's too much, Tony. *No.*"

She was breathing so hard she was on the verge of hyperventilating, but he didn't say a word. He just held her hips until she stilled. She tilted her head back and drew in sharp little breaths of anticipation. Tony lowered his head again, this time closing his mouth over her with a soft sucking motion of his lips and tongue that made her squirm all over again, but he held her in place, and after a moment, she wasn't fighting it and was even arching her body up to meet him.

He teased and tormented her, and she shivered beneath him. He could hear her breathing escalate, and when her shivers turned to shudders, he knew she was close. When she finally cried out, he glanced up to see her head thrown back, that wild hair spread across the pillow, her hands straining against the cuffs, and her whole body trembling with release. It was the most blatantly erotic thing he'd ever seen.

He needed to be inside her. *Now.*

After rolling on a condom faster than he ever had in his life, he pressed her knees apart and plunged inside her. Ah, God, she felt good, still convulsing from her climax, her muscles tightening around him, driving him to thrust with fierce intensity. Seconds later, a climax slammed into him, tearing a deep growl from his throat and battering him with one shattering pulse after another. Finally he fell against her, his head bowed, trying desperately to drag in a good, solid breath.

"Don't worry, sweetheart," he said. "I'll let you go. It's just going to be a little bit."

He lay there for several seconds, his cheek against hers, feeling her heart beating wildly against his chest. Finally he took a big, deep breath and sat up between her legs. He rested his hands on her thighs for a moment, then backed away and stood up.

He unlocked the cuffs, tossed them aside, and lay down beside her, pulling her into his arms. He felt as if he'd been mowed down by a freight train, and it was at least a full minute before his breathing slowed and his heart rate moved into the nonlethal range.

He turned to Heather. "And they both lived happily ever after."

She sighed with satisfaction. "I just love a good story."

"So you're not mad about the cuffs?"

"I was never mad about the cuffs."

"Just a little scared."

"A little. Until my strong, handsome, *virile* knight rode up. Is there a sequel to that story?"

He laughed softly and pulled her closer. "What do you think?"

Tony couldn't believe how good this was. Unfortunately, it was only for a few more weeks. But just as there was no reason to deprive themselves now, was there any reason they couldn't still sleep together after they split up?

Then again, that would be weird. They would be divorced, but still having sex?

He decided he wasn't going to worry about it now. Where Heather was concerned, he was going to live for the moment and think about tomorrow...tomorrow.

Chapter 19

During the next week, Heather went to McMillan's every night after work. First she ensured there were no sudden catastrophes she had to help Tony deal with, and then she went into his office to get some things done, whether it was planning for the grand opening, rearranging his filing system, or checking out his books to look for places where he could possibly save money. After a few hours, she left there and went to the apartment to take a nap before he got home so she'd be rested for whatever nighttime activity he had in store for her.

On the night he'd produced those handcuffs, at first she'd felt a shot of panic, thinking maybe Regina was right. Maybe she had married a sexual deviant. But before the night was over, she realized she'd never felt safer than when she was with Tony. After that experience, if he'd said, *Let's do it in free fall from twenty thousand feet before our chutes open,* she'd be scrambling into the airplane.

From that night on, his imagination had known no bounds.

On Tuesday night, even though she told him it was unsanitary to use the kitchen table for anything but eating, he told her he'd throw that one out and buy a new one if he had to, but he *was* getting his way. By the time they'd finished, they'd emptied half a can of whipped cream and most of a squirt bottle of Hershey's syrup, after which they moved the party to the shower.

On Wednesday night, Tony asked her if she'd ever made out in the back of a movie theater. When she said she hadn't, he stuck in a sappy romantic movie he'd brought home, curled up with her on the sofa, and turned out the lights. As he proceeded to give the term *heavy petting* an entirely new meaning, she began to wonder if what she'd told Regina about his movie theater fantasies hadn't been so far from the truth.

On Thursday night, she came home to see an old VCR hooked up to the television and a note attached to the remote: *A little nostalgia from my one year in a college dorm. Hit play.* She did, and she was shocked to catch Debbie right in the middle of doing Dallas. Being a nice girl, Heather flicked it off immediately. Then she thought, *Stop with the nice,* and hit PLAY again. By the time Tony got home that night, she was ready to implement a few of the strategies Debbie used to satisfy half the male population of Big D.

On Friday morning, she woke up to him sleeping beside her and thought, *You can't do this anymore.* He was ruining her for every other man she might possibly want to sleep with in the future. She'd compare every one of them to Tony, and the poor guys would be left in the dust. *Stop now,* she told herself. *Or at least taper off so you start to get him out of your system. Tell him no tonight.*

Then, as she was getting out of bed, he happened to

wake up. He grabbed her, dragged her back, and she thought, *Forget tonight. I can't even tell him no now,* and thoughts of kicking her dangerous new sexual addiction were sidelined. She just had to keep in mind that there was a reason Tony was so good in bed. He'd been with half the women on the planet, and he couldn't wait for the day he could start going after the other half.

An hour and a half later, Heather was hurrying along the downtown sidewalk toward the building where she worked, her briefcase in one hand and a sack containing the invitations to the grand opening in the other. No doubt about it. Sex in the morning was off-limits from now on. Her legs still felt like wet spaghetti.

She'd printed the invitations in Tony's office last night. If she mailed them this morning, people would have them in time to plan for the event, but not so early that they'd put it aside and forget about it.

She sidestepped a woman meandering along talking on her cell phone, and then a scroungy, sign-carrying pan-handler. She wasn't hurrying just because she was late. She had the final fitting for her bridesmaid dress that night after work, and she figured moving faster meant burning more calories. Yeah, that was dumb, but she'd had a dream the night before that only fifty calories had meant the dif-ference between being able to zip the dress and not being able to, so she wasn't taking any chances. Unfortunately, all the weight loss in the world wouldn't make the dress any less ugly.

She slipped inside the building and went to the mail drop in the lobby. Setting her briefcase down, she fished out handfuls of the envelopes and stuffed them into the slot until she'd emptied the bag. She tossed the bag into a nearby trash can, then reached into a side pocket of her briefcase and took out one more.

The one addressed to Don McCaffrey.

She'd debated long and hard about it all the way to work, finally reaching the conclusion that if the worst happened—if he got the invitation and didn't come—Tony would never know he had been invited in the first place. If he showed up after three years of not seeing his son, surely it would mean he wanted to reconcile, and eventually Tony would thank her for it. It would be okay either way.

With a deep breath, she stuck the envelope through the slot and let it go, sending it on its way with the others.

On Saturday morning, Tony and Heather got out of his car and walked down the sidewalk toward the formal-wear shop. Tony was more of a jeans-and-T-shirt kind of guy who opted for comfort over style, so the last thing he wanted was to put on a tuxedo. But the prospect of being in the wedding and therefore irritating Jason made it almost worthwhile.

"You'll be proud of me," Heather said. "Yesterday when I went to the final fitting for the bridesmaid dress, I could actually breathe in it."

"You have me to thank for that," Tony said.

"Excuse me? What did *you* do?"

"I put you on the sex diet. Works two ways. The activity burns calories, and if I keep your hands busy, you can't eat."

Heather stopped and stared at him.

"What?" he said.

"Leave it to you to take credit for *me* losing weight." She shook her head and resumed walking.

"So you think it was all that rabbit food you ate?" he said, striding along beside her.

"I *know* it was all the rabbit food I ate. And Regina was so kind. She told me not to worry about looking fat in the dress, that I still had a week to lose another five pounds."

"What are the chances she'll trip on the train of her dress on the way to the altar?"

"A hundred percent if I stick out my foot."

Tony grabbed the door, and he and Heather went into the shop. The tailor got the tux and sent Tony into a fitting room to try it on. When he emerged a few minutes later, Heather put her hand to her chest. "Oh, my God. You look *gorgeous.*"

Tony looked at himself in the three-way mirror. "I don't know. Wearing a tux makes me feel like kind of a wuss."

"A wuss? Are you kidding? Is James Bond a wuss? I don't think so. Look at the girls he gets."

"Hmm. Maybe you have a point." Tony stood up straighter, flexing his shoulders and tugging at the lapels. "So you're telling me that if I put on one of these, I'll be a real babe magnet?"

Heather screwed up her face. "Babe magnet?"

"You know, I can get all the chicks."

"Yeah, Tony," she deadpanned. "You can get all the *chicks* now that you're a *babe magnet.*"

Tony gave her a furtive smile. "I got you, didn't I? You said I looked gorgeous."

Heather turned to the tailor. "Give him high-water pants. The Pee Wee Herman look is in this year."

The tailor, who had zero sense of humor, marked the pants for hemming at the appropriate length, then examined the fit of the jacket, which turned out to be just about perfect. He told Tony it would be ready in time for the wedding and sent him back to the fitting room.

He changed back into his jeans and T-shirt, then started to push the curtain aside to leave the fitting room. As he did, he glanced between the curtain panels to the counter at the front of the shop.

No. It couldn't be.

His father?

Tony stopped short, clutching the curtain, feeling every nerve in his body go numb. At first he thought he must be imagining it. It had been three years since he'd seen his father. Could this man just resemble him?

Then the man turned to glance out the window, and Tony knew for sure. Don McCaffrey. There was no doubt about it.

Tony watched as his father pulled out his wallet and handed the clerk a credit card. He may have left the Navy, but the Navy had never left him. He looked every bit as staunch and upright as he had for the past thirty years, and he wore the same stoic expression. As a kid, Tony could still remember craning his neck to look up at his father's unsmiling face, searching for a glimmer of the kindness and understanding that had disappeared from his life on the day his mother died.

And finding neither.

His father signed the credit card slip. The clerk handed him the tuxedo that was hanging on the rack by the cash register. His father simply nodded thanks to the clerk, then strode out of the store.

Tony let the curtain slip out of his hand. He turned and leaned against the wall of the dressing room, a sick feeling rising in his stomach. He thought about all the times in the past three years when he'd almost picked up the phone and called, only to stop himself every time with the same thought.

Why hadn't his father contacted *him?*

As more time passed, Tony had actually started to think that maybe something had happened to his father, and that was why he hadn't called. Irrationally, he almost hoped something had. At least then he could reach some conclusion other than the fact that his father never wanted to see him again.

But clearly nothing had happened to him. He was here today, preparing to go to some formal event that required a tuxedo, moving through his days with no thought at all for the son whose life he'd made miserable.

I don't care. I don't need him. I don't need him ever again.

Tony stood there a moment or two longer, waiting for his heart rate to return to normal. Then he took a deep breath and pushed the curtain back. Heather stood up and smiled at him, and some of the sick feeling in his stomach went away.

"You took long enough in there," she said as they walked to the door.

"Sorry. I couldn't stop admiring myself in the mirror."

Heather grabbed the door and held it open for him. "Go ahead. See if you can squeeze your big head through the doorway."

He stopped and stared at her. "When did you become such a smart-ass? I missed the transition moment."

"Right after I met you. You know what they say. You are who you associate with."

As they left the shop, Tony was a little worried that his father might still be in the vicinity, but he didn't see him anywhere. He felt a little silly trying to avoid him, but what was he supposed to do after all this time? Walk right up and say hello?

As they strode along, Heather yawned. Then yawned again. "I have some errands to run. Then I'm heading home for a nap."

"Sleeping in this morning didn't help?"

"If you had let me *sleep,* it might have. Tomorrow's Sunday. I'm not getting up until at least ten o'clock, so it's hands off. Do you understand?"

"Sorry. Did you say something? I didn't hear you."

"Tony? What am I going to have to do to get some sleep? Get out the fuzzy purple handcuffs?"

She gave him one last look of admonishment as they got in the car. He couldn't help smiling as he thought about the night she'd tried to bolt from his bed, dragging that sheet along with her. And now she was talking handcuffs. She wasn't at all what he thought she was in the beginning.

She was a whole lot more.

Sweet and naïve on one hand, smart and sassy on the other. She was the only woman he'd ever been with who took absolutely no crap from him, and he was starting to understand the value of having that kind of person in his life. And if he was true to himself, after seeing his father now, he was realizing the value of having *any* person in his life who was there from one day to the next.

The sex might not be forever, he thought, *but when this is all over, we're staying friends. I'm not losing that. Not ever.*

⌒

Heather had told Tony how tired she felt today, but lack of sleep didn't catch up to him until after the lunch rush. He could barely keep his eyes open. Since Kayla was staying until the dinner shift, he told her he was going home for a few hours to get some sleep. Saturday afternoons were slow, but Saturday nights weren't, and he wanted to make sure he was up for it.

As he drove home, he imagined that Heather was already in bed napping. He'd just crawl right in beside her. Hmm. Maybe one thing would lead to another, and then...

No. You have to sleep. And that's that.

A few minutes later, he parked his car next to Heather's and went into the apartment. He tossed his keys on the kitchen counter, thumbed through his mail, then headed for his bedroom, only to hear a knock at the front door.

He walked back and opened it, and the moment he saw the woman who was standing there, he felt a rush of panic. She was tall and blond with spectacular breasts, wearing a navy blue uniform with little wings on her chest and pulling a suitcase on wheels.

Babette the Air France flight attendant. She was here

for their monthly rendezvous. He'd forgotten to call her off.

"*Bonjour,* To*nee,*" she said, giving him a lightning-white smile. "Aren't you going to let me in?"

Chapter 20

Babette glided into Tony's apartment, obviously assuming they were full speed ahead for a little afternoon delight. Tony looked over his shoulder, praying Heather was asleep and would stay that way until he could get rid of Babette.

Babette set her suitcase upright, then turned back and slithered up next to Tony, slipping her arms around his neck. "I have wonderful plans for you tonight, Tonee. I went to a darling sex shop in Amsterdam. You will *love* what I bought for us."

"That sounds real nice, but—"

"I have missed you so much," Babette said, her gaze roaming over his face as if she wanted to swallow him whole. "I told the cab driver to go fast all the way here." She inched closer, her lips grazing his. "To*nee?* Have you missed me?"

"Uh...sure. Of course I have."

"Then you want to kiss me, don't you?" Her voice fell to a seductive whisper. "Kiss me."

Without even waiting for him to meet her in the middle, she backed him against the wall and clamped her lips on his, kissing him with the kind of carnal wantonness that

only Babette could. Her hands seemed to be everywhere
at once—his face, his shoulders, his arms, his chest, and
pretty soon they'd traveled south to his zipper.

He'd just reached down to grab her hands when he
heard the bedroom door open. Before he could extricate
himself from Babette, Heather rounded the corner and
came into the living room.

"Tony? What are you doing home at—"

She stopped short and looked at him. Then at Babette.
Tony opened his mouth to speak, but nothing came out.

Babette turned to him with a perplexed look. "You
make me confused. You have another woman?"

Tony looked at Heather. What was he supposed to say
to that? *She's my wife, but not really, and we sleep together, but it's nothing serious, and she's living with me,
but not for long...*

"I'm his roommate," Heather said.

"Roommate?" Babette said.

Roommate? Tony thought.

"Yeah," Heather said with a smile. "And I'm so sorry
for interrupting. Tell you what. I'll just go to my room,
and you two can pick up where you left off."

With that, she walked into her bedroom, not his, and
closed the door behind her, leaving Tony standing there in
stunned silence. He'd imagined her having a lot of different reactions, but that sure hadn't been one of them.

Babette grabbed him by the shirt collar and dragged
him up next to her. "She is *so* right. We should pick up
where we left off."

And then she was all over him again, giving him a kiss
so indecent a porn star would cry with envy. Her hands
moved from his collar to his shirt buttons, flicking them

open so fast he was bare-chested before he knew it. In a matter of moments, they were going to be naked in his living room, achieving diplomacy between the United States and France in ways politicians could only dream about. Tony had always been willing to do his part for international relations, and he'd do so again in the future, too, but not until *after* he and Heather split up. And certainly not with her in the next room.

The question was, why had she told him to go ahead? And nonchalantly, at that?

After all their talk about being husband and wife right up to the time they weren't anymore, it wasn't like Heather to let something like this go on right under her nose. Something was up, and he needed to get to the bottom of it.

He pried Babette's hands from his zipper. "Hold on. I'll be back in a minute."

"But where are you going?"

"Don't worry. I'll be right back."

Tony went to Heather's room and knocked softly on her door.

"Yes?"

He opened the door to find Heather lying on the sofa bed, hugging a pillow, as if she were trying to go to sleep.

He nodded toward the living room. "Aren't you going to ask who that is?"

"She looks like a flight attendant to me."

"Yeah. Her name is Babette. We have...uh...a standing date once a month. I meant to call her off, Heather. I forgot."

"Whatever."

Whatever? "So what's with the 'roommate' thing? I thought we were supposed to be married."

Heather shrugged. "You were clearly having a wonderful time with Babette. Why should I mess that up?"

"Well, I guess because we're supposed to be making people think we're husband and wife."

"Does it matter what Babette thinks?"

"Well, no..."

"It's just one night, right? She'll be gone tomorrow."

"Yeah."

"And unless somebody comes crashing through the front door, no one will ever know she was here. Is that right, too?"

"Uh...yeah. I guess."

"She's a hot one, Tony. I'd suggest you go for it." She eyed his unbuttoned shirt. "Looks like you already have a pretty good start."

"Uh...yeah. But you know, lately you and I..."

"Have been having a good time together. But to tell you the truth, Babette's doing me a favor. I need a day off."

He was stunned. "A day *off?*"

"Yeah. I need some sleep."

Tony was surprised at how much that hurt. She was talking about having sex with him as if it were a job, and a tedious one at that. Their relationship might not be forever, but he'd thought they meant more to each other than that.

Then he got angry. When he walked in here, he was perfectly willing to send Babette on her way, but if Heather needed a *day off,* that was exactly what she was going to get.

"I just don't want you to be mad at me later and tell me I didn't live up to our agreement," he said.

"I won't be mad."

"It wouldn't be fair if you were, you know."

"I know."

"Okay, then. As long as we're clear."

"We're clear."

With a curt nod, he turned around and left the room. As he walked back to the living room, though, he felt even more bewildered than before. He couldn't believe this didn't bother Heather at least a little bit.

Never mind. She said she doesn't care. Take her at her word and let Babette take you to heaven. If all he wanted was recreational sex, did it really matter where it came from?

Tony found Babette draped across the sofa. She'd slipped off her shoes and her jacket and had unbuttoned enough of her blouse that he could look down her cleavage and see past France all the way to China. She gave him a provocative smile and a crook of her finger.

"Come here, To*nee*."

He sat down beside her on the sofa. The moment he hit the cushion, she stood, hiked up her skirt, and straddled his thighs. She unfastened the rest of her buttons and spread the shirt open to reveal a lacy pink bra that barely harnessed her generous breasts. She leaned into him, slipping his shirt off his shoulders and kissing her way along his neck.

In a minute, they'd move into his bedroom, get naked, and Babette would share whatever treat she'd brought from Amsterdam, which was bound to be something fun.

And then tomorrow night, Heather would still be there. What more could a man want?

Ahh. Life was good.

He slid his hands beneath her skirt and stroked her thighs, letting his mind go blank, telling himself to stop thinking and start feeling. And he was one hundred percent successful at that for approximately ten seconds.

Then Heather popped back into his mind.

She was in her room right now, acting as if she didn't have a care in the world. And the more he thought about that, the more it pissed him off. After having sex approximately a gazillion times in the past few weeks, she could have at least had the decency to be a *little* jealous. But no. How could she just lie there nonchalantly, as if—

And then it hit him. He knew why she was acting that way. Why hadn't he seen it before?

She *was* jealous. She just didn't want him to know it.

Yes. That was it. She was jealous. So jealous, in fact, that to keep it from him, she had to go overboard the other way, acting as if he could have an orgy in the living room and she wouldn't bat an eyelash.

Babette jerked his shirt all the way off, tossed it aside, and went for his belt buckle. But amazingly, all Tony could think about was how terrible he felt for Heather.

He had to talk to her. Get this straightened out. Make sure she wasn't in there crying or something.

He grabbed Babette's hands and eased her off his lap. "Tell you what, sweetheart. Why don't you go to my bedroom, and I'll be there in just a minute?"

"What now?" she asked.

"Just go on in there," he said, giving her a quick kiss. "I won't be long."

She looked at him suspiciously. "You are not being *you*, To*nee*."

"I'll be back to my old self in just a minute. I promise. I just have to take care of something first."

She started toward his bedroom, tossing him a skeptical look over her shoulder. That was okay. Babette was easily distracted. With a single wink, he could bring her right back up to speed.

He went to Heather's door, knocked a little, then opened it. Strangely, she hadn't been crying.

She'd been sleeping.

She blinked wearily and rose on one elbow, that wild cascade of hair draped over her shoulder and grazing the bed. And when she turned those clear blue eyes up to meet his, for just a few seconds he had a hard time finding his voice.

"Look, Heather," he said gently. "I know why you're doing this."

"Doing what?"

"Acting as if this doesn't bother you that Babette is here and we're...well, you know."

"It doesn't bother me."

"Hey, it's all right. Really. If it bothers you this much, I can ask Babette to leave."

"Tony? Do I look bothered to you?"

"Yeah, that's what you say, but I know what you're thinking."

"Oh, yeah? What am I thinking?"

"You wish Babette would go away, but you're too afraid to say so. So you're just sitting in here, acting as if you're sleeping, trying to make me think you don't care."

Heather shook her head with amazement. "I swear you have the biggest ego of any man I've ever known."

"Come on, Heather. Just admit it. You're jealous."

"Okay," she deadpanned. "I'm jealous. Now, can I get back to sleep?"

"Hey, college girl," he snapped. "Don't you think I know reverse psychology when I hear it?"

Heather sighed. "Actually, Tony, the psychology is pretty straightforward. You want to have sex with Babette. I don't care if you do. So if I were you, I'd go out there and get after it." Heather's gaze floated south of his waist, and the edge of her mouth turned up in a tiny smile. "Part of you clearly wants to."

"I'm a man, Heather," he said sharply. "That's what happens when I have two women taunting me."

Heather laughed. "*Taunting* you?"

"Yes! Babette's out there making a run for the international bedhopping championship, and you're in here...in here..." He waved his hands. "*Sleeping!*"

Heather's brows drew together. "Okay. Let me see if I have this straight. You think I'm trying to seduce you because I'm in the next room *sleeping?*"

For the first time, Tony realized exactly how stupid that sounded. "Well, no. Of course not. I just...." He let out a breath of disgust. "Oh, never *mind!*"

"Better hurry back out there. Your date's getting cold."

"Sweetheart, Babette doesn't get cold. She stays at a toasty three thousand degrees all day long. And now I think I'll go back out there and get hot right along with her."

He jerked open the door and left the room, irritated

beyond words. He'd very nicely offered to pull the plug on his liaison with Babette if it made Heather uncomfortable, and how had she responded? By pointing out that he had a hard-on and sending him straight back into another woman's arms.

Now he was going back to Babette and burning up those sheets. Let Heather lie in there and think about *that*.

⁓

Heather lay on that crappy sofa bed, gritting her teeth so tightly she was surprised her molars didn't crack. She hated to admit the truth, but it was impossible not to. This was driving her straight up the wall.

She just wasn't used to having regular sex. That was the problem. It turned her mind to mush. The more she had it, the more she wanted it. And to think of Tony doing it with somebody else was just about more than she could tolerate. She'd been so proud of sounding flippant, as if she didn't care if he dragged Babette into his bedroom and took her flying without a plane. What a crock that had been.

He'd said he would tell her to leave. So why hadn't she taken him up on that?

Because she knew how Tony's mind worked. He wanted her to say she was jealous only because he had an undying need to know that every woman within the sound of his voice wanted him. Well, she wasn't about to give him the satisfaction. He'd be doing it with plenty of other women in a few weeks, so she might as well get used to it now.

Then she heard something in the other room. Voices.

Commotion of some kind. She turned her ear toward the door, trying to hear, but she couldn't make out what was going on.

Slowly she eased off the bed and tiptoed to her bedroom door, putting her ear against it, listening for sighs of delight. Screams of passion. Something.

Now she heard nothing.

Wait. She did hear something. The front door? What was going on?

She put her ear against the door and heard a sound in the hall. Footsteps?

She backed away, but not quickly enough. The door swung open and smacked her squarely on the side of the head.

"*Ow!*" she said, holding her head and glaring at Tony. "What are you *doing?*"

"A*ha!*" he said, pointing at her. "You were listening at the door!"

"I was not!"

"Yes, you were! That's pretty strange behavior for someone who doesn't care what's going on in the other room, now, isn't it?"

"I wasn't listening at the door! I was just..." Her voice faded away.

"Jealous?"

"Oh, will you get *over* yourself? *God.* I'm standing here with brain damage, and all you can think about is *you.*"

His gloating expression melted away. "Are you okay?"

"I'm fine," she snapped.

He walked over and pulled her hand away from the side of her head. "It's starting to swell. And turn purple."

"Great."

"Come with me."

Tony took her by the hand and led her from the bedroom and toward the kitchen. She looked around the empty apartment.

"Where's Babette?"

"Gone."

"Gone? Why?"

"She got a phone call and had to leave."

Tony opened the freezer and took out a sack of frozen peas. He wrapped a dishtowel around it, then sat Heather down at the kitchen table and pulled up a chair beside her. He lay one hand against her cheek as he pressed the bag to the other side of her head. She sucked in a breath, wincing at the pain.

"Do I need to take you to the doctor?" he asked.

"No. Of course not. I'll be fine." She took hold of the peas, and he leaned away.

"In case you're still wondering," Heather said, "I wasn't listening at the door when you came in. I was just…"

"What?"

She paused. "Picking something up off the carpet."

"What were you picking up off the carpet?"

"Carpet fuzz. You know how I hate carpet fuzz."

"I thought you were sleeping."

Heather frowned. "How was I supposed to sleep when you kept barging through the door and waking me up?"

"So after I woke you up, you just happened to look over and see some carpet fuzz on the floor."

"Yes."

"And you thought you'd get up and throw it away."

"Yes."

"Let me get this straight. You were lying in bed, nearly asleep, but you saw the carpet fuzz, and you felt compelled to—"

"Oh, all right! I was listening at the door!"

A smile crossed his lips. "Too bad you cracked, Heather. I was actually buying the carpet fuzz story."

"Oh, you were not," she snapped.

"You're right. I wasn't. But it was entertaining just the same."

"Okay, smart-ass. I have a question. Who called Babette?"

"I don't know."

"So she just got up, answered the phone, and left?"

"Something like that."

"After flying five thousand miles for sex?"

"She didn't fly five thousand miles for sex, Heather. She's a flight attendant."

"Okay, so she drove thirty miles from the airport for sex. Then she just got up and left with no explanation?"

"Babette's flighty. Pun intended."

"I didn't hear a ring tone."

"She had her phone on vibrate."

"When I came into the living room, Babette was wrapped around you like an octopus. By that time, the vibrating phone was more sex toy than communication device."

Tony sighed. "You're going to keep this up, aren't you?"

"Uh-huh."

"Babette didn't get a phone call. I asked her to leave."

"You shouldn't have cracked, Tony. I was buying the phone call thing."

"Right. So why were you listening at the door?"

She stared at him evenly. "Why did you ask Babette to leave?"

He looked at her. She looked at him. No answers from either of them.

Stalemate.

"Look," Tony said finally. "I didn't want to be with Babette, and you didn't want me to be with Babette. She's gone, so we both got what we wanted, right?"

"Right."

"As long as we're married, it's going to be just us together. Anything else is just too weird."

"You can say that again."

"I was heading in to take a nap when Babette showed up. Shall we take one together?"

"Sounds good to me."

Tony rose from the table, and Heather followed him to the bedroom. He kicked off his shoes, and they lay down on the bed. He put his arm around her and pulled her over to lie against his shoulder. She put the peas to her temple, and he held them there with his other hand.

Heather drew in a deep breath, then let it out in a satisfied sigh. After a moment, Tony turned and gently kissed the top of her head, then let out a sigh of his own.

It felt so good to lie here with him like this, with the afternoon sun angling through the blinds to infuse the room with a warm, hazy glow. With her ear pressed to Tony's chest, she could hear the steady beating of his heart, and after a moment, his slow, rhythmic breathing told her he'd fallen asleep.

Don't get too comfortable. This is not forever.

In her heart, she knew the only reason he'd sent Babette away was because he was something she'd never imagined him to be: a nice guy. One who didn't like to see people hurt. It was the reason he'd concocted this crazy plan in the first place, and it was the reason she was lying here with him now. Once they had their annulment, though, she knew he'd be coaxing Babette right back into his bed again, along with any other tall, slender, gorgeous women he could get his hands on.

Or maybe not.

For just a moment, she imagined that Tony actually liked this taste of married life, that he was thinking about the possibility of making things permanent, that sometime in the next few days he'd tell her he wanted to hold off on their annulment, just for a little while, just to see where things might lead....

No. That was just wishful thinking.

Tony was what he was, and spending a month as a monogamous man was never going to change that.

Chapter 21

After Heather got home from work the following Tuesday, she met Alison for a quick dinner, and then they went to Neiman Marcus at Northpark Mall so she could get a wedding present for Regina and Jason. On their way to the housewares department, Heather saw a display of scarves. She looked at a price tag. A hundred and twenty dollars.

Neiman Marcus. It wasn't nicknamed *Needless Markup* for nothing.

"I can't believe this is the only place Regina's registered," Alison said as they walked. "This is going to cost you a fortune. Why didn't she register someplace like Target so people who aren't made of money can actually get her something practical?"

"Because *practical* isn't *prestigious.*"

When they reached the housewares department, they got a printout of the items on Regina's registry and looked at it together.

"What's the cheapest thing on there?" Alison asked.

"Let's see ... oh, my God. Will you look at the price of this flatware? Forty dollars for a single place setting?"

"How about a toaster or something?"

Heather scanned the list. "Okay. I can get her one of those. As long as I don't mind spending two hundred and twenty dollars."

"For a freakin' *toaster?* You can buy them all over town for twenty-five bucks!"

"But it wouldn't be a *prestigious* toaster."

Finally Heather settled on a set of four Waterford wineglasses for a hundred and twenty dollars. She gritted her teeth and handed the clerk her credit card, and a few minutes later, she and Alison were walking back down the mall. They passed the Body Shop, and something caught Heather's eye.

"Hold on," she said, stopping in front of the window display. "Look at that."

Alison stopped and circled back, looking where Heather pointed. "Scented massage oil?"

Heather smiled. "That could be fun. Come on."

"You're buying massage oil?" Alison said as she followed Heather into the store. "What have you two been up to?"

"You wouldn't believe Tony's imagination," Heather said, laughing a little. "The things he comes up with sometimes just boggle my mind." She grabbed a tester bottle of one of the oils and dabbed some on the back of her hand. "Oooh, this one smells like sugar cookies." She held it out for Alison. "What do you think?"

"I think you've gone off the deep end."

"Will you just *smell* it?"

Alison did. "It's all right, I suppose, as long as you fantasize about sex in a bakery."

After sniffing several more, Heather settled on two of the scents: coconut and sea breeze. After all, who *hadn't* fantasized about sex on a South Seas island? She paid for them, and a minute later they were walking down the mall again.

"Heather?"

"Yeah?"

"How do you feel about Tony?"

"What do you mean?"

"I've never seen you like this. You get positively giddy every time you talk about him."

"So what? We're having a good time. I also get giddy at DisneyWorld."

Alison grabbed Heather's arm and pulled her over to a bench to sit down, nearly sideswiping a woman pushing a baby stroller.

"You know once you get that annulment," Alison said, "he'll be out of your life."

"I know."

"He'll be seeing other women. A lot of them."

She thought about Babette. "I know that, too."

"Heather? How do you feel about him? Really?"

Heather started to respond with her usual brush-off, but then all at once it hit her. *You're crazy about him. Absolutely over-the-top crazy.*

As the realization struck her, the strangest little tremor slid down her spine. When had that happened? When had she gone from being levelheaded and practical to being the kind of dopey, starry-eyed woman she'd always thought was silly? She hadn't doodled his name on a pad of paper at her desk at work yet, but as she thought about it now, it wasn't impossible to believe that she might.

She looked away. "It's just the sex. I'm going to miss it."

"Are you sure that's all it is?"

She started to say yes, only to realize what a lie that was.

It wasn't just in bed where she was crazy about Tony. It was in the kitchen when she was making breakfast and he sat there looking rumpled and sexy. At the bar when they were trying to keep up with a rush of customers, and they'd lock eyes across the room and she could tell what he needed her to do without him saying a word. At the tux shop when she told him one more time what an egomaniac he was, even as she knew the truth: Tony was probably the least self-centered man she'd ever met. It was the way he made her feel, as if he valued her brain outside of bed as much as he desired her body in it.

In the back of her mind, she'd started to wonder if maybe there was another reason Tony sent Babette away the other day. Maybe he really was starting to think about her as more than just a temporary wife.

No. She had to be realistic. Tony just didn't like conflict. He wanted everyone around him to be happy. He'd do anything to make that happen, including passing up spending the afternoon with a hot Frenchwoman. Still, she couldn't shake the hope she felt when she thought about him sending away that beautiful woman just so he could be with her.

"Maybe it's more," Heather admitted. "A little bit."

"Oh, God," Alison said. "Why didn't I see this coming? Why did I push you into sleeping with him?"

"Oh, will you lighten up? You act as if the moment we break up, I'm going to take a handful of sleeping pills."

Alison tilted her head and looked at Heather sadly.

"No. It won't be that drastic. But you are going to cry, aren't you?"

Heather stared at Alison, suddenly feeling a little shaky. "I knew what I was getting involved in. I also knew who I was getting involved *with*. I have no delusions where Tony is concerned."

"Yeah, that's all very logical. But it won't make it hurt any less, will it?"

Heather stood up suddenly, grabbing her purse and the bag. "You're making too big a deal out of this. Once we have the annulment, we're calling it quits. And my life will go on."

"So the rehearsal dinner is Thursday night?" Alison said. "And then the wedding's on Sunday?"

"Yeah."

"You'll be splitting up soon after that."

"Yeah."

"What are you going to tell everyone?"

"It won't be as big a deal as you think. I'll just smile and say, 'Things didn't work out. In the end, we were just too different, but it was sure fun while it lasted.' If I'm not upset, nobody else will be, either."

"I guess the key to that is not being upset, huh?"

"Exactly."

But never in her wildest dreams could Heather have imagined just how difficult a task that was likely to be.

~

Before Heather knew it, Thursday had arrived, and she and Tony were heading to United Methodist Church of Plano for the wedding rehearsal. He'd put on slacks and a sport coat for the occasion, and she was reminded once again that no matter what he wore, or didn't wear, he was so handsome he practically glowed.

"Explain to me why they rehearse weddings?" Tony said. "You walk up the aisle, you repeat after the minister, you exchange rings, and you walk back down again."

"Oh, no. There are a lot of other things you can throw in. Like lighting a unity candle. Or having special music. Or reciting vows you write yourself."

"So how many of those things is Regina opting for?"

"Knowing Regina, all of them."

"Sorry. I can't see Jason writing his own vows."

"Of course not. Regina would write them and make him memorize them." Heather thought about it. "On second thought, Aunt Bev would write the vows for both of them."

They pulled into the parking lot a little before seven. When they went into the church, Heather saw that almost everyone had arrived.

Everyone but the groom.

Fifteen minutes after the rehearsal was supposed to start, Jason still hadn't arrived. Regina made breezy excuses for his absence, implying that he was such an important man with such important things to do that it was only natural that he might be delayed. But Heather didn't miss the way Regina's eyes kept flitting nervously to the door.

"She's making excuses for him again," Heather whispered to Tony.

"Why doesn't she just dump the bastard?" Tony whispered. "I'm not real crazy about Regina, but watching Bev, at least I can understand why Regina's the way she is. Jason's parents seem perfectly normal, so what's his excuse?"

When Jason finally came through the door, holstering his BlackBerry, Regina's relief was almost palpable. As the minister started the rehearsal, the bridesmaids were still chattering incessantly. Getting them to focus was like trying to get a litter of kittens to focus. Finally Regina's snooty wedding planner got them paired up with their respective groomsmen, and everybody took their turn going up the aisle, with Tony and Heather bringing up the rear. They went through the *blah-blah-blah* of the ceremony, and when Bev intervened to make sure Jason knew precisely how to lift Regina's veil when the time came, Heather glanced across at Tony. He gave her a subtle eye roll, followed by a smile.

Heather smiled back, thinking this wasn't the first time in the past few weeks she and Tony had shared a moment of silent agreement. As the days had passed, she found more and more that she was going to miss about him, and sometimes the sex was the least of it. And standing here in this church now, a bridesmaid once more, she wondered what the chances were that she'd find another man with whom she was as comfortable as she was with Tony, who also might actually want to settle down and become a married man.

She didn't even want to think about those odds.

When the rehearsal for the ceremony was over, they went back down the aisle again, and a not-so-subtle disagreement erupted between Aunt Bev and the wedding planner over the placement of the flowers. Uncle Gene tried to referee, but as usual, Aunt Bev gave him her sharp tongue and evil eye. He went over to a pew and sat down, undoubtedly thinking about how he was spending thirty thousand dollars to get bitched at when the majority of the time it happened for free.

Finally everyone left the church and headed to Forest Glen Golf and Country Club for the rehearsal dinner. Tony drove up the tree-lined lane to the clubhouse, a neo-Colonial brick mansion with white pillars and a fountain out front. Beyond the clubhouse were the rolling hills of the golf course, lit warmly by the setting sun.

When they reached the front door, they got out of the car, and Tony handed his keys to the valet. They went inside and started toward the double doors leading to the banquet room.

"You go ahead," Heather said to Tony. "I need to visit the ladies' room."

He nodded and continued on. Heather turned toward the hall leading to the restrooms, only to hear voices coming from that direction. Angry voices. She stopped just around the corner and listened.

"No. Turn it off now."

"Regina—"

"I said turn it *off!*"

Heather heard an angry huff, then the sound of an electronic device powering down.

"Now give it to me."

"No. I'm not going to—"

"I refuse to sit through dinner with your phone constantly ringing. It's *embarrassing!*"

"Christ, Regina! Do you have to be such a bitch about it?"

"You were late to the rehearsal, so don't you tell me *I'm* being a bitch about *anything.*"

"Fine," Jason snapped. "Take it."

Several seconds of silence. Then a shaky sigh.

"I'm sorry, Jason," Regina said, sounding contrite. "I don't want to fight with you. It's just that this is our *wedding,* you know?"

"I know. And I wish the whole damned thing were over with."

Heather heard footsteps, and she backed against the wall as Jason emerged from the hall and strode toward the banquet room. He never saw her because he never looked back.

Heather waited several seconds, and when Regina didn't emerge, she walked down the hall and opened the bathroom door. Regina was sitting on the sofa in the lounge area, her head bowed and a tissue pressed to her mouth. When she saw Heather, she immediately sat up straight and dabbed at her eyes.

"Allergies," she said. "Ragweed is terrible in north Texas, isn't it?"

"Are you all right?"

She sniffed. "Of course I am. Why wouldn't I be?"

Heather sat down next to her on the sofa. "You've been crying."

"You know how brides are. All those emotions. Anything sets them off."

"It's Jason, isn't it?"

"What do you mean?"

"I heard you arguing."

Regina started to deny it. Then, as if she recognized the futility of that, she feigned a laugh. "What couple doesn't argue?"

"Two days before their wedding?"

Regina's jaw tightened resolutely. "We both just have a lot on our minds."

"What's on his mind?"

"Work. He's so busy, you know. This is a bad time for him to be taking off, so he's a little uptight."

"He needs to forget work," Heather said. "This is his *wedding*."

Regina tried to hold it together, but a moment later, her face crumpled, and she couldn't stop the tears.

"This isn't the way it's supposed to be," Heather said gently.

"Right," Regina said through her tears. "I suppose you think you're an expert on marriage now that you're married."

"No, I don't. Believe me, I don't. I just think if you marry Jason..."

Regina sniffed, then turned to Heather. "What?"

"It's just not the right thing to do."

"It *is* the right thing to do! He's perfect for me! Everybody says so. All the other girls are telling me how dreamy he is and what a catch he is and..."

"You need to stop hanging out with those girls."

"They're my friends."

"They're morons."

Regina didn't respond, which meant she probably didn't completely disagree with that assessment.

"It's not too late to call off the wedding," Heather said.

Regina whipped around. "Call it off? I can't do that!"

"Why not?"

"Are you kidding me? My mother would freak out!"

"But it's not your mother's life. It's your life."

"No," she said, sitting up straight. "It's going to be okay. We just had a little argument. That's all. Once we're married and things settle down, everything will be okay."

She got up, went to the mirror, and repaired her makeup. Then she started for the door.

"Regina?"

She turned back.

"Will you just think about it? Please?"

"There's no thinking to be done," Regina said, sniffing a little, then taking a deep, shaky breath. "I'm marrying Jason, and that's that."

She turned and left the bathroom. A few minutes later, Heather headed back to the banquet room. The brides-maids were chattering away, which really grated on her nerves. Regina was smiling, but it was fake. Not the fake smile she usually wore while trying to put people down, but the kind of fake smile that hid a wounded heart.

Aunt Bev was oblivious to all of it. Her face was filled with excitement and triumph. This was what she'd always wanted. Her beautiful daughter marrying a beautiful man so they could produce beautiful children and she'd have a purse full of photos to show the other ladies at the club. *I did it*, those photos would say. *I raised the perfect daughter. And here's pictorial proof.*

Regina had moved over to take Jason's hand, smiling sweetly at the people he was talking to. Jason looked as if he'd rather be holding his BlackBerry.

Tony came up beside her. "You were in there a while. Everything okay?"

"I overheard Regina arguing with Jason, and then she went into the ladies' room. When I went in there, I found her crying."

"Oh, boy."

"If she marries Jason, her life is going to be hell."

"Did you tell her that?"

"More or less. She was horrified. She said she couldn't back out of the wedding because her mother would be upset."

"She's afraid of her mother? That's the only reason she's not calling things off?"

"Yeah. She didn't tell me she loved Jason and wanted to marry him. She said her mother would be upset if she cancelled the wedding. But she still insisted it was just a little tiff and things were going to be fine."

"Maybe they will be."

"Yeah. Maybe."

"You're sure worrying a lot about a cousin you don't even like."

"To tell you the truth, if I had Aunt Bev for a mother, I'd probably be just like Regina." She sighed. "I know she's been rotten to me, but in the end, she's family, you know? I just don't want to see her get hurt."

Heather could only hope that sometime between now and this Sunday, Regina would finally see the light and call off the wedding. If she didn't, she was going to be miserable for the rest of her life.

The next evening, Heather arrived at McMillan's just as Tony was pouring a very inebriated customer into a cab. He gave the cabdriver an address along with twenty bucks, and the guy nodded and took off.

"What was all that about?" Heather asked as they walked back inside.

"The guy's girlfriend dumped him this afternoon. Lisa didn't know he'd already been drinking when he showed up, so she didn't cut him off quite fast enough."

"The challenges of running a bar."

"Yeah. I'm just lucky the guy didn't barf all over the place. The cabdriver might not be so lucky."

"Yeah, I guess that would put a real damper on Friday happy hour, wouldn't it?" They went inside and Heather's eyes widened. "Wow. Good crowd."

"I know," Tony said with a smile. "Isn't it great?"

"Twenty-four hours and counting. Are we going to be ready for the grand opening?"

"Everything's under control. Chuck wants to talk to you about the buffet. And Lisa came up with a few specialty drinks I want you to try. But besides setting up the room tomorrow afternoon, I think we're good to go."

As Heather went to talk to Chuck, Tony thought about how much work she'd done to get them to this point. Not only had she designed and mailed the invitations, but she'd also run ads in the newspaper, arranged for the new sign, and had flyers distributed to the surrounding neighborhoods. She'd also spoken to two food and entertainment reporters she'd sent invitations to who said they were definitely going to be there. People Tony hadn't heard from in ages had received their invitations and called to say they were coming. And tomorrow night, McMillan's would officially become McCaffrey's.

He couldn't wait.

But the best thing Heather had done for him was to repeatedly tell him what a big success he was going to be.

As big a dream as this was for him, a small part of him had always doubted that he'd be able to pull it off, but Heather had made him believe he could actually do it.

Kayla had taken a call earlier in the day saying that a party of twelve was coming in at seven, so he and Heather pulled tables together. At five till seven, they'd just gotten the silverware and menus on the table when Erika hurried up to them.

"Chuck has a problem in the kitchen," she said. "I think you and Heather better get in there."

"What's wrong?"

"Just go look."

They hurried into the kitchen. As soon as they walked through the door, Tony barely stopped in time to keep from traipsing through a sea of water on the floor, and more was creeping toward them.

So much for everything running smoothly.

"I hit the water shutoff valve," Chuck said. "It was pouring out pretty good."

"Okay. We need to get this mess cleaned up so we can get the food out. Chuck, grab a mop. Heather, can you get on the phone and call a plumber?"

"I'm on it," she said, reaching for the wall phone.

Tony could see the mop wasn't going to do the job fast enough, so he grabbed paper towels to help sop up the mess.

Erika came through the door. "Anything I can do?"

"The water's going to be shut off for a while," Tony told her. "That means the toilets will flush only once. If we don't get this problem fixed quickly, I want you to stick out-of-order signs on the doors."

"Okay. I'll take care of it."

"And be sure to tell Lisa why her water isn't working at the bar. It won't be long before she runs out of clean glasses. I'll send somebody to the grocery store down the street to get some plastic ones if we need more."

As Erika left the kitchen, Tony looked at the stack of plates beside the grill. "Chuck? Are there enough clean plates for this shift?"

"Should be."

"I think we have plenty of silverware wrapped. Heather?"

She turned around, the phone pressed to her ear. "I've got a plumber on the line. He says he can be out in twenty minutes."

"Okay." Tony took a deep breath. "I think we're under control."

Kayla stuck her head back in the door. "That big party just showed up," she said. "Can you and Heather come out here for a minute?"

"What?"

"They asked to speak to both of you."

"What do they want?"

"They didn't say."

"You go," Chuck said. "I'll clean up the rest."

Tony looked at Heather. She shrugged. Kayla pushed the door open, and they followed her out of the kitchen. The big table they'd set up was full of people. Bunches of balloons were tied to two of the chairs, and there was a pile of presents on a nearby table. And the moment they caught sight of Tony and Heather, they shouted in unison.

"Surprise!"

Cameras started flashing. People clapping. What the hell was going on?

Then Tony realized he recognized a couple of the people. Fred and Barbara. And there was Regina. And wasn't that Bev? And about a gazillion other relatives of Heather's?

"Oh, my God," Heather said under her breath. "A surprise wedding shower?"

Chapter 22

Heather couldn't believe this. Tony had been freaked out over the idea of her parents bringing one gift to McMillan's for them to open, and now they had a dozen?

Her mother fluttered over with a big smile and hugs for both of them.

"Mom?" Heather said. "What is all this?"

"All newlyweds need a wedding shower, right? And the rest of the family hadn't seen McMillan's, so I thought this was the perfect place to hold it. I called here a few days ago, and Kayla was so nice to help us surprise you!"

Tony looked at Kayla. "So I take it there's no plumbing crisis?"

"Why, Tony," she said with a smile. "You sound disappointed."

Kayla didn't know just how right she was. If it was between suffering through a wedding shower with her family and taking care of a plumbing crisis, Tony would pick the plumbing crisis every time.

"I'll cancel the plumber," Kayla said to Heather. "Which one did you call?"

"I wrote his name on a pad by the phone."

Kayla waved her hands toward the table. "You and Tony sit down. We'll finish cleaning up the kitchen."

"This is Friday," Tony said. "Things are going to be busy. If something comes up—"

"You made me your assistant manager," Kayla said with a smile. "Let me do my job. I'll make sure everything's under control. You guys just sit here and have a good time."

As Kayla walked away, Heather whispered to Tony, "I'm so, *so* sorry about this."

"It's okay," he said, but Heather knew he was saying that only because they were trapped. It was all he *could* say.

They sat down in the balloon-decorated chairs, and Heather reintroduced him to her family members around the table. He'd met all of them that first afternoon at her parents' house, but everything had been so chaotic that she knew their names had gone in one ear and out the other. Tony did a good job of smiling and being congenial, and she decided that tonight when they got home, she'd have to go out of her way to thank him for that.

Erika came up to take their order, and Barbara asked for four appetizers for everyone to share, telling Erika they'd order dinner in a little while. Erika nodded, then went from person to person, asking for their drink orders.

Drinks? Appetizers? *Then* dinner? Heather cringed. They intended to stay all night, which meant she and Tony had to stay with them. He wasn't going to be happy about that.

"Regina's here," Tony whispered. "Where's Jason?"

"Probably off somewhere being important," Heather

whispered back. "He tries his best not to show up to any family stuff."

"Maybe she'll get lucky and he'll miss his own wedding."

The rest of the family, though, was in a party mood, smiling, laughing, and tapping their fingers along with the music. Heather was used to her family, but seeing them through Tony's eyes made her realize just how rowdy they could be.

"I really am sorry about this," Heather whispered to him. "I had no idea."

"I told you it's okay. Really. I'm happy to get the business."

After they had drinks and dinner, they opened their gifts, and Heather winced when she thought about how all of it would have to be returned in a few weeks. They got a blender from Aunt Sylvia and Uncle Burt, bath towels from Grandma Roberta, and a set of flatware from Heather's cousin Cynthia. Uncle Bev and Aunt Gene gave them some sort of overly elegant candlesticks that would look just stunning on Tony's mantel, beside the portrait of Grandma Frances. And Regina... good Lord. Did anybody really need a silver-plated candle snuffer?

Once all the gifts had been stacked aside, Erika brought out a big sheet cake that Kayla had picked up from Heather's mother earlier in the day. As everyone was finishing off a piece, her father turned to Tony.

"Pool table's open. How about a game?"

Tony paused, looking a little surprised. "Uh...yeah. Sure."

As they got up from the table, Heather shot Tony yet one more subtle look of apology. He gave her a quick wink to let her know it was okay, but he wasn't smiling. Putting up with her family was something he'd never expected to have to do. Then again, Tony liked to play pool, so what could one little game hurt?

⁓

Fred was one of those men who always seemed to be thinking far more than he was saying, so Tony felt a little wary as they walked to the pool table. He racked the balls, and each of them reached for a cue.

"Eight ball?" Tony said.

Fred nodded

"Your break.

Fred set the cue ball on the table and lined up his shot. "So. Tony. How's it going?"

"Good. You?"

"Can't complain." Fred broke, smacking the seven ball into a side pocket, then surveyed the table for the next striped ball he could drop. "How's business?"

"Coming along."

"Gonna be a moneymaker?"

"Hope so."

"Good. That's good."

Fred knocked the ten ball into the corner pocket, then the thirteen and the nine in quick succession. Tony wondered if he was going to play the rest of the game in silence.

Then all at once, he spoke again. "Heather surprised me that night, you know. Calling home at eleven at night, telling us she got married."

Tony's brain went on red alert. "Yeah. I imagine that was kind of a shock."

"I asked myself, Now, why did my smart, levelheaded daughter go and do something like that? Then I thought about how Heather's never made a decision in her life without thinking it through, so I had to trust that she knew what she was doing."

"Yes. Heather does know her own mind, doesn't she?"

Fred circled the table, looking for his next shot. "Yeah. She does. That's why I didn't spend too much time wondering about her motives." He paused. "But I sure as hell wondered about yours."

Tony felt a spark of anger. "What exactly did you wonder about, Fred?"

"Lots of things. Did you need a temporary wife for some reason? Did you need some help running this place? Did you con her out of money?"

"You think I'm *conning* Heather?"

"Didn't say that. I only said the thought crossed my mind." He pulled back his cue, then sank the eleven ball in a side pocket. "You're a guy who's clearly been around the block a time or two. Heather, not so much. Leaves me wondering what the story is."

"I would never—"

Fred raised his palm. "I'm just telling you that in the beginning, I thought something was up. You would have, too, if you'd been me."

Tony had to admit that was true. Who wouldn't think something was weird when two people got married after knowing each other only a few hours?

"Barbara and I have been going around and around

about this for the past couple of weeks. She tells me I'm being paranoid, that you're a perfectly nice guy. But she hasn't seen what I've seen. I was a cop for thirty years, so I know what people are capable of. That's why I ran a background check on you."

Tony couldn't believe this. "A background check?"

"Yep. Your employment history is a little spotty, but your credit's good. No outstanding warrants. Two speeding tickets, but they were over five years ago. You're pretty clean."

Hell, yes, I am, you son of a bitch.

"One thing I didn't understand, though."

He lined up his next shot. "You told us your father lives in Fort Lauderdale. He's never lived in Fort Lauderdale. He does, however, live in Plano."

Tony paused. "That's right."

"You got any reason to lie about that, Tony?"

"My family is no concern of yours."

"Your father appears to be respectable enough, so you're not lying to cover up a shady past. I'm guessing it's something between the two of you."

"That's none of your business."

Fred nodded. "Fair enough. As long as it doesn't affect Heather, I don't give a damn." He smacked the cue ball, sending it hard into the twelve ball, which dropped into the corner pocket. "In the end, I couldn't come up with a solid reason to be suspicious, and since Heather seems to be happy, I decided to give you the benefit of the doubt." Fred leaned over for his final shot—one a five-year-old kid could make. He knocked in the eight ball, then rose and leaned on his cue, fixing his gaze on Tony's. "But I'm giving you fair warning. If I ever find out that you've done anything to hurt my daughter, you're going to be answering to me. Do you understand?"

Tony couldn't believe this. "I'd never do *anything* to hurt Heather," he said hotly.

"Then there's no problem, is there? You and I are going to get along just fine."

But judging from the skepticism on Fred's face, he clearly didn't hold out a whole lot of hope for that. He eased away from the pool table, returned his cue to the rack, and sat back down at the table with the rest of the family.

Benefit of the doubt, my ass.

Barely keeping his anger in check, Tony walked back to the table, reaching it about the time everybody started checking their watches and standing up to leave. He kept his expression as pleasant as he could, enduring all of Heather's huggy relatives, all the while feeling Fred's gaze boring into him.

He and Heather waved good-bye to everyone, and the moment the door closed behind them, he turned and walked into his office. A few moments later, Heather appeared at the door.

"Okay," she said. "What did my father say to you?"

Damn. Did she have to be so *observant?* "Nothing. We played pool."

"I hope you don't ever try your hand at cards. You have a lousy poker face."

He bowed his head with a sigh of irritation. He didn't want to deal with this. He just didn't.

"Look, Tony. I know my father can sound very gruff, and it might seem as if he doesn't like you, but—"

Tony snapped his head around. "*Seem* as if he doesn't like me?"

"I don't know what he said, but whatever it is, I think you're reading too much into it."

"Okay, Heather," Tony said. "He told me that if I do anything to hurt you, I'm going to be answering to him. How many different ways are there to read that?"

Heather's mouth dropped open. "He threatened you?"

"I spent my whole life being browbeaten by my father. I don't need to be browbeaten by yours."

"My father was a cop. He's just suspicious, you know? He'll get over it."

"I won't be around long enough for him to get over it."

Heather nodded with resignation. "You're ready for those annulment papers, aren't you?"

"What?"

"Marriage isn't your thing, and this is getting to be a little too much like a real one."

She was right.

All at once, Tony felt smothered. As if he couldn't breathe. All he wanted was to go back to the way his life was before—mindless and feel-good, with nobody making demands of him and nobody threatening him if he didn't behave the way they thought he should.

He just wanted his old life back.

He put his elbows on his desk and rubbed his temples, then let out a heavy sigh. "Just go home, okay? I can handle things here."

"I know you can. You proved that tonight."

"What?"

"I meant to tell you earlier. You did a good job managing that crisis."

"The water leak? Come on, Heather. That wasn't really a crisis."

"Yeah, but you didn't know that. You did all the right things." She gave him a small, bittersweet smile. "After the grand opening tomorrow night, you'll be ready to handle everything by yourself. And that means you're not going to need me anymore."

With that, she turned around and left his office, closing the door behind her.

Tony sat there in silence, telling himself it was a good thing. He was more self-sufficient now. Things weren't going to fall apart. But he just couldn't imagine what it was going to be like when she was gone.

He muddled through the rest of the evening, trying to forget about the mess he'd created when he'd hatched this crazy plan with Heather. But later, in the quiet of his car on the way home, Fred's words were still bouncing around inside his head. And when Tony came through his apartment door, the first thing he saw was the stack of gifts beside the fireplace.

Damn. What a mess.

He glanced over the fireplace at Granny Franny, who would be leaving when Heather did. Oddly enough, he was actually going to miss that ugly portrait. Then he thought about Heather in the other room, and he realized that McMillan's wasn't the only place he needed to stop depending on her.

Things had just gotten too complicated, particularly after what had happened tonight. It was time to begin the process of mentally pulling back. That way, by the time those annulment papers came, he could shake her hand, kiss her good-bye, and get on with the life he'd been living before without so much as a twinge of regret.

Heather lay awake in Tony's bedroom, wishing her father hadn't said what he had, because everything changed after that. She knew why he'd done it, but she also knew that Tony didn't deserve a word of it. He'd never been anything but good to her, and it upset her to have her father think badly of him. But Tony was right. He wouldn't be around long enough for her father to see just how wrong he was.

Finally she heard Tony coming down the hall. He pushed the door open and came into the bedroom.

She rose a little and propped the pillow behind her head. "Hey," she said sleepily.

He looked surprised to see her awake. "Hey."

"How did the rest of the night go?"

Tony started to take off his clothes. "It was fine."

"Good. That's good."

A few moments later, he tossed his clothes aside and climbed into bed. He just lay there, staring at the ceiling, his arm draped across his forehead. When several minutes passed and he didn't reach for her, Heather felt a rush of disappointment. He was probably feeling hemmed in, counting the days until he could go back to playing the field. She thought about the hope she'd had that maybe their relationship meant something more to him. Obviously that wasn't the case. Clearly the good times they'd had together were wearing thin for him, and what had happened tonight had only made things worse.

"Tony?"

"Yeah?"

"I just wanted to say how sorry I am about what my father said to you."

"You don't have to apologize. You didn't do anything."

"I know. But you've done nothing these past weeks but try to keep me from being hurt, and now my father's making you out to be the bad guy."

"He's pretty damned good at it, too. For a minute there, I could have sworn I was listening to my own father. It was a real nostalgic moment."

Heather hated the bitterness she heard in his voice. "You said your father was tough to live with. But you never told me much about your mother."

"That's because I don't remember much."

"Did they fight a lot?"

"Yeah."

"What about?"

He paused. "Mostly about me."

"You? Why?"

"My father thought my mother was too soft on me, and he was always trying to counteract that. I was just a little kid, but he thought I ought to act like a man, anyway."

That single statement gave Heather a picture of exactly what Tony's childhood must have been like. He'd had a loving mother who understood her child perfectly, a demanding father who didn't, and there had been a whole lot of discord in between.

"A lot of fathers are at least a little bit like that with their sons, aren't they?" she asked.

"It wasn't just a little bit," Tony said quietly.

There was a long silence, and for a moment, Heather thought he wasn't going to say anything else. When he finally did speak again, his bitterness had only escalated.

"He was such a bastard," Tony said, his voice little more than a whisper in the dark. "Once when I was five or six, he overheard my mother and me reading a book together. *Peter Pan.* My mother used to do Wendy's and Tinkerbell's voices, and I did Peter's. My father came into the room and told my mother that no son of his would act like a flying fairy. They had a horrible fight, and the book ended up in the trash."

"But it was just *Peter Pan,*" Heather said. "All little kids should be able to read books like that."

"Not according to my father. But I loved that book so much that my mother bought another copy and hid it in her dresser drawer. She brought it out only when he wasn't there. I can still hear her whispering, 'Just don't tell your father.' "

Tony had told her how difficult his relationship with his father had been, but Heather had thought it was pretty much confined to his teenage years. She hadn't realized how torn apart his whole childhood had been. He'd spent it in two different worlds—his mother's filled with dreams and laughter, and his father's filled with rules and recriminations.

Now she knew. She knew just how deeply Tony's resentment ran. This wasn't just leftover discord between a man and his teenage son. This had roots in something older and much more hurtful.

"Your mother died when you were ten," Heather said. "What was it like with your father then?"

"He was transferred all the time. And he wasn't home much. I guess that was a good thing."

"So you were alone a lot?"

"Oh, no. I had company. The domestic staff was usually pretty friendly, assuming they spoke English."

Heather could only imagine how lonely he must have felt in a foreign place with no family around him at all.

"One Christmas Eve," Tony said, "my father was at some embassy dinner or something. I was home alone. I remember surfing around on the TV and landing on *It's a Wonderful Life*. About the only other things on were a *Seinfeld* rerun I'd seen half a dozen times and Catholic Mass, so I watched it."

In the dim moonlight streaming in through the window, Heather could see the curve of his throat, the silhouette of his eyelashes. He blinked quickly a few times, then swallowed hard.

"I felt like that guy."

"That guy?"

"In the movie."

"George Bailey?"

"Yeah. Everywhere I turned, it seemed as if my life was going to hell. My mother was dead. My father wasn't there very much, and when he was, he rode my ass constantly. I had no place to call home. Every house we lived in after my mother died seemed ice-cold to me. My father hired a whole army of domestic help and made sure whatever house we lived in was spit-polished from the floor to the ceiling. Our houses smelled like disinfectant all the time. I couldn't so much as put a damned poster on the wall of my bedroom without catching hell for it."

Oh, God. And what had she done? Cleaned his apartment within an inch of its life. Chastised him for anything that was out of place. She wanted to leap up right then and scramble things in the pantry or throw dirt back on the kitchen floor.

"My father had always been unreasonable," Tony went on. "When my mother was alive, she ran interference. When she was gone, I bore the whole brunt of it. We moved all the time, so I had no real friends. Yeah, I always had the guys laughing or the girls chasing me, but not one of them ever knew what I was really thinking."

Tony's voice was barely more than a whisper in the dark, an eerie reflection of something inside him that he never allowed to see the light of day. If only he'd had a loving family to fall back on, all the upheaval would have been okay. But he hadn't.

"As I sat there in front of that movie that night," he went on, "I didn't think there was anybody who would know or care if I lived or died. When George Bailey said he wished he'd never been born, I remember thinking, 'I hear you, George. I wish I'd never been born, too.' I missed my mother. Most of the time, I could put it out of my mind. But on that Christmas Eve, when I was all alone..."

"What?"

"I cried. I was a sixteen-year-old boy, and they sure as hell don't cry. Not when they have Don McCaffrey for a father. But that night I swear I cried myself to sleep."

And as she pictured that lost, lonely boy, Heather wanted to cry herself. "But the movie had a happy ending. George realized just how many friends he had."

"I don't have any friends."

"Tony, you have more friends than anyone I've ever known. I saw your address book. And how about all the people at the bar? Andy and Kyle?"

"Friends? Those are people I drink with. Play pool with. They're not friends. I could fill a thousand-page book with the things they don't know about me."

"What about me?" she asked.

"What?"

"I'm your friend."

"Maybe for now, but we'll be splitting up soon."

"That doesn't mean we can't still be friends."

"It won't work that way. You'll go back to your life, and I'll go back to what I was doing before we met."

"Playing the field?"

"You should always stick with what you're best at."

"Someday that'll change. You'll decide you want a wife and family."

"Heather, I know it's been good between us for a few weeks now. But we've just been playing house. No pressure, no long-term commitment. You know where I come from. I couldn't hold up my end of a real marriage if my life depended on it."

A real marriage.

In that moment, Heather realized just how real their fake marriage had become to her. But Tony was right. This wasn't real, and he'd never led her to believe for one moment that he wanted it to be.

"So I guess we'll be saying good-bye soon," Heather said.

"Yeah, I guess so. But I'm pretty good at it. I've spent half my life saying good-bye."

Watching Tony from afar, he seemed like a congenial, accessible, friendly man, with a good word and a back-slap for everyone. She'd never had any idea how many walls he'd put up around himself and why he kept his relationships with everyone, including women, at arm's length. She'd thought his friendliness and outgoing nature were gifts. He might use them to his advantage, but they weren't gifts. They were symptoms. Symptoms of something deep inside him so raw and painful he refused to touch it. In so many ways, he was still that scared kid who thought the only way to protect himself was to wrap up his feelings into a tight little knot and never let anyone inside.

Tony rolled to his side and looked at her. "Heather?"

"Yeah?"

"There's no way I can ever repay you for what you've done for me."

The sound of his voice—so heartfelt and sincere—sent shivers down Heather's spine.

"It was no big deal," she said.

"No. It was a very big deal. I wouldn't have been able to buy the bar if not for you."

"Now, Tony," she said. "What kind of wife would I be if I didn't support my husband one hundred percent?"

She expected him to laugh a little and say something flippant, but he didn't. Instead he looked at her intently.

"When we break up, I want you to tell everyone it was your decision. That you're divorcing me."

"But why? We can tell them it was mutual."

"No. I don't want anyone thinking I was the one who didn't want to be married to you. Do you understand? I don't care what you tell them, as long as you make me out to be the bad guy. Your father already thinks that. It won't be a tough sell."

"No. I'm not going to let them think badly of you."

"It doesn't matter, Heather. I'll never see them again. You'll see them for the rest of your life."

She smiled. "How about I tell them you wore me out in bed? That I'm leaving you for my own self-preservation?"

She waited for his snappy comeback. It never came.

"Promise me," he said.

She nodded. "Okay."

"Thank you," he murmured. "For everything."

"I should thank you, too."

"What for?"

"For keeping your promise. You told me that if I showed you how to make your business a success, you'd show me how to have more fun than I've ever had in my life." She smiled softly. "That's exactly what you've done."

He reached up to stroke his thumb along her cheek, staring at her intently. Up to now, he'd been a wonderful lover, making sex more fun than she'd ever imagined. But now there was something else in his eyes.

"I shouldn't do this," he murmured so softly she could barely hear him. "It'll only make things harder."

He pulled her into his arms and kissed her, and this time when they made love, there was no laughter between them. Not even a smile. Instead, he made love to her with an aching kind of tenderness that went straight to her heart.

After tonight, she knew why he thought this would only make things harder. When the day finally came for them to part, Tony needed desperately not to care. And it was the first time Heather realized just how much he did.

Heather had long since fallen asleep, but Tony lay awake, thinking about how their time together was almost over. The grand opening was tomorrow night, Regina's wedding the day after that. They'd let a little bit of time pass, and then they'd tell the world that no matter how compatible they seemed to be, they had irreconcilable differences and they were splitting up.

And that would be that.

He wondered how far Heather's father would go in thinking he was guilty of something sinister just because they were getting a divorce. The kind of condemnation Fred had heaped on him tonight had reminded him so much of his father that it had made the tiny hairs on Tony's arms stand up. They were so much alike.

And, oddly enough, Barbara was a lot like his mother.

In his memory, his mother was little more than soft eyes, warm brown hair, and a whiff of perfume, and with every year that passed, it grew harder and harder to bring an image of her to mind. He wasn't sure how much he'd idealized her in his memory, but even now, almost twenty years later, sometimes he missed her so much it hurt.

Pushing back the covers, he rose quietly and went to his spare bedroom. He flipped on a lamp, opened one of the bottom dresser drawers, and pulled out an old brown shoebox. He sat down on the sofa and opened it, taking out a small stack of photographs that were tattered and discolored with age.

The first one showed his mother in her early twenties. She wore a yellow halter dress and sandals, her shiny dark hair falling over one shoulder. She was sitting on a porch step, and she was laughing. His father had taken this picture when they were dating, and whenever Tony looked at it, he always found himself wondering when the laughter had stopped.

He flipped through the others. One was a wedding photo of his parents, his father in his Navy dress uniform and his mother in a lacy white gown. There were several of Tony and his mother together when he was a toddler, then a grade-schooler. In one of the photos, his mother looked thin and gaunt, and he knew that one must have been taken near the end.

He put the photos back and picked up a small book from the box—a storybook version of *Peter Pan*. Even now, he could still recite almost every word of it. He would never forget the sound of his mother's voice when she read to him and the lively, sunshiny expression she always wore whenever his father wasn't around. But the moment she heard the doorknob rattle, her laughter would die and her face would lock down, as if she was pulling shutters closed against an impending storm. After her funeral, Tony remembered lying awake in bed, staring at the ceiling, imprinting the sound of her voice on his brain so he'd never forget. Photographs helped him remember what she looked like, but the love and affection in a voice was something an image could never convey.

Then he saw the small black box. He almost picked it up, then reconsidered. It had been a long time since he'd looked at its contents, and it would probably be a long time until he did again. He wanted to remember the days she lived, not the day she died.

All the way up to her final moments of life, Tony always knew how much his mother loved him. But he'd never felt anything even resembling love from his father. Parents were supposed to shield a child from pain, not

cause it, and his father had caused him more grief than
any child should have to take.

~

At six thirty the next evening, Heather sat at the computer in Tony's office, butterflies fluttering around in her
stomach. She took a few deep breaths to settle them, telling herself there was no need to be nervous. Everything
was under control. The grand opening was going to be a
spectacular event.

She scanned the invitation list she'd pulled up to verify
the names of the two food and entertainment reporters
who were coming and scribbled them on a piece of paper.
She intended to give it to Tony so he could remember who
they were when they showed up, trying to do whatever
she could to help him make a good impression. Truthfully,
though, she didn't know why she was worried. Once he
turned on the charm, not a solitary soul could resist him.

Tony poked his head around the doorway, a big smile
on his face. "The sign's up."

"Thank God they finished in time."

"Come take a look."

Heather jumped out of her chair and followed him out
the front door. She looked up. There it was. And it was
beautiful.

"It's official," Tony said. "McMillan's is now
McCaffrey's."

She looped her arm through his. "How does it feel?"

Tony stared at the sign, nodding with satisfaction.
"Pretty damned good."

"I don't want you to worry about any management issues tonight," Heather said. "Kayla and I will keep things running in the background."

"Okay."

"People are coming here to see you, so I want you free to be Mr. Hospitality. Just relax and enjoy yourself, okay?"

"I'll try."

"Oh. Something else. You'll make a good impression if you can remember the names of the reporters coming here tonight. I wrote them—"

"Heather?"

She spun around to see Kayla sticking her head out the door.

"Chuck needs you."

"I'll be right there." She turned back to Tony. "I wrote them on a pad of paper on your desk."

"I'll get it. You go talk to Chuck."

They went back inside. As Tony headed for his office, Heather went to the kitchen, every nerve in her body buzzing with excitement. She answered Chuck's questions about the buffet, then checked her watch and took a deep breath. It wouldn't be long now.

Kayla came into the kitchen. "Where's Tony? Erika wanted me to tell him she's stuck in traffic on Central, so she may be a few minutes late."

"In his office. I'll go tell him—"

And then Heather remembered. *Oh, God. The invitation list.*

She spun around and raced out of the kitchen, circled the bar, and headed for Tony's office. She stopped short at his door, collecting herself, then walked in. And over his shoulder, she saw exactly what she prayed she wouldn't—

the Excel document that she'd forgotten to close when she went out to look at the sign. Tony turned slowly in his chair, his face tight with anger.

"Heather? Did you send my father an invitation?"

Chapter 23

Heather stood there helplessly as the most awful sense of dread spilled over her. If she lied and said she didn't send the invitation and then Tony's father showed up, Tony would be angry. If she admitted she'd invited him, Tony would be angry. It was a lose-lose situation if she'd ever faced one.

She decided it was time to tell the truth.

"Yes," she admitted. "I invited him."

Tony's expression turned hot with anger. "I told you I didn't want him here!"

"Tony, please don't be mad. I was just trying to help."

"Help? How is inviting that man here supposed to *help?*"

"Family is important. And regret is a terrible thing. I think you want to reconcile with your father. You're just scared."

"So you think you know me?" he said, his voice low and intense. "After a lousy couple of weeks, you think you know what makes me tick? I've got news for you, Heather. You don't have a clue." He stood up slowly, his blistering gaze causing her to take a step backward. "Do you have any idea what it's going to be like for me if he shows up here? Do you?"

"I didn't do it to hurt you!"

"I don't give a damn why you did it! It wasn't your decision to make!"

Her eyes filled with tears, her vision growing blurry. The sight of his usually smiling face so contorted with anger chilled her to the bone.

"I trusted you," he said, his voice quivering. "I thought you understood how I felt about this!"

Heather bowed her head. "You're right. I . . . I shouldn't have done it. I shouldn't have—"

"You're damned right you shouldn't have. This was going to be the biggest night of my life, and now you've ruined it. I hope you're happy."

He brushed past her and stormed out of his office. Heather drew in a deep, shuddering breath, cursing herself for what she'd done, misery spilling over her like an ice-cold rain.

She swallowed hard, trying to quell the anxiety that was building inside her. She could only hope that if Don McCaffrey showed up, he'd have a kind word for his son instead of trying to force him to live up to standards he couldn't meet and that it would be the first step on their road to reconciliation. That was the only thing that might possibly insure that Tony wouldn't hate her for the rest of his life.

Damn her. Damn her for doing this to me.

Tony's stomach was tied in knots, anger and apprehension eating away at him. He could only hope his old man had tossed the invitation in the trash, because if he decided to come, God only knew what he'd say.

Your drinks are too weak.

Apparently you have to hire slutty waitresses to keep a crowd in this place.

Don't you ever read the business page? This is one of the riskiest businesses you can possibly go into.

When seven o'clock came and people started showing up, Tony greeted them with big smiles and handshakes. One of his greatest gifts was the ability to put a smile on his face regardless of how he really felt, and by God, he was going to do that tonight if it killed him.

Then he had to endure Heather's family showing up with smiles and hugs. When Fred came up and shook his hand, Tony didn't miss the slight narrowing of his eyes that said *Look out. I'm watching you.*

He schmoozed the reporters, pouring on the charm, even as his head was swimming with anxiety. He kept looking toward the door, scared to death that his father was going to show up and ruin everything.

A few hours into the evening, the band took a break and Tony took the microphone. He thanked everybody for coming, made a few jokes, and told people about the plans he had for the future. But through it all, he felt dazed, as if he were standing outside his body hearing himself speak.

Other people showed up whom Tony hadn't seen in a long time, and all of them were thrilled that he had a business of his own. It should have been a heady experience, finally stepping up and doing something with his life with the whole world watching his success. But just as he'd start to enjoy himself, he'd remember what Heather had done, and his stomach would churn with dread. It was as

if she'd lit a stick of dynamite, and he was waiting for it
to go off.

But as much as Tony was afraid of his father showing
up, as the hours passed, an emotional tug-of-war started
up inside his head. He didn't want him here. Not if he was
going to cause trouble. But if he didn't come...

It meant he just didn't give a damn.

And as the evening came to a close, that was the only
conclusion Tony could draw. The dynamite hadn't gone
off. But in its place was a cold, dark feeling of loneliness
that he almost couldn't bear.

After he sent the last employee home, Tony went to the
bar and poured himself a shot of Scotch. He downed that
and poured himself another one. He knew Heather was
still in the kitchen. Doing what, he didn't know. In a few
minutes, he intended to be too drunk to care.

He thought about how her whole family had come
tonight, which had only highlighted everything that was
dysfunctional about his. The only family he had was a
few aunts and uncles in places he'd never even visited and
a bastard of a father who couldn't be bothered to come
ten miles across town to see his son on one of the biggest
nights of his life.

*Maybe he didn't get the invitation. Maybe he had
something else he had to do. Maybe...*

No.

There he was, doing it again, just as he'd done a million times while growing up. Making excuses for an old
man who didn't care and never would.

But his father wasn't the only person he couldn't de-
pend on. For the first time in his life, he'd laid himself bare
in front of a woman, telling Heather things he'd never told

anyone before, only to discover that she was the kind of person who would do things behind his back and screw up his life in ways he couldn't even imagine.

In that moment, Tony realized he'd been right all along, that there was only one person on this earth he could trust. And to find him, he needed only to look in the nearest mirror.

Heather had never spent a more miserable evening.

All around her, people had been smiling and laughing and having a good time. The band had rocked the place. She knew that they were going to get great write-ups in the media and that people would be coming back, probably bringing friends. But she couldn't concentrate on any of that. All she could think about was the anger on Tony's face when he found out what she'd done. A few times this evening, she'd turned and caught his eye, and that broad, brilliant smile had faded to an icy frown. To have him look at her like that after everything that had happened between them just about broke her heart.

But the worst part of all was her family showing up. Tony had put on a good face for them, and so had she. But as she pictured telling them in a few days that she and Tony were breaking up, it made her sick to her stomach. And knowing how wary her father was of Tony would make things doubly hard.

Now she sat alone in the kitchen, the silence hammering away at her. She knew everyone else was gone for the night, but Tony was still out there.

She couldn't leave it like this. She had to talk to him.

With a deep, shaky breath, she came out of the kitchen to find him sitting at the bar with a shot glass and a bottle of Scotch. That didn't bode well for his state of mind, but she had to say something to him. Apologize again. Apologize a thousand times over if that was what it took.

Taking a deep breath, she slid onto a barstool next to him.

"Hey," she said.

He was silent.

"I'd tell you I've been cleaning up some things in the kitchen," she said, "but I'd be lying. I was staying around to talk to you."

Tony downed the rest of the Scotch in his glass.

"I'm sorry," she said. "For sending that invitation."

"You already told me that."

"And I'm sorry your father didn't come."

Tony reached for the Scotch bottle. "You know what, Heather? I've been thinking about that. You actually did me a favor by sending him that invitation."

"What do you mean?"

He filled his glass again. "See, about a dozen times in the past three years, I've come real close to picking up the phone to call him. But I've always stopped. I was always afraid of him treating me like shit one more time, which would mean I'd know for sure I didn't have a father anymore. I just didn't have the guts to put that final nail in the coffin. But since you did it for me," he said, raising his glass to her, "now I know I can just write the bastard off and never think about him again."

Tony's tone may have been light, but his words weren't, and hearing him talk like this made Heather very uneasy.

So did the fact that he was drowning his disappointment in alcohol.

"Maybe there's a reason he didn't show up," she said. "Maybe he had something else he had to do tonight."

"If that was true, he could have called."

"Maybe he didn't get the invitation."

"Heather. He got the invitation. He just..." He stopped short, swallowing hard. "He just didn't want to come."

Heather saw a flash of sheer misery pass across Tony's face, and her heart broke for him. How hard must it be for him to know that his own father wanted nothing to do with him?

She reached out a hand and touched his arm, only to have him slap his palms on the bar and give her a big smile.

"Well," he said. "So much for that. The good part is that the grand opening was a big success. He can't take that away from me, can he?"

"No," Heather said warily. "He can't."

"I think this calls for a private celebration. Just you and me. Ah! I know." He circled around the bar, grabbed a lime and a bottle of tequila, and held them up. "Ever do body shots?"

"Tony—"

He held up his finger to silence her. He sliced the lime in half. Picking up one of the halves, he came back around the bar and grabbed a salt shaker.

"Now, there are a lot of ways to do this, but since you'll probably tell me it's unsanitary if I have you lie down on the bar, I'll use the lime-and-salt-on-the-neck technique."

"Let's just go home, okay?"

"I know, I know. You want to go straight to bed. Shame on me. I've spoiled you."

"I think it would be best if we both just got some sleep."

"Not until I've shown you this. You're gonna love it."

"Tony? What are you doing?"

"I told you. Body shots." He reached up and rubbed the lime in a slow, sensuous circle on the side of her neck.

"Don't," Heather said softly. "Please don't."

"Now, you need to tilt your head a little so I can sprinkle the salt, or it'll go right down your shirt."

She didn't move. As she stared up at him, knowing what was really in his heart, her throat grew tight and tears filled her eyes.

He leaned away, his smile vanishing. "Stop it."

Heather shook her head slowly, blinking to keep the tears at bay.

"Damn it, will you stop *looking* at me like that?"

"I know how much it hurts that your father didn't show up, no matter how much you try to act as if it doesn't."

"Let it go, Heather."

"Now I know why you have a different woman in your bed every night. Why you can't get close to people. I know why you wear that gorgeous smile most of the time, and I know what makes you lose it. I know you dealt with more crap growing up than any kid should ever have to. But if you don't stop keeping the world at arm's length, you're never going to have any kind of life."

He glared at her. "My life is just fine with me."

"No. You need relationships. You're starving for them. But still you go on sleeping with every woman you meet and pretending that's enough."

"Who the hell are you to judge me?"

"That's not what I'm doing. I'm just trying to make you understand—"

"That's *enough.*"

"—that if you don't do something to find some kind of connection in your life, you're going to turn forty, then fifty, and you'll have nothing but the memory of a thousand faceless women to keep you warm at night."

"I said stop it!"

"I can't stand the thought of that happening, Tony. I just can't stand—"

"Will you just get the hell out of my life?"

His shout reverberated through the empty room, slicing right into her heart. He slung the lime aside, huffing with anger. As loud as his voice had been before, the silence now was deafening. He was bitter toward his father, and he was still bitter toward her for making him face something he didn't want to accept. And he probably would be forever.

"Okay," Heather said quietly. "I'll leave." She walked around the bar and grabbed her purse, her knees shaking so hard she could barely walk. She came back around and headed for the door, only to stop halfway there and turn back.

"You know, I really am a fool," she said.

"What are you talking about?"

"For all the logic I brought to this situation, for all the warnings I gave myself, for all the times I told myself this was for a month and no more..." Her voice stuttered, and she swallowed hard to keep it steady. "It happened, anyway."

"What happened, anyway?"

Don't say it. Don't say it. You'll regret it. But still she heard the words coming out of her mouth.

"I fell in love with you."

Tony looked away, and a long silence stretched between them. When he slowly turned his gaze back to meet hers, it was cold as ice.

"Sweetheart, if I had a dime for every woman who's told me that, I wouldn't have needed a trip to Vegas to buy this bar."

Heather felt a jolt of sorrow that went straight to her soul. Even though she'd known it was impossible, one tiny part of her thought it might make a difference if he actually heard the words.

It hadn't made a difference at all.

"Like I said," Heather told him, "I'm a fool. Why else would I have fallen in love with a man who's not capable of loving anyone?"

On the verge of tears, she turned around and walked as calmly as she could toward the door, hoping to get out of there before she started to cry. But still she hoped he'd stop her. What he might say to her if he did, she didn't know, but she didn't want to leave it like this.

"Heather?"

Her heart jolted hard. She turned back around.

"Yes?"

"In case you're wondering," he said, "I'll be there for the wedding tomorrow. I won't screw that up for Regina."

And?

And nothing. What had made her think there might be something else?

"Then I'll see you at the wedding," she said. "And

don't worry. I'll move out of your apartment tomorrow morning."

"You don't have to do that."

"I'll go to Alison's. And then a few days after the wedding, I'll tell my family we're splitting up."

"I said you don't have to move out. I promised you that I'd stick it out until the end."

"Tony," she said. "This is the end."

His face never changed. He just looked at her with that cold expression, then turned back to his drink, dismissing her as if they'd never meant anything to each other at all.

Heather left the building, and once she was outside, she hurried to her car, fumbling through her purse for her keys. She clicked the door locks, barely getting inside before her throat tightened and the tears came.

She'd been denying it for some time now, telling herself she was just infatuated with Tony because of the good times they'd had together. But now that she realized it was something more, a feeling of despair overwhelmed her. It wasn't until tonight that she saw so clearly how much he needed a loving person in his life. She wanted to be that loving person, and he was never going to let her.

~

When Tony opened his eyes the next morning, shafts of morning sunlight stabbed through the window, penetrating his eyeballs and lodging directly in his brain. He snapped his eyes shut again and rolled away, which evidently was the cue for a jackhammer to start pounding away at his head.

He'd died and gone to hell.

He rolled over and saw the empty bed beside him and remembered.

Yes. It was hell, all right.

When he'd come home last night, his bed had been empty. The door to Heather's bedroom had been closed. No light shone from beneath the door. He'd gone back to his room and fallen into bed by himself, blessedly passing out the moment his head hit the pillow.

If only he could have kept on sleeping.

He swung his legs over the side of the bed and sat up, putting his hand to his head to ease the throbbing, dreading the thought of facing Heather after what had happened between them last night. He got up to go to the kitchen for aspirin and coffee, only to glance down the hall and see her bedroom door open. He looked inside.

She was gone. So were all her things.

He just stood there, staring at the empty room. She'd left that morning while he was sleeping, and he hadn't even heard her. She'd said she was going to do it, but he didn't think she actually would.

So it really was the end.

He staggered into the living room and glanced toward the fireplace. The wall above it was blank.

You hated that damned portrait. Be glad it's gone.

He headed for the coffeepot, only to see a small package on his dining room table, wrapped in shiny silver paper. There was a note beside it, written in Heather's careful script: *I was going to give you this last night before everything fell apart.*

He sat down at the table and picked up the envelope beside the package. He pulled out the card it contained and opened it.

Congratulations on your grand opening! I know you're going to be a huge success. Here's a little reminder that sometimes miracles do happen. Love, Heather.

Tony's throat tightened as he read that word. *Love.* When she'd written this, she'd meant exactly that. She loved him, and he hadn't even realized it. She'd looked up at him last night with that plaintive expression, as if she was begging him to understand something he was incapable of understanding. And he'd just sat there pretending not to notice her eyes clouded with tears and that damned *look* on her face.

She'd broken their pact. Fun and games, kiss and tease, but once it was over, it was over. *Damn it.* She wasn't supposed to fall in love. But somehow she'd edged her way into his life, taking over part of him he'd never intended to give away. All the family crap she thought was so important only made him wary, because sooner or later, it was all an illusion. The people you loved could be gone tomorrow. The people you loved might not love you. Every single time he'd given a piece of himself away, he never got it back. He'd spent his entire childhood and adolescence stringing pieces of himself all over the world, and there was only so much left he had to give.

He picked up the package and carefully ripped the paper away to find something in a small shadowbox frame.

A single ten-dollar casino chip.

Tony froze, staring at the chip, his mind rushing back to the thrill of that night, to the groundswell of exhilaration that had culminated in a wild ride to a wedding chapel.

Heather was right. Miracles did happen. And then sometimes they fell apart at the seams.

He set the chip down and dropped his head, rubbing his eyes with the heels of his hands.

You wanted me to follow in your footsteps, Dad? Well there you go. I finally have. I treated a woman who loves me like shit. Proud of me now?

Then he remembered. The wedding was this afternoon. Heather would be there, undoubtedly looking at him the same way she had last night. Good God, he didn't want to deal with that.

Then he looked over at the pile of mail he'd brought in yesterday but had been too busy to open. There were two identical envelopes, one addressed to him and one to Heather. They were from the Clark County Courthouse in Las Vegas.

It was official. They were no longer husband and wife. Tony just stared at the envelopes, feeling numb all over.

Suddenly his cell phone rang. He grabbed it from the kitchen counter where he'd left it last night and answered it.

"Tony?" Kayla said. "Where are you? Are you okay?"

"Uh...yeah. Sure. I'm fine. Why are you—"

Then he saw the clock on the stove. It was nearly noon. The day was overcast, so he hadn't realized...

"God, Kayla, I'm sorry," he said, rubbing his temple. "I guess I celebrated a little hard last night and overslept."

"Hey, you had a right to celebrate. The grand opening was a huge success."

"I'll be in just as soon as I can get a shower."

"Don't worry. The crowd's light. I've got it covered."

"Thanks."

Tony hung up, put on a pot of coffee, then hopped into the shower. Twenty minutes later, he left his apartment, and by the time he reached the bar, rain clouds hovered overhead, gray and dreary, a perfect commentary on his frame of mind. When he pulled into the parking lot, he imagined Heather's car there, as it had been so many times in the past several weeks. But it wasn't, of course. After what he'd said to her last night, once the wedding was over this afternoon, he knew he'd never see her again.

He went inside the building. Since it was Sunday lunch, the music was relatively muted, but still the bass seemed to pound right into his brain.

Aspirin. He needed more aspirin.

He started toward his office, only to glance to the bar, where one man sat having a drink. And when he saw who that one man was, he stopped short in disbelief.

His father, Don McCaffrey.

Chapter 24

Tony approached slowly, and his father turned around. He'd changed very little. He still had the military haircut, the piercing green eyes, the jawline that looked as if it had been carved from stone. Even in casual clothes, he looked as if he was ready for inspection.

"What are you doing here?" Tony asked.

"I got your invitation."

The invitation. The one Heather never should have sent in the first place. Tony felt that age-old anger simmer inside him.

"You're a little late. The grand opening was last night."

"I know." He looked down the bar, where Lisa was drawing a glass of beer. "Do you think we could go someplace and talk?"

"No need. You won't be staying long."

His father sighed. "Look, Tony—"

"No, *you* look," Tony said, dropping his voice to an angry whisper. "You get an invitation, and what do you do? You wander in here a day late. That's been the story of my life. You showing up late. If you bothered to show up at all."

"I just want a few minutes."

Tony glared at his father a moment more, then reluctantly led him into his office. He shut the door behind them and sat down in his desk chair, gripping the arms so hard his fingers ached, his heart beating like crazy. He hated that his father had this kind of effect on him, and he did everything in his power to quell it. His father sat down on the edge of the sofa, his elbows on his knees and his hands clasped in front of him.

"I would have come," he said, "but I was out of town."

"Also the story of my life."

"On my honeymoon."

Tony froze. "What did you say?"

"I got married. I know. It's crazy. But after all these years, I found a woman who'll put up with me. Imagine that."

Tony couldn't imagine that. Not for one moment. His father...*married?*

Then he remembered seeing him in that formal shop last Saturday. How could he have known the man was picking up a tux for his own wedding?

"Yeah, I know," Don went on. "I didn't tell you I was getting married. I should have. Rachel tried to get me to, but I was too damned stubborn."

"Rachel?"

"My wife. She told me I should ask you to come to the wedding. It was just a small one, but you're my son, you know? She couldn't understand why I wouldn't invite you."

"So why didn't you?"

"I don't know. I—" He stopped short, shaking his head

helplessly. "I guess things were so bad between us the last time we were together..."

God, yes, they were. Because you couldn't stop judging your son long enough to enjoy a single day together.

"Maybe I was afraid you wouldn't come," his father said. "I guess I was just too afraid to find out whether you would or not."

Until that moment, Tony had been certain the world would turn to dust before he'd ever hear his father say he was afraid of anything.

"We talked about it a lot on our honeymoon," Don went on. "Rachel told me regret is a terrible thing, so I had to try. And then we got home today and I saw that invitation..." He shook his head. "I realized you had more guts than I did."

But he hadn't had any guts at all. If not for Heather dropping that invitation in a mailbox, they wouldn't even be here talking.

But it didn't matter. None of this mattered. If his father thought a lifetime of pain could be erased this easily, he needed to think again.

"You can't just walk in here after all this time and expect me to forgive and forget," Tony said, his voice trembling. "You've made my life hell."

His father closed his eyes, and for a moment, Tony had a flashback to his childhood, to those moments when he'd angered his father and watched the calm before the storm. But when he opened his eyes again, there was no anger in them.

Just sadness.

"You're right," Don said. "I can't. I don't expect you to forgive me for a damned thing. I just wanted to tell you I was sorry I wasn't around to come here last night. I would have, Tony. If only I'd known."

Tony's stomach was in turmoil. It was coming. It had to be. No matter what his father was saying, sooner or later, Commander McCaffrey would reappear to start in on his son all over again. He'd find some way to find fault. No matter how successful Tony appeared to be, his father would find a way to slap him down.

"So how did the grand opening go?" his father asked.

"It was all right."

"I like that you put your name on the place. That's good."

There was a long, uncomfortable silence. Tony felt his emotions being pulled in ten different directions, and he stared down at his desk so he wouldn't give any of them away.

"Look, son, I just came by to tell you I was sorry for missing things last night. So I guess...I guess I'll be going now."

He started to stand up. Then he stopped, hovering for a moment before sitting down again with a heavy sigh. He turned his gaze up and looked Tony straight in the eye.

"Here's the truth, Tony. By all rights, an old bastard like me should have ended up dying alone. And then one day I turned around and there she was. Rachel. I'm actually getting a second chance to be a decent husband. And that scares the crap out of me. I'm not sure I'm up to the task, but I don't want to lose her, either. So I guess I'll just have to give it everything I've got and pray to God it's enough."

Tony had a flash of what he'd told Heather. *I couldn't hold up my end of a real marriage if my life depended on it.* In that regard, he was just like his father. Only his father was trying to get over it. He said he was, anyway. Could Tony really believe it?

"I didn't listen to Rachel about our wedding. I refused to let her invite you. But then when we came home and saw your invitation, she told me to get my ass over here or I'd regret it for the rest of my life." He shook his head. "I swear I never talked to raw recruits the way she talks to me sometimes."

Tony couldn't fathom that. He couldn't fathom anyone on earth talking like that to his father and expecting to walk away alive.

Except maybe the woman he loved.

"Your mother. I loved her, Tony. You have no idea how much. I know I didn't show it. My father was a hard-ass military man, and he raised me to be just like him."

Tony heard what his father was saying, but it still felt wrong, it *had* to be wrong, and every nerve in his body was strung so tight his limbs ached.

"And after she died," Don went on, "there you were, a kid I couldn't understand to save my life. Everything was a lark to you. You didn't give a damn about your grades. I can't count the times I got calls, telling me you refused to get serious in class and that you were getting in trouble outside of class. I wanted you to toe the line, but you wanted a different line altogether. And I just didn't know how to deal with it." He paused, a faraway look in his eyes. "All the crap that's happened between us...it's my fault. Every last damned bit of it."

Tony's mind was in turmoil. It just wasn't possible that his father had walked in here after all this time and was telling him things like this. And even if the man meant every word, what was Tony supposed to say? *Hey, Dad, no hard feelings? Let's go have a drink?*

"I didn't exactly make it easy for you," Tony said. "Especially when I was a teenager."

"Yeah, but you were a kid. What was my excuse?"

Tony didn't know what to say to that. He couldn't even look at his father. He just let the man's words tumble over him, telling himself he'd sort it all out later, once his brain was no longer in shock and his hands weren't shaking. Why were his hands shaking? He gripped the arms of his chair tighter still.

"I'd like you to meet Rachel," his father said. "And she'd like to meet you. But I'm leaving it up to you to decide if you want that. All you have to do is say when and where, and we'll be there. Night or day. Just say the word. But even if I don't hear from you"—he swallowed hard—"I'll love you just the same."

He rose from the sofa. He put his hand on the doorknob, then turned back, and Tony swore he saw his father's eyes glistening.

"It's a nice place you've got here, son. I'm proud of you."

With that, he turned around and strode out of the office.

Tony watched his father leave, fighting the tears that were welling up in his own eyes. He refused to be fooled. Nothing had changed. If his father really was the kind of guy he was acting like now, wouldn't he have been that way when Tony's mother was still alive?

But in his heart, Tony knew better. Somehow he knew it was true. A miracle had happened that had turned his father's life around. Given it meaning. Sent him down a

new and different path leading to a better life than he'd
ever known before. And what was that miracle?

He'd found a woman who loved him.

Suddenly all the terrible things Tony had said to
Heather crowded his mind. She'd told him she loved him,
and he'd thrown that right back in her face, sounding exactly like the man he'd been before he'd known her. A
cocky, aimless womanizer who thought he had it all together, when in reality he was so messed up he was lucky
to make it through life with any meaning at all. He had
nothing to hold on to. Nothing good. Nothing lasting. He
thought about how much he used to look forward to seeing Babette—all sex, no strings—and it made him sick
to his soul.

Women had told him they loved him before, and it
always struck him as horribly misguided. With those
women, it hadn't been love. It had been infatuation with
the man he showed the world. They'd fallen in love with
only that tiny part of himself he chose to show them.
He'd always lived with the knowledge that if any of those
women had realized just how incompetent he was at holding up his end of a relationship, they'd have run away
from him as fast as they could.

But Heather hadn't worshipped him because of his
looks. She hadn't fallen prey to his sexual manipulation.
It wasn't until she'd made him lay bare the man he was
inside that something had truly changed between them.
Somehow, some way, it was the man inside she'd fallen
in love with.

But now he'd driven her away, and the void screamed
so loudly he couldn't hear himself think. He'd realized
some time ago that he didn't want to lose her friendship—

ever—but suddenly just friendship wasn't enough. In his entire adult life, he'd never had anyone to love, or anyone to love him.

Until now.

His old man was trying to change. Was Tony going to wait until he'd collected twenty more years of regrets to do some changing of his own? He had a wonderful woman who was in love with him. What kind of fool would he be to turn her away?

When the lunch shift was over, he went home and changed for the wedding. Then he went to the dresser in his spare bedroom, opened the bottom drawer, and pulled out the ragged brown shoebox. He opened it, dug beneath the book and the photographs, and found the little black box beneath them.

He checked his watch. The wedding was in an hour. If he left now, he'd be there early. He could find Heather. And if there was room in his life for the same kind of miracle that had happened to his father, Tony prayed it would happen today.

～

Heather arrived at the church an hour before the ceremony. She found the bride's room, where the five blond bridesmaids stood at the mirror, chattering and fussing with their hair and makeup. Regina sat on the sofa in her slip, and Aunt Bev was poking at her hair. It had already been done by a stylist, but evidently it hadn't been done right enough for Aunt Bev. Regina just sat there looking miserable. Wasn't Aunt Bev wondering why the bride wasn't smiling?

Of course, Heather's own mother hadn't read *her* misery, either. When Heather talked to her this morning, her mother had gushed about how beautiful she and Tony were going to look as they came up the aisle together, which only proved that if somebody wanted something badly enough, they could overlook anything.

Heather changed into her bridesmaid's dress. Fortunately, it fit. Unfortunately, it hadn't grown any more attractive. But right now, she didn't care. Regina could tell her to go down that aisle in a gunny sack, and still the only thing she'd be able to think about would be Tony.

When Heather had agreed to Tony's plan so she wouldn't have to be humiliated in front of everyone at Regina's wedding, she'd never realized that would be the least of her problems. She'd never imagined feeling something worse than the pain of humiliation.

The pain of loving a man who was never going to love her.

She felt like such an idiot. She'd created the fairy tale in her mind she'd warned herself against, the one where Tony would fall in love with her and they'd live happily ever after. What a joke that had turned out to be. She couldn't believe he saw her as just one more in a long line of women who couldn't help falling in love with him. One of dozens. Just a face in the crowd.

After Aunt Bev helped Regina into her gown and put her veil in place, she told Regina she needed to talk to the wedding planner and left the room. Heather walked over and sat down next to Regina on the sofa.

"How's it going?" she asked.

"Just fine," Regina said with a brief smile. "This is my wedding day."

Heather hated how Regina was deluding herself. But it was her decision, and if she made the wrong one, there wasn't a damned thing Heather could do about it.

"Your hair is straight," Regina said.

"Yes."

"Won't Tony be upset?"

"You like it better this way. This is your day."

Regina nodded and looked back down at her lap. After a moment, she whispered, "Don't look at me like that."

"Like what?"

"You know what I mean."

"Regina? Are you sure about this?"

"I told you Thursday night. Of course I'm sure."

But then she looked up at Heather, and there were tears in her eyes. She looked away, blinking quickly. "It's just nerves."

Heather turned to the bridesmaids. "Will you girls leave us alone for just a few minutes?"

They kept chattering.

"Girls!"

All five blond heads swung around.

"Could you step outside for just a minute?" Heather said.

"What for?" Two said.

"Regina and I need to talk."

"You can talk with us here."

"We need to talk *alone*," Heather said.

Four turned to Two, screwing up her face. "What's eating her?"

"Got me," Two answered.

"I'm not going anywhere until I finish my eyeliner," Three said, turning back to the mirror.

"All of you," Heather said. *"Out!"*

They tossed down hairbrushes and makeup wands and scattered like startled deer, leaving the room and closing the door behind them.

Regina looked up, tears shimmering in her perfect blue eyes. "Heather? Can I ask you a question?"

"Yeah?"

"How did you get so lucky?"

"What?"

"I can't stand it anymore. I have to know. It took me two years to get Jason to ask me to marry him. Tony asked you in one night. How did you *do* that?"

"I don't know," Heather said, turning away so she didn't have to meet Regina's eyes. "It just...happened."

"I know everything I've said about Tony, but..." She sniffed. "He's wonderful. He's so handsome. He treats you so well. He pays attention to you. And he just fell into your lap. One day, you had nobody, and then all of a sudden, there he was. How did you get *so lucky?*"

Heather felt terrible continuing to lie to Regina and everyone else, but in spite of what had happened between her and Tony last night, she just couldn't make the truth come out of her mouth.

But her relationship with Tony really wasn't the issue here. The issue was Regina's relationship with Jason, which wasn't much of a relationship at all. And it needed to come to an end.

"I think you know what you need to do here," Heather said.

"But I can't! The guests are going to be here soon. The reception is waiting. My parents have spent thousands of dollars. I can't cancel this wedding!"

"What's your alternative? Would you rather get up the nerve to call off the wedding, or wait five years and get up the nerve to divorce him?"

Regina slowly turned her gaze to meet Heather's, her blue eyes filling with tears, looking as if she'd finally understood something that she'd been resisting for a very long time. "My God. That's what's going to happen, isn't it?"

"It's a strong possibility. And you deserve something better than that."

Regina sniffed again, then dabbed beneath one eye with a tissue. "Will you do me a favor?"

"What?"

She took a deep, shaky breath. "Go get Jason."

Chapter 25

Twenty minutes later, Tony was driving up Preston Road, heading for the church, wondering where all this damned traffic had come from on a Sunday afternoon. He felt so eager to see Heather and set this whole thing straight that he very nearly ran a red light and T-boned another car. He braked to a screeching halt, letting out a breath of frustration as he tapped his fingertips on the steering wheel.

He still couldn't believe how blind he'd been. Bit by bit, from that first night in Vegas to this moment and every second in between, he'd been falling in love with Heather. And he hadn't even realized it. His father coming by today had just been the brick to the side of the head he needed to knock some sense into him.

The light finally changed. He hit the gas, drove the last half-mile to the church, and swung his car into the parking lot. He got out of the car and started to go inside, only to have the door burst open and Jason come barreling out.

"Hey, Jason!" Tony said. "Do you know where Heather is?"

"Bite me," Jason snapped, and kept walking.

The door to the church opened again, and Jason's parents came tearing out, brushing past Tony and following

Jason to his BMW, where they stopped him from getting in the car. Jason looked pissed. His parents looked upset. And all of them seemed just a little bit manic.

What the hell was going on?

Confused, Tony went into the church, found the wedding planner, and asked her where the bridesmaids were. She pointed to a hallway that led to the bride's room. As Tony rounded the corner, he was surprised to see Heather standing outside the door, her ear planted firmly against it.

"Heather?"

She spun around, and in the next few seconds, he saw a range of emotions pass over her face. He saw her surprise that he was there. The pain she felt from the terrible things he'd said to her last night. Apprehension that he might not have finished hurting her yet. But through it all, he sensed something else she couldn't hide no matter how hard she tried. It was shining in those clear blue eyes, so raw and so real that it sent shivers down his spine.

She loved him.

Even after everything he'd done to her, it was still there. And he wanted to kick himself senseless for every single moment of anguish he'd caused her.

"Tony?" she said, sliding her hand to her throat. "What are you doing here? The groomsmen are in a room on the other side of the church."

"Forget them. I need to talk to you."

She flicked her gaze to the door. "No. I...I can't talk. Not now."

"But it's important. I have to tell you—"

"Regina called off the wedding."

Tony stopped short. "Oh, yeah? I guess that explains

why I saw Jason leaving in a huff. Well, good for Regina. I didn't think she had the guts to do it."

"But now Aunt Bev and Uncle Gene are in there. I'm afraid Aunt Bev is going to talk her back into it. And if she does, Regina's going to be miserable for the rest of her life."

"She just needs to stand up to them."

"She won't be able to. I know Aunt Bev. She'll browbeat Regina until she goes back out there and marries that jerk, telling her how embarrassing it will be for her if she calls off the wedding. I have to do something. I just don't know what."

Tony started to tell Heather that they'd deal with that in a minute, that right now she needed to listen to him. But when she put her ear to the door again, trying to hear what was going on inside the room, he knew this mess had to be settled first.

"Okay," Tony said. "Tell me exactly what you think should happen here."

"Isn't it obvious? I want Aunt Bev to go away. I want Regina to leave this church an unmarried woman. I want Jason to die a slow, agonizing death."

"Would you settle for two out of three?"

Tony pulled Heather away from the door and opened it.

"Tony?" Heather said. "What are you doing?"

Ignoring her, he went inside, and Heather followed. Regina was sitting on the sofa, her face streaked with tears. Bev was standing over her, looking like Godzilla on a rampage. Gene stood nearby, his eyes shifting back and forth between his wife and daughter, looking like a man who generally thought it best not to come between Godzilla and Tokyo.

"Listen to me, Regina," Bev said hotly. "There are going to be two hundred people in that church, waiting for you to get married. You can't back out now!"

"Of course she can back out," Tony said. "It's her life."

Bev whipped around. "What are you doing here?"

"Regina," Tony said. "Do you want to marry Jason?"

She sat in silence for several seconds, looking from one face to another. She bowed her head, sniffing a little.

"No," she said. "I don't."

"Good," Tony said. "Jason's an asshole. You're right to walk away." He turned to Bev. "You need to go."

Bev drew back. "*Excuse* me? Who are you to come in here and tell *me* to leave?"

"Bev," Gene said. "It's over."

She whipped around to Gene. "You do realize this is thirty thousand dollars down the drain, don't you?"

"It's worth thirty grand never to have to hear about it again. Next time, she's eloping." He looked at Tony. "The smart people bypass all this crap and just go to Vegas."

"That's easy for you to say," Bev snapped. "You're not the one who spent the entire last year planning a wedding!"

"And while you've been planning that wedding, how often did you consult with our daughter about what *she* might want?"

"She wants Jason!"

"So that's why she called off the wedding?" Gene turned to Regina. "I'm glad you're not marrying him. I never liked him, anyway. All he could do was punch that damned BlackBerry and talk about golf."

"Gene!" Bev said. "That's your future son-in-law you're talking about!"

"Nope," Gene said. "That's dead in the water. Now, you say you planned this wedding? Fine. Then it shouldn't be all that hard to get out there now and *un*plan it." He turned to Regina. "Will you be all right?"

"We'll stay here with her," Heather said.

Gene dragged Bev out of the room to break the news to the guests, and a few seconds later, five bridesmaids tried to pile in. Tony intercepted them and herded them out again. He shut the door, but still he heard them chattering outside like deranged chipmunks.

Regina took a deep, calming breath. "Please tell me I'm doing the right thing."

"You're doing the right thing," Tony said. "Life's too short to make stupid decisions. I've made plenty. That's how I know."

Regina nodded. "I don't think I ever loved him. He just seemed like the perfect catch, you know? And my mother was ecstatic. My friends thought he was wonderful. But you know what? None of them has to live with him for the rest of their lives."

There was a sharp knock at the door. "Regina!" one of the bridesmaids called out. "Come out here! You have to tell us everything!"

Regina dropped her head to her hands. "You're right, Heather. They're morons. And I can't take them right now. I just want to get out of here."

"Good idea," Tony said.

"But I don't have a car."

"Heather and I can take you wherever you want to go."

Heather looked at Tony with surprise. He'd made

it pretty clear after last night that there was no more "Heather and I." So what was he even doing here?

"Good," Regina said. "Let's go." She leaped to her feet and headed for the door at the back of the room that led directly to the parking lot.

"Regina!" Heather said. "Don't you need to change first?"

"My mother already took away the clothes I came here in. Will you please just get me out of here before she comes back?"

"Do you want me to tell her you're leaving?"

"We'll call her from the car," Tony said. "Let's go."

A few minutes later, they'd bundled Regina into the backseat of Tony's car, and he was backing out of the parking space.

"Where are we going?" Heather asked.

"I need a drink," Regina said. "Maybe two. Maybe even three. Tony, let's go to your place."

"Regina," Heather said. "You know you're wearing a wedding dress, right?"

"I don't care."

Tony looked at Regina in the rearview mirror. "You sure you want a drink right now?"

"I already had two half an hour ago. But it didn't work. After two shots of vodka, Jason still looked like a jerk." She slumped back in the seat, looking a little woozy, her dress billowing around her. "I hope he and that damned BlackBerry are very happy together."

At the BlackBerry remark, Tony shot Heather a furtive smile. She smiled back, even though she didn't have a clue why he was even there. Just sitting next to him made her want him so much she ached with it.

She looked at his hands on the steering wheel, remembering how he'd touched her more intimately than any man ever had before, sending her to heights of sexual satisfaction she hadn't even known existed. But it wasn't just the sex. It was the laughter they'd shared, the way he shook her out of her humdrum existence, the cozy contentment she felt just being with him. Those were the things she was going to miss the most. But while she'd been fantasizing about their marriage going on forever, Tony had merely been biding his time until he could go back to his old life.

And then she'd told him she loved him. How pitiful was that? She was going to feel foolish about that for the rest of her life.

"You should have seen Jason one night when we went to the symphony," Regina said, huffing with irritation. "They made an announcement that everyone was supposed to turn off their cell phones. He got up every fifteen minutes to see if he had a voice mail. I swear he could be standing in front of the president of the freakin' United States, and if that thing rang, he'd say, 'Mr. President? Could you hold that thought?'"

As Regina prattled on, her words slid right past Heather. All she could think about was Tony. She would have expected him to run far and fast once it was clear the wedding wasn't taking place. Instead, here he was, insinuating himself right into the middle of the chaos. Was he *trying* to drive her crazy?

Regina went on to cite approximately sixteen ways Jason had irritated her with his electronic device, and she was still going at it a few minutes later when Tony pulled into the parking lot at McCaffrey's. As they went inside,

Heather couldn't resist scooping up the train of Regina's dress so it wouldn't drag across the parking lot.

Inside the bar, it was a usual lazy Sunday afternoon, with a few guys at the bar and a couple of tables occupied. The Rangers game was playing on the TVs. Regina slid onto a barstool. Lisa walked up, eyeing her with surprise, then looked at Tony. "Can't wait to hear the story behind this."

"Martini," Regina said. "On second thought, make that two."

Heather sat on a barstool around the corner of the bar from Regina, and Tony took one next to Heather. Regina looked up at the boar's head on the wall above the bar, narrowing her eyes. "You know, that thing is kinda growing on me. Want a real conversation piece?" She ripped the veil off her head and set it on the bar beside her. "Stick *that* on it."

Heather turned to Tony and whispered, "Now she's really losing it."

"I'm not losing anything," Regina said. "In fact, I've never felt so clearheaded in my life."

When Lisa brought their drinks, Regina picked up both of her martinis with a flourish. "Here's to women, because all men are pigs. Present company excluded. You got one of the good ones, Heather. Hang on to him."

As Regina took a sip from each glass, Heather thought, *I only wish I could.*

"I wasted three years of my life on Jason," Regina said. "I gotta make up for lost time." She scanned the room and zeroed in on a guy at the end of the bar. "There. Heather, what do you think about that guy down there? The blond?"

"That's Andy. He's a player. He'll pick you up, have his way with you, then dump you."

Regina grinned. "That's perfect."

"I thought all men were pigs."

"They are. But what am I supposed to do? Become a lesbian?"

She scrambled off the barstool and picked up both martinis.

"Come on, Regina," Heather said. "You're not actually going to hit on a guy half an hour after calling off your wedding, are you?"

"Are you kidding?" Regina said. "I look fabulous in white. Why not take advantage of it?"

She kicked her train out of the way and headed down the bar. Andy pulled out a barstool for her and gave her a big smile. Bridal gown notwithstanding, the man wasn't blind. Even half-drunk, Regina was still a knockout.

"We probably shouldn't let her drink so much," Tony said, "but as long as she's smiling and not crying, let's go with it for a while. Besides, it'll give me a chance to talk to you."

Heather's heart skipped. "What about?"

"Just come with me."

Tony took Heather's arm and helped her off the barstool. "Lisa," he said, "we'll be in my office. If the bride tries to leave, step on her train."

"Will do," Lisa said.

They went into Tony's office. He closed the door, and they sat down on the sofa. Heather didn't have a clue what he was up to. Why had he intervened in this situation when he'd made it clear last night that he no longer wanted anything to do with her?

"First of all," he said, reaching for something from his breast pocket, "it's official." He held up two envelopes. "We have his and hers annulment papers. They came yesterday."

"So we're no longer married?"

"We're no longer married."

So there it was. In black and white. Why he was pouring salt in the wound, she didn't know. Couldn't he have just dropped them in the mail?

"Second of all," Tony said, "about last night—"

"I don't want to talk about that."

"No, we're going to talk about it."

"Tony—"

"I just want to tell you how sorry I am. I'm sorry for every stupid thing that came out of my mouth. I behaved like an idiot, and I should be shot for it."

Heather couldn't believe it. He was apologizing?

Wait a minute. Of course he was. Tony wanted everybody to be happy, no matter what the circumstances were. Well, her being happy with this situation was never going to happen, but she could certainly be adult about it.

"It's okay," she said.

"No, it's not okay. The things I said to you were *not okay*."

"You just had a rough night."

"Will you stop being so damned understanding? I don't deserve it. The things I said to you—"

She held up her palm. "Tony, if you don't stop apologizing, I'm going to feel compelled to start in again with my own apologies about the invitation, and we're going to be apologizing from now till doomsday." She sighed. "Can we both just forgive and forget?"

Tony smiled. "Yeah. We can do that."

"Thank God," Heather said. "I just don't want there to be hard feelings between us, you know?"

"I know. I don't, either."

"All I really want now is for us to be able to part as friends."

"Friends?" Tony's smile vanished. "No. We won't be able to be friends."

Heather's heart fell through the floor. "What happened to all that forgiving and forgetting?"

"We are forgiving and forgetting. But the friends thing—that's not going to happen."

"Why not? Because we were once married? Divorced people can stay friendly. They do it every day."

"But it isn't going to be long before some really smart guy grabs you and marries you, and before you know it, you'll be celebrating your fiftieth wedding anniversary with him. Somewhere in the middle of all that, you'll forget about me."

"Don't worry," she said glumly. "I won't be getting married anytime soon."

"Oh, yes, you will. Look what you have going for you. You have a good job. A smart mouth. Great hair. A work ethic that puts an entire congregation of Protestants to shame. Organizational skills out the wazoo. And sweetheart, the minute you show up in a man's bed naked, he won't let you go. Once he's got you, do you think he's going to take kindly to you being friends with your ex-husband? The answer is *no*."

"Well, he'll have to. He'll just have to understand that even though you and I got a divorce, we're still friends."

Tony shook his head sadly. "Sorry, Heather. It doesn't

work that way. When you have an ex-husband who's as handsome and charming as I am, the poor guy will feel threatened every day of his life."

Heather looked at him dumbly. "Do you *ever* turn off the ego? Or is it like Niagara Falls, where you couldn't stop it if you wanted to?"

"*So,*" Tony said, reaching into his pocket, "I decided that if your possessive new husband wouldn't let me be your friend"—he held out a small black box—"I'd have to become your possessive new husband."

He flipped the box open, and when Heather saw what it contained, she just about fell off the sofa.

The most beautiful wedding ring she'd ever seen.

Chapter 26

For several seconds, Heather's mind went blank. She couldn't think. She couldn't speak. Tony's words were gibberish in her mind. She just sat there looking at the ring, trying to connect all the dots and jump-start her brain. This couldn't mean what she thought it meant. He must have misspoken. She must have misheard.

She took a slow, controlled breath, then turned her gaze from the gorgeous ring to Tony's gorgeous face. Her eyes filled with tears. She wasn't a crier. She'd never been a crier. But she sure was turning into one now.

"The day my mother died," Tony said quietly, "she took off her ring and gave it to me. She told me that someday I'd fall in love with a girl, and when I did, I was supposed to give it to her. You're the one, Heather. The one she told me about."

All Heather could do was look at it, then look at Tony, then look back at the ring, as if she was afraid one or the other or both were going to disappear in a cloud of her own wishful thinking.

"But I don't understand," she said. "Just last night you said..." She shook her head in confusion. "What changed?"

"I wasn't kidding about another guy swooping in and marrying you. And when I thought about that happening...well, I just didn't think it was fair."

"What?"

"I'm the one who got you to let down your hair. I'm the one who showed you how Debbie does Dallas. I'm the one who taught you about furry purple handcuffs and told you dirty fairy tales. *I'm* the one who turned you into a sex maniac. So why should some other guy get to take advantage of that?"

That was so *Tony* that Heather couldn't help smiling, even as she wiped away tears.

"But in the end," Tony said, "it wasn't what I did for you." He paused, his smile fading. "It was what you've done for me." He took her hands and held them tightly. "I need you, Heather. I need somebody who'll keep me grounded. Who'll be there for me today and tomorrow and forever. I need that feeling you give me that I've finally come home." He traced his fingertips along her cheek. "When you said you loved me, did you mean it?"

"Yes. Every word."

"Then what's your answer? Will you marry me?"

"Yes," she said. "Oh, *yes.*" She wound her arms around his neck, and then there weren't just a few tears but a deluge of them. And when he slipped the ring onto her finger, she held it up, staring at it with wonder. "I don't believe it. It fits."

"Of course it does. It's fate. I'm a big believer in that, you know."

Tony hugged her again, this time whispering in her ear, "There's something I still don't understand. Maybe I never will."

"What's that?"

He pulled away and searched her face as if he'd find the answer there, only to come up short. He shook his head with genuine confusion.

"What does a woman like you see in a guy like me?"

Heather just sat there, stunned. She could never have imagined that question coming from a man who was at the top of every woman's dream list. But the truth was, she wasn't in love with the man he showed everybody else. She was in love with the man he'd shown her.

"I didn't even realize what I was missing in life until you came along," she told him. "I'm a different person when I'm with you. And I like her a whole lot better."

"We're good together," he said. "That's why we need to stay together."

As he leaned in to kiss her again, there was a sudden knock at the door. "Tony! Heather!"

Tony rose and opened the door.

"You'd better get out here," Lisa said. "The crazy bride is leaving."

Tony and Heather came out of the office in time to see Regina weaving drunkenly toward the door, Andy's arm wrapped around her shoulders. She waved at them. "Tony! Heather! This guy here and I are leaving. Thanks a bunch for the ride from the church. I'll see you . . . whenever."

Andy had a big, goofy smile on his face, as if he'd just struck gold. As they were walking out the door, Tony caught up with him and grabbed his arm.

"Hold on, sport. You're not going anywhere."

"Tony!" Andy whispered. "Will you cut it out? This one's too good to be true. She's drunk *and* on the rebound!"

"*This one* is my wife's cousin."

Andy let go of Regina as if she'd suddenly caught fire, holding up his palms. "Whoa. Hey, man. Didn't mean to mess with your family."

"Tell you what, Andy. From now on around here, let's make the drunk ones on the rebound off-limits, okay?"

"Uh...yeah. Sure."

"Why don't you head on home for today? That'll give you a chance to review the new rule before I see you back in here tomorrow."

Andy nodded. "Okay, man. Whatever you say."

As he walked out the door, Tony helped Heather prop Regina on a barstool. Heather looked over the bar to see a certain boar wearing a wedding veil, and she had to admit it was one hell of a fashion statement.

"Hey!" Regina said, looking around. "Wait a minute! Where's that guy? We were going to..." She stopped and looked at Heather. "What were we going to do?"

"Have a cup of coffee," Heather said.

"Oh, yeah." Regina put her elbow on the bar and rested her chin in her hand, looking as if she was about to drop off to sleep, only to catch sight of Heather's ring and sit bolt upright.

"Oh, my God!" she said, grabbing Heather's hand. "That ring is gorgeous!"

Flashing a beautiful diamond ring was like waving smelling salts under Regina's nose. Then she looked at Heather's face. "*Eww.* Your mascara is running."

Heather didn't think now would be the time to mention that Regina looked like a raccoon herself. And suddenly she had a queasy look on her face, as if the gin that had gone down might be getting ready to come back up.

"I think we'd better skip the coffee and get her home," Tony said.

"I think I'd better get her to the bathroom first. She's looking a little green."

Tony grabbed Heather and gave her a kiss and a smile. "Don't be gone long, now."

Heather smiled. She'd be counting the seconds.

Twenty minutes later, Tony pulled up in front of Regina's apartment. Heather had called Uncle Gene to tell him they were bringing her home, and by the time she got out of the car and walked Regina to her front door, he and Aunt Bev had arrived. Bev still looked as if she wanted to kill somebody, but since she wasn't saying much, it appeared that Gene still held the reins he'd yanked out of her hands. Heather felt confident that Regina was going to be okay. Or, at least, she would be once she got over the monumental hangover she was going to have in the morning.

As Heather got back into the car, Tony was flipping his cell phone shut. "We need to head back to the bar."

"What's up?"

"You know that pipe in the kitchen? It really did burst this time."

"Oh, great. Did they get the water shut off?"

"Yeah. But Chuck says there's a hell of a mess."

"Thank God this happened on a Sunday night instead of a Saturday night."

"No kidding."

"So we have to switch into crisis mode dressed like Ken and Barbie?"

"I'm afraid so."

"Fine with me. I never liked this dress, anyway."

Ten minutes later, they pulled into the parking lot at McCaffrey's. When Heather saw the new sign, she had a thought that warmed her all the way to her bones. Pretty soon the name up there wasn't going to be just Tony's. It was going to be hers, too.

But right now, they had a crisis to avert.

They hopped out of the car and hurried inside. But as Heather was making a beeline for the kitchen, Tony grabbed her arm and pulled her back around.

"Hold on, Heather. There's somebody I want you to meet."

"What?"

Just then, a man and a woman rose from their barstools and walked over, stopping in front of them. The woman had short, dark hair and lines around her eyes and mouth that said she was used to smiling. The man was tall and strikingly handsome, with thick salt-and-pepper hair.

"Heather," Tony said, "this is my father. Don McCaffrey."

Heather froze, sure she must have heard Tony wrong. "Your father?"

"Yes."

For the count of five, she couldn't breathe. She just stood there in complete astonishment, feeling as if her heart had stopped beating altogether. *Tony's father?*

"But I don't understand," she said, looking back and forth between them. "How...?"

"It's a long story. But I think..." Slowly Tony faced

his father, a wave of emotion passing over his face that seemed to sweep away the bitterness he'd held on to all these years. "I think everything's going to be okay now."

The men gave each other a meaningful look, and in that moment, Heather knew that something wonderful had happened. After all these years, somehow, some way, they'd come to some kind of understanding. A feeling of pure joy welled up inside her until she was sure she'd burst with it. She reached out to shake Don's hand.

"It's *so* nice to meet you," she said. "I'm Heather. Tony's wife."

Don looked at Tony with surprise, then turned back to Heather with a warm smile. "I have a daughter-in-law?"

"Yes," Tony said. "And I have a stepmother." He looked at the woman beside his father. "You must be Rachel."

Now it was Heather's turn to be surprised. "Stepmother? I didn't know—"

"I just found out myself a few hours ago," Tony said.

Tony reached out to shake Rachel's hand, but Rachel was a little more gregarious than Don and pulled him in for a hug. "I am so *glad* to finally meet you," she said, and then Heather heard her whisper, "You have no idea how much your father was hoping you'd call."

Heather glanced at Don. His eyes had begun to glisten, and when he looked away for a moment to collect himself, she felt her own eyes start to tear up.

Rachel turned to Heather and gave her the same kind of enthusiastic hug she'd given Tony. Then she backed away and looked at both of them. "My, you two sure are dressed up."

"My cousin's wedding," Heather said. "We were in the

bridal party. Or, we would have been if there had been a wedding."

"What?"

Heather smiled. "Never mind. Long story. Can you stay for a drink?"

"We'd love to," Rachel said.

Just then, Don zeroed in on Heather's left hand. He picked it up and stared at it, then turned to Tony with a stunned expression.

"My God. It's your mother's ring. You kept it all this time?"

Tony nodded.

Don turned back to Heather, speaking softly, emotion clouding his voice. "That's right where it belongs. Don't you ever take it off."

Heather felt a rush of pure pleasure, followed by the kind of bone-deep satisfaction that came with knowing what the future held, and it was wonderful beyond her wildest dreams. Something extraordinary had happened between the time she'd left Tony last night and the time he showed up for the wedding. Something that had allowed him to start down the road toward reconciliation with his father, a miracle she couldn't have imagined only a few hours ago. And somehow that miracle had led to another one.

She and Tony were going to be together, now and forever.

Later that night, Tony and Heather lay breathless on the bed, satisfaction oozing from every pore. His tuxedo and her dress lay in a messy heap on the floor, along with two empty martini glasses.

Heather rolled her head around to look at Tony. "James Bond captures a female spy?" She shook her head. "It's official. You really are nuts."

"Hey, we were wearing the costumes. I wasn't about to pass up that opportunity."

"Interesting method Bond uses to make women talk."

Tony grinned. "I thought you'd like that."

One thing was certain. Life with Tony was never going to be boring.

"I decided I'm going to ask my father to be my best man," Tony said.

"Best man?"

"Yep. We're having a wedding."

Heather smiled. "A wedding? Really?"

Tony rose on one elbow and looked down at Heather, stroking his fingers through her hair. "I want to start out right this time. I want everyone to hear me say that I love you. Your family . . . and mine."

Heather thought her heart was going to burst with happiness. He'd been so long without a real family, and now he had two.

"But nobody knows about our annulment," Heather said. "How do we explain that we're having another wedding?"

"We'll just tell everyone we're renewing our vows in front of our family and friends. Only the minister needs to know it's the real thing. I hear those guys are pretty good at keeping secrets."

"A wedding," Heather said softly, thinking about all the times she'd dreamed of one without knowing if the right man would ever come along. When she and Alison were in high school, they'd picked apart more than one issue of *Modern Bride*. Then it had been nothing more than a wishbook. Now all her wishes had come true.

Alison. She had to tell Alison. Her friend didn't know yet that she and Tony were staying married, much less having a wedding. She reached for the phone.

"Who are you calling?" Tony asked.

"Alison. I have to tell her she's going to be my maid of honor."

She punched in Alison's number. When Alison came on the line and Heather told her there was going to be a wedding, she wouldn't have needed the phone to hear her friend's squeals of delight five miles away. Alison didn't even remind her of their seventh-grade pact—unless both of them got a guy, neither of them did—but she did remind Heather of their pinky swear about bridesmaid dresses, and Heather took great comfort in Alison's pledge to make sure hers weren't ugly as sin.

When Heather hung up, Tony said, "Now it's time to call your mother. And this time it's for real."

Heather smiled, thinking about how she'd called her mother after their wedding in Vegas, and it had meant nothing. This time it was going to mean everything. She dialed her parents' number, and her mother came on the line.

"Hi, sweetie," her mother said. "Did you and Tony get Regina home okay?"

"Yeah, she's fine."

"It's too bad about the wedding."

"I know. But she did the right thing."

Barbara sighed. "You're probably right. Jason was a little...inattentive, wasn't he?"

Inattentive? Leave it to her mother to find a polite way of calling a jerk a jerk.

"It's just such a shame that it all went to waste," Barbara went on. "I was so looking forward to it. I *love* weddings."

"So would you like to go to another one?"

"Another one? Is somebody else getting married?"

"Yeah. Tony and I."

"But...but you're already married."

"I know. But our wedding was in Vegas and nobody else was there. Tony thinks we should have one here."

"A real wedding?" Barbara said tentatively, her voice escalating with hope. "In a church? With a minister? That kind of wedding?"

"Yep. Complete with flowers, bridesmaids, a reception—"

"Fred!" her mother screeched. "Fred! Get in here! Heather and Tony are going to have a wedding!"

Heather put her hand over the phone and whispered to Tony, "Did you hear that?"

He laughed. "Are you kidding? They heard it in outer space."

For the next ten minutes, Barbara chattered about everything from reception halls to cakes to nut cups to music, and Heather didn't think she'd ever heard her mother happier. Then, in minute detail, Heather described the ring Tony had given her, and she could practically hear her mother swooning on the other end of the phone. By the time Heather hung up, she'd agreed to take her mother the next Saturday on a trip to a bridal shop.

"What about champagne?" Tony said. "You didn't talk about that. We have to have lots and lots of champagne."

Heather closed her eyes. "I'm getting a hangover just thinking about it."

"And I'm taking you on a real honeymoon," Tony said. "How about Vegas?"

"Actually, I was thinking Cancun. You could lie naked on that beach again. I'd enjoy that."

"Would you lie naked with me?"

"I think you'd actually try to get me to do that. Which is why I'm never going to Cancun with you."

Tony dropped a gentle kiss against her lips. "You know what? That night in Vegas, I think we knew. On some strange, deep level, we knew exactly what we were doing."

Heather traced her fingertips over his cheek, amazed to feel this kind of happiness.

"Or we were just dead drunk."

She smacked him on the arm. He laughed and grabbed her hand, pressing it to the bed over her head; then he leaned in and kissed her, a long, deep, loving kiss that knocked the fight right out of her.

"Either way," he murmured, "we finally got it right."

They lay back down in each other's arms, and they'd just about fallen asleep when the phone rang. Heather looked at the caller ID.

"My mother again."

"Oh, boy. More wedding talk?"

"Hey, it isn't as if you didn't know what you were getting into."

She hit the TALK button. "Hi, Mom." She paused, looking confused. "Oh. Dad. It's you." She listened for a moment more. "Uh...yeah. He's right here." She held out the phone to Tony and whispered, "My father. He wants to talk to you."

"Me?" Tony whispered back. "Why?"

Heather shrugged. He took the phone from her, feeling a little apprehensive, even though he had no reason to be. After all, Heather was happy, which meant Fred was happy...right?

He put the phone to his ear. "Hey, Fred. What can I do for you?"

Fred cleared his throat. Twice. "Uh...Barbara and I were talking, and..."

"Yeah?"

"She tells me you and Heather are going to have a real wedding."

"Yeah, we are."

"Heather said it was your idea."

"Uh-huh."

"And that you gave her a ring. One that belonged to your mother."

"That's right."

There was a long silence, one that Tony nervously wanted to fill, but he kept his mouth shut. When Fred spoke again, his usual gruff tone had warmed and softened, and there was a note of awe in his voice.

"You really love her, don't you?"

Tony closed his eyes, his chest tight with emotion. Thank God he'd come to his senses. "Yeah, Fred. I do."

"Good. That's good. It's all I ever wanted, you know?"

"Yeah," Tony said. "I know."

"Well, then. I guess I'd better be going. I just wanted to

call and..." He stopped short. More throat-clearing. "Oh, hell. I can't lie. It wasn't my idea to call you."

"It wasn't?"

"No. It was Barbara's doing. She told me I needed to call and officially welcome you to the family, and if I didn't, she said she was going to make sure I regretted it. Your mother-in-law may seem really sweet and all, but trust me"—he paused, dropping his voice to a whisper—"you don't want to make her mad."

Tony just couldn't help smiling at that. Happy little Barbara taking on big, bad Fred. The women in this family were absolutely amazing.

"Thing is, she was right about you," Fred said. "And I was wrong. But Heather means the world to me, so I had to make sure you were on the up-and-up."

In that moment, Tony realized that Fred had threatened him because he loved Heather, so much so that he was willing to go to war with anyone who tried to hurt her.

"Maybe I should have done this sooner," Fred said. "But at least I'm doing it now. Tony?"

"Yeah?"

"Welcome to the family."

Tony felt so overcome by everything that had happened that day that it took him a moment to answer.

"Thanks, Fred," he said finally. "I appreciate that."

"Well," Fred said. "Gotta go. You two come by for dinner soon. I'll barbecue something."

Where Fred was concerned, that probably meant he'd shoot something first, *then* barbecue it, but that was fine by Tony. He'd eat barbecued yak if it meant being part of this family.

He hung up the phone and handed it to Heather, who looked worried.

"Is everything okay?" she asked.

"Yeah," Tony said. "Couldn't be better."

"What did he want?"

"To welcome me to the family."

Heather opened her mouth to say something, but nothing came out. Instead, tears sprang to her eyes.

"Hey, there's no need to cry," Tony said with a smile. "It's a good thing."

"I know. But after last night, I just didn't expect . . . and now everything is so good, and . . ."

Her voice trailed off, but she didn't need to finish the sentence for Tony to know how she felt, because he felt the same way.

"I love you, Heather."

"I know," she said. "I love you, too."

Tony pulled her into his arms and held her close, thinking about that one thing he'd been missing all these years, and he'd never even realized it. He'd gone to Vegas in search of twenty thousand dollars, only to find something far more precious than money: a woman who loved him. And he was going to hold on to her for the rest of his life.

ABOUT THE AUTHOR

Jane Graves began writing stories at the age of five, and she hasn't stopped since. She's a graduate of the University of Oklahoma, where she earned a B.A. in Journalism in the Professional Writing program. The author of fifteen novels, Jane is a six-time finalist for Romance Writers of America's Rita Award, the industry's highest honor, and is the recipient of two National Readers' Choice Awards, the Booksellers' Best Award, and the Golden Quill. She lives in Texas with her daughter and her husband of twenty-five years.

You can visit Jane's website at www.janegraves.com, or write to her at jane@janegraves.com. She'd love to hear from you!

THE DISH

Where authors give you the inside scoop!

From the desk of Susan Crandall

Dear Reader,

I'd like to share with you a little secret. It's one of those crazy writer things—you know, like making sure you have the right music playing, or just the right scented candle burning, or spinning around in a circle three times before you sit down to write. The kind of thing you simply cannot write without.

Superstitious, you say? Perhaps. A mind game? A crutch? Maybe. Doesn't really matter. As writers, we believe. And when your entire product comes out of your mind, you have to believe.

During those last grueling weeks before a book deadline, I indulge in a special writing snack. This snack is something I like to eat in mass quantities. Something I wouldn't normally allow myself to consume in such ridiculous amounts. But after seven novels, it's become obvious that the writing snack is integral in the process, necessary in order to properly tie off all of the plot threads, to make certain the villain gets his due, and the good guys get their happy endings.

And yes, I do require a serious diet and exercise program when all is said and done. But I do it for you, my dear reader. So the story is satisfying. So when you read that last page, you're glad you opened the first.

Like all of my books, PITCH BLACK (on sale now) had its very own writing snack. This novel is my first romantic suspense, so the choice was critical. I lost count of the number of boxes of Cheese Nips I went through as I wrote this story about a single-mother journalist whose adoptive son is the main suspect in a brutal crime.

Who knew romantic suspense required even more snacking than women's fiction? At the rare moment when I didn't have a backup box, I panicked. Luckily, I live close to the store.

I'd like to invite you to visit my Web site, www. susancrandall.net, to see the snack that accompanied each book. I have them listed on each book's description page.

While you're there, you can read an excerpt of my upcoming novel of romantic suspense, SEEING RED, which is slated for release in early 2009. Also, please stop by my message board and say hello. I always love hearing from readers, and it's a good place to connect with other book lovers.

Enjoy!

Susan Crandall

From the desk of Jane Graves

Dear Reader,

Did you know that over three hundred weddings are performed in Las Vegas every day? I learned that while researching my latest book, TALL TALES AND WEDDING VEILS (on sale now). So why is Sin City such a popular place to tie the knot?

Top Five Reasons to Get Married in Vegas

1. You've always loved Elvis, so having him perform your wedding ceremony is a dream come true, even if the Vegas version is fat and fifty and can't carry a tune in a bucket.
2. You figure marriage is a gamble anyway, so thematically speaking, it works.
3. It's between that and a New Orleans graveyard wedding performed by a voodoo priestess. The graveyard has spirits, but Vegas has martinis.
4. You can't resist the Austin Powers "1967 Summer of Love Groovy Baby Love Scene Wedding Package."
5. A woman you've just met helps you win a big jackpot, and after a champagne-soaked celebration in a stretch limousine, heading for a drive-through wedding chapel suddenly seems like a *fabulous* idea.

Now, how about that annulment?

Okay, that's not quite as easy. At least it isn't for Tony McCaffrey and Heather Montgomery, the hero and heroine, who spend the first morning of their married lives wondering how fast they can get *un*married.

When they made the drunken decision to marry in haste, they overlooked an obvious truth: No two people on earth were more incompatible. Tony's a handsome, sexy charmer who spends his life surrounded by women, and Heather's a serious-minded plain Jane whose idea of a good time is balancing her checkbook. But when an unexpected turn of events forces them to stay married for a month, slowly they begin to see each other in a whole new light. What started out as a drunken mistake just might turn out to be the best decision of their lives.

Hope you enjoy TALL TALES AND WEDDING VEILS!

Jane Graves

www.janegraves.com

Dear Reader,

Hope you enjoyed *Tall Tales
and Wedding Veils!*
Go to janegraves.com
for information about all my books,
including my previous title from
Grand Central Publishing,
Hot Wheels and High Heels.

Best wishes,

Jane Graves

Want to know more about romances at Grand Central Publishing and Forever? Get the scoop online!

GRAND CENTRAL PUBLISHING'S ROMANCE HOMEPAGE

Visit us at www.hachettebookgroupusa.com/romance for all the latest news, reviews, and chapter excerpts!

NEW AND UPCOMING TITLES

Each month we feature our new titles and reader favorites.

CONTESTS AND GIVEAWAYS

We give away galleys, autographed copies, and all kinds of fun stuff.

AUTHOR INFO

You'll find bios, articles, and links to personal websites for all your favorite authors—and so much more!

THE BUZZ

Sign up for our monthly romance newsletter, and be the first to read all about it!

VISIT US ONLINE

@ WWW.HACHETTEBOOKGROUPUSA.COM.

AT THE HACHETTE BOOK GROUP USA WEB SITE YOU'LL FIND:

CHAPTER EXCERPTS FROM SELECTED NEW RELEASES

•

ORIGINAL AUTHOR AND EDITOR ARTICLES

•

AUDIO EXCERPTS

•

BESTSELLER NEWS

•

ELECTRONIC NEWSLETTERS

•

AUTHOR TOUR INFORMATION

•

CONTESTS, QUIZZES, AND POLLS

•

FUN, QUIRKY RECOMMENDATION CENTER

•

PLUS MUCH MORE!

BOOKMARK HACHETTE BOOK GROUP USA @ WWW.HACHETTEBOOKGROUPUSA.COM.